Keep Your Friends Close

www.transworldbooks.co.uk

Also by Paula Daly

Just What Kind of Mother Are You?

Keep Your
Friends Close

Paula Daly

BANTAM PRESS

LONDON · TORONTO · SYDNEY · AUCKLAND · JOHANNESBURG

TRANSWORLD PUBLISHERS
61–63 Uxbridge Road, London W5 5SA
A Random House Group Company
www.transworldbooks.co.uk

First published in Great Britain
in 2014 by Bantam Press
an imprint of Transworld Publishers

A CIP catalogue record for this book
is available from the British Library.

ISBN 9780593071991 (cased)
9780593072004 (tpb)

Addresses for Random House Group Ltd companies outside the UK
can be found at: www.randomhouse.co.uk
The Random House Group Ltd Reg. No. 954009

The Random House Group Limited supports the Forest Stewardship Council® (FSC®),
the leading international forest-certification organisation. Our books carrying the FSC label
are printed on FSC®-certified paper. FSC is the only forest-certification scheme supported
by the leading environmental organisations, including Greenpeace. Our paper procurement
policy can be found at www.randomhouse.co.uk/environment

Typeset in 11.75/15 pt Minion by Falcon Oast Graphic Art Ltd.
Printed and bound in Australia by
Griffin Press

2 4 6 8 10 9 7 5 3

For my sister Debbie

'I fooled myself into thinking that *House Beautiful* should be subtitled *Life Wonderful*.'

Anna Quindlen

Seven Months Earlier

'So, WHAT'S BEEN on your mind this week?' she asks him.
'Besides the usual?'

She tilts her head. Looks on with mild disapproval and waits for him to answer more appropriately.

'Death,' he says. 'I've been thinking about death.'

'About dying?'

'Not dying per se . . . but wouldn't it be amazing if we got to choose the exact time of our deaths?'

Her expression is one of puzzlement. 'Can't we already do that?' she asks.

'I don't mean suicide.'

'But surely you don't actually want to die?'

''Course not.'

He's lying supine on the couch. There is the beginning of a small paunch forming, a concertina of trouser creases at his groin. He turns his head towards her, glances her way briefly.

'My youngest, Olivia, asked me what I'd do if I had three wishes,' he says, 'and it got me thinking. The one thing we're really scared of, the thing that unites all human beings, is the fear of death. Wouldn't it be great if you could just take death right out of the equation? If you could go through life knowing that everything's okay . . . because you're not scheduled to die for, say, another thirty years?'

'Would you live your life differently?'

'Maybe. Probably. Definitely. Wouldn't you?'

'We're not here to talk about me,' she says.

He smiles. Touché.

She uncrosses her legs.

Her skirt slides a little higher and she sees a flash of desire revealed in his face, though for now she pretends not to notice.

'How's work, Cameron?' she asks casually.

'I don't want to talk about work.'

'Any particular reason?'

'It's not been a good month, and, hell, I don't feel like talking about it today, not when I've got . . .' His voice trails off.

'Trouble with the workforce?' she offers.

He sits up. Swinging his feet to the floor, he puts his elbows on his knees and rests his chin on top of his now clenched fists. In the space of about a second he's become edgy. Latent energy brought to the surface in a heartbeat. She's touched one of his tender areas so now he begins reconstructing the armour. The defensive armour he supposedly comes in here to break down so he can *feel*. So he can love.

At least that's the general idea.

But that's not what actually happens.

She plays him, the poor bastard. She asks the questions he can't face. She toys with his problems for as long as he can stand it. Then she soothes him. Soothes him as only she can. Later she'll fan away his gratitude, telling him it is what she's here for. Showing him why it is only *she* that can help him on the long journey towards becoming himself.

'Tell me about Serena,' she says now. Her timing is exemplary, as always.

'Much the same.'

'Did you utilize the techniques we discussed? Did you stop trying to fix her problems? Did you really *listen* to what she had to say?'

'It's difficult.'

'It can take time,' she agrees.

'Serena's so wrapped up in the kids she doesn't see me. I touch her and she flinches.'

'Do you think she finds you unappealing?'

'No,' he says firmly, as though that's not an option. 'She just can't find room for me in her day any more. I'm another thing on the list. She can't stop running around after the kids. She puts everything she has into them.' He pauses, rubbing his face. 'Well, everything into them and the house.' Sighing wearily, he adds, 'I don't know how to make her happy.'

'You did suggest some help around the house?'

'She won't have it. Says they won't do the job as well as her.' He smiles briefly at his predicament. 'Anyway, she wants to do it herself, so there's not a lot more I can do.'

She puts her pen down and leans forward. 'But that means she has nothing left for you.'

He shrugs sadly.

'How does that make you feel?' she asks.

'Redundant,' he replies. 'Useless.'

She makes her voice soft. Lowers it and gives it a gravelly quality she uses on occasion. 'You know that you're neither of those things . . . logically, you do know that? A man doesn't get to your level of success by being redundant and useless. It's simply not possible.'

He looks away, unable to accept the compliment today. 'I've tried to love her,' he says, the words catching in his throat.

'I know.'

'I really have tried,' he repeats, his eyes filling.

'I know, Cameron. But she just won't let you.'

She rises from her seat and walks towards him, fingering the top button of her blouse. He closes his eyes and exhales. Exhales and tries to release the tension from his face, his shoulders, his fists. When he reopens his eyes she's standing right before him.

He looks into her face. 'Is it time to let her go?' he asks.

'You've done everything you can.'

Gently, she takes his hand and guides it beneath her skirt. Guides it up high along the inside of her thigh.

1

A RE YOU LIVING in the moment?
    Me neither.

I'm trying to. Really, I am. Periodically, throughout the day, I stop what I'm doing and say to myself, *This is it*. This moment is *all you have*. Enjoy it. Feel it. Embrace The Now.

So, right now, in this moment, I'm embracing cleaning fake tan from the walls of an en suite. It's a recently upgraded bathroom – solid marble wall tiles, twin Corian sinks – which one of the hotel guests decided would double up nicely as a St Tropez tanning booth.

I'm ignoring the fact that she's used the cream Ralph Lauren bath towels to home-dye her hair a deep magenta, and instead my attention flits between wondering what colour this woman would be in her natural state, and, if I were to nip home in the next hour, take a chicken out of the freezer, would it be defrosted in time for tonight's dinner?

I pile the ruined towels together in a heap in the centre of the bathroom and pour some bleach on to a toothbrush. I'm having real trouble removing the fake tan from the grout in between the tiles. This trick usually works so I set to, taking care not to splash any bleach on my suit trousers, all the while thinking: What am I doing in here? We have an army of staff for this.

But they won't attend to such details. You can train them till you're blue in the face and they'll still skim over the fine points, won't do the necessary extras to keep this place looking truly exceptional.

And that's why our guests come back. Because Lakeshore Lodge *is* exceptional.

If you've ever spent a night here, on your return, you'll get a personal greeting from either Sean, myself or the general manager – and we will remember to ask about your family, your journey to Windermere. Waiting in your room will be a miniature bottle of pink Moët, a box of six handmade chocolates and an individually wrapped Cartmel sticky toffee pudding. As well as a handwritten card saying, 'So pleased to see you again!'

For us it's about the extras. It's all about making the guests feel as though they really matter. And it's why we operate at 90 per cent occupancy, even when it's the low season. Even during November, when it can rain for thirty days and thirty nights consecutively and the filthy grey cloud is so low in the sky you can almost touch it with your fingertips.

There's a knock on the bathroom door. I stop scrubbing with the toothbrush and turn.

'Mrs Wainwright, I'm so sorry to bother you but there's a problem in the junior suite.'

Libby is one of the housekeepers. She's been here for three years and is one of my best cleaners.

'What is it?'

'That Indian family we had in last night? They heated up curry in the bedroom.'

I roll my eyes. Though this is not a major disaster, it happens from time to time. 'Just get the windows open, Libby, give it an airing. The next guests aren't due in until after eight tonight, so you've got plenty of time to give everything a good wash down.'

Libby squints and knits her brows together at the same time. Something she does when she knows I'm about to shout at what she has to say.

'What is it?' I ask sharply. 'Did they bring in extra bodies?' I hate to typecast here, but it's not unusual for additional children, babies . . . Grandma, to be smuggled in, unpaid for.

Libby shifts her weight from one foot to the other. 'They heated it up inside the kettle.'

'The curry?' I ask. 'Inside the electric kettle?'

She nods. 'I think the element might be kind of screwed.'

'Oh, for God's sake.'

I place the toothbrush by the side of the sink and begin kneading the back of my neck, swallowing the bark of abuse which was on its way out, as I have the beginnings of a migraine. It's at the base of my skull and if I were to lose my temper fully right now, it would jump straight behind my eyes, meaning the rest of the day would be a write-off.

'Well, that's a first,' I say softly, but Libby knows to keep her eyes low.

Because I can be unpredictable at times like this.

Often Libby will tell me the worst news: laundry room flooded, two housemaids called in sick . . . *a rat* . . . and I'll take it on the chin. I'll deal with it quietly and get on with the day. But other times I can go apoplectic over a dusty skirting board, a lone fingerprint on a mirror.

I'm not easy. I can be kind of prickly and I've been meditating to try to keep myself more balanced. Sean says he can see a clear difference, but I'm not so sure I'm getting anywhere with it.

'What should I do?' Libby asks.

'Go give the kettle to Sean. Tell him you need a new one from the spares store and tell him to check how many are left. He might need to order another batch. Tell him to look online and see if he can get a better price. Those glass kettles were stupidly expensive. Tell him to look at stainless steel instead.'

'Okay.'

When she's left the room I call her back.

'Libby? Second thoughts, tell him to stick with the glass. They're classier.'

Libby keeps her face impassive. Waits for me to change my mind another time.

'You're sure?' she asks tentatively.

'Sure.'

It's only when I'm rinsing the toothbrush and applying more bleach that I remember Sean's otherwise engaged this morning. His mother is here.

Penny, Sean's mother, visits Thursday afternoons. She spends a couple of hours with Sean; he takes her out. They might have a jaunt over to Sharrow Bay at Ullswater, or perhaps take afternoon tea down the road at Storrs Hall. Anywhere, really. Anywhere that's not Lakeshore Lodge – as Sean would face a constant stream of interruptions. And his mother generally demands his full attention. They normally return from their outing around 4 p.m., in time for the girls arriving in from school. Now, during the lighter evenings of British Summertime, Penny will stay for dinner. In the winter months she's back on the road, heading for the village of Crook, before darkness sets in.

Today is the first Wednesday in May. Not Penny's usual day to visit, but she's off to Nice for a few days with her photography club tomorrow.

I crash through the front door just before five, carrying chicken breasts, a small bag of morels (which I had to swipe from the head chef), a bottle of Marsala, and two books of carpet samples I need to look at before six – when the fitter is calling to get my selection. The hotel's conservatory carpet is showing heavy tread by the doorway and I should have made my choice by the end of last week, but the days have got away from me.

'Natty!' Penny exclaims, rising from the armchair as I enter the lounge. 'You look dead beat! Sean, go and make your poor wife some tea before she topples over from exhaustion.'

I place a kiss on Penny's cheek. 'You look really well from your trip,' I say to her, and tell Sean not to bother with the tea.

Penny is just back from visiting Sean's sister in Fremantle and her skin is leathery. It's a deep mahogany-brown. Penny has taken a lot of sun over the years, she's rail thin, and, you know when they put wigs on skeletons on the TV and it looks kind of funny? That is Sean's mother.

'Lucy's little ones all right?' I ask, kicking my heels off as the phone rings out in the hallway. Sean goes to answer it.

'Wonderful,' she answers. 'It's a joy to watch her with them. She has the time, you see, Natty? It makes *all the difference*. All the difference in the world. She's talking of having a third, now that Robert's finally got the promotion.'

'Another baby would be lovely,' I say brightly. 'Is she hoping for a girl this time?'

Penny dismissively waves away my words with her hand. 'Oh, she's not bothered in the slightest. She simply loves mothering. I do worry if she's getting a little *too* old for another child, though. But she assures me forty is not considered old these days.'

'More and more women are having babies at forty,' I say.

'She wouldn't let me do a thing while I was there, Natty. I don't know where she gets her energy from, I really don't. She's still up with Alfie half the night.'

'Nice for you to have a rest and enjoy the children.'

'Well, *of course*, she's still breastfeeding Alfie, so there's not a lot to be done there, and Will is such a kind boy. I can hardly believe he's five already. Where do the years go to? I just don't know.'

There is a subtext to this conversation. In fact, there's a subtext to every conversation with Penny, which is probably worth pointing out here.

I fell unexpectedly pregnant, aged nineteen and during my first year at university. Or perhaps, more importantly, during *Sean's* first year at university. We both left our respective courses and returned home to Windermere, Sean giving up a degree in law, me a degree in radiography.

It was a tricky time with Penny because in her eyes I'd ruined her son's future. 'Nineteen is far too young to be parents. What sort of life can either of you offer a child when you're still children yourselves?'

That's how she put it, but again, there was a subtext, this one being that she'd spent goodness knows how much on Sean's education at Sedbergh School, only to have him blow it on some silly local girl he should have got rid of ages ago.

To her credit, Penny softened when Alice arrived. She became the doting grandmother and I was able to tolerate the constant digs about our recklessness because, simply, without my own mother, I needed her.

'Lucy's starting to wean Alfie,' she says now. 'You should see the lengths she goes to, Natty. She has the most wonderful piece of kit – an electric steamer. It keeps all the nutrients *inside* the vegetables. Then she purées them or pushes them through a sieve and freezes the lot in ice-cube trays . . . The work that's involved, it absolutely amazes me. Like I said, though, she has the time. She can afford to do it properly.'

I smile weakly because, the thing is, I went through all the same palaver when Alice was born. I was so set on proving everyone wrong, so set on demonstrating that it was *not a mistake* for us to have a baby, that I tried my damnedest to be the perfect mother. I, too, steamed and puréed. I, too, breastfed longer than anyone was really comfortable with. I, too, carried my babies everywhere to give them the full *Continuum Concept* experience.

Penny just can't recall any of this because it was sixteen years ago. And I don't go reminding her about it now because I gave up playing the Who's-the-best-mother? game when my sister-in-law's first son got out of nappies. No matter what I said, in Penny's brain Lucy had got her life in order – emotionally and financially – *before* deciding to become a parent. The responsible way to do it.

Sometimes, over the past few years, it's been hard to remember that Lucy is actually a nice person. A person who Sean and I get along with very well. What is it with parents that they end up making you almost detest family members because of their proclivity for comparison? Their quick reminders of how their other child is doing a better job?

Sean comes back into the room. 'That was Eve on the phone,' he says. There's a mischievous glint in his eye which means that he, too, has been subject to his mother's stories of Lucy's marvellous puréeing. I probably got the edited version, actually. 'Eve's wondering if it's all right if she calls in tomorrow evening. She's finishing a series of lectures in Scotland and will be passing through.'

'Is that your friend from America?' Penny interrupts, chin raised. 'The clever girl with the good job?'

'Yes, God, I've not seen her in over two years. Did she say how long she was in the country?'

Sean shakes his head.

'Did you tell her it was okay to come?'

'I said if it wasn't, you'd call her straight back.'

2

SPRING WEATHER IN the Lake District is pretty much like the rest of the year. Changeable. This morning there's a fine drizzle, and low mist hanging in the valley above Lake Windermere. I stand looking out, coffee in hand.

Try to imagine every shade of green possible crammed into one small frame – khaki, bottle-green, sage, olive, lime, pistachio, right through to the paler shade of moorland grass, and you'll get something close to the view from my window.

Yesterday I rose to find brilliant clear skies and the valley filled with a thick, dense fog. Like a huge glacier it crawled southwards down the lake surface, enveloping everything in its path. Tomorrow I will have no view at all if the forecasted heavy rains arrive.

Bowness-on-Windermere is the busiest small town in the Lake District. It sits on the eastern shore of the lake, and both my home and the hotel are situated about a mile from the centre. Just close enough for the hotel guests to enjoy a pleasant stroll in, just far enough away for Sean and me to escape the crazy crowds of tourists who pack the place during the summer months.

I grew up here. And unlike most of my contemporaries, who, once grown, couldn't wait to escape for city life, I have always wanted to remain. Incidentally, most have returned now that they're raising families of their own. Bowness has a definite village feel – yes, everyone knows everyone, crime is low and people genuinely care about each other – but we have the amenities of a place typically much larger. An English village of a few thousand residents could not generally support a cinema, Michelin-starred restaurants and a supermarket. It's the influx of tourists that enables us to live a fairly cosmopolitan life while at the same time residing in a distinctly rural area, an area of outstanding natural beauty.

Still in my pyjamas, I rinse my cup in the sink and head out the front door with the bag of rubbish. Our tarmac driveway is slick and shiny; everything smells clean and new. I sling the black bag into the outside wheelie bin then give the lid a quick wipe-over with the cloth I've brought purposely for the job.

On my way back I notice that the night rain has sent splatters of grit up the lower half of the front door, so I grab the mop and give it the once-over. While I'm at it I decide to give the lamp above the porch a quick clean, too, and get rid of some cobwebs around the door frame at the same time.

Back inside the kitchen, Alice looks up at me from her mug of mocha. 'Have you started mopping the driveway now as well?' she asks, her voice laced with sarcasm, and I choose to ignore her.

It's quieter in the house than usual. Our younger daughter, Felicity, is on a school trip in France. Thirty of them left by coach on Sunday night and arrived in southern Normandy some twenty-seven hours later. She's due back on Saturday.

I can't decide yet if Alice is more difficult when Felicity is here or not. There are two years between them – Alice is sixteen, Felicity fourteen – and like most parents will tell you about their children, they are completely different in temperament.

What I *don't* say openly is that Alice takes after me in that she's a classic Type A. Both of us push ourselves to the point of breaking.

We're like toddlers who keep going at an unprecedented rate, only to snap at anyone close by before collapsing with exhaustion into uncontrollable crying. A well-meaning adult might smile on benevolently, sighing: 'Oh dear, I think she's ready for her nap . . .'

I check the calendar and on seeing the small asterisk scribbled in the corner of Saturday's box, take out a B vitamin, and slide it across the table towards Alice.

She's wearing her new leopard-print onesie. When she prowls around the house in it I find myself humming 'The Magical Mr Mistoffelees'.

'What's this for?' she asks, staring at the tablet.

'PMS – it's supposed to help.'

She glares at me. 'It's not me who's edgy, Mum,' she says, and takes herself upstairs, leaving me with the mild wounded feeling that follows most of our exchanges.

I get on with preparing her lunch. There's enough chicken breast left over from last night's dinner to jazz up a nice Caesar salad. I wash the lettuce, and as I dab it dry so it doesn't go soggy for her later, I begin mentally running through what we've eaten this week, before deciding on the menu for tonight's dinner with Eve.

We've had red meat twice, so that's a no-no. Carbs-wise, we've had potatoes once, rice once, crusty white baguette once – which means we're down to have pasta. But I don't want to serve pasta when I've not seen Eve for so long. I want something a little more special.

Eventually I settle on salmon in a champagne cream sauce and break my once-a-week-potatoes rule by planning to serve the fillets with some nice Jersey Royals and green asparagus. It's a touch early in the season for asparagus. I do try to keep things seasonal and locally sourced, but I've heard even the Italians eat tomatoes now in the wintertime. I know! I was pretty surprised by that as well.

After bagging Alice's dance kit, I pop her lunch in her floral school bag, making sure her phone is charged, and give the kitchen floor a quick whizz round with the mop before going to get showered.

Sean is sitting in bed, the laptop open on his knee. 'You've not moved yet?' I ask him accusingly.

'I'm looking at phones.'

'You've just got a new mobile, why do you need another?'

'I don't. I'm just looking. Anyway, I didn't get in till after eleven, I was networking.'

I roll my eyes at him. 'You mean *not* working,' and he smiles. Calls my name as I head into the bathroom and begin to undress.

'Natty?' he says.

'What?'

I come out, and he's still smiling at me, his boyish beauty catching my attention, the tanned musculature of his chest making my pulse flicker.

I know what he's thinking. I *know* that look.

But I ignore the heat in my groin because we're running late. And despite the fact he's patting the bed beside him, saying, 'Take a breather, Nat,' I don't. Because even though he says it good-naturedly, sexily even, it still irritates me. I try to smile. Try to mask the flash of anger, because he does this all the time.

I'll be running around the house like my arse is on fire, and he'll be lying in bed, or lounging on the sofa, flicking between the channels, and he'll say, 'Have a rest, Nat, you don't need to do this all at once . . . slow down,' and I'll want to run the Dyson hard into his shins, because, if I don't do it, if I don't make sure we're tidy and organized, if I don't make sure we're on time, in the right place, with all the right things . . . then who the hell will?

*

For dinner this evening I dress up a little. It's a given that with certain friends you have to make more of an effort, and, well, Eve is one of those friends.

I remember when I'd just had Felicity and we were mid-move, buying our second bed & breakfast. We'd gone from three guest bedrooms to five, and my standard attire back then was jeans, clean trainers, polo shirt – but because I'd just had a baby, I was still in leggings. My post-pregnancy belly had to be tucked inside my knickers and my boobs resembled two fried eggs.

Eve was over from the States and arrived unexpectedly on the doorstep: black shift dress, hair in a chignon – and I almost burst into tears upon seeing her. She didn't realize. She still doesn't. Eve's not yet had children so she doesn't understand how vulnerable a woman feels in the early stages of mother-hood. I don't hold it against her – you don't know what you don't know, after all – but since then, whenever visiting a new mum, I always make sure to turn up looking particularly shitty. Because it's the little things like this that really help a woman out.

When I'm more or less ready, wearing my black dress, I give my dad a quick call to check the homecare lady has been to help him shower. He's incapacitated because of two total knee replacements. After thirty-five years as a self-employed joiner his knees were shot. He had both operated on at once so he could return to work faster, but now I'm not sure it was such a good idea. His rehabilitation is taking longer than anticipated and he's not what you'd call a patient patient. At first he hated the homecare I arranged, but now I have the sneaking suspicion he's quite enjoying himself. A selection of chatty women come in to get him up; help him bathe; later, put him back to bed. He's playing his cards close to his chest, but I sense there's something developing – a romantic attachment – with one of them.

I stay on the phone less than a minute because the doorbell

rings and there's silence on the stairs, so it's left to me to answer. My dad says he's fine anyway, tells me he's got a bit of company planned for this evening, and he says no more and I don't ask.

Hurrying down the stairs, I do one last inspection of my appearance in the hall mirror before throwing open the door, squealing when I see Eve.

I throw my arms around her, gushing, 'I've missed you, I've missed you,' and I mean it.

Eve is probably my oldest remaining friend. I don't have a wide circle of friends; acquaintances have dropped away over the years as the girls have grown, and I've not sought to replace them, as I get more than my fill of socializing from the hotel.

But I don't see nearly half as much of Eve as I would like to, and when I clap eyes on her it's as if something clicks back into place inside me. I feel weirdly young again.

It happens every time I'm with her; I think because we have a shared history. We were at university together and so much happened that first year, so much that changed all of us, made us the people we are today, that no matter how close other women have become to me, there is never the same bond. Eve's the person I talk to when I'm struggling with a life problem, and the reason I turn to her is because she doesn't judge. I can vent. I can complain about Sean, call him unsupportive, lazy, feckless, and she will listen, even laugh along at how useless men can be, but she'll never criticize Sean. Never hint or suggest, as other friends might, that there are real problems within our marriage, because she knows that the stuff I complain about is, ultimately, trivial. She knows I love him deeply.

She holds me at arm's length, studies my face: 'God, it's good to see you,' and she brings me in again for another hug. We stay like that for – what is the optimal length of time for a hug? Four seconds? Five? Whatever it is, we exceed it and she says into my ear, 'You're thin again, Natty. Are you working too hard?'

'Don't start,' I reply playfully. 'You've only just got here.'

But she is right. Yesterday I caught sight of myself cleaning those bathroom tiles and was momentarily shocked by my appearance. I wouldn't say I'm desperately thin, but I am beginning to appear pinched and sinewy. The ribs above my breasts are jutting out like a rack. I studied geology in school and yesterday I found myself staring at my reflection, shocked, comparing my ribs to the fossilized thorax of a trilobite. Not a good look.

'You've got all night to analyse me and put me straight,' I tell Eve, closing the door. 'What do you want to drink? Red or white?'

'I could do with a caffeine jolt, actually.' Then she asks with a smile, 'Is that *Sean's* Maserati out there on the driveway?'

I nod, give her a mock-exasperated expression, and she follows me through to the kitchen. When I've taken her coat I set to, spooning Lavazza into the espresso machine. 'How's Brett?' I ask without turning, and she doesn't answer. After a few seconds I twist around to face her. 'Eve?' I prompt.

She closes her eyes. Not exactly fighting back the tears, more steadying herself for what she's about to reveal.

She gives one firm shake of her head and says, 'It's over.'

'Over?' I gasp. 'What? When? Are you sure?'

'Certain,' she replies, and I'm gobsmacked. I've never actually met Brett, but Eve seemed so settled. I forget the coffee for the time being and move towards her, putting my arm around her shoulders: 'Eve, can I ask why?' and she winces. 'Sorry,' I say. 'Sorry, that was clumsy of me. You . . . you took me by surprise. It's the last thing I expected to hear.' I don't add that I thought she was coming here to announce that she was pregnant.

She smiles at me feebly. 'It's okay. I probably should have told you before arriving. I suppose I didn't want my visit to be all maudlin, if you know what I mean.'

'Of course. Of course,' I prattle on. 'I totally understand. I tried calling you a few times last week but couldn't get through, was that because—'

'No,' she answers, cutting me off a little sharply. 'I've had a problem with my cell. I've got an iPhone now – remind me to give you the new number later.'

I look down, embarrassed. What I should have done is contact her office. Because she's on the road lecturing or else dealing with clients, we've had an arrangement for the past few years – I call her voicemail, and she gets back to me as soon as she's able to. Now I wish I'd persisted in trying to get in touch with her.

Not sure where to go next, I ask, 'Would you like a whisky with that coffee?'

And she smiles. 'Love one.'

Badly timed as ever, Sean walks in. He's barefoot, carrying a pair of clean socks in his right hand, his hair still damp from the shower. I can see wet patches soaking through his shirt. 'Hello, stranger,' he says, kissing Eve's cheek. 'Good trip?'

'Yes, thanks,' she says, instantly masking her distress to spare my husband. 'Are you dining with us tonight, Sean? Or are you at the hotel?'

Eve knows the drill. Knows that neither one of us can be missing from the place for too long lest we come out in a rash.

'I'm eating here,' he tells her, 'heading there for drinks later with guests, then I'll stay on to start setting up for Saturday. We're hosting the Pride of Cumbria Awards.'

'Oooh,' says Eve, suitably impressed.

'Shouldn't be late, though,' he says, grabbing a glass. 'I'm sure you two will still be up gossiping when I get back.'

'That new car's a beast, Sean.' Eve smiles, and he goes momentarily sheepish.

Sean's still not used to the idea of being flashy, but Christ knows we've worked hard enough to deserve a little luxury.

Eventually, when I could take no more of him browsing the procession of Maseratis on eBay (sellers upload engine noises now, if you can believe it), I told him to treat himself. Told him to get the thing before he gets too old to look good in it. Turned out he needed only minimal persuasion.

Sean pours himself a glass of Sauvignon Blanc and stops to kiss my neck as he passes on his way to the lounge, his fingertips brushing the delicate skin of my throat. 'You look beautiful tonight, Natty,' he whispers, and though this small act of love should be welcomed, I frown a little – though I hide it.

Sean and I have not had sex in – well, it's been a while. It's not him. It's me. In bed, he no longer nudges me in the back with an erection, expecting instant action. He does all the right things: beginning the bribery (ahem, *foreplay*) early on in the day, with compliments and caresses, lingering looks and unexpected kisses. But I've got to be honest: Right now, even though we've always enjoyed good sex, often great sex, it just feels like another thing to do.

I smile at Sean in a way that lets him know it's probably a no-go again tonight, and he holds my gaze, his face darkening suddenly as though to convey: *Then* when, *Natty? This situation can't go on for ever.*

Recently he asked me what it was I actually needed him for, and when I voiced everything I could think of, he told me we could pay any old dogsbody for those things.

The one thing he can give me, the one thing that no one else can, is the one thing I don't want, he said coldly.

Alice joins us for dinner and it's as if a surly girl climbed the stairs after school and a totally different one emerged just in time for Eve's visit. Metamorphosis complete, Alice is now charming and funny, interested in everything being said around the table. In short, she is a delight.

She has her red hair in a loose plait slung over her left

shoulder and is wearing a cream lace dress. On her feet she has sequinned flip-flops. It's early May. The temperature outside is still around twelve degrees, but Alice couldn't look more right. She has this knack for pulling together unsuitable outfits that on anyone else would seem silly and affected. But on her, because of her long-limbed, willowy build, her clothes are elegant. Elegant and cool at the same time. She's the only person I've seen wear biker boots with a tiny frilled skirt and a misshapen grey marl sweatshirt and look spectacular.

'Exams soon, Alice?' Eve asks her.

'Yay,' she replies flatly. 'I'm super-excited about that.'

Eve pours more wine: 'You'll do great . . . you've always had your father's brains,' and I bristle a little at this quip. Eve tips the neck of the bottle towards Alice: 'Are you having some?'

Alice throws her head back and scoffs. 'Mum won't let me so much as sniff it. Even though it's been *proven* that sharing small amounts of wine, as the French do, stops teenagers from becoming binge drinkers and alcoholics in later life.' She flashes me her best defiant glare.

'Plenty of alcoholics in France,' I counter.

'She could have a smidge, though, couldn't she?' Eve pushes.

I shake my head.

'Mum doesn't want me to become corrupted,' Alice says. 'She thinks one small sip and I'll make *all the same mistakes* she did.'

She says 'all the same mistakes' in a way that infers I've been going on about it every day for her entire life. Which I've not.

'Mum thinks if I get into drinking I'll throw away my future . . . that I'll be pregnant at sixteen.'

I raise my eyebrows at Eve and she smirks back at me.

'I don't know why you're so anal about it, Mum,' Alice continues unabated. 'It's not like it didn't work out for you, is it? You and Dad are living proof that teenage romance can last.'

'No wine, Alice,' I say firmly. 'Final answer.'

Half an hour later, around eight, when Sean has gone to the hotel and Alice is upstairs finishing the last of her physics homework, Eve and I laze on the sofa. I sense she is more tired than she's letting on after her week of psychology lectures. Her usual dewy skin is dull and her eyes have that vague quality that comes from not enough sleep. I can also see the beginnings of a set of small vertical lines encircling her lips, visible when she takes a sip. I'm thirty-five, Eve is a little older than me, but I don't yet have these wrinkles, so I assume she's taken up smoking again.

'What happened, Eve?' I ask, when there's a lull in conversation. 'What happened with you and Brett?'

She takes a gulp of wine and gives a sarcastic kind of laugh. 'He decided he didn't want children after all.'

'Oh!' I exclaim, putting my hand up to my mouth.

'I know,' she says. 'What a bastard, right? I'm thinking of not going home.'

'To the States?' This surprises me. 'But what about your practice?'

'I could do it here. I could start again. There's nothing to stop me; the change might be just what I need. It's not going to be easy heading back there, alone.'

'But isn't that running away?'

She looks at me levelly. 'That's exactly what it is.'

I don't have Eve's skills as a listener. In that sense our relationship is unbalanced. For every one time Eve has needed me, I've needed her ten. She has a rare quality, a quality I have found in no other friend. It's a kind of sixth sense, whereby she knows exactly what I need in the moment. I can cry, panic, be downright aggressive (usually when I'm trying to hide the fact that I'm ashamed of hurting another person's feelings), and Eve will be gentle, coaxing me along to the point where I am ready to face up to my actions, ready to listen to her advice on how to fix things and stop me from feeling so wretched.

I survey her sad, drawn face and wish I could offer her even a fraction of the comfort she has given me over the years, when we both jump. We're startled by the sound of the telephone. It's next to me on the sofa and I check the caller ID. The display reads: INTERNATIONAL.

I apologize to Eve. 'Really sorry, but I've got to take this . . . hello?'

'Mrs Wainwright?' says the voice.

'Yes.'

'It's Jenny Cruickshank . . . Felicity's French teacher?'

'What's happened? Is she okay?'

And it's as if the line goes dead.

Total silence.

I go to repeat the question, trying to keep my voice steady, but just as I'm about to speak I hear a faint sniffling sound. It's barely audible. Then I realize with sickening clarity that the teacher is crying at the end of the line.

'Please tell me,' I plead in a quiet voice. 'What's happened?' My stomach is suddenly in freefall. 'What's happened to my daughter?'

'I'm sorry,' she whimpers. 'Forgive me . . . Felicity is in the hospital, she's very ill. You need to come straight away.'

3

AM I OVER the limit? is the first question I ask myself. Am I too drunk to drive?

'Natty, who was that?' Eve asks.

'Felicity's in hospital. She's being operated on right now.'

I hear my words spoken from what seems like the other side of the room. I'm shaking. Not just shaking. It's shock. Where has all the blood gone?

'They didn't know,' I say without emotion. 'The teachers didn't know she was even sick.'

'What's wrong with her?' Eve asks. 'What did the teacher actually say?'

'They don't know what's wrong. She collapsed. They're not completely sure she'll make it.'

Eve bursts into action.

She doesn't comfort me, or tell me not to worry, or tell me Felicity will be okay. She grabs the phone, uses the speed dial to call the hotel and tells Sean in a businesslike manner that he needs to come home, there's an emergency.

'Why did I let her go to France?' I whisper. 'She's only fourteen, too young to travel alone. Why did I let her go? What was I *thinking*?'

Eve looks at me straight. 'They're fixing her, Natty. It doesn't make any difference that she's in France. They're saving her life. We need to get you there as soon as possible. Let me search for flights.'

'Do you think she'll die?'

'Go and pack a bag.'

The shaking is violent now.

Eve repeats slowly: 'Natty, go and find your passport and pack your bag.'

My guts have become a bucket of eels. I don't think I can stand, let alone board an aircraft. I stay fixed to the chair. If I just stay here, it will all go away. I put my hands between my thighs and squeeze tight to stop the shaking.

'Natty! Move!'

'I can't,' I say.

'You have to.'

I'm shuffling about the bedroom trance-like, picking up bits of underwear, T-shirts, when Sean appears in the doorway. He doesn't speak. We simply look at one another for an extended moment.

Is this it? we're both thinking.

Is this the rest of our lives? Do we move from the standard, the typical family of four, petty worries, petty fall-outs? Do we move into that *other realm*? Do we join the ranks of families who've lost a child?

My first thought hearing the teacher give me the news about Felicity was to whisper, 'Not this one. Please, God, not this child.' Then immediately I felt utterly wretched, because did I really want him to take my other child instead?

I've spent the last ten minutes bargaining with God. Even though I've not really been a believer since – well, since he deserted me, age nineteen. *Please save her,* I'm begging again now. *Please, I'll do anything. Take everything away from us, strip us of all that we know, but do not let my child die.*

Sean strides towards me. Puts his arms around my body, and I begin crying silently. There is so much terror inside my chest I cannot form sound. I'm struck by the realization that this is what it must be like to be attacked. Women, girls, say their voices simply leave them. Their bodies scream in fury, but nothing comes, their larynxes paralysed by fear.

'There's one seat left,' Sean says gravely. 'Manchester to Rennes. It leaves in two hours. I'll take it, Natty, you stay here. You're in no state to travel. You can fly out tomorrow morning.'

'What if we lose her, Sean?'

He shakes his head as though he's not about to answer that question. 'We need to decide. One of us needs to get on the road right now if we're to make it in time.'

'I'm going.'

'I'm not sure you can. Look at you,' he says, and he takes my shaking hands, lifts them for me to see, as if to drive home his point.

'But if she dies and I'm not with her, then how can I ever . . .' My words disappear in my throat.

'You can be there by eleven tomorrow morning at the latest. Stay here, Natty, let me do this.'

I pull my hands away. 'No. It has to be me.'

And I feel him relenting.

Another moment of quiet deliberation, and he says, 'Okay. Okay, let's get your things together. We need to move quickly.'

He pulls the overnight bag from the top of the wardrobe, unzips it and begins gently laying the small stack of T-shirts, jeans and underwear inside.

I watch him, knowing I should be running around, grabbing everything I need, but the thought of Felicity unconscious in the operating theatre without me by her side keeps me rooted to the spot.

Sean lifts his head. 'Natty?' he says, a cloud of fear passing over his face. 'Natty,' he says gently, 'which shoes do you want to take with you?'

'Huh?'

'Shoes? Which ones?'

'Oh, I don't know. Hang on,' and I walk to the wardrobe and stare at the choice, baffled. Then I turn back to Sean. 'What about Alice?' I ask him, frowning. 'If you come to France tomorrow, who will look after Alice? We can't leave her here alone. Christ, Sean, you know what she's like, she can't even open a can of beans. And your mother's away, and my dad's housebound and—'

'It's all right,' he says, grabbing my electric toothbrush, 'Eve has offered to stay.'

So, here I am then. *Right in the moment.* Everything I have is focused on the here and now.

I shuffle forward, clutching my boarding pass, my passport, thinking: *It has taken a disaster to put me in the present.* The mind chatter has stopped. All plans I must make for next week, next month, next year, have evaporated. The doubts, the lingering regrets from yesterday, from fifteen years ago . . . are all gone.

I remove my belt, my shoes.

I look ahead to an old guy about to put his belongings in the tray next to the conveyor; he is telling his wife to do the same, to take off her watch, but she doesn't want to. She's keeping it with her until told otherwise by a person in authority. This makes him anxious, and he glares at her as if to say: *Must you? Must you really do this?*

My gaze rests on the woman directly in front of me. She has three clear plastic bags stuffed full to bursting with cosmetics, and it dawns on me I've not brought along anything like that. Not a lipstick, not an eyeliner. In my race to reach the airport I've neglected to pack the usual things I need to face the world.

But this is not a usual trip. If I reach France with just my credit card, my phone, my driving licence and passport, it will be enough.

I close my eyes, swallow and steady my breathing. I place my bag inside the grey tray. I take off my coat and feel momentarily self-conscious because, in my haste to get here, I'm still in the short black dress I wore for tonight's dinner with Eve.

Seconds later I step through the metal detector and head towards the gate. My blank stare and purposeful stride belie the extent of my terror.

Three and a half hours later. Even though the satnav on my phone guided my rental car to the hospital in Mayenne, southern Normandy, I feel a small, misplaced sense of achievement. Or perhaps it's simply relief. I've driven on the right-hand side of the road only once before tonight, as Sean always does the driving when we travel, and I always had that nagging voice inside my head: *You should really crack this, there will be an emergency one day, and Sean might not be with you and . . .*

Well, now there is an emergency.

I pull into the car park. France is one hour ahead, so I'm not completely sure they'll let me into this small, single-storey, provincial hospital, which looks more like an outpatient clinic at this hour. I have no idea what I'll do if I *don't* get in. Sit and weep on the steps sounds like a plan.

I reach down to grab my handbag and it's only now that I've arrived that I allow myself to cry. For the past few hours I've been running on adrenalin. I spoke to no one; no one spoke to me. I've been giving off the aura of a wounded animal. Approach me and I'll give you a nasty bite. Maybe even break your arm like an angry swan. My entire focus has been on getting here fast, here to Felicity.

I make my way across the car park to the front entrance as a light rain falls. It's much the same as the damp drizzle I left at home, but the air here is less dense, the humidity lower. There is no one around, the place is completely deserted, though I do catch a waft of stale cigarettes. As I walk up the steps the smell becomes stronger: thick, lingering, dark tobacco, Gauloises, Gitanes, indicating it wasn't so long since there were people where I now stand.

The doors slide open automatically but the reception desk is unmanned.

Did I mention I can't speak French?

No, didn't think I did.

An intercom is built into the wall, so I press the button, hoping at least a skeleton staff operates throughout the night. After a few moments a gruff male voice responds.

'Oui?'

And the best I can manage in return is: 'Felicity Wainwright . . . *Maman.*'

And then I wait.

4

JOANNE ASPINALL HAS removed the clear polish from her finger-
nails, taken out her earrings and has been nil-by-mouth since
eight o'clock yesterday evening.

She's now so hungry she could eat the pillows from her hospital bed.

She's in a ward with three other women; two are to have
breast reductions, along with Joanne, and the other is to have
reconstructive surgery after a double mastectomy. 'Taking some
flesh outta me back,' the woman told Joanne as they waited, and
Joanne raised her eyebrows in a gesture of *The wonders of
modern medicine!*

For a while Joanne felt guilty about taking up this bed when
there were clearly more needy candidates than she. Again, she
wrestled with the idea that it was plain old vanity that put her
here, that if she were a stronger person, a more self-confident
person, perhaps if she were *in a relationship*, then this would not
be such a problem. Maybe the operation would not be necessary
after all.

But now, as she lies propped up on the polythene-covered
mattress and the sweat is pouring over her skin, trickling
down her armpits where the flesh of her breasts meets her
biceps, she has to admit that she can't go on like this for ever.
And, absurdly, she's gone up another cup size since Christmas –
even though she's not actually gained any weight. She even came

off the Pill in the hope it would make a difference. It didn't.

Much in the same way as pregnant women do for after the birth of the baby, Joanne's treated herself to some new clothes for after the operation. She's been told that once the swelling goes down she can expect to be a 36 C/D cup. She googled it and apparently that converts to a size fourteen in blouses and tops, so she can finally do away with shopping in Evans.

She's bought a finely knitted black rollneck. The assistant gave Joanne a look to suggest: *You'll never get in this.* Ridiculously, Joanne muttered something along the lines of how it would make a lovely gift for her Auntie Jackie.

And she's bought a dress. An actual dress.

Joanne has not been able to wear a dress since – well, since for ever. From adolescence onwards, Joanne's top half was four sizes bigger than her bottom half, which meant dresses were out of the question. She spent the next twenty years in a succession of black trousers and uninspiring smocked tops.

The anaesthetist is making the rounds. 'No,' Joanne is not allergic to anything, 'Yes,' she's had surgery before (tonsils out when she was seven). 'No,' she doesn't have problems with her heart or her breathing.

He asks her if she knows what she's in here for, and Joanne eyes him suspiciously. 'Yes . . .?' she answers, frowning.

'I need you to tell me what the operation is *out loud*,' he says apologetically, and Joanne realizes he's not being facetious, he's asking her this to prevent a mix-up. Like, she might wake up from surgery with the end of her right thumb missing, or her tubes tied or her ears pinned back neatly against the side of her head.

The four women don't yet know what order they'll be in, but they've been given a pre-med and as the next ten minutes pass the room becomes noticeably quieter. The chit-chat between them dies out as each patient starts to drift a little.

Joanne's wondering if this warm, contented feeling is similar to the response to opiates. Because if it is, she now totally gets how you could sell your own mother to get your hands on some. Everything is at peace and she can't think of a single thing troubling her. Any apprehension she had about the operation is melting away. She's flooded with an overwhelming sensation of love, of well-being.

Joanne glances down, and for the first time in over twenty years she's feeling A-Okay with her disastrous breasts. She looks at them for what is probably going to be the last time ever and feels almost sorry to see them go. She has a fond expression on her face, as if she's saying goodbye to an old lover.

Joanne understands she's not really with it and casts around the room to see the same spacey expressions on her ward companions' faces. Each woman is smiling, hands resting neatly on her tummy, a vague trusting look on her face.

'Joanne Aspinall?'

'Hmm?'

'We're ready to take you down now.'

The curtains are pulled around as a young porter positions a bed on wheels alongside her mattress.

'Do you need some help moving across?' he asks, and Joanne says no. No, she'll be fine, thanks.

She gets on to her hands and knees, her boobs swinging pendulously, and she resembles an old graceless Friesian stuck between two points.

Her muscles are not working as they should, and it's only now that Joanne realizes she's showing half her arse, as the hospital gown has fallen open at the back.

She reaches behind her, pawing clumsily, and touches not bare skin but the scratchy paper knickers she remembers stepping into earlier. Embarrassed, she lifts her head and looks straight into the eyes of the young porter.

Slurring, she says, 'Didn't I arrest you once?'

'Twice,' he replies. Then, smirking: 'Don't worry, Detective, I've seen it all before . . .'

5

I T'S 8 A.M. AND Felicity is yet to open her eyes. We are in a small private room; Felicity has a drip in each arm and a drain snaking from her stomach, along which putrid liquids flow.

Felicity's appendix burst.

When I arrived last night I was met by the surgeon who'd performed the appendectomy. He said it had been a perilously close call. When he opened her up she was full of gangrene: another hour and she'd have been dead. Now she is receiving IV antibiotics, saline and glucose, and they are monitoring her obs. every hour to check for a rise in temperature – a sign that peritonitis could be taking hold. As things stand, he expects Felicity to make a good recovery and thinks she'll be out of the hospital in about ten days.

So I'm calling Sean to tell him not to come to France.

I'm coping. I *can* cope.

There is only one small bed in the room with Felicity and I want to be with her 24/7. As long as she remains stable, it's best for Sean to stay where he is. He'll fight what I have to say, I know that, but the reality is – and this is going to sound like cold, hard business sense – I need him to take care of the hotel . . . and Alice, obviously.

There will be a ton of problems at work if he comes here, problems that will have snowballed by the time we return, and I'd rather focus entirely on Felicity right now. I can't face panicked phone calls every five minutes from the staff informing us of another disaster and, besides, it's not fair to ask Eve to stay. She can't just drop everything to look after Alice, she has her own business to think of, and it's not as if she's family, after all.

I step into the hallway and dial Sean. He picks up on the second ring. 'How is she?' he asks immediately on answering.

'Okay. She's still not awake.'

I've been giving Sean regular updates throughout the night. Neither of us has slept.

'I'm sorting out the last few things,' he says a little breathlessly. 'I called your dad, told him the score. I just need to find a set of keys for Eve, and then I'll be on my way—'

'Sean . . . don't come.'

'What?'

'Stay there, I can manage, I—'

'Of course I'm coming. I wouldn't leave you there alone. I have to come – why on earth would I stay—'

'Sean, listen, it's better you stay there and take care of things. Stay with Alice. I can be with Felicity every second, I don't have to leave her side. If you come, there's nowhere for you to sleep. You'll have to check into a hotel; it'll only complicate things. And then there's Raymond. He's got four days off booked from Monday, remember?'

Raymond's the general manager at the hotel. His parents are arriving from Slovakia and he's taking them to London, York, Edinburgh.

'Shit!' whispers Sean. 'I'd forgotten about that. Why do they always take holidays when—'

'Sean, it's okay. We'll be all right. Really, I need you to stay there. I can't get internet access on my phone, and they're already on at me for the medical insurance details. The teacher who stayed with Felicity during her op went straight back to the

45

camp and I don't know when one of them will return. I've got no numbers and no paperwork. You can sort all this stuff out for me . . . you can call the school, and I can take care of Felicity.'

He sighs, unsure if this is crazy talk. Of course he should come, he's thinking, but he knows there's some truth to what I'm telling him. If he leaves without arrangements in place, the hotel will suffer. And it's not always possible to recover from a hit if there are only junior staff on call; a minor grievance can develop into something insurmountable if it's not managed appropriately.

'I'll need you to book our return flights home, too,' I add, in case he's still wavering, 'and keep an eye on my dad for me.'

After a moment of silence he says, 'Okay. Okay, I get it. I can see that it makes sense. But you're sure you'll be all right?'

'Certain. Honestly, Sean, Felicity's come through the worst, and you know it's better to split our resources.'

He gives a small laugh at my obstinacy and tells me he loves me. Before he hangs up, he says, 'Thank God it's you over there, eh, Nat?'

Sean and I have always done pretty well in a crisis. We've never had people to step in, step up, never had that luxury. It's always been down to us. Back in my early twenties I used to fantasize about letting things fall apart, perhaps the way one might on the way to a big exam . . . 'If I just take my hands off the wheel . . . if I let the car glide across the road . . . all this pressure will be over.' But of course I never did. Too conscientious, too diligent.

Sometimes it felt as if we were being crushed by the weight of responsibility. We'd have guests complaining about there being no mobile phone signal, or the absence of a good fish restaurant in the village, or no sea view (the coast is twenty miles away), and either Sean or I would pacify them, talking them round with good humour while the other would be nursing a sick child with croup in the next room, or else out begging the bank manager to extend our overdraft, or wrangling with the *Mail on Sunday* to give our advert priority on the right-hand page.

My dad tried his best to help us out with the kids, but without my mum around to guide him he was pretty lost. And Sean's parents, though excellent at gushing over the girls on occasion, never once turned up saying, 'What can we do to help? Any ironing? Girls need a trip to the park?'

Understand, I'm not whining about this. They're our children, we had them. They are ours to look after.

Sean and I developed a way of working together so we could get through whatever was thrown our way. And I think our success was probably due to this attitude of not blaming, of getting on with whatever was in front of us without wondering if the other was pulling their weight. We've managed to get where we are without being beholden, without anybody's help.

I sit alongside Felicity's bed as a nurse finishes taking her temperature, her pulse.

'*Ça va?*' I ask the nurse.

'*Ça va,*' she replies simply, and leaves. For now, Felicity's okay.

With my fingertips I gently stroke her arm. Ordinarily, she's a healthy-looking child. She has Sean's dirty-blond hair, his golden skin that keeps a little colour right through the winter months. When they're properly tanned, both Sean and Felicity go that lovely deep-bronze colour, same shade as Farrah Fawcett in her tennis shorts.

There's a faint odour of meat on the turn coming from Felicity's drain site, and my eyes prickle with tears as I realize my poor baby was being poisoned from the inside out.

She'd been having mild stomach pains for a few months, and I now understand that what I'd casually put down to 'anxiety about school' was actually a grumbling appendix. I hadn't even taken her to the doctor, thinking it was silly to bother him with it when it was simply Felicity going through what all fourteen-year-olds go through: self-doubt, self-consciousness, the fear of not fitting in.

As I touch her hair I feel myself suppressing a guilty thought. Because it's not the first time I'd held off taking the girls to the surgery. Not the first time I told myself their ailments weren't important enough to warrant the doctor's time.

Now I look at Felicity's blanched skin, at the black circles beneath her lower lashes, at the freckles not usually visible across her nose, and I'm wondering if it was in fact *my time* that I was more concerned about wasting.

Out of nowhere a quote from Jackie Onassis pops into my head: 'If you bungle raising your children,' she said, 'I don't think whatever else you do well matters very much.'

Have I bungled motherhood?

Suddenly, I'm not so sure. Suddenly, it occurs to me that even though I've filled my time running around, tending to everything possible, I might just have been focusing on all the wrong things.

6

Dr Eve Dalladay sets Natty's kitchen table ready for breakfast. She arranges glasses of fresh orange juice, slightly stale chocolate croissants (which she's softened up in the oven) and vanilla cream doughnuts. Eve popped out at 7.15 a.m. and the Co-op had yet to have its first delivery of the day, so this was the best it had to offer.

She's dressed in skinny jeans, knee-high suede boots and a V-neck cashmere, lavender-coloured sweater. Her white-blond hair is held loosely in a ponytail at the crown of her head to accentuate her slim neck, and she has applied a fair amount of make-up. Today she's done it in such a way, though, to appear as if she's wearing none at all. She's gone easy on the perfume, too.

Alice shuffles into the kitchen, half dazed with sleep, and does a double take on seeing the doughnuts. 'Wow.'

'Thought we could all do with a bit of cheering up,' Eve says. 'Can I get you something hot? Coffee? Tea? Chocolate?'

Alice laughs. 'My mum would pass out if she saw all this sugar.'

Eve shoots Alice a worried look. 'Have I done the wrong thing?'

Alice shrugs. Her eyes are puffy from last night's crying and she has a deep red groove across her cheek. Eve doesn't mention it.

'Your dad's told you he's not going to France?' Eve asks.

'Yeah.'

Alice takes a bite from a chocolate croissant, licks the flakes of pastry from the corners of her mouth. 'He's staying to look after the hotel,' she says, taking another bite. 'Big shock there.'

'They've got a lot on right now.'

'When *haven't* they got a lot on?'

'It's the nature of the job, I suppose,' Eve reasons. 'The hospitality business never sleeps. The main thing is, Felicity's on the mend. Everything will be back to normal in a week or so.'

At the mention of Felicity's name Alice blinks hard a couple of times and reaches for her orange juice.

She had sobbed pitifully last night. As aloof as she could be around her mother, there's no doubt where she draws her strength from. Eve had watched carefully as Alice focused on Natty and, with Natty teetering on the edge of nervous collapse, Alice had no compass. No bearing. Simply no idea of how to cope with the news of her sister's plight. She'd cried uncontrollably for a good two hours, well after her mother had left for the airport.

Eve senses now would be a good moment to catch her off guard. She can't leave it too long, as Alice may not be in this fragile state for much longer, and after lying awake most of the night – Eve staring up at the ceiling, mulling things over – she'd arrived at the conclusion that she'd be an idiot not to act upon this serendipitous turn of events. Granted, the circumstances were not ideal. But when were they ever?

She chooses her words carefully. She stays by the range cooker, giving Alice plenty of distance.

'Alice, I don't want you to think I'm interfering in any way, but how would you feel if I were to stay for a while?'

'Fine, I guess.'

'I know you don't need me to look after you, you're quite capable of looking after yourself . . .'

'My mother clearly hasn't told you what a total disgrace I am in the kitchen then?'

Eve smiles. 'She might have mentioned something along those lines . . . I was thinking it could feel a bit empty here for you, what with your mum and Felicity not around and your dad stuck at the hotel most evenings. I could postpone my flight back to the States and keep you company.' Eve lifts her eyebrows questioningly. 'No pressure. I'm not trying to talk you into something you don't want or need.'

Alice stops eating. 'What about your work?'

'I'll rearrange things.'

'You can do that?'

'Sure.' Eve shrugs to make light of it. 'I don't really like the idea of you spending long periods by yourself, especially with your exams looming – I know how lonely revision can be. I thought perhaps I could stay just until your grandmother returns from Nice.'

Alice rolls her eyes. 'Can't wait for that.'

'She's not that bad, is she?'

'No, but she's like, "Did I tell you how clever *I was* at school?" like it wasn't, ohmygod, two thousand years ago. And she never stops going on about my dad, and how he was this super-talented kid who was brilliant at everything.'

Eve smiles. 'That's grandparents for you.'

'Yeah, but she can get hypercritical of my mum, and that gets kind of annoying. I'm looking at her, like, "What *is* your problem?" but I don't even think she knows she's doing it.' Alice folds the remaining pastry in two and pops it in her mouth. 'Have you told my dad you're staying?'

Eve shakes her head. 'I thought I'd run it by you first . . . but, Alice?'

'Hmm?'

'I'd just like to say that your mum has always been there for me. And I'd really like to help out if I can.'

Alice slips off her chair and bounds over to Eve. Now that she's properly awake she's no longer shuffling and once again has the elegant gait of a dancer: all loose, springy joints, long strides, feet turned out slightly. She plants a kiss on Eve's cheek and hugs her. 'I'd love it if you'd stay,' she declares, the fresh apple scent of her shampoo filling the air. 'You can tell me loads of really cool stuff about America.'

Alice goes to get dressed and Eve follows her upstairs. Rechecking her appearance in the bathroom mirror, Eve applies some white, pearly eyeliner to her Cupid's bow to accentuate her top lip and adjusts her breasts inside her bra. Then she takes her mobile from her back pocket so her arse is smooth and tight, rolls up her sweater a little at the rear. If she can find the opportunity to bend over, he'll get a quick flash of leopard print.

And leopard print to man is what shiny tat is to magpies. The response is primal. It's a reflex response. The image going from retina to dick, bypassing the brain entirely.

Eve gazes into the mirror until the sparkle in her eyes disappears and her expression is one of suitable concern. She arranges her ponytail for the last time, taking extra care to pull a few strands free so the thin, hairless, scar is not on show, and she's ready.

She opens the bathroom door and hears Sean banging around in the kitchen below. She's about to go downstairs when she pauses, eyeing the empty master suite across the hallway.

The back-up plan.

Sometimes all that's needed for the eventual unravelling is the initial seed of doubt to be sown.

So, after digging through her overnight bag, Eve takes the

black lace thong she wore yesterday and strides over to Natty's bedroom. She lifts the covers from the base of the bed and tucks it discreetly beneath the flat sheet, ensuring it won't be found immediately. Then she turns towards the open door, listening for any signs of movement coming her way.

When there is nothing, she surveys the room again. The décor is white – clean, simple, virginal. The only real colour comes from the antique brass headboard.

Climbing on to the bed, Eve kneels to face it. She presses her fingertips to her lips, one by one, making certain each has a little of the nude lipstick she's just applied. Then, gripping the cold brass in front of her, she leaves a neat row of prints – visible perhaps only to a person with a keen eye for cleanliness.

Satisfied, she makes her way downstairs.

Sean and Natty have always been very tight, a rock-solid couple since the very start. Because they've had to be. If they were to reveal the cracks, the buried secrets, if they were to disclose the blots on their history, then the show would be over and Mr and Mrs Perfect Lakeland Hoteliers' reputation tarnished.

They've had each other's backs for as long as Eve can remember. Sean is the type of guy to blow off drunken flattery from women with grace and good humour, never giving anyone an inch. And Natty, being so wrapped up with the girls, being so determined to get ahead, to make something of herself, proving to the world she's more than just a mother, has never really attracted the interests of other men anyway.

Together, the two of them make an impenetrable team.

But now, divided by a thousand miles, the stresses of having a sick child, and with Eve in the house, the one person aware of their weak spot – who knows what might happen?

Eve's going to take her chances because she's running out of time. And if there's one thing she understands, it's how to get inside people's heads. She knows how to get in there and fuck things up spectacularly. To the extent that they doubt everything they once knew to be true.

'How's it going?' Sean asks her as she enters the kitchen.

Eve smiles sympathetically. 'How are *you*, Sean? You don't need to put on a brave face for me.'

'Shitting myself, if I'm honest. I had no idea a person could get so sick in such a short space of time. It feels more like Felicity's been in a car crash.'

Poor Sean, he looks exhausted. The skin beneath his eyes is creased, the hair on the left side of his head sticking out at a right angle. If it weren't for the elegant cut of his suit and the whiter-than-white Italian shirt, open at the collar, you'd not give him a second glance if you passed him in the street this morning.

'Let me make you a coffee,' Eve says firmly. 'I can't begin to understand how worrying this is for the both of you. Heavens, I'm on the brink, and she's not even my child. Are you sure you don't want to go over there? Are you certain . . . because it really is no trouble for me to take care of things this end.'

He shakes his head. 'Natty's adamant she can manage. Thanks, though.'

'Well, if you change your mind . . .'

'Alice says you've offered to stick around to keep her company?'

'I'm in no hurry to go back,' Eve says, 'but if you think you'll be okay on your own, I'll get out from under your feet later on today.'

Sean doesn't speak. He's weighing what would be the right thing to do. Eve intuits his quandary and looks at him straight. 'How about I just stay until your mother returns, then she can be here for Alice – make sure she has everything she needs while she's studying?'

Sean shifts his weight. 'You mean, till Monday?'

Eve smiles innocently. 'Sure, till Monday.'

The kettle has finished boiling. Eve walks across the kitchen to fetch the milk. 'I think Alice might need a bit of support, Sean,' she says by way of an afterthought. 'She *was* very upset about Felicity last night . . . it'd be such a tragedy if it impacted on her studies.' She continues without turning: 'Natty says she's been working really hard recently. What is it she wants to do again? Medicine?'

'That's right, medicine,' Sean says wistfully.

'Such a clever girl,' Eve comments as she bends over to grab the milk from the bottom shelf of the fridge.

7

'Eve's staying until Monday?' I repeat back to Sean. 'That's thoughtful of her.'

'I'm not so sure,' he says. 'I'm not altogether happy at Eve being in the house without you. It feels a little weird.'

A scruffy orderly passes me in the hospital corridor and I'm immersed in a cloud of alcohol vapour. I'm wondering, if I were to pull out a match and strike it, would the air around me burst into flames?

I'm reminded of Alice's argument last night for the benefits of underage drinking, how the French – in allowing their children to drink wine at mealtimes – go a long way towards preventing binge drinking and alcoholism in later life.

I have seen no evidence of this so far. I've only been here a few hours and almost everyone I've come across reeks of either booze or cigarettes. Or both.

'Eve's not being a bossy-wife substitute is she?' I say laughing.

'No, but—'

'Eve's got her own problems,' I tell him. 'If she's offering to help out, let her. It'll take her mind off Brett, if nothing else.'

'They having a rough patch?'

'Before she left the States, he dropped the bombshell that he doesn't want children after all.'

'Ouch,' says Sean.

'I know. And she's no spring chicken either. So be nice. If she wants to stay and fuss over Alice, let her. Christ, Sean, we've got to learn to accept help from people now and again. Maybe this would be a good time to start?'

I end the call and return to Felicity's bedside. She opened her eyes for a few short minutes around ten this morning. Frowning a little when she saw me, she whispered, 'You're here?'

''Course I am. Does it hurt?'

'Not really,' she said, though her voice was desperately weak. 'What happened?'

'Your appendix burst.'

She tried to nod as it all came back to her. 'I didn't feel great on the trip over . . . I was sick on the boat. And then my stomach hurt really bad.'

'Why didn't you phone me?'

'Thought I'd just eaten too much processed crap,' she said, using my phrase, trying to smile.

I am always going on at the girls for eating *too much processed crap*. I have a friend whose daughter went away to university last September. She sent her mother a text saying: 'Guess what? I've not eaten a SINGLE VEGETABLE in over 3 weeks! What are you going to do about it?' and I laughed along merrily with my friend. Secretly, though, I was horrified.

'I love you, Felicity.'

And then her eyes went heavy again.

She's sleeping very deeply now as I watch her, and I'm trying to decide whether to chance leaving her to go and find something to eat while I've got the chance. The teacher who was at her bedside yesterday left a bag of individually wrapped cakes, snacks and crisps, but I'm not hungry for any of that. After wrestling with the idea for a few more minutes I make the decision to go out now, while Felicity's resting.

Rifling through my bag, the only paper I can find is my boarding pass, so I write across it: 'Gone for Food. Love you,

Mum xx', and place it on the bed by Felicity's right hand.

It's only when I'm out in the car park that I remember I've no currency. There wasn't time to get Euros at the airport last night. I look around, kind of helpless, because this is no holiday resort. This is rural France. The France that young English families embraced after the deluge of relocation programmes promised cheap property, old-fashioned values, and three-hour lunch breaks. The France of smallholdings, of friendly neighbours, bilingual children and good health care.

The France they tried their damnedest to escape when they realized there wasn't a whole lot going on.

Within my immediate sight, there are no shops, so I get into the car. The road on which the hospital stands is a single carriageway flanked by rows of plane trees. Their trunks are mottled with patches of taupe and olive, much like desert army combats, and their roots raise the road surface in places, cracking the asphalt. Shuttered houses lining the road are painted in various shades of French grey. Aged Peugeots and Citroëns, rusting around the wheel arches, jut out into the road. There is no shame in bad parking here. It's as if each driver has jumped out and abandoned his vehicle before coming to a complete stop.

I pass three ladies' hairdressers' and am just about to turn back and go in the other direction when I spot Aldi. Breathing a sigh of relief, I take a right.

I wouldn't be seen dead in a discount supermarket at home, but now, as I push through the glass door, I could kiss the assistant unloading plant seeds and potting compost from a big roll pallet.

The store is small. Four aisles stacked with the absolute basics I'll need to survive for the next week. And it accepts my debit card, which is the kind of small miracle I was hoping for.

I scan around and reckon I can be in and out of the place in five minutes. It's practically empty, just one other shopper – a woman with a toddler – loading up her trolley with supersized tins of Toulouse cassoulet.

I grab a baguette (half the weight of the French sticks in England), some Coulommiers Destrier – my all-time-favourite French cheese – and two tins of anchovy-stuffed green olives. Then into the basket I put tomatoes, apples, sanitary towels for Felicity, just in case, as I can't imagine hospital-issue pads will be welcomed by her, and lastly, as an afterthought, a bottle of Bordeaux. I have the feeling I'll need a drink once tonight comes around. I refrain from buying any goodies for Felicity, as the doctor said she won't be eating yet, and when she does it will be a diet of bland food to see how her digestive system copes.

I pay without trouble, the cashier even giving me fifty Euros cash back when I gesture to the till saying, '*S'il vous plaît?*' apologetically, and I'm almost starting to feel a little better about things, thinking I'm going to be okay here for a while, when I get a text from Alice. It says:

'Eve being absolutely brilliant!'

I read the words twice and feel a wave of queasiness wash through me. Like I've opened the fridge and got a whiff of food gone bad, but can't spot where it is. I tell myself to read nothing into it. It's simply Alice's way of letting me know not to worry about her, that everything is okay at home.

But I can't shake this feeling. Is this jealousy? Am I seriously jealous that another woman is taking good care of my daughter?

And I realize I am.

Disgusted at myself, I send Eve a quick text.

Thank you, I tell her. Thank you so much for being there for us.

8

'SHOCKED?' DC JOANNE Aspinall says to the surgeon. 'Of course I'm shocked. How would you feel under the circumstances?'

Three sets of eyes gaze down at Joanne, full of apology.

'It's one of those things,' says the surgeon briskly. 'Can't be helped.' His accent is cut-glass. He's sixtyish, an old-school type who most likely scares the shit out of his junior staff.

Joanne exhales. She can't believe this is happening to her.

The last thing she remembers is being wheeled down to theatre, that idiot porter grinning at her (she now recalls she arrested him for joyriding), she remembers the cannula going into her wrist, the anaesthetist telling her to 'Count backwards from one hundred,' she remembers the warm, wonderful feeling of something working its way up her arm, like being injected with 'Love Potion No. 9' and then . . .

Joanne's still pretty dozy, so she's not completely sure if this is real or not.

For all she knows, she might still be under. Or she might be in the recovery room – the room where patients coming out of anaesthetic thrash about in their beds. Where they moan and cry. Where they shout outrageous, filthy, sexual demands at the nursing staff. Her Auntie Jackie worked as an auxiliary nurse before changing to care in the community, so Joanne knows what goes on.

She glares at the surgeon. 'Am I dreaming this?'

'Afraid not.'

'Jesus,' she says, manoeuvring herself into a sitting position. 'It had to be me.'

'You understand we couldn't take the risk?' he says. 'I'm not being overly cautious, there is a *very real* risk of infection.'

'I know, I understand,' says Joanne. 'I'm just disappointed. I had the time booked off, I'd arranged cover . . . and I' – Joanne's unsure whether to say this next part – 'I really thought I'd be waking up a different person. This is the first day of the rest of my life kind of thing.'

'We should be able to get you back for surgery in around a fortnight's time,' says the nurse, who up till now has remained silent. 'I can't give you an exact date, we'll send out a letter—'

Joanne shakes her head. 'My colleague's having his wisdom teeth out. He's booked the time off. It'll have to be delayed until later this summer.'

The surgeon looks uneasy. He doesn't say anything, but Joanne can tell he's got something in the pipeline.

He's a wiry, sinewy-looking thing. Most likely a climber or a fell runner. Probably off to do the Inca Trail or K2 – something silly like that.

'I'll leave you with Hilary then. Let you two have more of a chat,' he says, and in true surgeon style he vanishes before Joanne has a chance to pose another question.

Hilary is mid-fifties, devoid of make-up, with short, sensibly cut, greying hair which Joanne reckons she will *never* resort to colouring. She's all business and detached. The perfect cosmetic surgeon's accomplice. Joanne thinks there must be a depository for this type of woman. Married for thirty years, Hilary will keep her home like a new pin, she'll take no nonsense from her grown-up children, take her summer holidays to coincide with Wimbledon and, though she never mentions him outside of work, she'd lay her life down in an instant for the sake of her boss. *The consultant.*

Hilary leans in towards Joanne. 'Shall we?' she says.

'If we must.'

Hilary unties Joanne's gown from behind her neck and lowers it, exposing the whole of Joanne's white chest. Joanne is immediately self-conscious. But who wouldn't be if their first boyfriend had referred to it as whale blubber?

'It's underneath the left breast,' says Hilary. 'Do you want to lift it?'

'I'd rather,' replies Joanne, and Hilary gives a tight smile.

Joanne lifts her breast upwards and outwards; it weighs about the same as an Accrington brick. She was told they would be removing around six hundred grams of tissue from each breast today, and Joanne had found herself imagining them to be almost weightless after the operation. Imagining not the normal incessant downward tug-tugging, but instead the light, lovely, buoyancy she feels when submerged in water.

Hilary takes out a pen from the top pocket of her tunic and points at the crease beneath Joanne's breast. 'There it is.'

'Where?' Joanne asks. 'I can't see it.'

'There,' replies Hilary.

Rather roughly, Hilary pulls the skin out of the way so Joanne can get a better look.

'Oh,' Joanne says, crestfallen.

'Yes, it's right where the incision line would be. If you were having a different type of reduction . . . if there weren't so much tissue to remove . . . it wouldn't be such a problem. But you're not a candidate for the vertical scar incision, you need the inverted T.' She takes away her pen. 'And *that*,' she says, as though she has a bad taste in her mouth, 'is right on the line.'

The *that* is a whitehead.

A large, angry, pus-filled spot about the size of a baked bean.

Slicing through it and then on into Joanne's skin and breast tissue would not be a very wise thing to do apparently.

'Bastard,' Joanne mutters under her breath.

'Yes,' replies Hilary, arching an eyebrow. 'It is a bit.'

9

'L ET'S EAT OUT tonight, shall we?' Eve says brightly. 'My treat. Where do you fancy, Alice? What's your favourite type of food?'

'Ooh, Chinese,' replies Alice enthusiastically. 'I'd really love a king prawn chow mein. Dad? Which is the best Chinese to go to? Is it the one behind St Martin's Church, or do you still go up to Windermere?'

Sean puts his mobile on the kitchen worktop and rubs his face. 'I don't know if I feel up to going out, I'm pretty drained. I'm operating on no sleep and I've got a killer day tomorrow. Could we have something here instead?'

Alice's face drops. She quickly becomes aware, however, that it's inappropriate to get excited about a meal out when her sister is so sick. And especially when her mum and dad are suffering with worry.

Foolish girl, Eve thinks, surveying her now. She's so childlike. Alice's emotions are displayed instantly, and in full view, for all to see.

'I just meant a quick bite,' she says gently, addressing Sean. 'To save us the trouble of cooking. I can pop out to get a takeaway instead, if that would be better?'

'Could you?' he says, trying his best to smile through the fatigue. 'Would you mind awfully? That'd be great.'

'Not at all,' Eve replies. 'And I was thinking, perhaps Alice and

I can come to the hotel in the morning, help get everything ready for the awards ceremony? Do you think we might be useful, or would we be getting in the way?'

Sean scoffs. Good-naturedly, he says, 'Alice hasn't so much as *set foot* in the place since we got her to chambermaid when she was fourteen. Natty thought it would be good for her to earn some extra money, realize how much hard work you have to put in to pay for a fifty-pound haircut.'

Alice straightens her spine. 'It was totally disgusting, Eve,' she spits. 'Can you imagine, people *actually leave* used condoms between the sheets for the staff to clean up? It's so gross.'

'We did provide you with gloves,' Sean reasons, grinning at his daughter's distaste.

'Never again,' she says. 'I'd rather clean up after farm animals than do that.'

'That's a firm no, then?' Eve laughs. 'C'mon, Alice, tomorrow's Saturday. We can go in for the morning, lend a hand and chill out in the afternoon. Watch a movie or something. It'll be fun.'

Every inch of Alice's being is screaming *No!* No, she does not want to go to her parents' place of work and be useful. No, that is not what she had in mind for tomorrow *at all*. But she looks at Eve and begins biting the side of her cheek. Eve can sense that the gently applied pressure is making Alice recognize she's acting like a spoilt brat. Eventually, Alice says, 'Okay,' reluctantly. 'Okay, we can go.'

'Great. Now that's settled, I'll go and get dinner.'

Half an hour later and Eve returns with the takeaway, just as Sean is finishing a phone call with Natty.

Eve can tell things are settling down in France. The desperate urgency and worried tone of Sean's voice is diminishing, and it's obvious from his words that practicality is setting in.

'I will,' he's saying, yawning. 'Yes . . . I know. No, I've not forgotten . . . Libby spent the afternoon wiping down the spare seating . . . Yes, we're putting him in the Lakeview Suite . . .'

He tells Natty to tell Felicity he loves her, and ends the call.

'How are they doing?' Eve asks.

'Better. Felicity's not up to talking, though. She's just due for another round of painkillers so she's pretty uncomfortable. Natty says the nurses seem happy with her progress.'

'And how is Natty bearing up?'

'Like the trooper you'd expect. She's holding it together much better now that she's at Felicity's bedside.'

'Had to be a huge shock.'

Eve begins unpacking the food, finds the large serving spoons and sets the table with the rest of the cutlery and three wine glasses. 'Do you want to give Alice a shout?' she says, before asking Sean if he's going back to the hotel later on.

'I should,' he says, a little guiltily, 'and I've told Nat I will be, but to be honest, I'm tempted to duck out, make an early start of it tomorrow instead.'

'If you don't mind my saying, you do look dead beat, Sean. I think you could do with a night off.' She reaches inside the other bag on the worktop. 'I picked up a few cans for you. Not sure if they're the right ones, I couldn't remember what you like to drink, so . . .'

She sees a mixture of relief and deep gratitude on Sean's face.

'Thanks,' he says.

'Any time.'

He walks towards her and goes to retrieve a pint glass from the cupboard, but as he reaches out, Eve touches his arm. 'Let me,' she whispers. 'Sit down, let me be useful.'

He stops and, for the first time since she's been here, Eve feels something alter. The space between them is changing and Eve knows from experience she's close to exposing that rare spot where Sean's blockade is weak. The spot where if just the right amount of energy is channelled, the blockade could very well fall apart.

Sean doesn't sit as Eve instructed, he stays right next to her as she pours the beer.

As the last of the liquid slips from the can, she hands him the glass, saying, 'For you,' and hooks a stray tendril of hair behind her ear, holding his gaze a moment too long.

She parts her mouth, moistening her lower lip with her tongue, and lets the possibility of her, the possibility of what she can do for him, start to sink in.

'You're letting me have *wine*?' Alice says, staring at the table. 'Seriously?' She turns to Sean, her eyes wide. She's dressed in MC Hammer 'Can't Touch This' pyjama bottoms and a pink Hollister hoodie.

'Half a glass,' Sean tells her. 'No more. Eve persuaded me, so you've got her to thank. Don't tell your mother.'

Alice is fit for bursting. She spins around to Eve. 'Oh . . . my . . . God,' she mouths, 'you . . . are . . . amazing.'

They sit down to eat and Alice downs her half a glass of wine quickly, too quickly, and starts babbling about how utterly lame it is that her mother won't let her drink. All her friends drink. Not stupidly, or anything. But their parents let them drink at home.

'Your mum thinks she's doing the right thing,' Eve says, 'and, to be honest, Alice, she is. You're only sixteen. If you lived in the States you'd have to wait another five years for your first taste of alcohol.'

Sean asks, 'Do they honestly stick to that?'

Eve nods. 'Pretty much. It's an offence in some states if you supply alcohol to anyone underage. So if you leave liquor in the house and the kids get at it, then you're liable.'

'That's nuts,' says Alice, twirling her fork in her chow mein. 'They're, like, "You can get married, you can have a baby . . . you can *even* have plastic surgery if you want to, but you can't drink."' She shakes her head. 'That is so totally screwy.'

'Where we live, lots of teens go across to Canada on the weekends so they can drink.'

Emboldened, Alice says to Sean, 'See, Dad? If you ban people from doing something, they will always find a way.'

Sean stands to get another can from the fridge. 'Is that so?' he says, amused. 'Eve? Can I get you anything?'

'I'd love another glass of white Rioja – can't get that at home.'

'No?'

'Washington state's a big wine-growing region, but there's not a huge variety to choose from.'

'What will you do when *you* have children, Eve?' Alice asks. 'Do you think you'll be all strict and unreasonable . . . like someone we know?'

'*Alice!*' Sean says, flustered by her faux pas. 'I don't think Eve wants to discuss—'

'It's okay,' Eve says. 'It's fine, Sean.' She smiles sadly at Alice. 'To be frank, I don't know if that's going to happen for me. I don't know if I'll ever get the chance to become a mother.'

'Oh,' says Alice in a quiet voice, 'but . . . but you'd be a great mum.'

Eve reaches across to Alice's hand, touching it briefly. 'Thank you, that's a lovely thing to say.'

'I mean it.'

Sean refills Eve's glass as she drops her gaze. For added effect, she blinks hard a couple of times before speaking. 'To be frank, Alice, I never imagined I'd find myself in this situation,' she begins. 'I always thought I'd have a brood of children by now. It just didn't work out that way, I guess.'

'But you're not too old, are you?' Alice says. 'I thought . . .'

Eve tries to smile. 'No, I'm not too old . . . but my relationship with my husband has ended and—'

68

Alice's hand flies to her mouth. 'Oh!' she blurts. 'Oh, I didn't know. Eve, I'm so sorry. I've really put my foot in it, haven't I?'

''Course not. It's no secret. I hadn't got around to telling you yet because of what happened to Felicity. It's okay, Alice, I'm not completely heartbroken.'

'You're not?'

'Things had not been right with Brett and me for a long time. It was best to end the marriage. I'm only trying to be realistic about the fact that by the time I meet someone else, someone I might want to marry and spend the rest of my life with – well, I'm going to be nearly forty. And then the chances of my becoming pregnant after forty are not as great. And the chances of meeting a man who wants a child, perhaps when he already has a family of his own . . . well, they're not so great either.'

Alice looks away as if she's suddenly going to cry. 'Everyone at school bangs on about not having kids till they're forty . . . but I never looked at it that way. I never thought that if you left it too long it might not happen at all.'

'Girls say that. Girls were even saying that when I was at school. And education is *the* most important thing, Alice. I took my education as far as it could go, and it's brought me the freedom and the chance to do countless amazing things I never expected. But don't leave having a family too late. You'll regret it, you really will.'

Alice nods seriously, digesting this new information.

Eve knows that Natty has pushed and pushed her daughter in school. Told Alice to not make the same mistakes she did. Told her not to get landed with a child at such an early age, cutting off her opportunities. And when you're fourteen, fifteen, that stuff makes sense. But when the hormones kick in, and the nesting instinct starts to strengthen, the desire to be a mother seemingly coming from out of nowhere, it can be a confusing time for girls. They become frightened to acknowledge what a few million years' of evolution is telling their bodies.

'And the reason I tell you not to leave it too late, Alice, is because I think you will make a fabulous mum, too.' Eve then makes like she's sneaking more wine into Alice's glass, even though it's in full view of Sean. He doesn't object. He's watching his daughter carefully. Proudly.

'But what if someone came along for you right now, Eve? Someone who wanted to get married. Then what?' Alice asks.

'Then I'd jump at the chance,' Eve replies. 'Because if I was really lucky, it might mean I'd get to have a daughter a little bit like you.'

When Alice leaves the table, going upstairs for a bath, Sean leans back in his seat and rests his hands behind his head. 'I'm glad you spoke to her in that way,' he says.

'Like what?'

'Like an adult. Natty has a way of babying her . . . perhaps "babying" is a little strong, but I think she's overly protective of her. I worry sometimes Alice might rebel against it.'

'It can be a fine line,' Eve agrees.

'Do you deal with many teenagers at your practice?'

'Sure. You know what they're like over there – kid starts acting out, *they have issues*. It's a different mindset. Give a British woman a wild child and she'll say, "This must be my fault. How did I cause this?" Give an American one and she'll say, "We need stronger meds and therapy" . . . I'm not complaining, though – kids are my bread and butter.'

'Well, you really know how to talk to Alice.'

Eve makes light of the compliment. 'She's a great girl.'

'No,' he says, 'I mean it. You get the best out of her. It's rare we see her relaxed . . . opening up like that. Lately it's been one long argument between her and Natty.'

'It's my job. Besides, I like to listen. Most people don't, but I do.'

Eve clears away the plates and takeaway cartons from the table. Sean goes to help but she tells him not to and grabs him another beer.

After he's downed half of it he asks, 'Are you really okay, Eve? About Brett, I mean.'

'I will be. There's a lot to sort out. I was telling Natty I'm not sure if I even want to go back over there. I might stay here instead. See if I can make a life for myself. What about you? Are *you* okay?'

'Of course. You know me.'

'Do I?'

He looks at her, confused. 'I'm not sure I follow.'

'I *did* know you, Sean. Once. I'm not certain I do any more, though.'

'Things change. *Life* changes,' he says. 'What I wanted at twenty is certainly not what I want now.'

'But does it ever get too much?'

'Does *what* ever get too much?'

Eve gestures around the expansive custom-built kitchen. 'This,' she says. 'The need to keep moving forwards, to keep succeeding, the incessant drive for the beautiful house, the perfect life—'

Sean stops her mid-sentence. He's mildly affronted. 'That's Natty,' he says quietly, 'not me.'

'I know,' she replies, and he looks away.

After a moment he tips his head back and exhales. 'It *can* get to be too much . . . sometimes,' he admits. 'I wonder what she's trying to prove, or to whom.'

'Does she ever get uptight?'

Sean laughs. 'Natty? When is she *not* uptight these days? It's become that she doesn't know how to be any other way.'

'What do you miss?'

'About Natty?'

Eve reaches out her hand and seizes his wrist. 'About *you*, Sean.'

'Whoa!' he says, and Eve panics she may have mistimed her approach. She stares at him, gauging his reaction, and to her relief he doesn't pull away, as she thinks he might. She sees a glint of interest in his eyes, rather than the cold rebuke she thought was on its way. 'Whoa!' he says again, sighing. 'Mrs Psychologist, you *are* good.'

'Not good,' she replies softly. 'Just concerned about an old friend.'

Sean thinks for a minute. After a time he says, 'I miss my youth. I miss feeling young and spontaneous. We became parents so early and since then Natty has had every year mapped out. We know what we're doing and when. Nothing ever just happens any more. The girls are almost grown, we're on the cusp of the first freedom we've ever had, but I'm not certain Natty wants that freedom. I keep trying to talk her into selling the hotel, but—'

Eve releases his arm and sits back in her seat. 'When did you last get a blow job, Sean?'

For a second he's thrown off balance. Shock registers on his face. Then, almost reluctantly, he says: 'I asked for one on my birthday.'

'And did you get it?'

He shakes his head, laughs derisively.

Eve moves from her chair and down on to her knees. She holds his gaze steady as she pulls off her sweater, removes her bra. He doesn't stop her. Even though his daughter is upstairs in the bath, even though she's just moments away, he doesn't stop her.

She releases his dick from his boxers and gives him a slutty smile. The sense of power she gets from this has always been a turn-on. The ensuing dependence these men have on her always useful.

She slides her tongue around the tip, lustily, and hears him say, 'Fuck,' breathlessly, when she takes him inside her mouth fully.

His hands are in her hair, on her face. His movements are urgent.

'Don't stop,' he whispers. 'Please don't stop.'

She looks up at him from beneath her lashes and his face is bordering on anguished; he's almost at that critical point. So she quickens her rhythm.

With his body braced and his hands locked to the sides of the chair, he comes violently, his entire body shuddering.

'Fuck!' he says again, astonished this time. 'You swallowed? You actually swallowed?'

And Eve looks deep into his eyes and frowns. 'Of course,' she says innocently. 'Why, doesn't everyone?'

TEN DAYS LATER

10

WE'RE FIVE MINUTES from home, driving along the Crook road towards Bowness-on-Windermere. I'm taking it steady, but the sharp bends, the rises and falls in the road, are making Felicity groan.

An Aston Martin is right up my rear end and, after having been patient with him for the first mile or so, he's starting to piss me off. I've taken to touching the brake with my left foot while at the same time keeping my right foot pressed to the accelerator. Each time he slows in response to my brake lights, I pull away from him. Smiling at my petty triumph, I look in the mirror and see he is not amused. Good.

Before leaving France I bought flowers and chocolates for the nursing staff and two bottles of *premier cru* champagne for the wonderful surgeon who saved Felicity's life. He's been a real sweetie. Popping in more than he probably needed to, helping me with the insurance forms, even bringing English DVDs from his own home for Felicity to watch. I developed a minor crush on him, which is only to be expected, I suppose.

Felicity is weak and thin but generally okay. She's eating almost normally now, though her skin still has that grey hue and they tell me it'll take time – around a month – for her to return to full health. So she'll be off school a while longer yet.

We pass the Wild Boar Hotel, Windermere Golf Club, and we're almost home. I can't wait to get her there, can't wait to get

Felicity into her own bed and spoil her rotten. And Sean really needs us back where we belong. He hasn't been coping at all well on his own – I could hear it in his voice.

He has been uncharacteristically quiet on the phone, and though he was insistent nothing was wrong, it's clear he's been lonely. He's one of those men who doesn't do well without his wife; without regular meals and his usual routine, he goes all to pot.

I am longing to see him. Longing to love him. After one day in France I found I was aching for his presence, and it occurred to me that because we are together almost every minute, I have been taking our love for granted. I couldn't get rid of the thought: What if I put *us* first? What if I put us above the girls, above the hotel? What would our life look like if I simply shifted emphasis?

Every time I imagined this scenario Sean was smiling (and naked). And, uncharacteristically, so was I.

Of course, Eve's been a godsend. Thank heavens she was able to stay for a time to take care of Sean and Alice – though, sadly, she's now gone, flown home to Washington state. While in France I finally managed to get an internet connection on my phone, so I sent flowers to say thanks for all the help she gave us. I'm totally indebted. And I only hope they were there when she arrived back to brighten things up a little, because I hate the thought of her returning to an empty house.

I look across to Felicity. She's happy. 'It's so pretty, isn't it, Mum?' she says. 'Every time we go away I forget how lovely it is around here.'

'I know. We're lucky.'

There have been floods while we've been in France. Nothing catastrophic, just excess surface water after days of persistent rain. Rain that fell on to already saturated ground.

Today there are large pools in the fields adjacent to the road, with Scots pines standing oddly erect in the water. I say 'fields', but this is not really farmable acreage, not ploughed regular spaces used for growing crops. Mostly, they're used for sheep.

South Lakeland fields are small, small and scattered with the same giant, rocky boulders that were broken up and used to build the dry stone walls which enclose them.

Felicity gestures through the windscreen to the new spring lambs on the rocky outcrops gathering together to avoid the wet, just as we hit a flooded patch of road and water sprays up high in sheets. Everything is a deep, lush green. British racing green.

We pull into our driveway and see Alice has hung a banner above the front door: 'Welcome Back Felicity!' and Felicity turns to me, arches an eyebrow. It's starting to sink in that there might be some mileage to be had in almost dying.

'She might be nice to me for a bit,' Felicity says mischievously.

'Enjoy it while it lasts,' I reply.

I climb out, and I'm about to go around to Felicity's side to help her when in my peripheral vision I'm aware of Sean approaching from the house. I go to greet him and stop for a second because, immediately, I see something is wrong.

I stare at him, frightened.

'What?' he says, walking up to the car, trying his hardest to smile. 'You look like you've seen a ghost, Natty.'

'What's happened? Where's Alice, is she all right?'

He lays his hand on my shoulder, something he never does, and I am panicked beyond measure.

'Alice is fine,' he says soothingly. 'Absolutely fine. She's at school. She didn't want to go this morning, obviously. She wanted to be here for when you two got back. I told her she had to—'

'Who's dead?' I demand.

'What?' he laughs awkwardly.

'Has someone died? Where's my dad?'

'Natty, calm down. No one has died. Everyone is fine.'

'What is it, then? Sean, I can tell by looking at you something bad has happened. Tell me. You look like you've not slept in a week. Are you ill? Have you been to the doctor?'

He sighs. 'Let's go in.'

'No. Tell me now.'

He holds my gaze for an extended moment before shaking his head. His whole body appears conflicted and I don't know what to make of it.

He bends forward to talk to Felicity across the driver's seat.

'Hey, Miss Wonderful!' he says jovially. 'How are you doing? Shall we get you inside? Wait till you see what Alice has done to your bedroom – you're going to love it.'

He makes no comment on her pallor, which I'm grateful for, and I watch through the windscreen as Felicity goes to lean towards him. Without warning, though, as she attempts to kiss his cheek, the pain in her abdomen forces her back in her seat and, reflexively, Sean and I bolt to her – Sean around the back of the car, me around the front.

Sean gets to her first. 'Don't move, love. Please don't move. I'll carry you to the house,' he's saying from his crouched position. 'Where does it hurt? Can you show me?' He shoots me a quick look as if to ask, *Is this normal?* but before I can respond, Felicity is saying, 'It's fine, Dad.' She's smiling because she thinks he's fussing, though it's clear she is in some discomfort. 'I'm okay to walk,' she tells him. 'I just forgot and moved a bit too quick.'

'All right,' he says, glancing at me again, still worried. 'Don't get out straight away. You catch your breath and then I'll swing your legs around for you.'

He strokes her upper arm tenderly, frightened to touch her too firmly lest his daughter is hurt once more. He's telling her he loves her and how much he's missed her. I try explaining that she will be okay to climb out in a moment, but he's not listening.

Before leaving France, Felicity and I practised getting in and out, up and down, and, though she needs to go slow, she *can* do it.

Sean kisses Felicity's cheek and rises silently.

He turns, and again we're face to face. And it's only now that I see his panic is not simply down to Felicity. There is more. My first instincts were right: there is something terribly wrong here.

Go on, my eyes say to him, bulging, scared. *Go on, tell me. What is it?*

And with a bereft look, a look of complete despair, he whispers, 'Natty, I am so, so sorry.'

Upstairs, Felicity is settled in bed, TV on, music on, laptop open, as I stand in the kitchen shaking. *He has lost all our money* is what I'm thinking. The stupid sod has been dabbling in shares and now we've got nothing left. I always knew it was a bad idea.

'Spit it out, then,' I say.

He closes his eyes, takes a deep breath, and, steady as his nerves will allow, replies: 'I'm in love with Eve.'

I do a double take.

'You're *what?*'

He repeats: 'I am in love with Eve Dalladay.'

'After two days?' I say. 'No, you're not. How *can* you be?'

He shifts his weight to his other foot. 'It's been a bit more than two days actually.'

I'm scowling at the information he's giving but, to be honest, I feel nothing yet. No anger. More like confusion. As if I've been presented with a naughty toddler, and I know on some level he has done something very, very wrong, but I can't organize my thoughts to proceed with the best course of action.

'You love Eve,' I say without emotion. A statement.

'Yes.' He's wincing, trying to gauge if I'm playing dumb. Not sure what to expect next.

I try to get this straight. 'So you're saying that while I've been in France, tending to our sick daughter, sleeping in a hospital room, counting the hours till we could all be together again, you've been having a thing with *my friend*?'

He nods, shrinking away from me.

I roll my eyes and go to flick on the kettle. 'I don't believe you.'

He doesn't press it and there's a moment, a pause in the proceedings, during which I survey him fully. He's pale and wan-looking, not unlike Felicity, and it occurs to me that he could very well be anaemic. I pick up the phone. I'll call the doctor, get him booked in for some blood tests.

'Natty, are you listening to what I'm telling you?'

'But she's gone home, Sean.' I emphasize the words. 'Eve has gone back to America. I don't see how you can think you've got something together when she's not even in the country.' I replace the handset and move towards him. 'Sean,' I say gently, 'does Eve know about this? Have you talked to her about it? Because I'm pretty sure you're suffering from some sort of delusion here.'

My face is showing concern but, inside, I'm terribly embarrassed. What if he made a move on Eve and she had to flee? God, that would be awful. How do I go about beginning *that* conversation?

'She's staying at the hotel,' he says.

'Which hotel? Ours?'

'She didn't go back to America,' he explains. 'Under the circumstances, we thought it best to say that she had.'

My brow furrows in confusion. 'Which room is she in?' I ask, shakily, because . . . could this possibly be true?

'What does it matter?' he says.

''Cause it fucking matters, okay?'

He starts to prattle on with explanations, apologies, reasons for all of this, but I can't hear him. I can't understand the words pouring from his mouth. I hold up my hand to stop him from speaking, because here it comes. Here is the anger. I feel it rising. In the space of a split second I've gone from numb, devoid of emotion, to possessed.

There's a thrashing, ugly creature inside of me and it needs to come out. Feels as if it's going to split me right in two when it does. And I try to get a hold of my breathing but—

'YOU WANKER!' I scream at him. 'You total fucking wanker!'

He backs away. Closes his eyes, takes the hit.

'How can you be in love with her?' I demand. 'How? Tell me!'

'I'm not sure I could explain it even if I wanted to.'

'Try.'

'I don't know. People don't choose to fall in love with other people, Natty. It's something that just happens.'

'What a load of shit.'

'Neither of us wanted this, believe me,' he says.

His words are desperate, pleading. All the clichés rolling out of his mouth in a steady stream.

'That's the thing,' I tell him, 'I don't believe you . . . I don't understand how, in the space of a few days, you can—'

'It was more than a few days, and you have to believe it,' he says intently. 'You have to believe it, because it's true.'

My heart is hammering. The glass vase on the kitchen worktop catches my attention. I start to eye it, feel my hand edging towards it.

'Don't throw that at me,' he says tiredly, rubbing his face.

And I scrunch my eyes up tight. We stand in silence. Me, my world falling apart, and Sean, wondering if I'm going to go for him.

'Fuck,' I whisper, the pain beginning to swell. It continues until it has the force of a blow. A real, physical blow to the gut because, Christ, he actually means it. I stare at his face and see only resignation. He means it when he says he loves her.

How the hell did this happen? How did this happen in just over a week? Is that how long it takes for your whole life to be handed over to another person?

Now I start to cry.

'You've been fucking her, I assume?'

He doesn't answer.

'What am I saying? Of course you've been fucking her.'

He nods and I screw my face up again as I try to be brave, try to thwart off another blow to the gut.

'Jesus, Sean,' I whimper. 'Jesus, this *hurts*. Have you really thought this through, because this is really hurting me? It's killing me to stand here listening to this.'

'I didn't want to tell you today. I was going to wait. I wanted to wait until you and Felicity were settled in and were more in a position to—'

'To what? So you were going to sleep next to me? You were going to tell me tomorrow? What if I wanted to make love? What if—'

He cuts me off gently. 'You wouldn't have wanted to make love, Natty.'

I swallow and look down at my hands.

I feel almost ashamed, because he's right. Even though an hour ago my need for him was desperate, primal, when the opportunity arose I was sure to have flinched when he touched me. Because I'd be worrying about Felicity. Worrying about something, anyway, because that's who I am now. That's who I've become.

I try to gather myself. 'Is this about, you know, the past?'

He shakes his head.

'Is this punishment for what you did for me? Is that what this is? Birds finally come home to roost?'

'That's unfair,' he says.

'*This* is unfair!' I cry. 'You're not even giving me the chance to fix it, you're looking at me like it's already over, no discussion, and you're not even giving me a chance to say my side of things. Have you been *that* unhappy, Sean?'

'I've been happy,' he says.

'Not happy enough, though.'

He presses his lips together into a lame, sympathetic kind of smile. 'Sorry,' he whispers.

'What about marriage guidance? What about fighting for what we've got?' I plead. 'Surely we deserve some shot at this?' My voice is starting to screech as I get more and more desperate. 'I don't even know what I've done wrong.' I walk towards him, my face beseeching, but he steps back. 'Tell me what I've done and let me fix it.' I go to put my arms around him, but he won't let me. He pushes me away.

'Natty, listen, you *can't* fix this. There is nothing to fix. You've done nothing wrong. You have been the best wife, the best mother, you could possibly be.'

'What then?'

And he shrugs helplessly.

'Is it because I'm not her? Because I'm not Eve?'

He won't answer.

Turning towards the worktop, I put my head in my hands. I don't know what to do. Don't know how to make him stop saying what he's saying. I feel as I did when I got the phone call about Felicity, when I thought she might die. It feels the same.

'Please change your mind, Sean,' I whimper. 'You have to. I can't do this without you.'

I feel the palm of his hand on the small of my back. It's a weak attempt at comfort, and for the first time in my life I can sense he doesn't really want to touch me. He's doing it because he thinks he ought to, because he doesn't know what else to do.

I look at him. 'Please?' I say again. 'I'll be better, I'll *do* better. I'll change, I know I've not been—'

'Natty,' he whispers. 'Don't.'

'Don't what?' I sob.

'Don't do this. Don't make it harder than it already is.'

'I can't believe you're walking away now. After all we went through together. After how hard we had to fight to keep everything. Explain to me why, Sean, because I don't get it. I know it hasn't been easy, we've had our problems, but every couple has problems.'

'I've never been loved like this,' he says simply. 'I've never been *wanted* like this. It's like nothing I've ever known. To be needed so much by someone, it's . . . it's as though I've got no option. I can't turn my back on it, it's too strong.'

His eyes are wet with tears and I know he didn't want to have to tell me that.

'Look,' he says after a minute, trying to gather himself but still with an audible catch in his voice, 'I promise I'll do my best by you and the girls. I'll make it as painless as I possibly can.'

'Painless?' I sob. 'And how d'you suppose you're going to do that? Sean, you're *my* husband, not hers, does that not mean anything to you?' But I can feel the fight draining from me as I realize it's pointless to continue to beg. His energy is changing. He wants to get out, wants to leave, and I see I've lost him.

'I love her,' he says firmly. 'And I can't stop, Natty. I really wish I could, but I just can't.'

11

So HE'S GONE.
Alice returned home from school and Sean asked her to join him in Felicity's bedroom, whereupon he did his best to explain why he wouldn't be living with us any longer. Unable to face it, I sat outside the door crying quietly as Alice screamed furiously at her father and Felicity asked questions about our future. She wanted to know the practicalities: Would we stay in this house? Would Sean and I continue to run the hotel? Questions I hadn't even thought to ask yet myself.

That was four days ago and, apart from shuffling around the house, tending to Felicity, I have remained almost constantly in bed. I'm filled by what I can only describe as a deep emptiness, a kind of non-feeling, or void. I want to cry. I want to shout and scream. But it's as if my emotions are in standby mode.

Of course, the first night after Sean left I terrorized myself with images of him and Eve together. I drank a litre of wine and it sent my thoughts spiralling. I lay in bed, head throbbing, wondering: *How did it all start?* How did they go from polite enquiry about each other's lives, gentle banter and courteous, friendly chit-chat, to actually fucking?

Did they talk about me? Did Sean confide in Eve about *me*?

Filled with equal parts outrage and self-loathing, I found myself thinking about France. When I was there, did they sit on the sofa, exchanging glances, waiting for Alice to go to bed? Did they watch TV, checking their watches, Eve's legs tucked beneath her, innocently asking Alice about her day before they could get upstairs?

Did he send Eve text messages, the type he used to send me?

'Meet you at home in an hour ... plugs and points? Or is there time for a full service?'

Did he run her a bath? Talk about her marriage? Did he tell her she looked good naked? Better than me? (She does, by the way.)

How exactly *had* it started?

Had they fallen in love with each other's minds, or had Sean behaved as any warm-blooded male would behave in the company of a lone female? I mean, Arnold Schwarzenegger wasn't immune; he slept with his maid. Why? Because she was beautiful and amazing? No, she was just nearby. As in *inside the house*.

Jude Law did the same.

These women were there, they offered it, and the men said, 'Go on then. Why not?'

Why should Sean be any different?

My dad telephones every few hours, but I can't speak. The muscles of my throat are taut and constricted; I feel as if I have a large pill lodged in it that I am unable to swallow. And, besides, there is nothing to say. 'I won't kill myself, so you can stop calling,' I tell him this morning, and for now it seems he may ease off. I tell him I *will* get up eventually. Sean's mother has been round to the house. I didn't let her in. Put my head beneath the pillow and let Penny bang away on the front door, let her go on for as long as she could be bothered to do so. And there have been dozens of messages on the answer machine, acquaintances desperate to console me, but, again, I don't talk. My instinct is to stay close to the wall, shutting out life for as long as it takes.

The girls are in a daze. Initially, Alice continued in exactly the way I'd expect Alice to – yelling at her father, demanding he come home *this very second* and witness what he was doing to us. And, in fairness, he did come. But he could only say the same thing over and over: how he hates himself for what he's done to me, to *us*, how sorry he is, but there is no going back. Alice came to me crying when he'd left, her red hair frizzing up around her face, her eyes raw. 'Has he lost his mind?' she said. 'He doesn't even have a proper explanation. What's happened to him, Mummy?'

Today is the first day I've eaten. I stood by the sink, breaking Carr's water biscuits into pieces, pushing them into my mouth methodically like coins into a slot. They are the only things I can come close to stomaching without throwing up. And still I gag when I think of him fucking her.

There's a memory I have. A memory of Eve arriving by train from Southampton a few years ago. She hadn't been lecturing that day so she was dressed casually – sweater and jeans – but when I pushed open the door to the guest room, carrying a cup of tea, I found her crouched over her luggage in what I can only describe as burlesque lingerie.

'You travel in that?' I asked, marvelling at her ability to tolerate both thong and jeans on an eight-hour trip.

'What? Yes,' she'd answered, smiling, totally unembarrassed. 'I find it comfortable. And,' she added mischievously, 'you never know who you might meet.'

She was joking, of course, but I couldn't help wonder if that attire was in fact the norm. If it was *I* who was unusual in plumping for comfort over appearance. I'd told Sean about it and he laughed it off, saying she sounded very high maintenance, saying he found me sexy whatever I wore.

The night Sean left I couldn't get the memory of it from my mind.

Had she left the guest-room door ajar and Sean had caught a glimpse of her? Is that how it started? Or was I being totally ludicrous in blaming Eve?

It's so tempting to blame her instead of him, and I have to keep telling myself: 'It's not all about Eve.' Sean has a brain inside his head, too. I mustn't become one of those pathetic wronged wives, the type who say, *It's entirely the other woman's fault*. And Christ knows, regardless of what's happened, Eve was my friend. It's not like she's some nameless, faceless dominatrix who tempted away my husband. It couldn't have been easy for her either.

It's around 5 p.m., I have two frozen pizzas in the oven for the girls' dinner and Alice is at the kitchen table, studying. She has her GCSE examinations in a couple of weeks, but I can see her brain has turned to mush. When I walked in I found her staring at her books blankly as if everything that was once written there is now in Urdu.

'Why don't you hate him?' she asks, her voice a whisper, barely audible.

'I do,' I lie.

'You don't seem as if you do.'

I smile weakly.

'I hate him,' she says firmly, and I think of all the times I've seen this scene play out in movies. The mother soothing the child, saying, 'Don't hate your father. You mustn't hate him. He loves you. He will always love you.'

But 'I know, hate him, Alice' is the best I manage to say to her.

The doorbell rings and Alice looks up. 'I'll get it,' she says, and I don't bother arguing. It's probably Sean's mother, and I'll have to talk to her eventually.

However, from the hallway I hear Alice say, 'Oh,' and her tone is startled, childlike. 'Oh,' she says again, 'it's you.'

I don't hear a reply, so I make my way towards her, guessing it's Sean, wondering why he hasn't used his key, and are we at *that* stage already? but then I see it's Eve standing there.

She has a doleful expression, but God she looks good.

'I had to come.'

I'm not sure what to say. Under normal circumstances the sight of Eve provokes a reaction of warmth within me, a rush of love towards the friend who has always had my back. And for a moment that feeling begins to swell, my body betraying me in such an appalling way, as though it hasn't yet been able to process the latest necessary information.

'I understand I'm the last person you want to see right now, Natty,' she continues carefully, 'but, all the same, I had to come.'

'Why?' I ask her.

'Because it's breaking my heart to know that you're suffering.'

Alice steps towards her. 'Maybe you should have thought of that before you went and—'

'Alice,' I say, laying my hand on her shoulder. 'Don't.' Alice shoots me a look as though I've lost my mind. 'Let her speak. In fact, Alice, could you leave us? I think this is something Eve and I need to discuss alone.'

Alice marches off and I look at Eve, waiting for what happens next.

'I never wanted to hurt you,' she begins.

'But you did.'

'I know. But if you were only aware of how Sean and I wrestled with this, if you could see how hard we tried to stop it.'

'Is that supposed to make me feel better?'

She drops her head. 'No,' she answers. 'But I want you to know that this was not done lightly. I want you to know that we both love you, Natty. That what happened totally stunned us, that it came out of nowhere. We weren't prepared for it.'

Her voice quivers and I have to prevent myself from reaching out to her.

'Sean says he's never been loved like this,' I tell her quietly. 'Any idea how it feels to hear that?'

She shakes her head. 'No.'

91

'It feels like shit . . . Anyway, Eve, why exactly are you here?'

For a second, I think she might break down at this point, fall to her knees and beg for forgiveness, but she doesn't. Before answering, she hesitates. She holds my gaze and her mournful demeanour vanishes. It's replaced by cold steeliness, visible in the whites of her eyes. 'I know you're not anywhere close to coming to terms with what's happened, and I really don't expect you'll want to see either of us for a substantial amount of time, but I'd like you to consider something that's always helped me in the past . . . helped me when I've had difficult times.'

'And what's that?'

'Forgiveness is a gift you give to yourself, Natty,' she says earnestly, and my eyes widen in response.

'Well, Eve,' I say bitterly, 'I'll try to remember that,' and I close the door before she has chance to say anything else.

Mad Jackie Wagstaff is cleaning my dad's front room when I arrive three days later. She has a wet cloth in one hand and a clean tea towel slung over her left shoulder, for drying off. The first thing she says to me is, 'Well, you know what I'd do . . . I'd chop the bastard's balls off, an' serve 'em to that bitch on a plate.'

I manage only half a smile as I sit down on the leather sofa.

My dad is opposite. He is perched on a tall, wing-backed chair. A friend who owns the residential home in Windermere let me have it when Dad came home after his knee surgery. It makes it easier for him to go from sitting to standing, standing to sitting. I survey my father now, and he looks misplaced. The dated tapestry upholstery of the chair is incongruous in here with the room's taupe décor and its clean lines.

My dad is incredibly house-proud. He's what you'd call 'handy' (he can do almost anything, or has a mate who can). Often I'll turn up to find him re-plastering, or fitting double glazing to the porch, or plumbing in a new gas fire. Strictly speaking, he's not supposed to work with gas because he's not Corgi registered, but he reckons that's only a problem when you come to sell the house.

He calls himself: Ken Odell PhD . . . Plumbing, heating and Drains.

The house is an old stone semi-detached on a street off the main road, about halfway between the villages of Windermere and Bowness. There are more cars than spaces so it's always impossible to park, which drives me nuts when I visit. Especially if I'm loaded up with groceries and need to make multiple trips to the car.

I grew up in this house. It was just the three of us. My mum died when I was fourteen and, a few years later, Dad did have a couple of short flings – relationships he was very discreet about – but Jackie is the first woman acting like she might actually become a permanent fixture.

'You don't need to do the cleaning, Jackie,' I say to her absently, gazing at my dad's slippers, thinking they're a bit past their best. 'I'm not paying you to do that.' Jackie is employed by the carers' agency I hired to help my dad out after his operation.

'No bother,' she replies. 'May as well do it whilst I'm 'ere.'

She and my father exchange a guilty look. They're building up to tell me about their relationship. Their reticence is endearing, totally understandable because of the state I'm in.

My dad is careful with me, concerned. 'How is Alice?' he asks.

'Still livid,' I reply.

'And Felicity?'

'Still quiet.'

'Do you want me to talk to him?'

I frown. 'To who? Sean? And say what?'

He tilts his head and smiles sympathetically. 'You never know, Natty, I might be able to knock some sense into him.'

My dad and Sean have always got along; they've always been

close. More than once Dad's claimed that Sean is like a son to him.

I dismiss his offer. 'You'd be wasting your time,' I tell him, thinking of the black lace thong I found hooked around my big toe when I woke this morning. I've not told anyone about it. It's too humiliating. The thought of Eve's underwear festering between my sheets turns my stomach.

My dad persists. 'He might listen, he might if I can get him on his own—'

I cut him off. 'He won't.'

Sensing he wants to press the issue further, I glare at him. I am not up to discussing the ins and outs of this in front of Mad Jackie. She's a nice enough woman – I've got nothing against her – but I could really do without her presence today. It's not as if I really know her, and here we are, talking openly about my break-up, my break*down*, right in front of her.

My dad sits up in his chair. He adjusts his feet, grimacing as his new knees send a jolt of pain into the surrounding tissues. Though considering he's had major surgery, he looks the healthiest I've seen him in ages.

He's always looked older than his years – his beloved roll-ups are probably the reason for that. He's sixty-one and he smokes far more than he lets on. When we went for his orthopaedic appointment a few months back he claimed to get through fifteen cigarettes a day. I'd raised my eyebrows at that until he muttered, 'Could be closer to twenty.' When asked what medication he was on, he answered, 'Real ale,' but the nurse was not amused.

'Have you been to the hotel yet?' he asks me.

I shake my head. '*She's* there.'

'Are they allowed even to do that?' Jackie pipes up. 'Is your husband even allowed to let her live there? The pair of 'em have got such a bloody cheek. Can't you get her out?'

I sigh wearily. 'And how am I supposed to do that?'

Jackie stops cleaning and turns to face me fully, hands on hips, jaw set. 'Go and see a solicitor. Tell that bitch you'll kill her if she doesn't get off your property. Tell Sean he'll not see his children.'

I bow my head. 'I can't do that.'

'Why not? 'Course you can. Everyone starts off playing fair, Natty, but they soon change their tune once they realize the gloves are off.'

'It's Sean's name on the deeds. Sean's name on the alcohol licence.'

'So?'

'And they've moved out from the guest bedroom now,' I reason. 'They're staying in the staff accommodation in the attic, so it's not as if it's actually costing the hotel anything. We're not losing money by them being there.'

'That's as may be,' Jackie presses, 'but how can you even stand for her to be in there *at all*?'

'I can't. I hate it that she's there.'

'Why are you being so soft about it then?' she says. '*Do something.*'

My mouth gapes open and I look at my dad helplessly, trying to indicate that I really can't handle this barrage from Jackie right now. But he's nodding his head like a donkey, like a silly old front-bench politician backing up the Prime Minister.

'Sean needs to run the hotel,' I explain patiently. 'We can't just shut up shop, whatever's happened. And I'd rather he was there doing it than my having to face all the staff. That would be excruciating. It's bad enough all of them know.'

Jackie goes to argue the point again and stops. Opens her mouth then closes it. After a moment she takes the black and white photograph of the girls from the wall and wipes it clean. It's the professional one I had done of Alice and Felicity when they were seven and five. They're adorable in old-fashioned nightdresses, barefoot, with their hair loose and tangled. Alice has four teeth missing top and bottom. At the sight of my daughters, my breath shudders inside my chest.

'Well, what *are* you going to do about the hotel?' my dad asks. 'You're going to have to sort something out. Will you sell it and split the money down the middle?'

'Dad,' I cry, close to tears now, 'I've not even begun thinking about selling the hotel. I'm barely able to get myself dressed at the moment. Do you not get it? Do you not get how hard this is for me?'

Jackie stops dead and turns. 'You've got to toughen up, Natty. Because, sure as eggs is eggs, that woman'll be getting her claws into everything that's yours. By the time next year rolls around, she'll have got your husband squirrelling away all the money . . . you'll come out with nothing.'

'Eve doesn't need my money, she earns plenty from her practice and from lecturing. And she'll have half her soon-to-be-ex-husband's wealth to come as well. Besides, Sean's always been very fair with money, Jackie,' I say.

'Not any more, he won't be.'

I shake my head at her. 'You don't know him.'

She snorts loudly. 'Last time I looked, neither did you.'

I know what happened to Jackie and her husband. There aren't many people around here that don't. I understand that losing everything can make you cynical. Understand that if your husband sold off your house and scarpered with all the takings, you may not be the most trusting of women.

But Sean has always had such a keen sense of fairness where money is concerned, and I really can't see him trying to cut me out of what's rightfully mine. Particularly when he's the one who's been at fault here.

'Watch yer back,' Jackie huffs, before getting down on to her hands and knees to clean the skirting board. Her expression is one of *Don't say I didn't warn you!*

By the time I leave I'm more fraught and tearful than when I arrived. I can't make my mind up if it's Jackie's unsolicited advice that's really got to me, or if it's my dad, supporting everything she has to say – nodding along without question, as if her assumptions about Sean have some merit.

I'm not ready for all that. I can't sit around planning ways to get back at him, ways to get back at Eve. It's all too raw. Jackie's idea of revenge is not the kind of thing I could ever go in for. Volcanic emotion and primal recklessness is just not me. It's so easy for Jackie and my dad to babble on about selling the hotel as if this all happened months ago. As if I haven't invested *every single thing* I've got into the building, the business, the gardens, the staff, the guests. I can't possibly sell simply so Eve won't get her hands on it.

I drive up to Windermere, scanning the pavements, the oncoming cars. I need to pick up some food for the next few days but I am filled with dread at the prospect of bumping into somebody I know.

I feel humiliated.

I'm embarrassed I couldn't keep hold of my husband. I don't feel wronged, or righteous, I'm ashamed. I can hear what people will be saying: 'If he was getting some at home, he wouldn't have gone elsewhere.' And 'She's always looked down her nose, it's about time she got what was coming to her.'

Today I wish I didn't have this silly, showy car. I'd prefer to be in something discreet rather than this ostentatious red Porsche Cayenne GTS. I drove a standard Cayenne last year, in silver, which was fine. But Sean exchanged it for this pimped-up thing and I've never really got used to it.

I pull in to Booths' car park and see a scruffy woman who was in my class at junior school. She's pushing her trolley alongside another woman I'm not acquainted with and they exchange glances, smirk, when they catch sight of my car. They know. Everybody knows.

Inside, I keep my head low and move through the store, avoiding eye contact. I stick behind an annoying mother in her mid-forties who's picking up vegetables and naming them loudly for her child. Probably scared Jamie Oliver will turn up at school unannounced and her son won't recognize a cauliflower.

I stand at the cheese counter – some prick in a Driza-Bone hat with a booming voice is making a big fuss ordering white Stilton with apricots, as though he wants everyone to know he likes sophisticated cheese. For a moment I contemplate ordering an obscure Yorkshire sheep's milk blue but stop short when I realize it makes me just as bad as him, and getting into a Who can order the cleverest cheese? competition is not what I really need. I'm perusing the selection of unpasteurizeds when there's a gentle nudge at my elbow.

I turn, and my heart sinks.

It's Alexa Willard and she has a mournful look on her face. I can't abide this woman and I know she's only stopped me so she can gloat.

She clutches my arm. 'Natty, I've heard. How absolutely dreadful, how *utterly* horrific. I can't imagine how you must be feeling.'

I'm tempted to say, *Can't you, Alexa? I thought your husband played away from home every chance he got.* But I don't. Because I'm not like that.

Instead I flush red and say, 'Got to put on a brave face, Alexa. I've not really got any choice.'

She nods furiously and her eyes widen as she speaks. 'I admire your spirit. Poor you. *Poor you.* Obviously, it goes without saying . . . *if there's anything I can do* . . . How are the girls? They must be devastated. And after what you've just been through with Felicity's appendix . . . how is she, by the way?'

'On the mend.'

She takes a fast breath in and closes her eyes, shuddering as she considers my ordeal. 'Bloody men!' she hisses.

'Quite,' I say, and thank her, ordering half a pound of creamy Lancashire and hoping Alexa will leave me alone and move on. She doesn't.

She can be very trying. One of those women you can't wait to get away from. She's known for, amongst other things, allowing her children to watch DVDs only if the language function is changed to either French or Spanish. I'm one of the few people around here who make the effort to be nice to her. Now I wish I'd never bothered because she'll be straight out, spreading the word, saying she's seen me and that I looked *utterly dreadful*, saying she's *so desperately* sorry for me.

Which, of course, she isn't.

I can tell she's secretly quite pleased. And I'm not judging Alexa unfairly here, because she's not alone. I know we all take some pleasure in the downfall of others. It makes our own lives more bearable if someone who seemingly has it all no longer does.

The British press have the reputation for building people up only to knock them straight back down again. Which they're often criticized for. But after reading about Jennifer Aniston's latest break-up, or another heartache for Kylie, do you not walk away thinking, *Well, I suppose there is a price to be paid for being rich, famous and beautiful after all?* Do you not go back to your own little life, reflecting that things aren't so bad, you're not really missing out by being you?

I do.

And if you look at it that way, the press are actually providing quite a good service.

So I don't blame Alexa for getting a small thrill from my situation. I just wish she'd fuck off so I don't have to discuss it with her in public.

Eventually, she says her goodbyes, telling me again how sincerely sorry she is, and flees. I watch her abandon the last two aisles and head straight for the tills. I can't see over there, but I wouldn't be surprised if she dumps her basket and gets on with calling her cronies, telling them the latest.

Inwardly, I curse Sean for doing this to me. He's left me exposed, vulnerable to the likes of Alexa, and I hate it.

To my left, in the meat section, one of the young butchers emerges from the fridge carrying a new fillet of beef in his arms. Lovingly, he places it inside the glass counter and I feel a jolt. A yearning. I realize I suddenly want steak.

A nice thick fillet in red wine and garlic, with a big blob of Saint Agur cheese on top. Refocusing on the cheese, I ask for a slice of the French blue and lick my lips, because I'm salivating. For the first time in days I've got an appetite.

I buy three steaks, grab a good bottle of St Emilion, a couple of leeks and some oven chips, and I'm good to go. *I can do this*, I'm thinking, imbued with a sense of empowerment as I leave the store, slinging my carrier bag on to the passenger seat of the car. I can come here and hold my head high. I've done it once, I can do it again.

And that's when I spot Sean's car. The Maserati.

I'm just about to back out of the space when I see it pass in my rear-view mirror. Eve is driving. And she appears absolutely fine. She's singing along to the stereo, not a care in the world.

Following her, I head to the recycling area at the far end of the car park. She stops and I hang back, waiting for her to get out. She turns sideways a little, perhaps to retrieve something from the passenger seat, and I urge myself to leave. Spying on her like this will only end in misery. If she steps out looking together and beautiful, as she did the other day on my doorstep, I will go home feeling even more shitty and inadequate.

I move my foot off the brake, about to pull the wheel to the right, and, without warning, I'm filled with hatred.

It's as if all the thoughts, *all the misery*, of the past few days come crashing to the forefront, and I have to grip the wheel just to try to keep hold, to stop myself from what I am about to do.

But it's no use.

I see red, and the primal recklessness I didn't know existed until now rises within me. There's a whooshing sound in my ears, like a flying shuttle across a loom, and my vision is occluded, the peripheral zone gone. It's as if I'm staring through the sights of an air rifle.

I hear Eve's words inside my head: *Forgiveness is a gift you give yourself, Natty.*

Eve straightens in her seat, checks her appearance in the mirror and spots me behind.

So I hit the accelerator.

There's not enough space to gain any real speed, but I'm in a tank and she's in the shag magnet.

I slam into her. Hard. I am braced for the impact and it feels good. Christ, it feels unbelievable.

I don't wait to see what happens next, I don't wait to see if she's injured. I'm reversing fast. I must be off centre, though, as I scrape the side of my car on the railing of the trolley park as I back up.

I ignore it and within seconds I'm ready to go again.

Flooring it, I slam into her, and this time I see her body jolt as I hit.

So I go again. And again.

12

DETECTIVE CONSTABLE JOANNE Aspinall pops home for a bite to eat rather than waste money on a pre-packed sandwich. Her Auntie Jackie must have had the same idea because as Joanne enters the hallway she can hear Jackie slamming around in the dining room.

Jackie's standing on the weighing scales in her bra and knickers. In an untidy pile on the table are her carer's uniform, clogs, watch and tights. Joanne stays in the doorway, saying nothing, as Jackie picks up the scales and moves them to another spot over by the kitchen.

'They're wrong, these,' she says to Joanne. 'I'm two pounds heavier over here.'

'You had any lunch?' Joanne asks.

'I'm not eatin'. Diet Club this afternoon and they shout out how much weight you've lost to everyone. It's embarrassing if you've gone up.'

Joanne nods and goes into the kitchen at the back of the house. Squatting in front of the fridge she picks up some smoked turkey that's curling around the edges and gives it a sniff. 'You didn't say you'd joined,' she calls through to Jackie.

'First rule of Diet Club is: You *do not talk* about Diet Club.'

Joanne smiles and stands, spotting some minestrone Cup-a-Soups next to the sink. She reaches for the box and goes into the dining room, where she finds Jackie back on the scales, now over by the gas fire. 'Can I have one of these?' she asks.

'Help yourself. I don't like 'em. They taste of soil.'

'You weigh any less over there?' Joanne asks.

'Don't know. It's saying "Error" now.'

Jackie picks up the scales and fiddles underneath. There's a switch that changes the reading from stones to kilograms to pounds. Jackie flicks it backwards and forwards a few times before placing the scales on the floor again and stepping on.

'How's the romance coming along?' Joanne asks her. 'Is he up to much with those bad knees?'

'They're not bad knees, they're *new* knees. And he's too much of a gentleman for any of that yet.'

'Must be a novelty having you around then.'

As Jackie gets dressed Joanne disappears to make her soup and sandwich. She's due back at the station for in-service training on a new computer system; it starts at 2 p.m. so she needs to get a move on. And it's Ron Quigley's last day before his wisdom teeth op, so they want to get the training done as quickly as possible to get out for a drink.

Joanne pours hot water on to the dried-soup mix and gives it a stir. Jackie's right. It does smell like soil. When she goes through to the dining room Jackie's back in her tights, pushing her arms inside her tunic.

'Where's it held?' Joanne asks her.

'Diet Club? The Methodist church. The women there drive me mad, listing *every single thing* they've had to eat for the past week. Like anyone's going to be interested.'

Joanne doesn't comment, as Jackie has that exact same habit.

'Have you lost much?' Joanne asks.

'A bit,' Jackie says. 'Put it back on again, though, when I ate all those pork pies at Margaret Hughes's funeral.'

Jackie fastens the remaining press studs at the top of her tunic and primps her hair a little in the mirror above the fireplace. Dissatisfied, she pulls a fine-toothed comb from her handbag and starts backcombing the crown, to make it look fuller. 'I saw his daughter this morning,' she says.

'Whose? Ken's?' asks Joanne.

Jackie nods. 'Husband walked out on her. He'd been sleeping with her friend while she was in France nursing their daughter back to health. She's in a right mess. I tried talking some sense into her, but she wouldn't have it.'

Joanne winces. 'Bet she loved you for that.'

'He'll take her to the cleaners if she doesn't sort herself out. Kenneth's worried sick. He doesn't know what to do for the best. He wants to talk to the husband, but she won't let him.'

'I thought Ken couldn't get out of the house.'

'He can't,' Jackie says, 'but you know what I mean. He wants to help. He knows she still loves him and he wants to see if he can get him to come back.'

'What happened to the wife?'

'Kenneth's wife?' she asks, and Joanne nods. 'Car crash twenty years ago. She came off the road on a patch of ice going over Shap Fell. On her way back from Christmas shopping in Carlisle, I believe.'

'That's sad,' says Joanne. 'Has his daughter got any kids?'

'Two girls. They're good kids, Kenneth says, but spoilt rotten. Private school, dance lessons, music lessons, horse riding, skiing . . .'

'Who pays for all that?'

'They do. They've got Lakeshore Lodge down on the Newby Bridge road. She's the one paying for us to look after Kenneth. She's too busy with the hotel to do it herself.'

Joanne pushes the last of the turkey sandwich into her mouth. 'What does she make of you getting it together with her dad?'

'We've not said owt yet.'

Joanne imagines Ken's daughter will not be completely happy when she's informed. People who don't know Jackie very well think she can be a bit volatile. Those that do know her tend to be of the same opinion.

Joanne dusts breadcrumbs from the table on to her plate. 'Anyway,' she says, 'isn't there some kind of rule against heavy petting with the invalids?'

And Jackie swipes the top of Joanne's head with her hand in response. 'He's no invalid,' she replies, slipping on her jacket and grabbing her handbag.

'Right then,' she says. 'I'm off. I've got to meet the district nurse at Irene Slater's before I go and get weighed. Her husband wants her catheter whipping out again.' She shivers at the thought. 'Filthy bugger gets us to take it out once a week so he can have sex.'

As it turns out, Joanne rushes back to work for nothing. The training is cancelled because the instructor can't get across the Yorkshire Dales from Skipton – she's driven her car through a flooded patch of road and it's gone and died. The region is littered with discarded cars at the moment. People daft enough to think they can make it through a foot of water, wrecking their engines in the process.

Joanne spends the afternoon writing up a final report instead. Two months ago Cameron Cox, a businessman from Kirkby Lonsdale, twenty miles south-east of Windermere, put a shotgun in his mouth and redecorated his conference room. Joanne hadn't attended the scene, but she'd been called in shortly afterwards, as his wife – one Serena Cox – was making allegations that her husband was murdered by a woman he'd been having an affair with.

However, after lengthy investigation, they weren't able to

trace the mystery femme fatale, and it ended up looking more like a case of investments gone wrong, a business on the brink. His poor wife had no idea of the mounting debts and seemed delusional to the last, claiming he'd been shafted by a leggy blonde who'd scarpered with all his money.

Joanne submits the report and is about to grab her parka and head out to the pub to meet Ron Quigley and the others when DI McAleese asks her to step inside his office.

'Something's just come in for you, Joanne,' he says gruffly.

When Joanne asked if she could return to work early after her abandoned breast surgery McAleese had stuttered and stammered on the phone, telling Joanne that she could come back straight away, if that's what she wanted.

She's not exactly sure what's happened to him, but since his separation from his wife a few months ago, DI McAleese has not quite been himself around women. It's as if he suddenly doubts his competence. As if he's not sure who he is any more, and his normal unflappable demeanour has been replaced by something quite different. The man in front of Joanne now is anxious, edgy.

'There's been a problem at Booths' car park, Windermere,' he tells her officiously, shuffling papers on his desk. 'Not many details yet. Appears to be a case of a wife's revenge.'

'What's the name?' she asks.

'Natasha Wainwright. She rammed her Porsche Cayenne repeatedly into the back of a Maserati.'

Joanne sucks in her breath as a long whistle, but McAleese doesn't react, doesn't even look at her, and she's left feeling a small stab of embarrassment, as if she's responded inappropriately. She's beginning to think McAleese is particularly abrupt with *her*, more so than with the other female detectives in the department, and she doesn't know why this should be.

'It was her husband's car that Natasha Wainwright smashed

into,' he says, 'only he wasn't driving it, his girlfriend was behind the wheel. Eve Dalladay was the once close friend of Mrs Wainwright, and she's been smashed up pretty bad, apparently. Anyway, she's pressing charges.'

'Section 20 assault?'

'I reckon so. We've got no witness statements as yet, we need the CCTV, and we need to get a look at her car because—'

'Hang on a minute,' says Joanne. 'This Mrs Wainwright's not from Lakeshore Lodge, is she? The hotel in Bowness?'

'Yes. Why, do you know her?'

Joanne shakes her head. 'Not directly.'

There's a moment of silence as DI McAleese looks up and holds her gaze. It seems as if he's about to say something more. The tips of his ears colour red and he takes a breath in, then clears his throat. 'Joanne, I was wondering if maybe you . . .' And he pauses.

'Sir?'

'Nothing,' he says quickly. 'Doesn't matter.'

He pushes a slip of paper across the table. 'I want you to go and talk to her – this Mrs Wainwright. That's the address. Check out the car, because we've only got Eve Dalladay's word it was her . . . but she's got previous.'

'Who has? Natasha Wainwright?' Joanne is surprised; it's not what she was expecting to hear.

'Yes,' he answers. 'Bit of a turn-up. It sounds unlikely, but Mrs Wainwright got herself a six-month suspended prison sentence, back in 1998.'

13

I WATCH THE RAIN pelt the kitchen windows as my mobile vibrates inside my pocket. No point in checking who it is. I know who it is. Sean has been calling and texting all afternoon, but I am yet to answer. Sitting at the table with my feet tapping the floor tiles beneath, I chew on my bottom lip feverishly.

Felicity comes in to make herself a hot chocolate. 'How come you're sitting in here on your own?' she asks me. She's up and about quite a lot now, says she might like to return to school sooner rather than later. I think watching daytime TV is not as much fun as she first thought – especially with her dad gone and her mum hanging on to her sanity by a thread. I'm not sure she's ready, though. She tires easily and I still see her wince as she rises from a chair.

'Just needed some space to think,' I answer, and she asks if I'd like a cup of Earl Grey. 'Please,' I say, trying to force a smile. 'That'd be great.'

I've chewed the skin down the side of my thumbnail and it's stinging terribly. I try sucking it but the heat from my mouth intensifies the pain so I blow on the area a couple of times instead.

'Are you sure you're okay, Mum?' Felicity asks.

'Yes, why?'

'You seem worried. Is it Dad?' She takes a coaster and places it in front of me before setting down the tea, spilling it a little as she does so. Ordinarily, I would complain at this. I'd ask her to pass a cloth from the sink to wipe the base of the cup, stop it from dripping on my clothes, the floor. Today I refrain from my usual chiding. 'Only a little worried over you two,' I tell her. 'About how all this is going to work out with your dad and Eve.'

'We'll be okay,' she says tenderly.

Trouble is, Felicity has no idea if she will be okay or not. None of us does. She's telling me we'll be fine because that's what she's seen kind, thoughtful, teenagers say on *Hollyoaks* or *Glee*. She has no experience of divorce. The only couple she knows who have split are her granny and grandad – and that wasn't exactly straightforward. Sean's dad had a nervous breakdown five years ago and his mother, Penny, had no alternative but to file for divorce.

At least, that's the official version.

The other version, the version we *never ever* talk about in Penny's presence, is that David left Penny for another woman.

After deciding he'd been putting lipstick on the pig for long enough, David fled and shacked up with a young redhead from Elterwater. He had his vasectomy reversed and went on to have a couple more kids. (I'm told the youngest is a real handful.)

People mock Penny in secret when she refers to David's 'mental breakdown', but she really does believe that's what happened. As in, *What other reason could there possibly be?* And misguided though this is, I can't help but admire her attitude on the matter, because it certainly saved her a lot of heartache in the long run. She completely avoided the appalling period of self-examination that comes in the aftermath of a split, the period where you ask yourself: What did I do wrong?

Alice comes in and regards Felicity, says in the offhand way she reserves for her sister, 'Made yourself a nice cup of selfish, have you?'

Felicity gives me a look. 'What would you like?' she asks Alice. 'I've made hot chocolate, but there's no cream left.'

'Hot Vimto, please. I've got a sore throat . . . Mummy, where is that ear thermometer thingy? I feel hot and I have a headache.'

'In the first-aid box in the cupboard beside the wine rack. Let me feel your head.'

Alice sits down beside me, sighing dramatically. 'I told my English teacher about Dad today,' she says as I lay my palm across her brow.

'Oh?'

'I'm just not with it. I can't concentrate at all, and when she asked me to read aloud from *Of Mice and Men*, I couldn't do it. And some idiot boy had written "Lenny dies" on the first page, so that didn't help. I wanted to cry.'

'You do feel a bit warm,' I tell her, now feeling the back of her neck. 'It might be best to have a bath and go straight to bed.'

'I've too much revision to do,' she says.

'What did your teacher say?' I ask.

'She told me to go to her any time I needed to talk.'

'That's nice,' I say softly, masking my hurt and annoyance, because I really don't want a twenty-something English grad-uate giving life advice to my daughter, no matter how well-meaning she is.

'What did you go and tell *her* for?' Felicity asks her sister.

'Because I *needed* to,' Alice flares. 'I needed someone to understand what we're going through here.'

'Needed attention, more like,' says Felicity. 'I can't stand Miss Bellamy, she's such a fraud.'

'She is not a fraud,' Alice replies. 'You're just jealous because she only teaches the top sets.'

'She doesn't.'

'Girls, stop,' I plead, but it falls on deaf ears.

'Miss Bellamy *always* teaches the top set in each year,' Alice says, spitting her words at Felicity. 'You're doing the classic stupid-kid thing of being in denial. Poppy Ferguson is always claiming she's top set in English. It's totally tragic. You don't want to be like her, Felicity, it's embarrassing.'

Felicity rolls her eyes. 'Who was it thought Stephen Hawking was American again? Oh, yes, Alice, that was you.'

Alice goes to get the thermometer out of the cupboard. 'I don't know why you're always bringing that up. It's so lame. Is that, like, the only argument you have . . . it's not as if I'm the only person in the entire world who didn't know he was English. If you weren't such a—'

The doorbell rings and my heart stutters. I stare at the table. 'Don't answer that,' I say quietly. 'I don't want to see anyone today.'

But Alice is off. 'Mum, we can't hide for ever. It's probably Granny. She said she was calling in to talk to you. She's bringing some of her yellow pea and ham soup.'

A moment later I hear Alice's words coming from the hallway: 'Yes, she is, come in,' her pitch an octave higher than usual. 'She's in here . . . Mummy? There's a lady here to see you, a police officer.'

Alice returns to the kitchen. For a second I'm confused, because the woman following her is not wearing a police uniform, she's dressed in a cheap navy suit that doesn't fit properly.

'I'm Detective Constable Aspinall,' she says. 'Are you Mrs Natasha Wainwright?'

I nod mutely. Try not to look as alarmed as I feel.

'Is it all right if I ask you a few questions, Mrs Wainwright?'

Again, I nod. Unable to speak.

'Good. Okay if I sit down?' she asks.

'What? Yes, sorry, of course,' I say, stumbling, 'Alice, get the detective a drink.'

'Tea would be great,' she says, without being asked. I was thinking water so I could get rid of her quicker.

I can feel the two girls exchanging mortified stares behind me. 'What's happened?' Alice asks. 'Are you here about my dad? Has he done something wrong?'

DC Aspinall's face gives nothing away. She's like an undertaker, trained to remain unruffled no matter what's put in front of her. 'It's probably for the best if I talk to your mum alone,' she suggests.

Alice comes to my side. 'Mum?'

'Make the tea and go through to the lounge, Alice. I don't think this has to do with your dad.' I glance at DC Aspinall, who gives one small shake of her head.

We sit in silence as Alice makes the tea, not something she's particularly good at. So far she's set two kettles on fire by forgetting to fill them with water.

Felicity tells us she'll be upstairs, and when the tea is ready Alice leaves us as well. I'm fully aware they'll be eavesdropping, but I'm also aware that if I make a big deal about excluding them, their curiosity will be raised almost to danger level.

DC Aspinall takes a gulp, grimaces and takes out a notepad. Alice has given her the Earl Grey. It's not for everyone.

'We've had a report of an incident occurring this afternoon in Windermere from Dr Eve Dalladay.'

'Hmm-mm.'

'She says you repeatedly drove your car into her at Booths' car park before driving away, leaving her with serious facial injuries requiring medical attention.'

I do my best to appear shocked. 'What?' I say, and DC Aspinall reaches for her mug, before thinking better of it. 'That's what she said?'

She looks at me levelly. 'Yes. That's what she said. She wants to press charges.'

'But that's simply not true,' I say.

DC Aspinall tries to get the measure of me before speaking

any further. Eventually, she says, 'Mrs Wainwright, you're newly separated, yes?'

'Yes.'

'And this Dr Dalladay is the lady who is now with your husband?'

'Yes, but that doesn't mean I'd try to hurt her. We were friends and I'm really not that sort of person, I—'

'I noticed on my way in here that your car has been in an accident. It's actually quite smashed up . . . That is *your* car outside? The Cayenne?'

'Yes,' I say quickly, 'but that's not what happened. I didn't do what she's accusing me of.'

DC Aspinall maintains an air of tolerance. 'Mrs Wainwright, I should tell you that as soon as it's available I will be viewing the CCTV footage of the car park. I suggest you tell me now exactly what happened, because it's clear your car didn't get into that condition on its own. So, did you ram Eve Dalladay's car, or not?'

I'm about to answer when there's a small yelp from the doorway. Alice and Felicity are both standing there. Alice has her hand over her mouth. She lowers it to her throat, and says, horrified, 'Mummy, you didn't do that, did you?'

'No,' I say, and again I address DC Aspinall. 'Eve is lying. I was behind her car and out of nowhere she slammed on the brakes. I went straight into the back of her. I thought a child must have run out into the road, but she did it for no reason. As if she wanted me to crash into her. On purpose.'

'Odd that your airbag didn't inflate, don't you think?' she says.

'I wasn't speeding. My airbag didn't go off because I must have been doing less than thirty miles per hour. And hers didn't inflate either, so I can't have hit her *that* hard.'

'Or, as she is claiming, she was stationary. And had already removed her key from the ignition,' DC Aspinall says accusingly. 'That also would prevent her airbag from inflating.'

'No,' I say firmly, 'we were moving. We were definitely moving.'

'Why didn't you contact the police?' she asks.

'There was no reason to. It's not like we had to exchange insurance details. Sean owns both cars.'

'And where did this happen?'

'Coming out of Booths.' She jots down the details. 'Have you actually seen Eve's face?' I ask. 'Because I'm sure she must be making more of this than it really is.'

Without raising her head, DC Aspinall says, 'I've not seen her, no.'

I fold my arms across my chest. 'Well, then.'

I glance at the girls as DC Aspinall continues to document my version of events, and I can see they are rattled by the presence of a detective in the kitchen. Naturally, they hate Eve. They can't stand what she's done to us by stealing their dad away. But they must be wondering if their mother has really gone and done something as crazy as ramming her car. They must not know what to think.

Even ramming the car as I did, it wasn't possible to get any real speed up, so I can't imagine Eve is injured. I did it to humiliate her. I did it to piss her off. I didn't do it to harm her.

'Surely this is a domestic issue?' I say to DC Aspinall, taking the opportunity to divert attention away from the actual incident. 'What a waste of police time!' I scoff. 'It's a disgrace that Eve should contact you when this is clearly something between me and her.'

DC Aspinall raises her head. 'Perhaps,' she concedes, 'but then there's that deep scrape along the right-hand side of your car, Mrs Wainwright. I'd say that's inconsistent with a simple shunt collision, wouldn't you?'

'I . . .'

'And of course there's the issue of your suspended prison sentence, because as much as I'd like to—'

There's a sharp intake of breath again from the doorway as Alice blurts out, 'Her *what*?' She strides in to face the detective. 'I'm sorry, but what did you just say?'

'Alice, don't,' I whisper, now aware that my lie is spiralling into something more altogether.

'Mummy, what is she talking about? She's saying *you've been to prison*? Mummy, whatever does she mean?'

DC Aspinall hesitates a moment and explains, 'It was a suspended sentence. Not a custodial sentence.'

'Well, what is *that*?' asks Alice, her voice shrill with terror.

'It means she didn't have to go to prison, moron,' mutters Felicity. 'It means she did something wrong, and instead of sending her to prison, they gave her another chance.'

With my head in my hands, I part my fingers to see Alice spin around, her mouth gaping open. 'So, what did you do, Mummy?' she cries out. 'What on earth did you do?'

14

I MET EVE ON my third day at Manchester University. It was
September 1997 and I'd arrived in the halls of residence under
a cloud of melancholy, nursing a wound I wasn't sure I would
ever recover from.

Formal lectures were not about to start for another few days.
This was Freshers' Week. And Freshers' Week, I'd learned from
former Lakes school pupils who'd been there and done that, was
the week you made lots of new friends, only to spend the next
three years trying to get rid of them again.

With this in mind I began my time in Manchester cautiously.
I'm not sure I could have behaved in any other way, but this was
the excuse I told myself. I decided *against* tagging along with a
gaggle of girls to the Students' Union bar before we'd even
unpacked; decided *not* to stay up the entire first night with the
three sociology students next door drinking 20/20, necking Bols
Blue straight from the bottle, flashing my tits out the window at
four in the morning, thinking it was just about the funniest
thing ever.

By day three I was desperately lonely. I missed my mother in
a way I'd not experienced in the longest time, and the home-
sickness seemed to be cleaving away at my spirit. At fourteen, I'd
suffered episodes of depression after Mum died; periods of a few
weeks, sometimes extending into a couple of months, when my
dad didn't know what to do with me, hoping it would pass. And

eventually it did pass – the antidote to my grief coming in the form of Sean. Looking back, I'm not sure if claiming he filled the scooped-out parts of me is placing a little too much merit on the shoulders of the young, gentle-natured lad Sean was then. But that's how it felt to me at the time. Now I think perhaps he just took my mind off things. And when I moved to Manchester he could no longer do that.

Sean and I met at a sixteenth-birthday party. We lived pretty near to one another but he was a weekly boarder over at Sedbergh School. When he returned to Windermere at weekends we were inseparable, spending every available minute together. His mother was kind, courteous, always made me feel welcome in her home – right up until we got our A-level results.

Then, catastrophe.

Encouraged by his parents, Sean and I had made the very grown-up, rational decision (we thought) of attending separate universities. He would go to Manchester to study law, and I would go to Edinburgh to study biology. Not so far apart that we'd never see each other, but far enough for us to have an independent university experience – ensuring we came out of it with new friends, new interests, conceivably even a new world view.

It was a sensible approach and, even though I dreaded being away from Sean, I was sufficiently level-headed to know that this was a once-in-a-lifetime opportunity. This was the moment you put your academic future above any notions of romance. And it hadn't escaped my notice, either, the looks of utter relief I'd had when telling well-meaning adults of our plans for separate cities. Put bluntly, if you follow your first love to university, you are a total saddo. Everyone knows it spells disaster in the long term.

So I accepted an offer from Edinburgh in the March, and was, outwardly at least, happily preparing to go. But when in mid-August I received my grades, achieving only two Bs and a C, instead of the requisite A and two Bs, I had to re-evaluate my options. Fast. Because the clearing process allows only a matter of days to secure your university place, and my options were now woefully limited.

It was a frantic time of crazy ideas. Should I switch fields to study marketing? Philosophy? Urban planning? All I was sure of was that I didn't want to attend some second-rate polytechnic on the outskirts of a town I'd never heard of. Did I love biology that much?

Eventually, I rejected the idea of biology. After taking advice from the careers advisor at school, I plumped for a vocational degree with a guaranteed job at the end of it. My choices were physiotherapy (though I didn't really want to touch people's bodies), podiatry (categorically didn't want to touch people's *feet*) and radiography (the most reasonable and palatable option). In three years' time I would come out with a ready-made career. A career that would take me anywhere in the world, if I so wished, and one which I could dip in and out of later on, should I want children.

And wouldn't you just know it? The only university with a spare place available and willing to accept my grades was Manchester.

I was elated. Totally thrilled. And so was Sean – he was round at my house, declaring: 'We had done everything practically possible to stay apart.' This was providence, he said. Fate somehow intent on keeping us together. It would work out. It was going to be—

'Natty?' my dad called up the stairs, an uneasy edge to his voice.

I looked at Sean and shrugged, the joy of the moment spilling over into rational thought and not for one second thinking my dad's tone could indicate anything other than all the brilliant things to come.

'Natty,' he repeated, 'you best come down. Someone here to see you.'

At the foot of the stairs was Sean's mother, Penny. She wore a pale turquoise suit – the shoulders on the jacket a little too wide, a wedding outfit left over from the eighties, possibly – and very tall stilettos.

I descended in a bit of a daze, confused by her presence in our hallway, because she'd never visited before. As I got closer she made an attempt to smile, but her face was rigid with tension. It had the effect of baring her teeth – like an old horse with its head over the stable door – and I stopped dead in my tracks.

Something was wrong.

'Sean,' I called out to him, 'your mum's here for you,' because I assumed she'd come to collect him. I assumed he'd done something he shouldn't, maybe not been where he was supposed to be. Missed a dental appointment.

Penny turned to my dad. 'Is there somewhere we can go to talk?' she asked. And my dad, more attuned to her mood and motive than I was, said, 'Of course.' We could talk in the lounge.

Long before everyone went cream, mushroom and taupe with their contemporary décor, before the arrival of the big chocolate leather sofas in Dad's lounge, there were two plain, hessian-coloured sofas in our lounge. And *before that*, back when I was in secondary school, my dad had two rather fussy apricot sofas with a turquoise stripe. I remember thinking Penny matched the sofas rather appropriately in her suit as she perched on the edge of the two-seater, her snakeskin shins, scaly from too much sun, sticking out from beneath her skirt.

Sean appeared and she requested he sit down. He did as she asked and I watched his face carefully, trying to discern what Penny's presence here might mean. But there was nothing other than the usual quiet watchfulness Sean displayed around his mother.

'Mr Odell,' she began.

'It's Ken, please,' my dad replied.

'As you wish,' said Penny stiffly. What followed was a moment of awkwardness as she readied herself to talk.

Penny cleared her throat. 'I'll start by saying that my husband, David, was due to accompany me here today, but he's been called to Carlisle on urgent business. You can rest assured, though, that my views are his views, and what I'm about to say has been discussed at length between the two of us. We are united on this issue and he sends his apologies to you, *Ken*, and hopes to meet you at some point in the future.'

My dad made a face to imply this was duly noted and then began rubbing his chin thoughtfully.

My stomach tightened. It was in moments such as this that my dad was in the habit of calling a halt in the proceedings. He'd start rolling a cigarette, claiming he could only listen properly to what was being said if he smoked. I prayed hard he wouldn't do it today.

'I'm afraid,' said Penny, turning to address me, 'that this situation which has arisen, Natty, is untenable.'

She waited for me to speak.

'I don't know what that means,' I said honestly.

She tried to smile, finding at the last second she had to avert her eyes. 'I mean that you accompanying Sean to Manchester is just not going to work for us as a family.'

Sean cut in by saying, 'Natty's not *accompanying* me, Mum . . . she's going there on her own to—'

Penny held up her hand. 'You'll get a chance to put your views across in a minute, Sean. For now, I'd appreciate it if you kept silent.'

The three of us – me, Sean and my dad – exchanged worried glances.

'What are you suggesting?' my dad asked carefully.

'Well, I don't have anything firm,' Penny replied, 'but David and I thought one option would be for Natty to defer her place at university, perhaps for another year.'

'Why would I want to do that?' I asked.

'Yes, why would she want to do that?' repeated Sean.

'Don't take that tone with me,' Penny warned, and Sean shrank back into the sofa, sulking at being reprimanded, but not challenging his mother all the same.

It dawned on me that in every conversation we'd had about university in Penny and David's kitchen, UCAS forms spread out across the table, a frisson of excitement in the air, it had never once occurred to me that the reason Sean's parents didn't want us to attend the same place had nothing at all to do with him being distracted by a girlfriend, it was that they didn't want a girlfriend like me. It later became evident the reason for this was because they wanted a privately educated girl for Sean. Someone with better breeding.

Suddenly I felt deeply hurt, as if they'd been pretending. My pride fought hard to push this rejection away and as I studied Sean's reaction it became clear that this was not exactly news to him. I sensed he'd been arguing the case for me for some time.

My face hardened, and Penny, sensing she was about to delve into territory she didn't want to get into, quickly tried another tack.

'Natty,' she said, 'let me ask you something. Do you really want to study radiography? Is that *really* what you see yourself doing for the next ten, twenty, perhaps thirty years?'

Did I? I thought. I wasn't sure. Possibly. Probably. It's not like I'd wanted to do it my whole life or anything. But who did?

Eventually I answered her. 'I think so,' I said.

'You think so,' she repeated flatly, lifting her chin. 'Natty is a bright girl, Mr Odell,' she said. 'I'd hate to see her waste her future on a subject she has no real interest in, just to ensure she and Sean can be together.'

'But that's not what's going on here,' I protested. 'I—'

'Wouldn't it be more sensible for her to repeat her final year of A levels?' she continued, as if I'd not spoken. 'Wouldn't it be more prudent to take the time *now* to strive for excellence, instead of accepting second best, instead of—'

'Mrs Wainwright,' said my dad gently, 'that would be for Natty to decide. And I reckon she's already made her choice. How about you tell us why you're really here. An' I'm thinking it's probably best if you talk frankly from now on, so as not to confuse matters. No sense in beating about the bush.' He sat back in his chair, deciding then that, indeed, a roll-up was in order after all.

To my total mortification he withdrew the Players' tin from his pocket and began, slowly and carefully, as was his way, to assemble one.

Penny straightened her spine. She placed both hands on her knees, took a deep breath in and steadied herself before speaking. 'All right,' she said. 'All right, I'll explain as best as I can . . . We are not awash with money, David and I. We are not what you'd call a rich family.'

'Join the club,' muttered my dad with a half-smile.

'Yes,' she said. 'Quite,' and she shifted in her seat. 'My husband and I decided very early on, though, that we would forego the luxuries afforded to other families, instead making Sean and Lucy's education paramount.'

I think she may have been expecting plaudits of some sort here, because she paused. When none were forthcoming she went on.

'It has not always been easy. In fact on occasion it was nigh impossible to scratch together the money necessary for two sets of weekly boarding-school fees. But I'm proud to say we managed it. And Sean has made us exceptionally *proud of him* by attaining the results he has.'

Sean got three As, by the way. History, English and Economics. Bastard.

'And now that he's got the chance of fulfilling his dream of becoming a lawyer,' said Penny, 'I would hate to see anything get in the way of that.'

'And you think Natty will get in the way of that,' proposed my dad.

'Exactly,' she answered. 'I think any distractions at this stage of Sean's education are best avoided if at all possible. And Natty, while we remain incredibly fond of you, and would hope that you and Sean can still be good friends, we would like to see an end to the relationship as it stands.'

I felt as though she'd slapped me.

My dad raised his eyebrows. He blew out his breath, saying, 'You don't think Sean is going to be distracted by *other* girls for the next three years?' he asked. 'Just Natty. That's what you're saying?'

'Mr Odell, I realize that it might sound a little far-fetched to you. So, no, I don't think Sean is going to' – she paused here, trying to find a suitable word – '*abstain* completely whilst away, but what worries me is the intensity of Sean and Natty's relationship.'

Sean and I traded glances at this assessment of our union. Intensity. It's a word we both found rather pleasing. We were happy with what we had created; happy that it was taken seriously enough for his mother to deem it necessary to try to pull us apart. We felt accomplished.

My dad lit his roll-up and inhaled deeply. 'What if she refuses?' he asked her. 'What if Natty refuses to give up her place? She might not want to leave it till next year . . . she's a mature girl, mature for her age, like you said, and she might not want to wait a year to study with the younger kids.' He looked to me. Tried to throw me a lifeline. 'What d'you say, Nat?'

Penny didn't give me time to answer. 'Well, then we'd have to reconsider Sean's place at Manchester,' she said abruptly.

Sean bolted upright. 'You're not serious.'

'I'm completely serious, Sean,' she replied. 'I had very much hoped it wouldn't come to this, but if Natty is intent on—'

'I won't go,' I said weakly, pretty tearful by now.

'Of course you'll go,' argued Sean.

'No, it's not fair on you. *You're* the one with the good grades,' I said. 'You're the one with—'

My dad stood up. I went quiet. Three sets of eyes were upon him and I prayed he had something useful to say.

He didn't.

It was clear Penny would rather cut out her own tongue than send us off to Manchester with her blessing. And so, reluctantly, eventually, we reached a compromise and agreed to a period of separation. We were to be at different campuses, live in different halls of residences, to limit our interaction. Sean suggested a six-month trial split, his reasoning being that if we went with what his mother wanted now, later, when we were well into our courses, we would have more bargaining power. Reluctantly, I acquiesced and over the next few days I made a series of phone calls to him, begging Sean to explain the reasons for his parents' decision, but he either wouldn't tell me, or else couldn't.

Ultimately, it was my dad who got me to drop it. He caught me crying on the stairs and sat down, squeezing in alongside me. He put his arm around my shoulders, and said, 'Natty. *Oh, Natty.*' His words were delivered with the same level of compassion as just after Mum died. He meant: surrender. Surrender to *what is.*

I flared at him, saying, 'Why should we let that woman decide what happens? Why won't *you* stand up to her?'

He pulled me in close. 'You stay with Sean . . .' he said softly, 'you stay with that lad . . . and that woman's liable to dictate your entire life. Now might not be such a bad time to let it go, Natty.'

So it was with an empty and lonely heart that I showed up at Manchester University. And it is quite possible I would have bolted home to Windermere had I not met Eve on that third day. She sensed I was fragile – the whole sorry tale about Sean coming out within a couple of hours of our meeting – and a kind of mothering instinct was ignited within her. This blossomed into the long-term friendship we enjoyed for the next sixteen years.

She came across me in the bathroom. It was 9 p.m., Friday night, and I was in my pyjamas brushing my teeth. Eve was applying eyeliner in the mirror and I knew the instant I saw her she was older. She was so self-assured, there was no way she could be eighteen.

'Why aren't you going out?' she asked me. A direct question to ask someone you've only just cast eyes on.

I shrugged, not really having a proper answer.

'You don't look dorky enough to be staying in on your first weekend here,' she said. 'Come out with me if you like. I know my way around.'

'Thanks,' I replied, 'but I don't really feel like—'

'What?' she asked accusingly. She spun around to face me. 'You don't really feel like *what?*'

'Going out.'

'Why?'

'I'm pretty tired,' I said casually.

She pulled out a tube of mascara from her make-up bag, dipped the brush a few times before turning back to face the mirror. She opened her mouth wide, as one does when applying mascara, and began stroking the brush through her lashes, blinking periodically.

I felt compelled to watch. As though this person had some kind of immediate hold over me.

'You don't *look* tired,' she said, not glancing in my direction. 'You look sad.'

Unable to think quickly on my feet, I just nodded.

'A boy?'

Was she about to laugh at my pathetic behaviour? Her face seemed open, no hint of mockery, so I said, 'Yeah, a boy.'

She zipped up her make-up bag and smiled.

'Go and get changed, then,' she instructed, 'fast as you can . . . because I have *the best* cure for that.'

Eve waited in my doorway as I rummaged through my drawers for something to wear. I opted for jeans, a vest top and a fitted checked shirt which I planned to leave unbuttoned. 'This okay?' I asked, and Eve chewed the inside of her cheek as she looked me over.

'You got anything a bit more dressy? It's not a student bar we're going to.'

'Oh, okay,' I replied, a bit deflated, and pulled on a baby-pink halterneck I'd recently bought. It was a shade on the tight side and had the effect of squeezing my breasts upwards and out-wards. When I turned around for Eve's opinion a shadow fell across her face.

'That might be *too* dressy,' she said curtly. Instantly, I felt foolish. It was clear Eve was altogether cooler and more know-ledgeable than I, dressed as she was in a metallic snakeskin top with 'Red or Dead' printed across the front, and I'd just demon-strated my woeful ignorance about the Manchester bar scene.

Eve marched across the room and pulled out an uninspiring black top and thrust it my way. 'Here,' she said, 'this is great. Get a move on.'

I did as she asked and, as I applied some make-up Eve filled me in on the quick details of her life so far. She'd started at Manchester, studying psychology, this time last year, but had to pull out on account of a swelling which had developed on her brain.

'Meningitis?' I asked, remembering, because the press was full of articles about students succumbing to the infection. Kids who'd gone off to uni and spent their first weeks kissing everyone in sight, were, if you believed the stories, dropping like flies.

'No, nothing like that,' explained Eve. 'I had an aneurysm when I was a baby.'

'An aneurysm?'

'I had a clip fitted . . . See this?' and she bent forwards slightly and dipped her head, parting her hair with her fingers.

Barely visible, half an inch from the hairline, was a fine, thread-like scar where the hair didn't grow.

I looked at her, dismayed. 'Are you okay now?'

'Completely,' she said, matter-of-fact. 'Just, for some unknown reason, last year I ended up with swelling. I'd never had any problems like that before.' And she shrugged as if to say it wasn't such a big deal.

'Shit,' I said. 'That must have been scary. Were you in hospital? Did they give you . . . *brain* surgery?'

She laughed. 'No. But they thought about it . . . I've got one of the old clips, they use a different type now and in the end they decided to see if the swelling would go down on its own.'

'And did it?'

She nodded. 'But by the time that happened and I was okay to come back, I'd missed too many lectures. The psychology department didn't think I'd be able to catch up, so I took a gap year.'

The idea of a year off seemed so exotic to me back then – backpacking around India or Mexico; working around America.

But Eve didn't tell me what she did. She rearranged her hair and told me we'd better leave right away or we might not get in.

Half an hour later, and Eve carried a tray of tequila shots, shots she'd paid for with a fifty-pound note (the first I'd seen), over to a large rowdy group of young men at the back of the bar. Laying the tray at one end of the table, she said, 'Guys, this is Natty. Natty had her heart broken. So I want you all to be extra nice to her.'

Within seconds the table erupted into chaos as they clambered to get to both me and the shots. They were mostly second- and third-year medical and engineering students, and Sean was largely forgotten that night. Forgotten for the next fortnight, actually, as I became immersed in a beautiful boy from Surrey.

His name was Will Goodwin.

15

Mrs Wainwright is not planning to tell her daughters what she did.

'Is there anyone you can call?' Joanne asks her. 'Because I'm going to have to take you in for questioning. I'm sorry, but in light of the circumstances, protocol dictates it.'

Joanne's being as sensitive as she can here, but there's not a lot else she can do. If Mrs Wainwright decides to go ramming her husband's lover, to the point that the woman breaks her nose, Joanne's got to take her in. And that's even if Mrs Wainwright *hadn't* whacked some poor student unconscious with a golf club, back in her former life.

'Mrs Wainwright?' Joanne repeats. 'How about your husband? Would you like to call him to stay with your daughters? It could be late when you return.'

Mrs Wainwright can't look her daughters in the eye. Clearly this is the first they've heard about their mother's record, and not for the first time in her career Joanne's thinking: Just like a lover scorned to bring all the skeletons marching out of the closet.

After a few tense minutes of silence, Joanne decides to take charge of the situation and addresses the more level-headed of the two daughters. 'What's your name?' she asks.

'Felicity.'

The elder girl – the arty, neurotic one – sits shaking at the kitchen table alongside her mother. She won't be much use.

Joanne smiles kindly at Felicity. 'Can you call your dad and ask him to come over, soon as he can?'

'Sure,' she answers, and leaves the kitchen.

'Don't ring him, Felicity!' the older sister shouts. 'He's not welcome here after what he's done!'

Joanne takes a breath. Raises her eyes to the ceiling before saying, 'Your mum is in trouble. We need to make this as uncomplicated as possible.'

'Is she under arrest?' she demands.

'No.'

'Then you can't take her!' She turns to her mother. 'Mummy, don't go. I believe you! I know you wouldn't do that to Eve. You're right, she's lying to make Daddy hate you, she—'

'The interview must be recorded,' Joanne says cutting in. 'Mrs Wainwright, if you come in right away there's a good chance you'll be back here within a couple of hours.'

This makes her stand. Seemingly mustering every ounce of fortitude she's got, Mrs Wainwright says, 'I'll be with you directly, Detective. Just let me have a moment with my daughters.'

Joanne nods and waits for her by the front door.

At the station, Joanne's office is deserted as everyone is at the pub with Ron Quigley. Joanne sends a quick text saying she'll be with them soon as she can. She sets up the interview room with DC Angela Blackwell assisting, and tells a frightened Natasha Wainwright to sit herself down in the seat opposite.

'Okay if I call you Natasha?' she asks.

'I go by Natty.'

'Natty, then. I'll try to get through this quickly. I can see it's a difficult time for you and your girls and they need you at home. So we're clear, you haven't been charged with anything yet, you are not under arrest, the purpose of your being here is to answer questions relating to the attack on Dr Eve Dalladay which occurred earlier this afternoon. At this point I must ask you if you would like a solicitor present.'

Natty shakes her head. 'No. I just want to get home.'

'Okay, we've been through this, I know, but for the purposes of the tape could you tell me what happened earlier this afternoon when you crashed into Eve Dalladay's car.'

'Sean's car,' she states. 'It was nothing really, I was following her out of Booths' car park, about to join the Crescent Road in Windermere, when for no reason whatsoever Eve slammed on her brakes and I had no choice but to hit her. I checked if she was okay, saw that she was fine and came straight home. Obviously I was pretty shaken up, things being how they are.'

'Because your husband, Sean Wainwright, and Eve Dalladay are in a relationship?'

'Yes, and because Eve was my friend.'

'How do you explain the damage along the driver's side of your car?'

'I did that reversing out of the garage yesterday morning. I was hassled and stressed.'

'When I asked you that question earlier, you said you didn't know how it got there.'

'No, I didn't say that. I didn't answer. I didn't want the girls to know I was such a wreck. I've been trying to hide how much all this is affecting me.'

Joanne drops it for now and moves on. 'Do you and Eve Dalladay go back a long way?'

Natty gives an awkward glance to the side before saying, 'Since university. She was Eve Boydell then.'

'What happened there?'

'With regards to what?'

Joanne gestures to the file in front of her. 'It says here you attacked a student with a golf club. Says you fractured his skull, gave him a concussion.'

Natty Wainwright's eyes go wide. 'No one knows about that,' she whispers.

'You've not told your daughters?'

'*No!*' she says emphatically. 'And I don't want them to know either.'

'Surely your husband knows?'

'Well, yes, of course. And my dad . . . and Eve.'

'Eve?'

'She was there at the time.'

'At the time of the attack?'

'No.'

'Why did you attack him, Natty?'

'Because he left me.'

'Seems a little extreme,' Joanne says.

'I was upset. He humiliated me and then dropped me . . .' She pauses here, glances down at her hands. 'What you must understand is that I was very young.'

Joanne rests her hands on the table.

'Did you intentionally ram Eve Dalladay's car this afternoon?'

'No. I am not a violent person. That thing with Will Goodwin was a one-off. I've never been in any trouble of any sort since, and I did not drive into Eve looking for vengeance.'

'I have to tell you again that the CCTV footage from the car park will be available for us to view shortly. If there's anything you want to tell me, anything you want to add, I suggest you do it now,' Joanne says. 'You really won't want to be amending your statement later on, will you, Mrs Wainwright?'

Natty Wainwright folds her hands in her lap primly and straightens her spine. 'I have nothing further,' she says.

16

B Y THE TIME I arrive home it's after 8 p.m. I'm dropped by a
squad car on the driveway. I'm expecting to see the smashed
rear of the Maserati, but it's Eve's car outside my house.

I didn't wait for Sean to arrive before going in for questioning. We left as soon as we knew he was on his way. I made
an excuse to the girls and to DC Aspinall, saying the sooner we
went, the sooner I could get back. But in reality it was because I
couldn't stand to see the look on Sean's face.

I can fool the girls with lies about ramming Eve, keep my
story straight relaying events to the police, but Sean would be
my undoing. He knows what I'm capable of, he's aware I've
spent the last God-knows-how-many-years creating a life I can
be proud of to try to cover up the past.

Duping Sean would not be easy.

I put my key in the Yale lock and push down on the handle.
The door doesn't move. It's been bolted from the inside.

Instantly, I'm angry. How dare he lock me out of my own
house? I ring the doorbell, keep my finger on the button so it
sounds continuously, and with my free hand I rap loudly on the
wood. After a moment the door opens and there is Eve. She has
a lint dressing across her nose and one on her forehead.

'What the hell are you doing here?' I say to her, and she steps
towards me as if to block my passage into the hallway. 'Where's
Sean?' I demand.

'He's in the shower. We're staying here tonight, Natty. It's probably best if you go before the girls see you.'

I glare at her, fuming. 'You're doing *what*? Not a chance. Move out of the way.'

She stays right where she is.

'And what's wrong with your face?' I add, taking a proper look at her. She has the beginnings of two black eyes and a row of ugly stitches on her chin. Scowling, I say, 'There's no way I did that to you. No way. What the hell have you done? Thrown yourself down the stairs?'

She doesn't answer so I barge past, shoving her against the front door, and come face to face with Alice – who's sitting at the foot of the stairs in her leopard-print onesie.

She's sniffling into a handkerchief and, as I approach, she shrinks away as if she's actually scared.

'What have they told you, Alice?' I say, incensed that they've been poisoning the girls' minds the first opportunity they got. 'What has . . . what has *that woman* said to you?'

'Nothing,' Alice stammers, taken aback. 'Nothing, Mummy. What's happened? Daddy said the police might keep you there all night so he had to stay here . . . and Eve can't be left alone because . . .' she starts to cry '. . . Eve can't be left alone because of the trauma to her head. Mummy, did you do that to her? Daddy said you almost *killed her.*'

I put my hand on her shoulder and she stares up at me, unblinking.

'Alice, I did not do that to Eve. I promise you, I did not do that.'

I turn around and see Eve standing a few feet away, a wide-eyed, doleful expression on her face.

Eve is wearing a Laura Ashley tea dress with a silly white Peter Pan collar at the neck. It's the kind of outfit a savvy lawyer would place his defendant in to give her an air of purity and innocence.

134

'What did you do?' I hiss at her. 'Did you smash your face against the wall like Myra Hindley? So that you'll be less menacing?'

Eve always was ever so slightly rodent-looking; she'd spend hours at university trying to 'open up' her small eyes. Using a combination of liquid liner and brown eyeshadow at the outer edges, she'd declare that, with clever application, she knew how to *enhance her beauty*. But, really, the effect was minimal.

'Natty,' she says compassionately, 'please stop. This is not helping anyone, least of all Alice. I understand your emotions got the better of you today, and I'm really sorry about what you're going through. But what you're accusing me of is just pre-posterous ... and besides,' she says, her tone slightly mocking now, 'there's no evidence that Myra Hindley ever actually did that. It's a rumour never proven to be true.'

I turn back to Alice and can tell by her face she thinks Eve is being reasonable. I'm losing her confidence and I don't know what to do.

'Will you have to go to prison?' Alice asks me in a quiet voice.

Suddenly, I am drowning. I want to run at Eve and punch her. I want to grab her by the hair and drag her out of my house. But my daughter is watching my actions carefully, like she's not quite sure who I am any more. I am paralysed from doing anything about it.

Just then, Sean appears on the stairs. He is clean and dewy-looking, fresh out of the shower. In his hand is my overnight bag.

'I've packed a few things for you, Nat,' he says. 'I've told your dad you'll be staying there for a while.'

My mouth gapes open. 'Not a chance. This is *my home*. These are my children. You two stay here over my dead body.'

Eve clears her throat. 'Natty, have the police viewed the CCTV yet?'

'I'm not sure,' I lie.

'Well,' she begins, 'we're under the impression that they've not. They will be watching it first thing tomorrow morning, and you know what they're going to find, Natty. You know what it will show.'

I don't speak.

Sean descends the last few stairs, taking care not to nudge Alice's head with the bag. He ushers me towards the door and, softly, so Alice can't hear, says, 'I don't think it would be good for the girls to see you taken in again. We've played it down so far, Natty, but they're not stupid. Do you really want them to witness your arrest tomorrow? Is that what you want?'

'But I won't *be* arrested,' I say. 'Eve caused those injuries herself. She's done it to trap me, Sean. She's done it to get her hands on my kids and—'

Sean puts the bag down and closes his eyes. 'Natty, just listen to yourself. This is absurd. Neither of us wants it to be this way, we don't want you to lose the girls, but this needs dealing with. And the last thing I want is for Alice and Felicity to see their mother as a criminal.'

'I'm not a criminal!' I shriek.

Whispering, he replies, 'But the law says that you are. Do you really want the whole thing dragged out in front of them?'

I wring my hands helplessly. I'm trying to think, but I can't. I look over at Alice on the stairs, and I'm trembling. She can't find out like this.

He leans in and speaks into my ear. 'Go now. Don't let them see what you've done. I'll make sure they never know, but you've got to play fair, you must leave Eve alone.'

One last glance at Alice and I see I have no option. I have to comply.

Sean opens the door and we go outside. I take the bag from his hand and my keys from my pocket.

'Let me order you a taxi, Natty,' he says, 'your car's not fit to drive . . . look at it.' The car is a real mess. The front is a total wreck and the side has a deep gouge the whole way along it. 'You might get pulled over by the police because the headlights are out.'

'It'll be fine,' I say. 'If I'm going to leave I need to go now.' He drops his head. He doesn't want this, he doesn't want to send me away from my home, I can feel it.

'You won't sleep in our bed again, will you, Sean?' I ask him, tearing up. 'You won't let Eve into our bed?'

And he says, 'No.'

Still looking downwards, he shakes his head. 'No, I won't do that, Natty.'

I sit here sobbing as my dad slowly and methodically rolls the Rizla back and forth between his thumb and forefinger. He licks along the edge and lights it, and the pungent smell of Drum tobacco and cannabis resin fills the air. He's always enjoyed the occasional joint. I've tried reasoning with him to stop, but he simply won't.

Wincing as a thread of smoke catches his eye, he says to me, 'You want some?'

I stop crying for a second and glare at him. 'Don't be ridiculous.'

'Might make you feel better?'

'Dad, there is *another woman* in my house. How is a joint supposed to make me feel better?'

He shrugs as if to say, *It might.*

'I'm losing my home,' I snap at him crossly. 'I'm losing my home and my kids to a woman who was supposed to be my friend. And you want me to sit around getting stoned so we can end up discussing – what? The Vikings? Or how the pyramids were built?'

'It got me through when your mum died,' he says reasonably.

'Yeah, well, I'm not you. And hold that ashtray beneath that joint, will you? I can't go sending the chair back to the nursing home full of rock burns.'

I shake my head. 'I'm getting a drink,' I say, rubbing the back of my neck. 'Do you want anything?'

'No. See if you can get the cat in while you're up.'

Gazing into the darkness, I stand at the back door sipping water, trying to calm myself. It's a mild night, low cloud, no sign of any stars. Shaking the Cat Crunchies box up a couple of times, I call out, 'Morris!' and do that ch-ch-ch-ch thing cats answer to.

People say they're either a cat person or a dog person. I am neither. Nothing against them per se; it's the fur I can't stand, gets all over everything. Pets, or the lack of, has been a running battle in our house since the girls were small. The closest we ever came to being pet owners was bringing home the school guinea pigs for the weekend. But, amazingly, we were struck off that rota when I forgot to take them back and had to return the guinea pigs at Monday lunchtime in a taxi. (In my defence, there was a particularly difficult guest at the hotel I had to attend to.)

I shut the door and go through to my dad. 'The cat doesn't want to come in.'

'Try him again in an hour,' he says. His words are slowed; they've already taken on that sleepy quality. 'There's some brandy in the cupboard above the kettle, Natty,' he says. 'Pour yourself a glass.'

'I don't want any.'

'Come here,' he says gently, and I think he wants to hug me. 'Come here, love.'

I walk towards him, my arms open, but he doesn't reach out to receive the embrace as I expect. Instead he says, 'Take a look,' gesturing to the large mirror hung above the fireplace.

'*That,*' he says, signalling to the angry, contorted reflection staring back at me, 'is why you need a drink. Go and get one.'

In the kitchen I find the brandy. Usually, my dad stocks cheap Metaxa 3 stars – alcohol that doubles as lighter fluid – which his friend brings back from Greece twice a year. Tonight, though, there is a large, unopened bottle of Hennessy. I down a shot and immediately pour another.

'Sure you don't want one?' I call to him.

'Aye, go on then, I will.'

As I carry in the glasses, he's stubbing out the remainder of his joint. 'Marvellous,' he says, reaching for the tumbler.

'What time is the carer coming to help you up to bed?'

'It varies.'

Frowning, I say to him. 'Should you really be smoking dope in front of them, Dad? I mean, it doesn't look good.'

'I'm sure they come across worse things.'

'What if they report you?'

He chuckles. 'To who?'

'The police.'

Amused, he raises the glass to his lips. His eyes are already bloodshot – as if he's stepped out of a chlorinated bath.

'What's so funny?' I ask him.

'It's me who's supposed to be paranoid,' he says, motioning to the ashtray, 'smoking this stuff.'

'I'm not paranoid,' I protest, and he tilts his head, smiling a little.

'You're not paranoid,' he repeats neutrally. 'You're not para-noid, yet so far you reckon Eve's smashed her face up – so she can curry favour with Alice and Felicity. And now you think my home help are police informants. You're lacking – what do they call it, love? – hard evidence?'

'I just think you should be more careful about openly breaking the law in front of people you don't really know.'

'I'm not breaking the law,' he says, and I toss my hair dismissively, thinking: *Great, here we go. The justification speech of the seasoned dope smoker.* He'll now launch into the mind-opening properties of cannabis, the stats proving it less harmful than alcohol, the low incidence of violence at Dutch football matches.

But I don't get the lecture. Instead he says, 'Natty, you rammed a woman's car this afternoon. You did this with a criminal record for assault . . . Now, who d'you reckon ought to be giving out the advice here? Me or you?'

I close my eyes and sink deep into the sofa.

'Jesus,' I say in a strangled voice. 'What am I going to do?'

'Tonight?' he says. 'Tonight, you do nothing. Get back to thinking sensibly and drop this nonsense of conspiracy theories – you're acting like you've got a screw loose. Sean is not the first man to leave his wife for another woman, it happens every day. Drop the paranoia, Natty, and get on with living again. If it's only for the sake of the girls.'

'But you didn't see her face, Dad! There's no way I did that kind of damage.'

'How many times did you ram her?'

'Two or three times.'

'Which was it,' he asks, 'two, or three?'

'Four,' I say sheepishly, 'but there's absolutely no way I—'

'All right,' he says, cutting me off. 'All right, let's say she did it herself, if that makes you feel any better. It doesn't change the fact that as soon as the police check the cameras, they'll see what you did. And what happens then?'

I toss the remainder of the brandy down my throat. 'They'll come for me.'

'That's right,' he says sadly. 'They'll come for you.'

He rests his glass on the arm of the chair and sighs heavily.

'What made you do something so bloody stupid, Natty?'

'I don't know.'

'Well, we've got till morning to come up with an explanation. After that . . .'

He doesn't finish his sentence.

17

A SK ANY MOTHER what her biggest fear is and she'll likely say something bad happening to one of her children. Get that out of the way and you're in the realm of spiders, heights, enclosed spaces – that sort of thing.

For me, it's always been snakes: I'm helplessly treading water in a murky jungle pond when a venomous yellow water snake zigzags its way towards me.

Well, there's that . . . and prison.

I imagine going to prison is not top of most women's list of fears. The chances of it happening are as remote as, say, choosing to holiday in Baghdad. Logical thinking deems it pretty unlikely.

But what if you *were* going? What if suddenly that woman on the front of the newspaper is you?

Not going to happen, you say. I'm not that sort of person. I don't lead *that* sort of life.

Okay, but ask yourself this: Would you ever kill another person out of desperation? Would you ever kill another person out of jealousy or hatred?

No, me neither. But somebody has. *Somewhere.*

Maybe a woman a little bit like me or you has done such a thing. She didn't rob a bank, or commit credit-card fraud or traffic drugs. She simply did what she's here to do – love her family fiercely. And when her family was threatened, she reacted with one of the primitive emotions that exist inside us all. The emotions we're conditioned to override if we are to live inside a civilized society. She protected her family and now she is being punished.

It's 5.50 a.m. and as I lie in the narrow bed, in my childhood room, I know there is a reasonable chance I could be on my way to prison.

For a first offence, a person committing grievous bodily harm, or the lesser charge of wounding without intent, would be eligible for bail. For a second offence? Not so much.

So I try to think about what to do. Because this is my second offence. But trying to think cogently about my options while paralysed with fear is hopeless. I get as far as perhaps grabbing my passport, making for the ferry port, when—

SLAM. The comprehension I'll never see my kids again knocks me sideways.

Maybe I *do* take the penalty. Maybe I go to a women's prison, serve my time for whatever it is they decide to charge me with – I won't be in for more than a few months at the most, and—

SLAM. I won't see my kids. And if I do see my girls, they'll be visiting me *in prison*.

Now I can't think of anything because I'm swamped by the hatred of Eve and the whole injustice of it. I'm so enraged with myself for letting her get me into this, the very worst of lose–lose situations.

I get up, I go downstairs to make a cup of tea, see if I can get the cat in after all. As I walk through the lounge I hear pawing at the bay window, so I double back to the front door, chiding him as I open it. He rubs past me, meowing loudly. He's a great big brute of a cat – with a black, glossy coat and white belly, he is a close cousin of Looney Tunes's Sylvester, but he has a smattering of indistinct black spots on his chest, like the dotted fur lining the Queen's St Edward's Crown. My dad calls it Morris's Regal Fur.

It's almost daylight, but still the street lamp outside sends a shaft of amber my way, illuminating the doorway and revealing a white envelope at my feet that I failed to spot a moment earlier.

'Natty Wainwright' is printed across the front. There's no address or postmark; it must have been hand-delivered during the night.

I close the door and go to the kitchen. After shaking out a few Cat Crunchies for Morris, I open the letter and a sudden coldness hits my core.

It says:

EVE HAS DONE THIS BEFORE. DON'T LET HER TAKE WHAT'S YOURS.

I stare at the note, my mind running at a hundred miles an hour. It's handwritten, the letters printed in small, neat capitals, and if I had to guess I'd say it's from a man. Simply because men tend to stick to capitals – though I could be wrong.

The paper on which it's written is a raggedy scrap, torn from a yellow, lined notepad. I'm trying to figure out if this is significant or not when the front door bangs shut and a woman's voice shouts, 'Only me!'

Mad Jackie.

I'm at the kitchen table, clutching the note in my hand, when I hear heavy footsteps coming my way. She's straight to the kettle, filling it, before she's aware of my presence.

'Jesus!' she exclaims. 'Bloody hell, I didn't see you. What are you doing here?'

'Long story.'

She's a little ruffled. She opens the fridge and quickly closes it again when she spies her stack of Weight Watchers ready meals on the middle shelf.

'They yours?' I ask, gesturing.

And she smiles back at me. 'What's that?' she says brightly, pretending she's no clue.

'Ocean pie, salmon and broccoli melt, chicken hotpot . . .'

'Oh, those,' she says. 'Yes, they're mine. How's yer dad doin' this morning? Has he had a cuppa?'

'Not yet, I don't think he's awake.'

She's about to say something more when she notices the paper in my hand. She doesn't ask what it is, but I hold it out to her anyhow.

She pulls a pair of glasses from the breast pocket of her uniform and slips them on. They still have the sticker in the corner displaying the lens strength +2.00. They're the type of specs you pick up from the petrol station or from next to the tills at Sports Direct. Jackie looks very schoolmarmish with them perched on the end of her nose.

'Where did you get this?' she asks.

'I just found it. Must have been delivered here sometime last night.'

'Who's it from?'

I shrug. 'No idea. I think the sender wants to remain anonymous . . . or else they would have signed it?'

She nods. 'Strange thing to say, don't you think? What does it mean, she's done it before? Done *what* before?'

'I assume it means stolen a husband.'

'What you gonna do, confront her? Ask her who else she shacked up with?'

I swallow, not sure whether to divulge yesterday's events. My dad will tell her anyway, so I may as well come clean. 'I'm in a bit of a fix, actually,' I begin. 'I crashed into Eve's car yesterday—'

'On purpose?'

I grimace, about to answer, but before I have the chance, she says, 'I bloody hope so. She deserves some grief after what she's done to you. If it was me I'd have gone the whole hog and—'

'There's more to it,' I cut in. 'She reported me to the police.'

Jackie pulls a face as though to say: *Well,* they *won't be bothered. Stop worrying about it.*

I look down. 'It's not that straightforward. I did something else, something a long time ago. I've got a criminal record.'

Jackie's eyes widen, before she retracts her chin in surprise. After a moment of consideration she gives a bark of laughter. 'Well,' she says, 'aren't you the dark horse? I had you down for Miss Butter-Wouldn't-Melt. Yer kept that quiet. Does yer dad know?'

'No one knows,' I say firmly. 'Well, *he* does, obviously . . . but we don't like to talk about it.'

Mad Jackie removes her reading glasses and mimes zipping her mouth shut with her index finger. 'Safe with me,' she says.

When she's poured the tea Jackie disappears upstairs to get my dad moving. I hear the combi boiler firing up as she runs the hot water, and I hear them laughing.

Twice a day a carer comes in and does the necessaries for my dad, and he's friendly, amenable, never shy or difficult. With Jackie, though, the tone is different. It's cheery, jovial, and I wonder how he's *really* felt about being on his own all this time. He's always brushed it away when I've enquired in the past, professing to enjoy his own company. When pressed, he'd even go as far as to say he relishes his solitude. Now, I'm not so sure. Now I wonder if it was for my benefit, and I feel a sting of shame that I took his proclamations as genuine.

I hear my dad come down the stairs on his bottom – the physios at the hospital insist it's the safest way. When he reaches the last step the gentle banter between them ceases and I sense they are discussing me. I hear the metallic crunch of his elbow crutches as he makes his way into the lounge and, hearing him exhale with relief as he sinks into the chair, I go to say good morning.

He's wearing black jogging bottoms and a red fleece. His knees are still twice their usual size, the swelling visible through the fabric, and now I'm feeling guilty for haranguing him last night about getting stoned. It must be dreadfully painful.

'Morning,' I say.

Before he can reply, Jackie's behind me, announcing, 'I told him about your poison-pen letter.'

'It's not a poison-pen letter,' I mumble. 'It's a note.'

'Who sent it?' he asks. 'How did it get here?'

I shrug.

'Let's see it, then,' he says.

I hand it to him, and he looks at it, perplexed. 'That's it?' he says after a moment. 'That's all there is?' I nod. 'Well, that could have come from anyone, anyone with an axe to grind.'

'You don't think it's strange?' I ask. 'That she's done it before?'

'Not really. Women who commit adultery tend to make a habit out of it . . . I'd be surprised if she *hadn't* done it before. Nothing weird there,' he says, and hands the note back.

I go to speak – and stop.

There's a memory of a thread of a conversation playing around the edges of my thoughts.

It takes me a few moments to retrieve the words spoken, but what remains clear to me was how ruthless Eve could be, even then.

She and I had just returned to the halls of residence after a night out together. We were in her room and I was lying on her bed, a little drunk, flattered by all the attention I'd been receiving from Will Goodwin, saying, 'Oh, I *do* hope he likes me.'

'He likes you,' Eve answered bluntly as she brushed her hair, 'but you want to snare him fast if you plan on keeping him.'

'Snare?'

'Hmm-mm.'

I sat up, immediately on the defensive.

'You're saying I need to trap him?'

'Yes,' she replied.

I scoffed at this idea, it totally going against my notion of romance. 'You think I need to trap a guy into liking me?'

Eve made a face to imply: *Yes – God, you're naïve.*

'But I want a guy to fall in love with *me* – the real me.'

'Prepare to be on your own, then.'

I felt pretty offended, but Eve continued on, unabated, as if she considered it her duty to instruct me in the ways of the world.

'Do you really think Will Goodwin's going to fall in love with you if you withhold sex until the third date?' she asked. 'Do you think he's going to value you, respect you? Take you home to meet his mother?' And she laughed openly when she saw by my face that, yes, this had in fact been my plan. 'That's all fine in theory, Natty,' she said, 'but these are men we're talking about. They don't operate like other creatures. The trick to making a guy fall in love with you,' she declared, 'is to find out what he wants . . . and become *that.*'

'But he needs to love me for who I am,' I argued.

'No, he doesn't. Become what *he* wants you to be. And when you've done that, find out how he sees himself and praise *those* traits. See him for the way he wants to be seen. The way he wishes he were seen. Respond to his opinions as if they are the most insightful, the most thrilling things you've ever heard. And, of course, give him lots of blow jobs in inappropriate places. Try it, Natty,' she told me, 'it's the only fail-safe method.'

I look at my dad and Jackie now, and see they're regarding me sceptically, waiting for me to continue.

'What if,' I say to them, 'what if, for some crazy reason, Eve did set out to do this? What if she planned to steal Sean?'

And they exchange pitying glances.

Mad Jackie claps her hands together. 'How about a nice bit a breakfast?' she asks.

'No, thank you,' I reply. 'I'm going out.'

My dad's expression falters. 'You're doing what?'

'Going out.'

'But what about the police?' he stammers. 'Shouldn't you be lying low? The police might see your car and—'

'I'm glad you mentioned that,' I answer brightly. 'Okay if I borrow the van?'

18

JOANNE FLASHES HER warrant card. 'Detective Constable Aspinall. I spoke on the phone to Martin North.'

'Ah, yes,' replies the supervisor. 'Follow me, I'll take you through to the office.'

Booths supermarket is not open to the public at this hour; its doors are unlocked at eight. Joanne decided to come straight here this morning rather than the station. If there's anything on the CCTV, she can pick up Natty Wainwright directly. Save doubling back.

As she makes her way through the store Joanne says hello to three people she knows. Half of Windermere works here, but it wasn't always that way. The building was converted from the old Victorian railway terminus in the eighties. Joanne remembers the outcry from local shop owners at the time, but that's all changed now. She still hears the objections from the death-of-the-high-street brigade when another bakery is replaced by a gift shop, another butcher's by a holiday letting agency. But Joanne wonders just how many people would actually be willing to work six full days a week now. And do their bookkeeping, trips to the wholesaler, on their days off. Not many, she suspects. She suspects part-time hours, holiday pay, sick pay and a regular wage will probably win out with most in the end.

'Hi, Martin,' Joanne says as she enters the office. 'Been away? You're nice and brown.'

'Turkey,' he replies.

'Any good?'

'I believe it's nice at Christmas.'

Joanne groans, and Martin adds, 'So sorry, terrible joke.'

Joanne's dealt with Martin North a few times; he's always been very accommodating during investigations. Last year she arrested a woman from Booths' accounts department for embezzling funds; the year before that a driver was caught stashing marijuana in containers inside one of the large freezers. And six months ago one of the café staff stabbed her husband with a bread knife. She leapt from behind the coffee machine when she saw him exiting the store carrying a bag of Pampers he had bought for his ex-wife's baby.

Martin North motions for Joanne to sit down in his office chair, its vinyl beginning to split, while he remains standing. He's comically thin. He wears plain-fronted Farah trousers – in what Joanne reckons must be about a 26-inch waist – and a polycotton white shirt and plain tie. He *always* wears a vest beneath his shirt, whatever the weather, like an Italian waiter ordered to by his mother.

'Kids all right?' Joanne asks, and Martin nods, flushes with pride at the mention.

It's not something Joanne's always done – ask after people's children. But it's a useful tactic in getting people to talk. To get the most out of them. She began noticing how DS Ron Quigley started almost all conversations with a personal enquiry, and she saw how people responded: guards down, faces relaxed.

'Do you want to take this with you?' Martin asks, meaning the CCTV footage.

'Okay if I look at it here instead? I'll have to make two trips if I take it with me to Kendal.'

'No problem.' He lines it up for Joanne to see. 'It's pretty funny, actually,' he says.

When Joanne doesn't comment, Martin looks abashed. Apologetically, he adds, 'I do hope she wasn't too badly hurt.'

'She'll live,' says Joanne.

Joanne watches as the Maserati pulls alongside the recycling bins, watches as the brake lights go out. Moments later the car is slammed from behind by a Porsche Cayenne.

Martin sucks in his breath as the driver reverses and hits the railing of the trolley park to the right. 'Bet that's expensive,' he says quietly.

The Cayenne goes out of shot for a second, then it's back again. There is no movement from inside the Maserati. Eve Dalladay must be sitting, shocked and injured, because anyone with their wits about them would have jumped from the car, trying to escape the onslaught.

The car is rammed twice more, and then nothing.

Martin says he's got footage of the Cayenne leaving the car park from another camera if Joanne wants it, but she tells him not to bother. There's no doubt it's Natty Wainwright's Porsche.

No doubt it's her, and no doubt she didn't run into the rear of Eve Dalladay's car while driving through Windermere, as she claimed to have done, either.

My dad persuades me to wait until later before heading home and brandishing the note at Eve. It's one thing to turn up when they're half asleep, he says, quite another to do it with accusations flying. He thinks I'm jumping the gun, thinks I'm behaving in the quintessential wronged-wife fashion, and I should forget all about the note.

I don't take his advice, though, because I'm buzzed and eager, ready to confront. I spend the next hour twitching, checking my watch and tutting at the banality of breakfast TV. At eight I'm on the road, driving my dad's van. It's jammed full of tools, even though he has one of those 'No equipment kept in here

overnight' stickers on the rear door. It's the only embellishment
on the aged white Transit.

The van's interior reeks of cigarettes and some kind of lubri-
cant – a WD40 type of smell – and the inside of the driver's door
is covered with tiny circles of ash. Eyeing the burn marks brings
back memories of being small, of Dad taking me along to a job
somewhere. He would open the window, just a fraction, and it
always amazed me the way the smoke and ash was sucked out
when the van got up to speed. That, and how he managed to
steer with his knees if he needed to roll another.

I join the main road, crunching the gears a little, as the clutch
is heavy, and drive down the hill towards Bowness. I wouldn't
usually be in the village at this hour. After getting the girls out
the door, typically I hightail it to the hotel, greet the guests for
breakfast, then spend the morning in the office dealing with
problems, anticipating potential problems. Often I spend way
too much time heading off the various sales people who call
throughout the morning, only to reach 11 a.m. not having
achieved anything I set out to do. I need to get back there. I can't
hide myself away for ever. Perhaps I'll call, make an unscheduled
visit like an AA inspector, keep the staff on their toes.

I drive past the rows of shops and cafés setting up for the day,
hanging baskets being watered, pavements swept, delivery vans
blocking the road, and it feels strange to be incognito in the
Transit. I pass a number of pedestrians I know by sight, as well
as drivers who would ordinarily raise their hand, flash their
lights, upon seeing my car.

I pass two women from the girls' school, walking dogs I didn't
know they owned; pass the hotel gardener, chatting outside the
sandwich shop. He's with a plumber I sometimes use when I
can't get hold of my regular guy. They are laughing together, and
I wonder what Sean has told them about me. About us.

The hotel staff are paid to be discreet, but of course that

doesn't mean they don't gossip. Has Sean taken a leaf out of his mother's book and told them I've had a nervous breakdown? I suppose, in a way, I have.

A few minutes later I pull on to my driveway. I leave the van in gear as I cut the engine and, because I forget to keep my foot on the clutch, it lurches forward unexpectedly.

I feel like a fool.

I have the urge to go in there and fight for what is mine. But am I being absurd?

All at once I'm not so sure about this. Perhaps this is one of the stages of grief. Have I gone from Denial to Anger to Bargaining and then to Irrational without even realizing?

But someone left me that note, wanting to help me see the truth. Or, what if it was Eve who sent the note? What if she sent it knowing I'd come here, further cementing my craziness by throwing accusations at her?

Or am I being completely crazy by even thinking *that*?

I don't know.

My heart is pounding the way it does when you've had a close call with a lorry on the motorway or nearly fallen down a flight of stairs. A cold sweat has sprung between my shoulder blades and for the first time in my life, I am questioning my sanity.

Then the front door opens and out comes Eve.

She is walking towards the van, and her face is set. She walks with such purpose you'd think this was *her* house, and it is *I* who am trespassing.

Instinctively, I lock the door. She approaches and stands at the driver's-side window in her dressing gown. Her eyes are blacker now than yesterday, but she has removed the lint from her nose and it doesn't appear broken. I look at her out of the corner of my eye but keep my head fixed forward. 'Natty,' she says in an almost bored manner through the glass. 'Why are you here?'

I don't respond, so she taps on the window.

'I'll call the police,' she threatens. 'Is that what you want?'

Instantly, I'm riled by her air of propriety. I wasn't expecting a welcoming committee, but still.

Without speaking, I slap the note hard against the window. She recoils backwards then frowns slightly as she reads it.

'Well?' I mouth at her.

And she shrugs dispassionately as if to say: *Well what? So what if I have done it before?*

Incensed, I fling open the van door and march inside the house. Eve is trailing behind, can't keep up in her slippers, and if she's speaking to me I can't hear her – so intent am I on finding Sean.

I head to the kitchen first, but he's not there. Nor in the living room, or the utility, where he sometimes shines his shoes before work.

So I run upstairs, two steps at a time, and find him in the guest room. He's perched on the edge of the bed, trimming his toenails. The sight of this stops me dead. What an utterly normal thing to do. How can he perform such a pedestrian task when my life is in tatters? I stand in the doorway until he registers my presence.

'Nat?' he says, concerned, knitting his brow.

'This came.' I shove the note towards him.

Eve is now in the hallway, so I spin around. 'You stay put,' I warn, and she doesn't argue.

Methodically, Sean gathers the nail clippings and places them in a neat pile on the bedside table. He reaches for the note. After what seems like an eternity, he says, 'I don't know what you want me to do, Natty.'

I try to keep my voice steady. 'She's done it before, Sean.'

'I know,' he answers. 'Eve has been fully clear about her past. I'm aware of the extramarital affair that happened early in the relationship with Brett.'

We're supposed to be friends, and this is the first I've learned about her stealing someone's husband. What else has she kept to herself, I wonder?

Trying to mask the hurt I'm feeling at this – another betrayal – I ask, 'But what if she planned all of this?'

'Planned all of what?'

'This,' I answer, and gesture wildly around the room.

'Felicity's appendix?' he asks, his tone sceptical. 'She planned Felicity's burst appendix? How on earth did she do that?'

He waits for me to respond and, when I can't, says, 'You were the one who didn't want me to come to France, Natty. *You* were the one who said it was fine.'

Ignoring his words, I plough on. 'Sean, you need to listen to me. I don't think she loves you, I think she's tricking you. This is what she does, she *told me* this is what she does. This is how she operates.'

He shakes his head.

'It's true! Do you really think she loves you?' I demand.

'Yes,' he says. 'I really do. Natty, stop this, before the girls come in. Stop being—'

'She doesn't, you know. She—'

'Look, I'm not justifying it any more,' he says, losing patience. 'I've told you it's over between us, I've done it the best way I can, but' – he sighs his breath out wearily – 'but . . . you are making this unbearable—'

'Do you think I told *you* the truth?' I ask, my voice shaking with anger.

'I don't know what you mean.'

'Do you think I told you the truth all these years? Do you think I really liked listening to *The* fucking *Doors*, Sean? Do you think I like your mother? 'Cause I don't. I really don't. That's what women do, you idiot. We say what you want to hear . . .'

He's staring at me as if he doesn't recognize the person in

front of him. As if it's dawning on him that he's *never really known* me. But I keep going.

'You want kooky and interesting?' I ask nastily. 'We can do that. You want intelligent and slutty? We can do that, too. You want sex outdoors? That's what we do to snare you, Sean. *That's what women do!*'

He drops his head.

After a moment, he speaks. 'But you didn't do that, Natty . . . you stopped doing all those things a long time ago.'

And I burst into tears.

'That's because I was fucking busy!' I shout, and then I throw my keys at him.

19

IF I'D BEEN thinking straight, I would have grabbed my laptop. But I wasn't. So I didn't.

I leave the guest room, screaming at Sean, screaming at Eve, only to come face to face with the girls, standing shocked and bewildered in the hallway. They'd barely heard me swear before today (well, aside from the occasional *shit!* when someone pulls out on me in traffic). Felicity is dressed in her uniform for her first day back at school and Alice is holding her lacrosse stick out in front of her – as if for protection.

'I need my passport,' I mutter vaguely as I descend the stairs, and they nod, repeatedly, as you might to a crazy thief . . . *Anything you want . . . Take anything you want.* I don't say goodbye, such is my focus on retrieving the passport – my thinking being that, if I leave it behind, any chance of escape from the law is nigh impossible. It's only when I emerge from the office – heart pounding, brow sweaty from frantic searching – that I see the girls gathering their belongings, and I stop short and realize what it is that I've just done.

The girls are speaking in hushed tones, their movements are exact and purposeful – exaggerated, really – and instantly I feel shitty about making them so uneasy in their own home.

Felicity catches sight of me. 'You okay there, Mum?'

I rush towards them. 'I'm so sorry about all that,' I say, straightening my clothes and hooking my hair behind my ears

158

in an attempt to appear less chaotic. 'Are you both okay? Felicity, are you sure you're well enough to go to school? How is your tummy?' I survey her ashen face and I'm gripped by inner rage at Sean's appalling timing. Could he not have at least waited until Felicity was better to start screwing my friend?

'I'm a bit sore,' answers Felicity, 'but I've got a note from Dad to say I can't do any exercise, and I've got a pretty easy day.'

'You'll call me if it gets too much? Call me, and I can be there in five minutes to collect you.'

Felicity nods, as Alice leans in. In a forced whisper, her eyes wide, she asks, 'Mummy, *what is* going on? Why were you telling Daddy that Eve is lying to him?'

'It was nothing,' I say. 'I thought I had proof that would alter things. But it turns out it was nothing.'

Alice looks dubious, as though I'm sparing her the details because I don't trust her to be adult enough to deal with them. 'It was nothing,' I say, more firmly this time, and she puts her arms around me. Gives a kind of awkward half-hug on account of all the kit she's carrying.

'Just don't do anything else, will you, Mummy?' she says, more relaxed now. 'Don't do anything to Eve, because Daddy's, like, super worked up about it.'

'I won't.'

I tell them I love them and moments later pull off the driveway, head back towards the village. I come to a stop about a hundred yards along at the entrance to an unused track. Turning the passport over in my hands, I close my eyes, thinking: *What the hell use is this, Natty? Where are you going to run away to, Acapulco?*

Shaking my head at my own absurdity, I look left across Lake Windermere; at the thick grey clouds arriving from the south-west, at the chocolate-box houses perched on the other side of the valley. It's almost the exact same view I see from my bedroom window every single day. The view I gaze at when I have a problem; when I'm worried or anxious.

'So what now?' I say out loud. 'What do I do now?'

The girls had watched like I was a monster. As though I was sabotaging what little I had left with them. And when that rotund detective turns up again, saying, 'Sorry, but we need to arrest your mum,' I can just picture them, relieved, replying, 'Yes, *could* you? She seems to have lost her mind.'

All at once I'm regretting being so detached when in the company of the countless newly separated women I've known over the years, their faces full of disbelief at having the rug pulled out from under them.

I remember one woman, particularly, saying it wasn't selling her home that was her undoing, nor saying goodbye to her lifestyle, but the big expanses of time she now had to fill. The whole empty weekends that once took care of themselves. In the past she'd run her son to football, washed uniforms, perhaps gone to the DIY store before settling down to watch *The X Factor*, the day disappearing without a thought. 'Who watches *X Factor*,' she cried to me, as I stood choosing a card for Sean's mum in WHSmith, 'who watches *X Factor, alone?*'

There's a hollow, empty feeling as I now contemplate my abandoned future. Realizing that for almost half my life I've planned, dreamed, wished for what was to come, with Sean in mind. What happens now to the trips to Bologna, to La Rochelle? What happens to driving through France in a Mercedes Benz 230SL like Albert Finney and Audrey Hepburn in *Two for the Road*? What happens to spending whole Sundays in bed with the newspaper, or selling the hotel and buying a hillside villa in Sorrento? What happens to *all that*, Sean?

Fat drops of rain begin to fall, as if on cue. Fumbling with the switch for the wipers, my attention is caught by a nondescript grey car, its headlights on, heading my way. Upon seeing the driver my heart begins jackhammering inside my ribs, because it's the detective from yesterday. I dip my head and freeze, watching in my wing mirror as she indicates right and swings into my driveway.

DC Joanne Aspinall stands outside Natty Wainwright's house in the rain and rings the bell. She marvels again to herself that it's a beautiful home. The lower section is Lakeland stone, the upper finished in white, pebble-dashed render. Must be worth around two million, perhaps even more because of the view across the lake. Most of these big gentlemen's residences were built at the end of the nineteenth century for Lancastrian mill owners, this being one of the remaining few that hasn't been split. Many were sectioned into smaller residences – two, sometimes three or four units – and sold off separately in the fifties, mainly because the whole house was impossible to heat. Impossible, that is, without a small army of staff to tend to the open fires in each room.

Joanne tries the bell again and lifts her hood. The rain is really coming down now and it's the type of rain that soaks a person right through. Eventually the door is answered by Eve Dalladay in her dressing gown.

'You just missed her,' Eve says, a flat, malevolent tone to her voice.

'How are you feeling today, Miss Dalladay?' Joanne asks pleasantly. 'Your face looks to be healing nicely.'

Eve ignores the question, says, 'Natty was here a few minutes ago, causing problems again. Did you see the CCTV? Have you seen it yet?'

Joanne smiles. Gives nothing away. 'Any idea where she went?'

'Her dad's,' replies Eve. 'Well, I assume that's where she went. She's staying there now.'

'Moved out, then, has she?'

'Yes. It'll be better for everyone.'

Joanne keeps her face blank as she muses on the fact that Eve Dalladay hasn't wasted much time getting her foot in the door. 'Do you have the address?' Joanne asks. She knows which street the house is on – on account of Jackie half living there at the moment – but she's unsure of the exact number. She retrieves her notebook from her inside pocket as Eve gives a tight smile.

'An address for whom?' asks Eve, playing dumb.

'Mrs Wainwright's father.'

'I'll see if I can find out for you,' she says, and she shuts the door in Joanne's face. Leaving her to stand in the rain.

Mad Jackie grabs three cups from the kitchen cupboard and proffers a bag of something herbal. 'Do you want some of this dyke tea?' she asks me.

'What type is it?'

I'm thinking I'm in for a sermon on decaffeinated redbush, or the antioxidant properties of organic camomile. But no – Jackie shrugs, as if she has no idea what kind of tea it is.

'I'm off milk,' she explains: 'Think it's that that's causin' me bloatin',' and she rubs her tummy tenderly. 'So your husband didn't want to know about the note then?'

I shake my head.

'You can't blame him,' she says, running the cloth around the taps. 'He'll be thinking with his dick for now. Give it a few months till the shine wears off . . .'

The kettle boils and Jackie dips the tea bag in and out of the cup repeatedly. She opens the fridge and I see she must have nipped to the shops while I was gone. There are now masses of Yakult probiotic drinks in there – next to the ready meals. I don't bother to tell her that they're made from milk.

She hands me the cup and I take a sip. 'This is peppermint,' I tell her.

'Yeah, one of me clients gave me a bagful,' she explains. 'Just takin' up space in the cupboards since his wife died, he said.' Jackie sips from her cup, pulls a face before flinging its contents down the sink. 'Not keen on that one,' she says. 'It's like gripe water.'

She refills the kettle and turns back, regarding me for what feels an uncomfortably long stretch of time.

'What?' I ask.

'Just thinking.'

'And?'

'It might have been a bit daft you going over there this morning, waving that piece a paper in his face.'

'I kind of worked that out for myself, thanks.'

She pauses for a moment, then speaks. 'If you're gonna get them to listen to you . . . and I'm not sayin' it'll make any difference, mind, because I'm not convinced there's anything to that note, but if you're gonna get them to take you serious, you need something proper on that woman.'

'On Eve?' I ask. 'Like what?'

'You tell me. What d'you know about her?'

I shrug. 'We were all at university together, Sean and I left, she stayed and got her doctorate . . . then she moved to the States, where she's been lecturing and running her therapy practice ever since. She's squeaky clean. I've never known her do anything out of the ordinary.'

Jackie gives me a look. 'No one is squeaky clean.'

I sigh, wrapping both hands around my cup. 'She is.'

'Person who sent that note doesn't reckon so. What's her husband like?' she asks.

'Never met him.'

'You never what?' Jackie says. 'How come?'

'Because I'm not allowed inside America, Jackie . . . and Brett's never been over here, so . . .'

Jackie frowns. With a thoughtful expression she repeats what I've just told her, but slowly. 'You're not allowed inside America.'

I wait. Widen my eyes a little, hoping she'll catch my drift without my actually having to spell it out.

She doesn't.

'Because of my criminal record?' I offer.

This piece of information is clearly news to Jackie, because she goes uncharacteristically quiet. Eventually, she says, 'So, if you've got a criminal record you can't never ever go there?'

'That's what I said, yes.'

She nods, processing this. Then she starts chewing the inside of her cheek and I know what she's doing. She's trying to come up with an example of someone with a criminal record *who has* been allowed into the United States.

So, before she can blurt out, 'George Michael!' I save us some time and tell her, 'There are exceptions, but you need a visa. And for that you need to go to the US embassy in London and have an interview. Sean and I looked into it when we wanted to take the girls to Disney, but in the end we decided not to go ahead. We didn't want to run the risk of anyone finding out, and it seemed like a lot of palaver when we could just go to Paris instead.'

Jackie's considering this when the doorbell rings.

She ignores it momentarily, asking, 'Have you got Eve's work number?'

'Yes, but I always ring her on her mobile.'

'How about giving her secretary a call, see what you can find out?' The doorbell sounds again and Jackie gives me a sideways glance. 'Make yourself scarce,' she orders. 'This might be trouble.'

Jackie tramps towards the front door, and I'm tempted to follow her, to see who it is, but a warning glare from my dad signals me to retreat. He's seen something from his chair. Probably saw the caller walking up the pathway. He motions for me to leave by way of the back door, but I hesitate: I want to know who's there.

Jackie's voice bellows through: 'She's not 'ere, Joanne,' and I think: *Joanne?* Who is Joanne? Jackie's clearly shouting for my benefit, but who is—

Then it dawns on me: Joanne is the first name of the police officer who questioned me yesterday; the detective I just saw turning into my driveway. She's come straight from my house to here. Someone has told her where to find me. I hear more words exchanged and my palms start to sweat. It's clear Jackie knows this woman personally. I raise my eyebrows to my dad, who whispers, 'Her niece,' by way of explanation.

I lean against the wall. 'You're quite sure she's not in there?' the detective is asking Jackie.

''Course I'm sure,' Jackie replies crossly.

There's a pause, and the detective says, 'Can I come inside?'

'Not unless you tell me what you want.'

'I want to speak to Natty Wainwright.'

'And I told you, she … is … not … here,' Jackie repeats slowly, as if her niece is stupid. 'Not seen her since earlier. Are you gonna arrest her?'

My dad is staring at me fiercely while at the same time tipping his head repeatedly towards the dining room, like he has a mad tic. He seems at once determined and fearful.

'What?' I mouth.

'*There*,' he whispers.

I follow his line of sight and upon moving a step forward realize he's motioning to his stash. It's positioned just behind a couple of empty glasses on the table.

I lift my eyes to the ceiling in exasperation and grab the pack of king-size Rizlas and the old worn Player's Navy Cut cigarette tin. He's carried that tin around with him for as long as I can remember. 'I told you to be more careful with this,' I hiss.

And he gives me a look as if to say: *That woman is not here on account of me.*

I move to the kitchen door and crane my neck a little to hear what's being said.

'I just want a word with Ken Odell,' the detective is saying. 'C'mon, Jackie, I'll charge you with obstructing a police officer if you don't let me—'

'No, you won't,' says Jackie dismissively. 'What do you need to talk to Kenneth for, anyway?'

'Just want to ask him a few questions. I can't help this woman out if you won't let me do my job, Jackie. Maybe her dad can shed some light on things, maybe he can give me something I can use to take the heat off her . . .'

Jackie huffs and gives in. 'Oh, all right, all right,' she snaps. 'If you must. But you'll have to give me a minute to get Kenneth decent. He's sittin' in there still in his drawers.'

20

I WALK FAST, HOOD up, head down, along Queens Drive, making my way in the rain along the back streets of Windermere. Though the town took its name from the lake when the railway opened in 1847, it lies a good half-mile from the lakeshore, so consequently it has fewer hotels, fewer B&Bs than neighbouring Bowness – the more popular tourist destination.

At this time of year the town of Windermere appears tired. Scaffold adorns many of the terraced houses as owners start to repaint, repair, and begin their losing battle against the cruel weather this region receives. Heavy November rains are followed by frost in December, and by the time we get to the sunshine of spring, the buildings have peeling paintwork or else are covered in a green, algae-like layer.

Property repairs are never-ending here. Fall behind and you're likely to have leaking sills, overflowing gutters, damp patches on interior walls capable of cultivating a large variety of mushrooms. Chimneys are blown clean away by the strong winds of March, and it's not uncommon to rise after a particularly blustery night to find a tree emerging from somebody's attic bedroom.

Walking now, I carry only my wallet. I left my Fendi tote in the kitchen cupboard, hiding my dad's cannabis paraphernalia inside the washing machine before stealing out the back door, exiting via the gate at the end of the yard.

If I were looking for me – someone like me, I mean – the handbag would be a dead giveaway. So I try to blend in because you don't get many *women like me* walking these streets. We tend to stay inside our 4x4s. Inside, with our handbags on the passenger seats, our golfing umbrellas in the boot, our D&G sunglasses in the glove compartment, ready to pop on top of our heads should there be a brief respite from the rain.

I remember picking up Felicity once from her friend's house on the next street over, and my dad, in the passenger seat, thought it was hysterical I should text Felicity from outside the row of terraced houses. 'Why don't you go and ring the door-bell?' he asked, and I didn't really have an answer for him, other than this was just how we did it. He'd chuckled, saying, 'Bet you'd get out if it was a big posh detached,' and of course I protested vehemently. Though, to be honest, there was probably some truth to his words.

At the T-junction at the top of the hill I take a right, then dip immediate left on to the public footpath beside the beck. This area is not visible from the road. I used to run through here as a kid.

Remember when you were convinced that any deviation, any detour from the usual route was a short cut? Making sure you ran *twice as fast* just to prove the point to your friends? I'd emerge from here, shoes thick with dog shit, triumphant, and spend the next hour arguing with some kid about who was the faster.

Now I check over my shoulder to make sure I'm not being fol-lowed and rest for a moment to allow my breathing to return to normal. It's not that I'm unfit. More the act of giving DC Aspinall the slip has flooded my blood with adrenalin and I'm feeling kind of buzzed and heady. So I pull out my mobile and call Eve's business line. After letting it ring and ring, it dawns on me that of course there will be no one at her office at this hour

– when an answer machine kicks in. 'You have reached Nordstrom Seattle. Opening hours for this store can be found on our website . . .' My throat goes tight. I hang up and stare at my phone. This was definitely the number Eve gave me. Could I have entered it incorrectly?

I blow out my breath and drop my shoulders, do the yoga breathing that's supposed to lower your blood pressure. Closing my eyes, I'm momentarily startled by the alarm call of a vexed-looking mistle thrush resting in the leaves beside my feet. He's clearly perturbed by my being here, so I move on.

Because now I have a plan.

It's not a particularly sophisticated plan, but it's a start: If I stay out of plain sight, using the streets and cut-throughs of my childhood, I can get to Windermere Library unseen. And it's not far. Only a ten-minute walk.

Once there, I can hide for as long as necessary while I do some research. Because Mad Jackie is right: *Why* blindly accept every-thing Eve has told me? She's demonstrated pretty clearly she's not who I thought she was, so perhaps there *is* more. Perhaps I can find some dirt on her, something that happened over in America.

Outside the library there are two cars with disabled badges in the window and a beat-up old Bedford Rascal van – the type with the small, comical wheels. I don't recognize any of the vehicles so I go on in, keeping my head low. At the desk is a tradesman in blue overalls unenthusiastically telling the librarian that he's, 'All finished . . . and if you've got a dustpan and brush then I'll tidy up.'

The librarian scoots out from behind the desk to go and find him one. I resist telling her that this is an empty phrase uttered by tradesmen. You're supposed to reply, 'Oh, don't worry about that! I'll clear up the wood shavings.'

They don't actually expect you to *go and find a dustpan and brush.*

Minutes later, she's back, victorious. 'I didn't even know we had one!' she says, jubilantly, and he takes her offering without a word, trudging across the hallway.

I move forward. 'Yes?' she asks.

'Can I have an hour on the internet, please?'

'Have you got your library card?'

My heart sinks. 'No,' I say, wincing. Bloody hell, my plan is thwarted before it even got going.

'Are you a member of Windermere library?' she asks, and I begin searching back through the far corners of my mind. Way, way back to when the girls were small and—

'Yes!' I exclaim. 'I'm sure I *used* to be. Yes, definitely. I am.'

The librarian casts me an uneasy glance before tapping the keyboard.

'Can I have your name?' she asks.

'Natasha Wainwright.'

It takes her a few seconds before she looks up and smiles. 'Found you,' she says. 'Would you like to apply for another card? I can get it processed while you use the computer . . . if that suits?'

'Perfect,' I reply, and she tells me she's put me on number four.

I peer to the right, to the computer area, and see only two seats are occupied.

'Number four's opposite,' she tells me, helpfully. Which means I'll be visible from the front desk. I almost ask for an alternative – one with more privacy – but I decide against it. Causing a fuss over this will only attract more attention than if I simply duck behind the monitor should I see anyone I know.

Suddenly it strikes me that perhaps I am being over-cautious. What if *I were* to see someone I knew? What am I worried about? That when the story of my avoiding apprehension hits the papers, someone will say, 'And there she was, *brazenly* typing away in Windermere library . . .'

I settle myself into the seat and tap in the code the librarian gave me to log on. I'm a little uneasy. Not because I have a detective following me. But because, you know on TV when they tell you about computer keypads, about remote controls carrying more bacteria, more microbial faeces, than, say, a public toilet? And some pleased-with-himself doctor asks, 'How many people actually clean those things?'

Well, I do.

I'm the person who cleans those things *every* day. Sometimes twice. So I'm rather edgy touching this keypad with its bits of food lodged around the space bar. And before you ask, it's not OCD. OCD is purposeless cleaning and repeated checking. My cleaning is not without purpose. If I don't remove traces of the person who used these things before me (perhaps a sweaty guy picking his nose), then who knows what I might catch? Norovirus? Impetigo? I dread to think.

I look around, a little helpless. I could do with some hand sanitizer.

To my right is a woman in her early twenties, hammering away. She has long black hair down to her waist and a diamante nose piercing. Its setting has tarnished to a greeny-grey and stained the skin around the stud to the same colour.

She stops typing and peers my way. 'You need help?' she asks in accented English.

'Sorry?' I reply.

'You need help . . . with computer?'

'Yes, actually I do,' I say, fixing a smile. 'Do you have any wipes?'

She knits her brow, confused.

'Wipes?' I repeat, and make as if I'm removing my mascara. 'Wipes . . . for make-up?'

'Aah,' she says, grasping what I'm on about. 'One moment,' and she leans to her right and begins searching through her handbag.

She hands me a travel pack of Wet Ones, and I thank her. Then she watches with a bemused expression as I withdraw a couple and set about sterilizing the keyboard. Not forgetting the mouse.

When I'm done, I sense she wants to say something. '*Neurótico*,' she whispers, shaking her head.

I resolve to let her think what she wants. I have other things on my mind.

I type 'Eve Dalladay' into Google and sit back in my seat, hoping something magical will appear. Something to call into question Eve's motive for screwing up my life.

But nothing. I get the usual: Did you mean Eve Halliday? Eve Holliday?

Thank you, no. I meant Eve Dalladay.

I scroll down. There's a Facebook entry for a couple of different Dalladays, but no news items. So I try searching with Bing instead – but just get the same search results.

After a couple of fruitless variations I go back to Google and try 'Dr Dalladay' this time, expecting to *at least find the wrong* Dr Dalladay on LinkedIn.com. But no, again, there is nothing.

I'm confused. It's as if she never existed.

I try Dalladay + Washington, adding in Seattle, psychologist – to no avail.

Then I have a brainwave.

'Brett Dalladay,' I type. There has to be something on Eve's husband. I hit Enter with a flourish and put my hands behind my head, waiting to be rewarded for my quick thinking.

Then I slump back, because the screen clears and again it displays: 'No results found.'

21

E VE DALLADAY SITS at Natty's dressing table viewing her face from different angles in the three-section mirror. She likes what she sees. Just enough bruising to make a person gasp, but not so much as to cause any real, lasting damage.

Every time Sean looks at her, his expression collapses into wretched remorse. He couldn't be any sorrier for what he thinks Natty did to her.

Stupid Natty.

Of course Eve would capitalize on her recklessness. She'd have to be a fool not to.

Eve had actually given Natty more credit than she deserved. She thought it was going to be significantly harder to get sympathy from Natty's girls, thought she'd have to manipulate their minds more deeply before she gained any kind of approval from them. But Natty was just making it all so easy.

As long as she keeps digging her own grave, Eve thinks now, as she dabs concealer beneath her lower lashes, I won't have to do a thing.

Eve opens the top drawer of the dressing table and gives a spiteful laugh at what she finds there. She'd always known Natty was a control freak. It's always easier to step inside the shoes of a woman who's concentrated on the irrelevances of life. Always easier to disarm a woman who's so busy making sure everything is perfect she fails to see the threat right in front of her. And this type of woman is more common than ever before. Eve puts it down to insecurity – this quest for perfection. The fact that they need to do more, *be* more. Once they've had the children, remodelled the house, returned their figure to its former glory, they set about proving they're much more than just a wife and mother – studying, starting a business, finding their calling, moving up to the next level. They become so focused on this goal that Eve can spot them a mile off, and it is always surprisingly easy to instigate an affair with the neglected spouse.

Eve has managed to accrue cars, clothes, cash, a mews cottage in London and an apartment in Seattle, to date. Sadly, the properties had to be sold a few years ago when she ran short of funds and had to flee after a particularly nasty confrontation with a wife holding a grudge. Eve *does* regret the way she left that woman. No child wants to find their mother's body, after all – she knows that; she's not totally heartless. But you turn up shouting your mouth off when Eve is dining with a prospective client and, needless to say, there will be consequences.

Natty has all her cosmetics in neat tidy rows with the aid of drawer dividers. Eve picks up a barely used tube of Retinol night cream which Natty must have shipped from the States, Retinol not being available in the UK without prescription, and squeezes the entire contents on to a tissue. She's never fully understood why these small acts of mischief bring her such pleasure, but they do.

After the Retinol she scoops out the Crème de la Mer face cream in one big handful; rubs it into the skin on her shins, her feet. Then she sets to stabbing a cotton bud into Natty's various lipsticks – the Chanel Rouge Coco, the Dior Diorific. Each is rendered a sticky mess.

When she's finished with the top drawer, she moves on to

the one below. She takes Natty's birth-control pills and ejects them one by one from their foil wrapper and begins mashing them with the back of a hairbrush.

She's reminded of the act of crushing coriander seeds in a pestle and mortar, and thinks how nice an aromatic curry would be this evening. Sean's mentioned more than once that Natty won't allow curry in the house – the smell lingers, she says, and the turmeric stains her granite worktops.

Eve applies some more Touche Éclat to the bruising beneath her eyes, then looks past the mirror, through the window to the lake beyond.

The rain of earlier has cleared. Sunlight breaks through the clouds and glances off the lake. Perhaps she'll take a walk down to the lakeshore. Hop on a passenger ferry and do the tourist thing. Sean was saying you can buy a day pass now, take in Ambleside, Newby Bridge, Fell Foot Park – perhaps stop for a bite to eat at the visitor centre at Brockhole.

Eve's not been to Brockhole since she was eleven and came to the Lakes on a school trip. She remembers learning how to build a dry-stone wall, seeing her first monkey puzzle tree, which she's told is now gone. Mostly she remembers standing on a jetty, smiling at the thought of her friend, Andrea, crying in the gift shop minus her cherished five-pound note.

Eve recalls the sweet thrill that came over her as she fingered the money inside the front pocket of her shorts. She'd been sent on the trip without any cash of her own but had no intention of spending Andrea's.

What did Eve want with a pen with a fluffy creature on its end? Or a scented eraser? Pointless.

That's not why she took the money.

She wanted to enjoy the crestfallen look on Andrea's face. To enjoy Andrea's tears when she sobbed that she'd been unable to buy anything in the gift shop. She took it to upset the teachers, to 'Take the shine off a perfectly good day,' as they would later tell the class with stern disappointment.

When she let the money fall into the water, the note dropping cleanly between the slats of the wooden jetty, the sensation she got from this small disruptive act was like a shot of pleasure. An energy-charged jolt she felt from the back of her knees all the way up to the top of her scalp.

The teachers subsequently blamed Karen Wilcox for the lost money. Karen was a smelly girl, one of seven kids, who wore the same clothes day after day and had to wear her knickers and vest during swimming lessons as she didn't own a swimsuit.

Eve never bothered to tell the teacher otherwise.

She studies her face in the mirror now, watching for any sign of emotion to surface as she thinks about Karen being unjustly accused.

Nothing.

22

HOW CAN EVE not exist? How is that even possible? There must be some trail of Eve Dalladay, surely. Anyone running a business has to be listed *somewhere*.

Feverishly, I type in anything I can think of to find some kind of link. I go way back through Eve's history – type in her maiden name, searching for Eve Boydell from Cheshire. Eve Boydell at Manchester University, Eve Boydell at—

'Natty?' comes a voice. 'Natty, *is that you*? Good Lord, it is you!'

I look up. Sean's mother is striding my way. She's clutching two audio books to her chest. The pink Radley handbag I bought her last Mother's Day is swinging from the crook of her arm.

'Hello, Penny,' I say. 'What are you doing here?'

Her mouth gapes open, her face displaying both confusion and contempt, as though she's come upon a trusted member of staff, their fingers inside the till.

'W–what . . .' she stutters, '. . . what *am I* doing here?'

I nod.

'I'm collecting these for Valerie Warburton,' she says, frowning, and holds out the audio books. The top one is a Barbara Taylor Bradford. I can't see the one beneath.

She waits for me to respond, she's expecting an explanation for my being here, and I find myself glancing around the room

– as if something might rescue me from this discussion.

'Aren't you supposed to be with the police?' she hisses. 'Sean told me the police have been at the house and—' All at once, she notices the girl sitting next to me is watching her. Penny drops her voice to a forced whisper, a look of distaste coming over her as she notices the girl's nose ring. 'Sean says the police are *looking for you*, Natty.' The ferocity of her glare makes her chin shoot forward. 'He told me you got yourself into an altercation with Eve.'

'That's right, Penny, I did.' She flinches at my honesty.

'Well,' Penny continues, 'Alice and Felicity are terribly upset about the whole thing, terribly upset. I plan on seeing them this evening when I've fulfilled my obligations with Valerie. The WI has a rota in place . . .' Her accent becomes prim and dictatorial at the mention of the Women's Institute. She lifts her chin a little as she speaks. 'In fact,' she adds, 'I must remember to pick up the prawn salad when I . . .'

Her voice trails off as she thinks through the logistics of what she needs to do.

Incidentally, I have no idea who Valerie Warburton is. I assume I am supposed to know. She's probably a woman of great standing in the community, probably a formidable woman who is now incapacitated – thus sending each member of the Windermere WI into a frenzy of usefulness and duty.

'So,' Penny says, snapping her attention back to the here and now, 'I'll take the girls out for an early-bird dinner, see if I can't take their minds off all this nonsense. Is it Alice who likes Italian, or Felicity? Perhaps I'll just take them for a roast. I imagine it's been an age since they had anything decent to eat.' Then she pauses.

'Natty,' she says, her tone questioning, serious. 'Natty, Sean says you rammed Eve's car.'

She says this as if to suggest *it can't possibly be right, can it?*

And before I can answer the girl next to me snorts, flicks her head around.

'Whose car you hit?' she asks me.

'My husband's lover's.'

The girls eyes widen. 'Bravo.'

'Thank you,' I tell her, and glance up at Penny. 'I did hit Eve's car, but there's more to it than you've been told, and—'

'I always knew you'd do this,' Penny snaps, dismissing my attempt at explanation.

'Knew I'd do *what?*'

'Knew you'd . . . never mind,' she says, shaking her head. 'We need to talk about this somewhere more private. Follow me,' she instructs. Then she takes one last, disdainful look at the girl to my right and says, 'Make sure you bring all of your belongings, Natty.'

I don't bother telling her I haven't got my handbag with me, that my purse is inside my pocket. Instead I rise silently from my chair and traipse after her to the library entrance, next to a dinosaur display from the local primary school.

'Right,' she says. 'The most important thing now is of course Alice and Felicity. And I have to say, Natty, you're setting a terrible example. Whatever must they think, conducting yourself in such a manner?' I go to speak but she lifts her index finger, silencing me, and I'm reduced to giving a tortured little smile. 'It goes without saying I understand what a terrible situation this is for everyone, and *Lord knows* I am not condoning Sean's behaviour . . . but ramming Eve's car, Natty? What on earth were you thinking?'

'I wasn't really thinking anything,' I mumble.

'Evidently not,' she says, 'but you're going to have to start. You can't go on pottering mindlessly through the days feeling sorry for yourself, and you certainly can't go attacking Eve. So my question is this: What *are* you going to do?'

'What am I going to do about what, Penny? I'm not following you.'

Penny exhales and reaches out, clutching my wrist with her hand.

'You need to build a new life, Natty. You need to get back into the swing of things instead of mooching around after Sean. How do you think I felt when David had his nervous breakdown and went off with that . . . that *child*? I'll tell you, I was grief-stricken. I felt like I'd never get through a full day again. But I did. I absolutely did. Because I *made* myself. Now, you needn't say yes to this straight away, because I appreciate there are things you'll need to organize. And I know you can't just drop everything . . . but they're positively crying out for help at the Save the Children shop.'

I withdraw my arm.

'I don't think so,' I tell her.

'Why ever not?'

'Penny, as of yesterday, your son has installed another woman in my house, in my home, and you think the answer to this problem is . . . charity work?'

'If you don't keep active, Natty, you're certain to become depressed. And you might think me forward in my approach here, but, as a mother, the one thing you should never ever do is let your children see how a breakdown in a relationship is affecting you. Sean and Lucy were never witness to David's illness; I shielded them from it. And that's exactly what you should be doing with—'

'David's illness?'

'His nervous collapse.' She looks at me questioningly. 'You remember that, Natty, surely?'

'Penny, David was never ill. He left you.'

She gapes at me, genuinely astonished, as if I've slapped her hard across the face. 'How can you say that?'

'Because it's true!'

She backs away, saying, 'I assure you *it is not true.*' Her eyes are prickling with tears. 'I assure you David had a series of complicated problems long before any of that started.'

She places her audio books on a display table and rummages inside her handbag for a clean tissue. Dabbing her eyes, she casts me a wounded look and instantly I feel terrible.

'Aww, Penny,' I say, reaching for her, 'I shouldn't have said that, I'm—'

But she folds her arms across herself.

I stand helpless, not able to find the right words. Wishing I hadn't let her push my buttons, because I know – have always known, in fact – that sustaining the lie about David is the only thing keeping Penny from unravelling spectacularly. The only thing keeping her functioning like a normal human being.

Eventually, she's able to bring herself to speak. 'I'll thank you to keep your opinions to yourself in the future, Natty,' she sniffs, and it's bordering on tragic, because I know she's trying to say this forcefully, but it comes out strained and weak.

As she gathers her things to leave, she says, 'I *do* hope you know I was only trying to help you.'

I nod sadly, watching her disappear into the fiction section. There's a sudden whoosh of air behind me as the automatic doors are thrown open.

I turn around and freeze.

'Hello, Mrs Wainwright,' says Detective Joanne Aspinall.

My face must register instant alarm because she tries her best at a consolatory smile. 'I'm here to take you in,' she says, carefully gauging my reaction. 'I expect you'd prefer for me *not* to read you your rights in a public place?'

'You're arresting me?' I ask.

She places her hand on my elbow and begins guiding me towards the door. 'Let's get you straight to the station and there'll be no need for a scene,' she says. 'I don't think we need the cuffs, do we?'

'What?' I gasp, confused, then realize she's being serious.

'No. No, of course not,' I say, and follow her out.

23

IN THE END Eve decides against a trip on Lake Windermere. It's drizzling, again, and she can't stand the wet. In the short time that she's been here it has done nothing but rain.

In the village, at the hotel, at the hospital, Eve's heard people joke that last summer occurred on the second Tuesday in June. Following it up quickly with: 'Of course, if we didn't have all the rain . . . then we wouldn't have the beautiful lakes.'

Eve's not sure the lakes are actually that much of a trade-off. How *do* people spend all year in this dank, dreary corner of the world? How, when there is day upon day of thick, low clouds, the horizon blurred between the sky and the fells?

And there are no decent shops. Just gift shop after gift shop selling brightly coloured crockery. Selling high-waisted smock dresses with gaudy embroidery along the hem. Selling tall, ugly, wedge-heeled boots for ladies with thick calves.

Eve would have thought the combination of bad weather, restricted sunlight and limited choice of consumer goods would have an effect on the common psyche – as it's purported to do in, say, Alaska. But she has seen no evidence of this so far. The people here seem happy – particularly the pensioners. Eve's noticed that they appear fitter, more cheerful, *more vigorous* even, than pensioners in other parts of the country. Naturally, she has no intention of staying here long enough to become old herself. No, she'll stay as long as it takes to get a decent payout from Sean, and then she's off to Malaga. She'll try her luck on the Costa del Crime with all those rich Russians. That is, unless she can persuade Sean to leave the girls and sell up. That could work, at a push.

Today Eve determines it's more important for Sean to desire her rather than feel woeful about her injuries. If he stays in that sorrowful state for too much longer, he might be liable to forget why he left Natty in the first place. And Eve can't take the risk.

So it's for that same reason she decides to remove every scrap of her pubic hair.

Better, yes, to have it done professionally. She knows that. But Eve's not going to chance using one of the provincial waxing salons in Bowness. She'll take care of it herself.

But should she go for the whole vajazzle, she wonders? Perhaps not. Sean is fairly traditional when it comes to sex: too much sparkle and he may get spooked.

She picks up the phone and calls him.

He answers on the third ring. 'Come home,' she whispers, and he tells her he's on his way.

She puts on the blood-red lipstick she saves for occasions such as this, applies two coats and a layer of gloss. She runs a comb through her hair, twisting it, securing it, into a loose chignon with a number of shiny pins. Then she strokes a coat of mascara through her lashes.

She brushes shimmery highlighter along her cheekbones, remembering to dust a little on to her breasts before fastening her bra, and pulls on her stockings – seven denier with black lace at the top. She clasps her suspender belt – wears no briefs for now – and slips her feet into her heels, walking over towards the bed.

Lying on her back, she begins rubbing almond oil into her newly shaved skin. After a few minutes of kneading, the flesh there is engorged, baby-soft and plump. Almost ready.

She slips a finger inside to be certain she's thoroughly wet, and, satisfied, she turns on to her tummy. She lies in her bra, stockings and shoes, facing towards the brass headboard, so that, upon seeing her, Sean will benefit from the full rear view.

And now she waits.

When she hears the front door slam and Sean's eager footsteps on the stairs, she parts her legs. Looks over her shoulder, sexily, from beneath her lashes.

Sean arrives in the doorway, panting.

Before he can speak, Eve shoots him a filthy smile and gets up on to her hands and knees.

I try Sean's mobile for the third time. 'This person's phone is switched off . . .' comes the haughty, pre-recorded voice of the Vodafone woman. I've always thought they could get somebody far nicer for that role. It's bad enough that you can't get through, without her making it worse. A lovely, lilting Highlands accent would be such an improvement . . . *Och, dearie, this person's phone is—*

'Perhaps you could try calling someone else?' DC Aspinall says flatly. She casts the desk sergeant a quick glance: they're beginning to lose patience. 'What about your father? Maybe give him a call?'

I shake my head. 'He can't help me,' I mumble, because I'm thinking: Where is Sean? What the hell is Sean doing?

We've always had a rule about mobile phones: They never get switched off when the girls are not with us. They can be set to silent. But phone calls from family cannot be ignored. No matter what time of day, no matter what we're doing. No exceptions.

Of course, I know Sean and I are not technically family as of late, but still. The girls are at school and so Sean's phone should be on. And if I go wasting my one phone call on somebody else, it will be just that: a waste.

Finally, on the fourth attempt, it goes to voicemail. 'Sean,' I say, my voice shaking with emotion, 'Sean, please ... I'm at Kendal police station, I've been arrested. I need the name of the lawyer you mentioned ... you know, the guy you met at ... I can't remember where you met him.' I pause, the gravity of my situation starting to sink in as I speak it out loud. 'I don't know who else to ask, Sean. Please hurry, I'm on my own here.'

I lift my head to see the desk sergeant busying himself, pretending not to listen. He's dressed identically to the bar staff at the hotel – black polo shirt, black pressed trousers. He's slim-hipped, with strong, sinewy forearms – joiner's forearms – and is experimenting with pointed sideburns. For a moment I'm distracted, because, since when did police officers stop wearing shirts and ties? When did the chequered Juliet Bravo epaulettes disappear?

The desk sergeant meets my gaze and I snap back. Dropping my voice, I finish the call. 'Sean, I've got no one else to ask ... *please* get in touch with the lawyer. They're waiting to question me, and I'm scared.' As an afterthought I whisper: 'Don't tell the girls I'm here.'

I replace the receiver and turn to DC Aspinall. She's already read me my rights and I have been arrested on suspicion of assault: grievous bodily harm and dangerous driving. I used my vehicle as a weapon.

'What happens now?' I ask quietly.

'Not a lot,' she says. 'We wait for your solicitor.'

'But what if he can't get here? What if he can't get here till tomorrow? I don't know where he's based, so it could be ...' My words evaporate as I try my hardest to recollect the conversation Sean and I had about this guy. All I remember is Sean saying he was nicknamed something corny like Dr Fix-it, because he had quashed numerous motoring charges against idiotic Premier League footballers.

DC Aspinall shrugs, giving me a sympathetic smile as if trying to convey something obvious that I'm failing to grasp. 'If you're declining the services of the duty solicitor, then there's not a lot we can do.'

I sigh. 'Can I go home?' I ask her. 'I promise not to leave the country.'

She shakes her head. ''Fraid not,' she answers. 'We can't let you go . . . not this time.'

I look at her aghast. 'You mean, I actually have to stay here?'

'Yes.'

'Really?'

'Yes.'

'Surely there must be something,' I say helplessly. '*Some* reason you can find that will allow me to go home.'

DC Aspinall's face is impassive. She thinks I'm acting like a silly, spoilt woman, but that's not it at all. I'm terrified. Beyond her is a skinny man arguing with an officer. The officer is trying to calm him. The man, emaciated, no more than seven or eight stone, has bad skin and a terrible, twitchy manner. He is swearing loudly and I'm finding it deeply unsettling. Someone has bumped his car and he's incensed that the police are claiming it's an insurance matter. The man is warned to lower his voice or else he'll be removed from the station and, as he slams his fist down hard on the counter, we all shudder.

'I cannot stay here,' I whisper to DC Aspinall, my voice pleading. 'You don't understand . . . this is not *my life*.'

'Mrs Wainwright, you don't have a choice.'

Suddenly I can't seem to catch my breath. Logically, I knew on the way here that being arrested meant I was likely to be charged. Which meant I would have to appear before magistrates in a few days' time for sentencing. I said all this to myself, said, 'Brace yourself, Natty.' But in the fifteen minutes it took to get here – DC Aspinall hurtling through the floodwaters in a way a person would do *only* in a company car – I didn't actually conjure up the image of my being led to a cell. Of sleeping behind a locked door. Of pissing on a low toilet without a seat in the corner of the room.

Sensing my terror, DC Aspinall touches my arm.

In a steady, controlled tone, she says, 'I'll make this as clear as I can, Mrs Wainwright. Unless Dr Dalladay changes her mind and decides to drop the charges against you, you will remain here until questioned. And then—'

I go to interrupt but she stops me.

'And then, if charged, you may well be released on police bail. But I can't guarantee that, on account of your previous conviction.'

'You mean I'll be remanded in custody?' I cry, horrified. 'You're telling me I'll be shut away until I go to court?'

'That's usually how it works, yes.'

I fight back the tears. 'Don't do this,' I beg. 'Please don't do this, this is not who I am.' And I can only think of my mother. She hadn't brought me up with all that love, all that integrity, for me to end up here. She hadn't invested so much of her good, decent self in me, for me to be locked up.

Sean's mother was right. What sort of an example do I set for Alice and Felicity?

I am an embarrassment.

DC Aspinall tilts her head. 'You'll be okay,' she says, guiding me by the elbow towards the cells. 'It's not going to be half as bad as you think.'

The problem with noisy sex, thinks Eve Dalladay, as she comes loudly and aggressively on top of Sean, is you're not always aware that someone's approaching until it's too late. And Eve always comes loudly.

Men are such simple creatures, after all, and with an innate need to please. 'Like loyal mongrels,' Eve has mused more than once; dogs whose entire sense of well-being comes from pleasing their masters.

And what could be more pleasing than making a woman's legs shake, making her shout out with pleasure? All the while under the happy delusion that you are *the only man on earth* capable of such a feat? This is what makes Eve such a good fuck. It's not what she does in the bedroom, but how she reacts. This is what makes her a generous lover. A lover that men have a hard time giving up.

She climbs off Sean's naked body and tells him they have a problem.

He's out of bed in an instant, pulling on his underwear, his socks, his shirt. Striding around the room in a state of utter despair.

'You're sure?' he asks again. 'You're absolutely sure?' The fear is clear in his voice.

'It was definitely Felicity,' Eve repeats. 'She headed towards her room.'

'Jesus,' he says. 'Jesus!' He picks up his mobile from the dresser and stares at Eve, horrified. 'My phone's been off. She's probably been trying to call me from school.'

He turns it on just as the ring tone blares out. His face registers further alarm. 'Natty,' he says, by way of explanation.

He cuts Natty's call, puts his phone inside his back pocket.

'What am I going to do?' he asks. 'What the hell do I say to Felicity? She's fourteen. She should not have seen that. No child should see that.'

He pulls his fingers through his hair. Wincing, Eve supposes, as he relives the scene: the bodies. The noise. The animalistic, almost bovine, groaning that comes from deep within Eve when she's about to come.

'Let me talk to her,' she says.

Sean's mouth drops open. '*No!*' he says emphatically. 'Absolutely not. That would be worse. That would be so much worse.'

'Would it?'

'Christ, what am I doing?' he says. 'What am I doing letting that happen? What kind of father goes and . . .' His words fade in his throat as he gags, and Eve thinks he's about to vomit.

She gets off the bed and stands. She's still in her heels and bra. 'Close the door, Sean,' she says gently, and he does as she asks. 'Just wait for a moment. Don't do anything rash. You'll regret it, I promise.'

He starts pacing again. 'What have I done?' he asks her, and Eve tries not to panic, lest he lose it completely. She senses this might not just be about Felicity; the way he says it suggests a wider implication.

'Sean,' she says firmly, 'I can handle this. Have some faith. I know what I'm doing. If you go in there and apologize, start stuttering your words, falling over yourself with regret, you are sending very mixed messages to a vulnerable young woman. She needs an explanation. A full explanation about what it means to be an adult and how confusing it can seem at times. I promise you I will take it steady and I will certainly not push our relationship on her. But I must handle this professionally, because you will get it wrong and she won't know what to make of it. We could risk scarring her for a very long time.'

'I don't know. I just don't know.'

Eve slips off her heels and steps into her Laura Ashley dress. She decides to remain barefooted. 'You need to trust me here. I don't want to tell you how to deal with your daughter, but remember, this is what I'm trained for . . . Sean, this is what I *lecture on*, for heaven's sake.'

He's startled by her last sentence. Eve sees him flinch, but then, little by little, he starts to let go of the tension. She's given him a lifeline. Given him an excuse not to face the problem looming in front of him. Someone more qualified should handle this, he's thinking. Yes, absolutely.

He sits down on the chair by the dressing table and covers his face with his hands.

Eventually, he says, 'You're right. It would be so much worse coming from me. Christ, Felicity would be mortified if I went in there explaining what she just saw. You do it. That would be best.'

Eve nods. 'Okay,' she says. 'I'll do it now, before she has chance to get upset.'

'What are you going to say?'

'I'll be led by her. Let her air her feelings first.'

'Will that work?' he asks.

'I think, as long as she feels like I've really heard her and we're taking her feelings into account, we should be okay.'

'Okay, that sounds good.'

Eve makes a quick trip to the en suite bathroom to remove her slutty lipstick, replacing it with a more neutral toffee colour. On her way back she pauses in front of Sean, kissing the top of his head.

He lifts his chin and grabs her hands, their eyes locking. His eyes brim with tears. 'Thank you,' he says. 'Thank you for doing this.'

'I'll make it better, Sean,' she tells him. 'I promise.'

24

I AM TRYING TO be brave. Really, I am.

I'm filling my head with the images of poor, desperate women from around the world: refugees fleeing war zones; mothers on the backs of covered wagons, on donkeys, clutching their hungry babies, carrying their whole lives with them in one shoddy satchel.

I'm trying to imagine what that feels like. Imagining the fear, the not-knowing, the grief of leaving behind a former existence. And I'm looking around my police cell and telling myself that things could be much, much worse. Women endure far worse fates than this.

I mean, in truth, if I squint a little, turn my head to the side – blocking out the barred window and the metal door – I could actually be in a Travelodge.

The walls are breeze block, painted magnolia, and a royal-blue carpet covers the floor. 'The only cell with a carpet,' DC Aspinall remarked as she led me in, and I told her I was grateful.

I lie on the bed that's affixed to the wall, atop the sleeping bag, trying not to think of cleanliness at this moment. I begin stroking the floor with my hand. The carpet has a strange, wire thread running through it that sticks up at odd angles, offensively, like the first grey hairs to appear on the crown of my skull.

I find myself pondering if the wool used to make the carpet

came from a really old sheep. Or a Herdwick, perhaps. The breed gives a good flavoured meat; they were once kept by Lake District author and farmer Beatrix Potter. But the wool is very tough, not at all suitable for making clothes.

At the hotel, the guests would go a bundle on Herdwick lamb when it came into season.

'*Herdwick.*' They'd say it reverently, as if eating something sacred. Our menu is littered with similar dishes: Salt Marsh Lamb, Goosnargh Chicken, Galloway Beef.

Bizarrely, meat has now become like wine and books – if you don't put an 'AWARD-WINNING' sticky label on it, the consumer will not buy. I used to wonder what would happen if you were to switch around those tags in the supermarket – exchange the book clubs for the award-winning sausages. The gold-medal-winning wines for the champion black puddings.

But I digress. There's a sharp pang of grief as I think about the days, weeks, the months, before Eve came. I went through those days blindly. Attending to everything in front of me, worrying about the things to come. Ticking off events with relief when they'd passed by.

I made it so very easy for her.

Eve waltzed in, fixed her attention on Sean, something I'd not been doing for way too long, and she beckoned him away with something as simple as … remember the Bisto commercial? Kids playing in the street, pausing from play as they caught the scent of Mum's gravy wafting through the air? That's how I imagine it happened with Sean.

There's a noise from the door. Keys in the lock, the sound of the bolt being slid across. Immediately, I sit up, demurely perch on the edge of the bed, ankles delicately crossed, my hands held in my lap. I am Princess Diana in one of the early portraits. My aim is to give the person on the other side of that door the impression I have been wrongly incarcerated.

An officer I've not seen before pops his head around. 'Solicitor's here for you.' He gives a well-practised smile.

I stand, dusting down my clothes, picking off the stray hairs and bits of lint, and wait, expectantly.

A second later, he's back. 'You not coming, then?' he asks.

'What?' I say, flustered. 'Oh, I thought the solicitor was coming here.'

'Nah,' he says, 'they don't do roughing it. C'mon, love,' he says, holding the door for me, 'I'll take you on through.'

Whatever I'd been expecting in a solicitor, this person is not it.

For a start, she's a woman, and immediately I become aware of a latent prejudice I didn't know existed in me. Yes, I know women can do the job just as well as men. Better, in most instances. And yes, *of course*, women must be equally repre-sented in the workplace, paid the same money, have the same opportunities to lead, govern, inspire.

But what if this solicitor suddenly has to rush home to her kids? What then? This is my *life* we're talking about, not some utopian model of equality.

I want a male solicitor. I don't want a multitasking female. I want a person capable only of focusing on the job in front of him.

I want a single-minded, selfish, arrogant man.

'Mrs Wainwright,' she says, extending her hand, 'I'm Wendy Hogg from Foster and Updike. How are you?'

I regard her uneasily. 'Scared,' I reply.

She's early fifties, with a round face of loose flesh, no eye-lashes that I can discern, and stands at around five foot one. Her face is clear of make-up and her coarse, colourless hair is cut sensibly into a Victoria Wood-style bob.

She looks less like a solicitor and more like a social worker. One who has recently returned to work after being on long-term sick leave.

Has *Sean* sent this woman? Has Sean sent her to make certain I have no way out of this?

We're left alone, and Wendy Hogg lifts a briefcase from beside her chair and places it on the table. As she withdraws a thick-barrelled fountain pen, she says, 'I'll get on with the particulars in a moment. Your husband, Mr Wainwright, kindly gave me a brief recap of the incident when he requested our services. If you could just begin by telling me how many times you rammed the car, Mrs Wainwright . . . and why.'

I check over my shoulder to make sure we're alone and sit down opposite. When I don't answer her, Wendy Hogg tilts her head. 'Mrs Wainwright?' she prompts. But I've read the Michael Connelly books (not the Harry Bosch ones, not so keen on those, but I've read the ones featuring Mickey Haller – *The Lincoln Lawyer*, etc.), so I know that the client absolutely *does not* reveal their crime, not even to their own lawyer.

'I didn't ram the car,' I tell her decisively.

'You didn't?' she asks, frowning. 'So that wasn't you on the CCTV footage I just viewed? It certainly looks like you.'

I drop my head. What am I supposed to tell this woman? What if I admit to this, and she's totally incompetent, and what if she has no idea of how to—

'I can get you out of here tonight,' she says without emotion.

At once I'm snapped to attention. 'You can?' I reply. 'How?'

'You tell me exactly what happened, and I'll proceed with how we expect to deal with the case after that. First, I'd like to hear your side of the story, make sure we don't miss anything.'

'But I thought I wasn't supposed to admit to hitting Eve's car, I thought—'

She cuts me off. 'You thought wrong. Now, let's start again. You admit to ramming the car, yes or no?'

I glance away, as if I'll find inspiration beyond this featureless room.

'Yes,' I answer miserably.

'Three times?'

'Possibly four,' I say, and sit forward in my seat, 'but can I ask you something? I don't mean to be rude, I don't mean to question your suitability or anything, but I was under the impression it was Mr Updike who handled this sort of thing.'

As she jots down notes, she says, 'Mr Updike will represent you in court. I'm employed by Foster and Updike to do the legwork in cases such as this, by which I mean driving offences. Now, was Eve Dalladay wearing her seatbelt?'

I'm about to answer no, when I stop myself.

I *had* assumed Eve had removed her seatbelt prior to my slamming into her, but now I can't remember her flailing forwards a great deal as I made contact.

'I think she could have been wearing her belt, actually.'

Wendy Hogg makes a note of it. She looks up, and for the first time there's the hint of warmth in her face. 'Just so you know,' she says, 'I'm the person who looks for inconsistencies, I'm the one who's finding reasons for you to avoid being charged.'

'There *are* inconsistencies!' I blurt out, almost leaping across the desk. 'I tried to tell the police and they wouldn't listen. I *did* ram Eve, but I know I didn't cause the damage to her face.'

'You're saying she did it to herself?' she asks. 'For what reason, do you suppose?'

For a minute there I thought she was on my side. Now she's asking the same questions as everyone else, making out like I'm paranoid.

'I'm not testing you, Mrs Wainwright,' she adds. 'Feel free to speak openly. I'm trying to ascertain the motivation of Eve Dalladay. Can you shed any light on the matter?'

'She stole my husband,' I tell her, and to my ears this is starting to sound a bit feeble. 'I even received a note to say that she's done it before. And now I suspect she doesn't love him and

196

she's attempting to make me seem like a madwoman. *And* I can't find any trace of her on the internet. It's as if she never existed.'

'Interesting,' Wendy Hogg says, nodding. 'The fact that she wants your husband could be motivation enough.'

'Really?' I ask. 'You don't think I'm deluded?'

'Not sure we can do much with the note you received, but no, I don't think you're deluded.' She sits back in her chair, places her pen by the side of her notepad. 'On my way here I made a visit to Windermere train station and viewed their CCTV. As you know, the station sits alongside Booths' car park. There's a very clear side-view image of you ramming Eve Dalladay from across the tracks.'

'There is?' I ask, not sure if that's actually a good thing.

'Yes,' she says, 'there is. And it *does* appear as if she was wearing her seatbelt. What's more, in the footage, her face never comes close to hitting the steering wheel. Not once.'

Eve had found Felicity with her eyes locked on the screen of her laptop, headphones completing the barrier between Felicity's immediate environment and the wider world beyond her bedroom.

Eve surveyed her from the doorway. She'd known Natty's girls since they were babies. Not well, needless to say, but she played the role of absentee aunt rather effectively, misleading Natty with tall tales of travel and responsibilities from across the Atlantic which were only partially true. Eve turned up when she had nothing better to do. Spoiling the girls with sweets and cinema visits, when the occasion called, but not because it gave her any real pleasure. She did it to appear normal. Did it because that's what people do for a friend.

Eve could remember the girls being around six and four. She had taken them to the viewing platform at the top of Orrest Head in Windermere. It was quite a hike for short legs and Alice, always eager to please, marched ahead, discussing pine cones, acorns, pieces of wood she found along the way that were shaped like animals.

Felicity, however, held back. She didn't seem to trust Eve.

She watched Alice and Felicity play from the summit. It was a cool day in late autumn. The trees were bare and the view of Lake Windermere was spectacularly striking: the water a deep sapphire blue, the sky already pinking nicely over in the west, though it wasn't quite yet three o'clock.

Eve sat alone on the bench, the worn wood feeling more like a slab of granite beneath her. She watched as Natty's girls ran around happily, their cheeks ruddy from the cold, and as they moved a little near to the edge she called out to them, 'Come back over here, girls!'

But they ignored her. Pretended that they couldn't hear her, and she had the overwhelming urge to smash their skulls against the bench. Over and over.

The urge had come upon her quite suddenly, as was often the way, and she could think of no real grounds for her compulsion besides scratching the itch to aggrieve Natty. She wondered what it would be like to truly eviscerate someone who considered Eve a friend. Someone who thought they were shielded from the world because they used the most expensive car seats, never left their children unattended, gave their family a perfectly balanced diet with no additives, no colours, no fun. As it turned out, Eve didn't get to indulge in that particular curiosity until a few years later, when an opportunity presented itself that she couldn't pass up.

Felicity removed her headphones. 'What?' she said to Eve now.

'You came home early, Felicity. Is everything all right?'

'Fine,' she replied flatly, and faced the screen. 'You can go now.'

Eve felt herself drawn towards the angry teenager in front of her. Felt propelled to the chaos inside Felicity's head. Chaos Felicity was doing her damnedest to conceal with a mask of insolence. 'I told your dad I'd talk to you about what you just saw.'

'I didn't see anything.'

Eve smiled. 'We both know you did.'

Felicity kept her eyes averted and said, 'Okay, so we talked. You. Can. Go. Now.'

Eve had been in this situation once before, funnily enough. Shortly before the Cameron Cox debacle, she'd signed a six-month rental agreement on a plush office unit over in Richmond, North Yorkshire. As usual, the clients had come thick and fast, there being a gap in the market for an attractive therapist radiating success, and Eve almost immediately began screwing a guy who'd come for help with his insomnia.

She moved in with him quickly – as planned – and everything was going well, until his teenage son came by unexpectedly, caught them and went apoplectic. His father had his face lodged hard between Eve's legs as she writhed and bucked on the Queen Anne dining table.

Eve had taken charge in that instance, too. Explaining to the boy that this was adult behaviour – *This is what adults do* – as he well knew from the variety of porn sites he'd been visiting recently. It was unfortunate that he'd seen them, she said, but she would not apologize for something that was entirely normal, entirely *human*. She told him he would be free to partake in these activities himself if he ever decided to bring a girl home.

The boy had accepted Eve's scalding rebuke with tears rolling down his face and told her he was sorry for judging her, and, yes, he did agree that his father was entitled to some love after so many years married to a person who found him repulsive.

It had actually gone rather well, considering.

Eve regarded Felicity now and decided that the same approach was unlikely to be successful this time.

'You're still here?' Felicity said, one eyebrow arched.

And Eve marched across the room, grabbing hold of her by the chin.

'You fuck with me and I will destroy your mother.'

Felicity stared back at her, at first too shocked to speak.

'Do you understand?' Eve repeated.

'You're hurting me.'

'I know things about your mother that—'

'Yes, and I know things about you too, Eve,' Felicity whispered. 'It's not the first time I've seen you like that.'

Eve slackened her grip. 'What do you mean?'

'Christmas, two years ago? At the hotel? I walked in on you and that tosser who comes by helicopter each year. The married guy?'

'I don't remember,' Eve said dismissively.

'Yeah. Sure you don't. You didn't look that into it, if it helps.'

Eve narrowed her eyes as Felicity stared back defiantly. She waited a moment, then slapped her. Slapped her hard across the mouth.

Leaning in, only inches from Felicity's face, Eve warned her once more. 'You heard me the first time. Fuck with me and I will ruin your mother. I know things about this family that will kill her. Now, for the last time, is that what you want?'

Felicity shook her head.

'Say it. Is that what you want?'

'No!' cried Felicity. 'No, I don't want that! Don't do anything to hurt my mum. Please.'

'Good,' Eve said, smiling then at Felicity. 'Glad that's all settled.' And she left the room.

25

IN THOSE FIRST few weeks at university I felt like a different person.

I'd stare at my reflection in the mirror, my brow wrinkled in perplexity, as I asked: *Who are you? Who are you, Natty?* And I was excited by the options.

All at once, I loved learning. Because this was *real* learning. Gone was the cosseted classroom environment of school. Gone the feeling of humdrum familiarity, of tedious repetition. Now I was in huge lecture theatres with two hundred students. In the John Rylands library with its basement rooms and ancient desks, the students either working hard to cultivate an air of apathetic indifference, or else, like me, wandering around the place in a state of awe.

It was as far away from provincial village life as you could get, and I wanted to soak it all in.

I loved the course. Within radiography there was so much human biology to study, in the way of anatomy, physiology, pathology. To get a taste of things to come, I spent a day in the radiography department at Hope Hospital, Salford. It was a newish department – very plush, not at all standard NHS issue. There was even fresh coffee. And I had the most fantastic afternoon with a young radiographer who tested me on the contraindications to MRI, CTs, X-Rays – all the stuff we'd been covering in the past week. I came away inspired, absolutely firm in the belief I had chosen the right course. I was also a little indignant at Sean's mother's suggestion that I had made a mistake, and my new passion brimmed over into making sure she would eat her words at some point in the future.

Sean.

I'd not seen him. Not even bumped into him by accident, and, coward that I was, I hoped it would stay that way.

He'd called the payphone in the hallway several times. I'd return to my room to find a Post-it note stuck to my door saying: 'Ring Sean Wainwright' or 'Some lad phoned' – but I never returned the call.

What was I going to say? That I was fine? More than fine, in fact. I was fine and in love with someone else and I'd forgotten all about him.

I think back to that tearful time with lead in my belly, because how long had it taken? No more than a few days for me to jump into another boy's bed. Perhaps the reason for this was because Sean had turned his back on me. Was I punishing him? Maybe. Was I replacing one love for another because I'd been rejected? Definitely.

Will Goodwin was a bad boy. Total opposite of Sean. He was a third-year engineering student, strikingly good-looking, well-bred but dangerous (his dad was a big-shot editor at *The Times*), and within hours of meeting him I found myself in that very worst state: infatuated. Easing my broken heart with the love of another.

It was shocking to me, the attraction I felt. Shocking the speed with which my thoughts of him became all-encompassing. And it's not like I'd not been in love before. Because I had. With Sean.

Out of the blue I understood how girls could make disastrous fools of themselves, give themselves away so readily, prepared to stamp over their self-worth, their friendships, to get to a boy.

We were driven by something outside of ourselves, and no

amount of reasoning would register. Sean's mother had been right in that respect. If it hadn't been for the volume of work engineering students needed to complete each week, then my studies would have been in real danger of slipping, because I couldn't tear myself away from Will.

So when I turned up at Will's halls of residence on a bleak night of wind and rain, my feet soaked, the water dripping down the back of my neck, to tell him I thought I was pregnant – *knew* I'd fallen accidentally pregnant with his baby – I wasn't unduly worried. I knew he was as into me as I was him. It was shitty timing, no doubt about that, but my mind had already gone into overdrive about the life we were about to have together.

This was the late nineties, remember, when babies were billed as the ultimate accessory. Nothing could be more perfect than a young, handsome guy carrying his baby in a sling. Perfume ads, the press, even holiday brochures, were filled with images of intrepid couples, their active, exciting lives enhanced by the arrival of their offspring. And I had totally bought into the bull-shit, like, I suppose, most other young women had.

A baby won't stop me doing what I want to do! Hell, I can do anything!

Unsurprisingly, Will Goodwin did not feel the same way.

'You're *what?*' he said to me.

'Pregnant.'

'But you're on the Pill.'

I laughed a little, made out like these things do happen, and shrugged.

'What?' he said. 'What the fuck does *that* mean?' mirroring my shrugging action in an exaggerated way. He pulled a face like a French footballer claiming innocence after a particularly nasty tackle. 'You have been taking them, haven't you? The pills?'

'Of course,' I said, astonished he would doubt me. 'It's just that—'

'It's just what?'

'The Pill's not always a hundred per cent guaranteed to work, that's all. Not if you've been sick, or had diarrhoea, or been drinking heavily . . .'

'Bollocks,' he snapped. 'That's what girls say when they've been skipping pills to make sure they *get* pregnant. Oldest trick in the book.'

'I . . . I wouldn't do that.'

He fixed me with a chilling stare. 'Wouldn't you?' he said flatly.

The breath knocked out of me, I slumped down on his single bed. How had this happened? He loved me. He'd told me he loved me. Why was he behaving like this?

All at once, I was nauseated. Like I was going to throw up in my lap. I bent forwards, put my head between my knees. The room was hot. Hot, with a sickly, cloying odour that felt thick in my throat.

I raised my head. 'What's that smell?'

'Dunno. I could probably do with a shower.'

'It's sweat,' I said.

He busied himself with a stack of papers on his desk. 'Me and Dave have been at the driving range.'

'Have you had someone in here?' I demanded, my hands starting to shake. 'Has someone been here . . . with you?'

'Only Dave. He can get a little ripe after exercising.'

'Will,' I said carefully, 'it's sex I can smell, isn't it?'

At first, he didn't answer. Just paused what he was doing and stood stock still. Then he turned, and his whole being radiated arrogance. 'Yeah,' he said, 'it is.'

He gave a cruel bark of laughter. 'I can't believe you're fucking pregnant,' he said. 'I can't believe what shit luck—'

Laughing at me? Laughing while he was sleeping with someone else?

There was a baby inside me and I was eighteen years of age. What was I supposed to do?

I wanted to hurt him. I really wanted to hurt him.

Without thinking, I picked up what was to hand, what I later learned was a seven iron but which I knew only as a golf club at the time, and I held it high above my right shoulder.

He didn't think I'd do it. And I probably wouldn't have if he'd not grinned at me like I was ridiculous.

I swung it once, aiming for his shoulder.

But he ducked. The stupid prick ducked, and, regrettably for me, the seven iron connected with the side of his skull instead.

26

I ARRIVE AT MY dad's house just after ten. I was offered a lift by a uniformed officer at Kendal police station, to which I said thanks, but no thanks. The thought of sitting in a squad car making polite conversation was the last thing I needed, so I requested a taxi.

What I really *need* right now is to go home. I have no change of clothes, no toothbrush, nothing. I feel dirty from the inside out, after eating crappy processed food for the past couple of days. But what I want more than anything is to talk to the girls. Tell them I've been charged with the lesser crime of aggravated assault and I'm allowed home. Of course, I *really* want to tell them Eve is a total bitch fraudster who's hoodwinking their father . . . but I must bide my time with that one. If I'm going to rebuild any kind of trust between us, I should tread carefully. Not plough straight ahead, like I did before.

But I yearn to see them. They're mine. They belong with me. Marital breakdown is one thing, but the crushing weight of sadness at the thought of another woman with my children, in my home – well, it's agonizing.

I pull my keys from my coat pocket and sort through the multitude until I find the one for Dad's front door. Inserting it in the lock, I find the door's been left open. Not unusual – my dad would only lock the door on his way to bed – but the lights are off, meaning the carers have already been and gone.

I'm irritated and begin rehearsing the complaints I'll tell the agency first thing in the morning. *Let it go, Natty, or your head will explode.* I flick on the hall light; the house feels warm and welcoming. My eyes prickle with tears as it hits me just how close I came to being incarcerated this afternoon.

That could have been it. The end of everything. Stuck inside the system, unable to get out.

The cat sits on the bottom stair. He stares at me, round-eyed. 'Hello, Morris,' I whisper, and he's unresponsive. He regards me in a manner as though to convey: *Your presence here is meaning-less to me.*

'Jackie?' comes the throaty call from upstairs.

'No, Dad, it's me.'

'Natty? Where've you been, love?'

'Kendal.'

'At this hour?'

I give a small laugh. 'Hang on,' I tell him, 'I'll be up in a few minutes,' and head through to the kitchen.

In the fridge beside Jackie's Yakults and the Muller Light yoghurts I find a block of mature Cheddar and some seedless grapes. I fix myself a small picnic with a glass of milk and a few crackers, pouring some milk into a saucer for Morris, who is snaking between my shins. Now that there are dairy products on offer, suddenly he's a lot more interested.

'Fickle, you are,' I say, resting the saucer down carefully, though tipping it at the last second. It's the spilt milk that Morris begins lapping, so I don't bother to clean it. I'm bone tired – bone tired and running on empty. I feel the essence of what makes me *me* leaching away with each hour that passes.

At the top of the stairs the door to my dad's room is ajar. He's turned his bedside lamp on and he's propped on three pillows.

'Did I wake you?' I ask.

'No, Polly's not long left. Just lying here with my eyes open.'

'She left the door unlocked. Are you expecting Jackie?'

I can tell by his face that he's not but he doesn't want Polly to get into trouble. 'She said she'd probably pop over,' he tells me, 'but it might be getting on for after twelve 'cause she's on a late.' He's lying. He's a terrible liar. 'I've just been watching an old Clint movie to kill the time,' he adds, to divert my attention.

'Any good?' I ask.

And he makes a face. 'It had Sondra Locke in it. I turned it off after half an hour.'

'Clint's Yoko,' I remark absently, and my dad nods in agreement.

'Sean must have arranged to have your car taken in for repair, because it's gone from the front.'

'Oh,' I say, because I hadn't noticed.

'What were you doing in Kendal?' he asks.

'I was arrested.'

His face registers alarm. 'By that copper who came here?' he asks. 'The woman?'

'She found me in the library.'

He swallows. 'Bloody hell, love, why didn't you ring me?'

'What could you have done?'

His face is grey with concern and I sense he may have said something to tip off DC Aspinall about where I was. Said I was out to find evidence to prove Eve was lying. And DC Aspinall's no fool. It wouldn't take a genius to figure out what I was up to.

'I feel awful not knowing you were there,' he says. He's shaken, so I don't press him about what was said in my absence. 'You've been there on your own all this time?' he asks. 'Were you in a cell?'

'It's fine, Dad. *I'm* fine. Sean sorted me out a good solicitor. Get to sleep . . . I'll fill you in on the full story in the morning.' As I leave the room, I turn. 'Okay if I borrow the van again tomorrow?'

''Course, love,' he replies. 'Any time. What d'you need it for?'

'I've got a few errands to run.'

7.30 a.m. and I'm in the middle lane of the M6 heading south near Preston. Last night was the first time I'd slept in days. I'm rested and ready. I've put aside the emotion of everything that's happened because it's too exhausting and I need to be fully focused on my task.

Really, I should have set off a little later, because I'm sure to get caught in the 8 a.m. gridlocked traffic when I hit the M60. But it was either this or wait around for another hour, risk dodging questions from Dad and, most probably, Jackie too. I left a note saying I had lots to do and made an early start.

The Transit is only happy at seventy miles an hour. The van's sweet spot. Slightly faster or slower and the steering wheel vibrates thunderously – which I'm sure is no problem for my dad's muscular joiner's hands to control, but very difficult for me. And of course I can't see out the back. There are no rear windows, only wing mirrors to view what's behind, and twice already I've switched lanes and almost wiped out a car in my blind spot. So I'm taking it steady.

I'm running through the questions I'm planning to ask. Hoping I'll be given some solid answers but knowing, realistically, that this could be a waste of time. I'm not even sure what I'm looking for. But it's a start. And I have to try.

Over an hour later I'm in Manchester city centre. I find a space at the car park on Booth Street West, just off Oxford Road, and from here I make my way the short distance to the School of Psychological Sciences.

The pavement is busy with students and I'm swept along amongst them. It hits me that this will be Alice in only two years' time. She will be in this crowd, at a university somewhere, as I was eighteen years before her. Will she feel the same way I did, lost and bewildered? Unlikely. Alice is Alice. Words which spring to mind are 'forthright', 'determined', 'energetic', 'confident'. She's sure to cope better than me.

I'm almost at the entrance when my mobile vibrates in my pocket. It's Felicity, and I hesitate in answering because, as much as I need to talk to her, right now is not the time.

But we *always* answer the girls when they're not with us. Whatever the circumstances.

'Mum,' she says, 'where are you?' Her voice is quiet and strained.

'What's happened, Felicity? You sound upset.'

'No,' she says, a little too quickly, 'I'm just . . .' She takes a breath, and I'm not sure if she's about to cry. You know how it is with girls. They get the first sentence out all right and then you can get a full two minutes of choking breaths before another word is possible. 'I tried calling last night,' she says, still quiet, but not crying. '. . . You didn't pick up.'

'The phone died,' I lie, 'and I didn't have the charger at Grandad's.' Before she has the chance to catch me out, to ask how I managed to charge it this morning, I say, 'I'm sorry you didn't hear from me, love, I've been in a bit of a mess, what with Eve and everything. I just needed some time to lick my wounds.' A young male student passes beside me, holds the door to the building open and raises his eyebrows. You coming in? he asks, wordlessly, and I shake my head.

'Are you coping okay without me? Is Dad feeding you?' I say to her, in a tone that belies just how much it hurts to ask these questions.

'Yes,' she replies.

'Is your tummy okay? How's your scar? It's not oozing, is it?'

'No, it's pretty neat.'

'Doesn't smell or anything?'

She heaves a sigh. 'It's *fine*, Mum.'

'That's good. Really good news. Listen, love, I need to be somewhere, so I have to dash. We'll speak later, okay? I'll call you when I'm done.'

'Mum?'

'What is it, honey?'

She hesitates, and my mouth goes dry. I sense she needs to get something out, and there's a tightening in my chest as I think about the unthinkable. Have Sean and Eve told the girls about my past? Have they told them *everything*?

'Never mind,' she says, cutting the connection without saying goodbye.

Will Goodwin's father was, as I said, deputy editor at *The Times*, and he moved heaven and earth to keep my attack on his son out of the papers. Journalists can do that, you know – call in favours from friends, arrange a blanket ban on something being printed. Terence Goodwin had hopes his son would enter politics one day and didn't want the facts of our violent liaison scuppering his chances. Will was despatched back down to Surrey to recover. Meanwhile, Sean and I went home, tails between our legs, ready to face his mother. Sean took the full force of her wrath, and we knew that the only way to get through it was never to tell anyone of Alice's true parentage. Pretend that we'd gone against Penny's wishes, never split up, and the pregnancy was the result.

A few months later, I was handed a suspended sentence, but the only people to know the full extent of what happened in Manchester, besides Will and his family, were Sean, my dad and, of course, Eve Dalladay.

Why did Sean do it for me? The ultimate altruistic act. To this day, he's never fully explained it. What I remember was Sean being fiercely defensive of me at the time. He adopted the role of protector, wouldn't let anything upsetting near me. And I became quite docile in response. I wanted him to fix things, to take over. I'd turned up at his dorm asking him to help me arrange an abortion, because I was too ashamed to talk to anyone else. But he flat out refused. Told me he loved me enough to live with the situation, take on the child as his own, and then, astonishingly, he took me home.

Trying not to dwell on my conversation with Felicity, I step inside the School of Psychological Sciences. To my right there's a run of offices, perhaps five or six in total, the doors all closed. Names are clearly displayed, and it's immediately evident that everyone here is a doctor. It occurs to me there should be a way to tell the difference between a PhD graduate and a medical doctor. Like, in the States, they use the initials MD. *Medicinae Doctor.*

I study the names, but nothing rings a bell so I keep walking along the passageway. There's activity coming from the far end. A sign hanging from the ceiling overhead reads 'Reception This Way'.

The reception area has a large curved desk in a blond beech laminate with two rows of funky art deco chairs in front of it. The smell of polyurethane resin hangs in the air, and the carpet beneath my feet is shedding. Clearly, a renovation has taken place.

I approach two women at the desk. One is in her mid-sixties, nesty hair, glasses on the end of her nose, crepe skin around her gullet – you could teleport her to any doctor's reception in the world and she'd fit right in. She would tell you, abruptly, that no, the doctor does not do home visits unless it's an absolute emergency, and yes, there is a thirty-pound charge to countersign your passport application.

The other woman is early twenties. She's wearing two sets of false eyelashes and has drawn a big brown beauty spot on her left cheek, *à la* Marilyn Monroe.

I approach Marilyn and say in an overly apologetic voice, 'Hi, so sorry to trouble you, but I used to attend here . . . some time ago . . . I'm hoping to find some information on a former student.'

'We don't give that out,' says the woman next to her, without looking up from her work.

'No,' I say, addressing her now. 'I completely understand that policy. But it's not personal information I'm searching for. I'd like to just have a chat with one of the professors. Would that be possible?'

'Try the main admin office,' comes the brusque reply.

'But I've driven down from Cumbria, and it's a professor I really—'

'Have you?' she says flatly. 'Admin's out the main doors, turn left.'

Signalling that the conversation is over, she gets up from her seat and carries a file across to the row of cabinets behind her. She pulls out a drawer and begins flicking through the folders, tutting loudly to suggest that someone (I'm guessing Marilyn) has returned a document to the wrong place.

I look back to the young receptionist. I give her my best defeated look, to which I expect her to smile sympathetically. Or else roll her eyes dramatically, like, *See what I have to put up with here? That old sourpuss?*

But she doesn't. She puts her hands up on either side of her head as if she has a pair of ass's ears, then widens her eyes to convey something.

'What?' I mouth silently, and she waggles her hands. Bucks out her teeth and gestures with a flick of her head in the direction I've just come from.

I have no idea what this means, but I do as she says. Head back to the passageway, and it's only when I reach the third door along that it makes sense.

Dr Phil Hutch.

The ass's ears were bunny ears.

I dilly-dally outside the door for a moment, my rehearsed speech floating around the top of my head in a cloud of sound bites. I can pull out fragments of sentences, but where has my actual speech gone?

'Shit!' I say, under my breath, just as the door handle levers downwards. I pretend I'm mid-knock as a tall gentleman in a shirt and tie, bit of a paunch, Buddy Holly specs, walks straight into me.

'Whoa!' he says in an accent I can't immediately place. 'Almost knocked you straight off your feet there.'

He smiles at me warmly, a flicker of interest in his eyes, and I think: Bingo! A flirt.

My luck is *in*.

'Have you got a moment?' I ask.

'Always got a moment for a pretty face,' he replies. 'Come on inside. What can I do you for?'

As we stand, I regard him, hold his gaze for an extended moment. I smile, but I'm immediately thrown by the colossal blackheads across his nose. They are really quite something; they pucker his skin. Like strawberry seeds raised over the flesh of the fruit.

'Your accent,' I say, gathering myself as we sit, 'it's really . . .'

'Phoney?' he offers.

I laugh. 'I was going to say "interesting". Where are you from?'

There's a photo on his desk. Two boys, tanned and healthy-looking, each posing for the camera while straddling a jet-ski. The water beneath is brilliant aquamarine.

'I was born in New York,' he replies, 'but I've been here for . . .' he waves away the words with his hand as if he can't be bothered to count up the years. 'I like to think I have the mid-Atlantic accent of Cary Grant, one of those old Hollywood stars,' he says, 'but I'm told I sound affected, more like Naomi Campbell.' He reaches across the desk, proffers me his hand. 'Phil Hutch.'

'Natty Wainwright. Pleased to meet you. So, you're a doctor of psychology?' I ask him.

'For my sins.'

'And you've worked here for . . . for how long?'

Still smiling, he furrows his brow. 'Are you a reporter, Miss Wainwright?'

'Gosh, no! Goodness.'

He sits back in his chair, crosses one ankle on to the opposite knee and grins. I'd put him at around fifty-four. Firmly middle-aged but with a certain something – charm, I suppose. I imagine he's one of those lecturers who can make a student feel special, make them feel he's *one of them*. I've never really trusted this type. Always much preferred teachers who didn't try to befriend you, who didn't have favourites. The ones without an ego who were simply there to teach.

'I'm not a reporter,' I tell him, dipping my head a little and blinking coyly. I'm not naturally playful on a first meeting, but I sense this is the way to go. 'I'm looking for information on a former student – she was here quite a while back,' and I moisten my bottom lip.

'Not sure I'll be able to help with that,' he says mildly. 'Lotta people pass through these doors.'

'She was here for some time. She stayed on to do a PhD.'

'Oh,' he says, his tone brightening. 'Well then. Perhaps I *can* help.'

He turns to the monitor and types in his password. Waits. Glancing at me, he rolls his eyes, 'Terribly slow, this morning,' he drawls, and resumes typing.

'The person's name is Eve Dalladay, but you would have known her as Eve Boydell.'

He pauses. His shoulders tighten. It's an almost imperceptible change in his demeanour, but it's a change nonetheless.

'A PhD, you say?'

'Yes.'

His eyes remaining fixed on the screen, he says, 'You're certain? Because I can't recall a student by that name.'

'She would have attended here in 1997 – well actually, she was here the year before but had to drop out on account of illness. Her family were from Alderley Edge, Cheshire.'

He raises an eyebrow. 'More champagne consumed per square mile in Alderley Edge than anywhere else in the UK.'

'So I've heard,' I say. 'Must be all the footballers' wives.'

He clicks the mouse a couple of times and frowns. 'You're sure your friend didn't do the undergraduate course and then attend elsewhere? Because that does happen.'

'Quite sure.'

'Well,' he says, 'there's nothing listed.'

Something tells me he's lying. Either that, or there really is no record of Eve – which isn't totally impossible given that there's no trace of her on the internet either.

'Well, I'm afraid I can't help you, Miss Wainwright,' he says brightly, signalling that our meeting is now over. 'And I'm sorry, but I really must be going. I've a first-year lecture to deliver in ten minutes.' He turns off the monitor, but I can hear the hard drive continuing to hum.

'Pavlov's dogs?' I ask.

He smiles. 'Amongst other things. What is it exactly you want to know about this former student anyway? Because, even if she was in the system, I couldn't give you any personal information. Have you tried her parents?'

'It's her parents – well, actually, her father, who I'm trying to locate,' I lie. 'It's an odd situation, but Eve and I were very close at university, have remained close, more by phone than anything else. She turned up on my doorstep a couple of weeks ago very distressed, after having broken up with her husband in the States. And then she just disappeared.'

'Oh?'

'Yes, there's no trace of her. I've tried calling all the numbers I have. Numerous times. Tried to locate her, but I can't find anything. And I'm worried. Really worried.'

'You've been to the police?'

'Of course. They've filed a missing persons report, but I keep getting the same line: If a person wants to disappear, they're well within their rights to do so.'

'She's not with her parents, then?'

'That's why I'm here. Eve's mother died when she was twenty-three. It was her dad she was closest to . . . but he remarried and I'm not exactly sure what happened but I don't think Eve got along with his new wife. I think it played a part in her decision to move to America.'

'And if you can trace her father—'

'Then he might know where she is.' I look down at my hands. Make my voice soft and tender. 'I just need to know that she's all right. That she's not lying in a ditch somewhere . . . and no one seems to care that she's disappeared, and . . .' I sniff a little. Make as if I'm rooting for a tissue in my pocket.

He opens the top drawer of his desk. Hands me a box of man-sized Kleenex.

'Thanks,' I say, and blow my nose. 'I don't know what else to do.'

'You must be terribly worried,' he replies gravely.

There's a short period of silence. His face is concerned, serious, but as I regard him I see him wince involuntarily as if in response to a private thought. As if he's torn in some way.

I've come here hoping to shed some light on Eve's where-abouts after I left university. Hoping to find anomalies in her life story. It occurred to me last night that Eve's version of my attack on her in the car park might just be the tip of the iceberg. She may well be a compulsive liar, and if I'm to prove to my family she's not who she says she is, then I need evidence. Because no one gets to be a Doctor of Psychology – teaching students, treating clients – without leaving some sort of paper trail.

Phil Hutch clears his throat. His palms are pressed together in the manner of prayer. 'I really wish I could give you something to go on, but it's' – he looks away sadly – 'it's as if your friend never actually studied here, never mind graduated . . . I'm so very sorry I'm unable to be of use, but—'

There are two sharp raps on the door, and we're both startled.

'Phil,' comes the stroppy voice. 'I've got UPS at the desk delivering some equipment and they won't take a signature from me, it's got to be a head of department, can you—'

It's the dragon from reception. 'Oh,' she says, her narrowed eyes settling on me, 'it's you.'

I smile meekly, but my heart quickens under her stare.

'What are you doing in here—' she starts, but Phil Hutch is out of his chair in a split second, guiding her from the office by her elbow. Which is odd. Why the urgency?

'Shan't be a moment,' he says awkwardly as the door closes behind them.

I take a couple of long, unsteady breaths. Put my hand to my neck and feel that the skin there is hot to the touch. I know without looking I'm covered in blotches. I am rubbish at misleading people . . . never could have been an actress.

I should go. I should go right now before Phil Hutch returns and I trip up with my story about Eve's disappearance. Yes, leave now, Natty. Stand up and walk out the door.

But that hard drive is humming. It's calling to me, softly, hypnotic . . . *See what secrets I hold, Natty* . . .

I swallow my trepidation and stand, opening the door just a fraction to check the passageway is clear. The carotid pulse in my neck is throbbing wildly.

Okay, I've not got long.

I move around to Phil's side of the desk and switch on the monitor. I'm so jittery that I knock over the waste-paper basket with my foot. The screen goes from black to . . . *what the hell?*

Up pops Ladbrokes betting website.

He'd not even been looking at student records as we spoke. Christ, I am so easily hoodwinked by people in authority.

I close the window, and I'm now looking at some kind of homepage for the psychology faculty. It's not easy to read, and I can't really make sense of—

There are muffled voices outside the door. I freeze and listen.

Do I pretend that I've not been snooping?

No. I'm never going to get this chance a second time. Screw the consequences. I must set about finding Eve as fast as I can.

Within minutes, I have her.

27

SAFELY BACK AT the car park, inside the van, I calm myself. There's activity all around me: students in and out of their brightly coloured Fiat 500s, their Mini Countrymans. I notice their easy laughter, their sense of entitlement, their good teeth.

A woman reverse parks a clapped-out Ford Escort to my right. She gets out; she's in her mid-fifties, looks harried. Her right wing and door are dented to such a degree that she can't lock the car; she tries twice and gives up. Doesn't even notice my presence as she strides away, clutching a stack of folders to her chest. She must be a lecturer. I observe her in my rear-view mirror – suede boots almost as old as her car, tatty chunky-knit cardigan, woollen tights that should have been thrown out last year, and as I watch I think what a strange state of affairs it is, when students have more free cash than their teachers.

I am wired. Ready to take on that bitch Eve, and, now that I know where to go next, I'm filled with the certainty that this will be over by bedtime. She will be gone and I'll have my family back.

With the key in the ignition, I'm about to set off when I feel my mobile vibrate in my pocket. It's a message from Felicity, asking where I am. 'Back soon,' I reply and hit send. And it's then that I notice there's a voicemail from Alice. It must have come through when I was in Phil Hutch's office. 'Mummy, it's me,' she says.

She uses 'Mummy' when she's unhappy, or vulnerable, or she wants something. Any time there's heightened emotion going on. Which I suppose is pretty much all the time with Alice.

'Mummy, I need to speak to you. It's really important. Felicity won't talk to me. She's gone really quiet and moody, and it's not me. At least, I don't think it's me. I suppose *it could be me*, but if I've upset her then I don't know how . . . I think she needs you. I think something bad has happened and she won't spill. Anyway, gotta go,' she says, dropping her voice to a whisper, 'I should be in first period by now but I thought . . . Oh, I miss you, Mummy.'

I close my eyes and heave a heavy sigh. Clearly, Felicity needs me. Clearly, Alice needs me. But I can't forfeit this new lead. It's too valuable. I cannot leave yet.

Pushing away the guilt of deserting my children, *again*, I turn the ignition and put the van into reverse. As I glance down something catches my attention and I see that the fuel warning light is illuminated. Great. Just great.

I slam the steering wheel with my fist in frustration. Then look up at the ceiling of the van as if addressing God directly: 'Cut me some slack, will you?' I yell. 'I'm really trying here!'

Ten minutes later, and I'm queuing on to the Shell forecourt, rain hammering, aggressive drivers sandwiching me to the front and rear. And I'm quietly shitting it, because I don't know which side my fuel cap is on.

If I'd been thinking clearly when I saw the warning light, I'd have jumped out of the van and had a quick check. As it is, it's inevitable I'll drive to the wrong side of the pump. When I do, my only option will be to leave the petrol station, rejoin the bumper-to-bumper traffic on the dual carriageway, do an illegal U-turn at the lights and double back.

So I get out. Just as the van in front pulls forwards. I'm caught in the should-I-shouldn't-I action of a cricketer at the stumps, undecided whether to check or to get back in.

I move to the rear of the van and eventually spot a flap next to the passenger door. And *of course* the fool behind feels the need to sound his horn. How could he not? Moments later, though, I'm at the pump, filling the tank, happy with myself for getting back on track. But still reeling from the information I found. Because, listen to this: Eve was thrown out of university.

A few months after I left Manchester, Eve was found to be having an affair with a professor (no prizes for guessing which one), and she left the course after studying for less than a year. With no qualifications, and certainly no doctorate to speak of.

Which begs the question: How has she managed to forge a career for the last fifteen years out of a subject about which she has no clue?

I shudder to think.

No doubt Eve would have some smooth answer ready if I were to go accusing her of lying about her job. And, besides, I managed to stumble upon something a lot more interesting.

Eve's parents are not listed as living in Alderley Edge, home of the Cheshire millionaires, but in Bolton. Bit of a difference.

I'm supposing (and I could be way off here) that 32 Wilkinson Street is not the affluent area she claims but more likely to be within a row of red-brick terraced houses. So that's where I'm heading now. It's not far. Once out of Manchester, I should be there in half an hour.

I replace the fuel pump and totter across the forecourt to pay. Once inside, I take my place behind the queue of people: men in suits; builders wearing Mastic-smeared jeans and those strange yellow work boots. There's a woman with a high ponytail in a pink Juicy Couture tracksuit near the front, a vivid yin-yang tattoo at the nape of her neck.

When I reach the counter I punch in my PIN and the spotty

cashier tells me, 'That card's rejected. You want to try it again or use another?'

'What?' I ask. Certain I've heard him incorrectly.

'Declined,' he says. 'The card.'

'Impossible,' I reply. 'There's at least—'

I stop myself from claiming there is thirty grands' worth of available credit on the card. Because that would sound preposterous in here.

'Would you mind trying it again?'

'Take your card out,' he says in a strong Salford accent, 'now put your PIN in.' Someone catches his eye over my shoulder. 'Iyor,' he says, and there's an incomprehensible exchange about Manchester City, points and league tables. Might as well be in Russian, because it means nothing to me.

The machine beeps. Declined.

'I'm sorry,' I say, mortified, fumbling in my purse. 'Could you try this one?'

We go through the entire process once again, this time with the card from my and Sean's joint account. The other is registered to the hotel and, though this card has a lower credit limit, there's still plenty left on it. I clear the balance each month without fail.

Declined.

'What happens now?' I say, quietly as I can.

'Stand over there,' he says, not unkindly, nodding his head towards the racks of Ginsters pies and pasties. 'You'll need to contact your bank.'

Fuck.

Fuck. Fuck. Fuck.

I want to cry.

'Isn't there some way I can pay for it later?' I ask, desperate. 'This once happened to a friend of mine, and I'm sure she was given twenty-four hours to return to pay.'

'This is a franchised garage,' he replies. 'Owner doesn't give credit.'

'Well, it's not like I can put the fuel back?'

'Your best bet is to ring your bank,' he says, and looks past me, signalling me to move so he can deal with the next customer.

My triumphant state has now been completely eclipsed. It feels like such a petty victory over Eve. Inconsequential. I decide against calling the bank and instead call Sean. There's no answer on his mobile, so I dial home.

Eve picks up. 'Hello,' she says, as if she's always lived there.

'Why are you answering my phone?'

'Because you were in custody,' she replies.

'I'm not. I'm out. They reduced the charges against me, you . . .'

The people waiting to pay for fuel are staring. My card has been rejected and I am now hissing into my mobile the words: 'reduced the charges'.

Not great.

'I know you're out,' Eve says. 'I was told last night. The Crown Prosecution Service will still investigate, though, so you're not exactly home and dry.'

'Is Sean there? Does he know why they dropped the charges? Did you tell him about the inconsistencies in your story, Eve?'

'He's not here.'

I'm guessing from her answer that Sean has not been informed about the new CCTV footage.

'Where is he?'

'Oh, you know,' she says vaguely, as if he's probably around there *somewhere.*

'No, I don't. That's why I am asking you. I need to get hold of him urgently. My credit cards have been rejected and I am trying to buy diesel. I need him to call the bank and get it sorted out straight away. I can't leave until I've paid . . . obviously.'

'Those cards have been cancelled, Natty.'

I go to reply, but I have no voice. I am wordless.

'Cancelled?' I say to Eve, stunned. People are trying not to stare but, sensing my heightening panic, they can't drag their eyes away.

'The joint ones, yes,' she answers, matter-of-fact. 'Sean's cancelled your credit cards and moved half the money from your joint current account into your personal one.'

'Why? Why has he done that?'

'Why wouldn't he? He's not done anything wrong, Natty. You'll get a new card and you've got the same money as you had last week, it's simply not in the joint account any longer. Since you haven't been running the hotel, it's hardly fair for you to have access to the funds. Just use your debit card to pay for the petrol . . . it's no big deal.'

'But I haven't got my debit card on me,' I say, the panic escalating. 'It's in the pot on the kitchen windowsill. Alice took it with her to Costa last week and I forgot to replace it in my purse.'

Eve doesn't respond. I hear her footsteps across the kitchen tiles. She's wearing heels. 'Oh, yes, you're right,' she says. 'Here it is. I suppose you'll have to leave your car there and get a taxi . . . hang on, your car's being repaired, isn't it? What are you driving, Natty?'

'My dad's van.'

She laughs. 'Hang on, I'll see if Sean's got time to come and bail you out. Where are you?'

I don't answer.

'Natty?' she prompts, as if she hasn't got all day.

'In Manchester.'

'Manchester? What are you doing down there? You've only just got out of custody. Strikes me as a very odd thing to do when—'

She stops.

Carefully, she asks, 'What are you up to, Natty?'

And I try to hold back, but the words fly out of my mouth before I can stop them.

28

'I WASN'T ASKED TO leave,' Eve says. As if she's totally bored speaking to me, 'I left of my own accord. Whatever *evidence* you have, Natty' – and she stresses the word 'evidence' as if using air quotes – 'whatever you have is unreliable.'

She is completely unruffled by my accusation. And I can't decide if that's a good thing – as in, it shows just how capable she is at lying under pressure – or if it's totally scary, because it shows just how capable she is at lying under pressure.

'We'll see,' I say to her, defiant.

'I could have saved you the trouble of your little investigative exercise. If you'd only asked, I would have told you I left Manchester and continued my studies at Salford. I had a short affair with a lecturer and we both decided it best if I transferred before it became public knowledge.' She scoffs at the memory. 'I'm not the first person to do it. It's not as if it's illegal. The only reason I never mentioned it was because I promised the guy I'd keep it hush-hush. He was married.'

I try to swallow my disappointment.

'Come back to Windermere, Natty,' she says. 'You're wasting your time down there.'

In a rush of anger and desperation, determined she won't have this victory, I cry, 'Yes, well, it wasn't the only thing I found out about you!' and I hang up, panting and shaking like a madwoman.

I look up.

The spotty cashier is watching me. 'Get through to the bank, did you?' he asks.

'Not yet,' I snap.

He raises his eyebrows in response, and I remember I am not in the position to be snippy here. I cannot pay.

'Just popping back to the van,' I say, 'to see if there's any cash in the glove compartment. I'll move it over to the car wash so the pump can be used. I won't drive off.'

He gestures to a plethora of CCTV cameras positioned outside and shrugs as if to say it's no skin off his nose. I'd be picked up by the police in less than a minute if I were to make a run for it.

After furiously searching every nook and cranny of the Transit, I scrape together £2.47. Add to that what I have in my purse, and I have a grand total of £17.80.

I am short by fifty pounds. In one last desperate attempt I rifle through my handbag, hoping desperately to find a source of cash.

And that's when I spot them.

Tucked between my diary and a slim catalogue for staff uniforms, I find the girls' National Savings bank cards. Joint accounts between both me and the girls, and each has around four thousand pounds in it. Money deposited from relatives for birthdays, money that Sean and I deposited each time they achieved good grades at school. Halle-fucking-lujah.

I stride confidently over towards a slim young woman replacing her petrol cap. 'Hi,' I say, smiling, 'I'm in a bit of a fix. Would you be able to drop me at the nearest Post Office? I need to withdraw money to pay for my fuel.'

'No,' she says, and walks off.

As I look after her, the guy on the other side of the pump is laughing, shaking his head. 'Very accommodating,' he says. 'What's happened, have you lost your purse?'

He's wearing a high-vis jacket with 'United Utilities' printed on the breast pocket.

'Kind of,' I tell him. 'My husband's cancelled my credit cards. And he didn't think to tell me.'

The guy screws up his face. 'That's a cunt's trick,' he says, matter-of-fact. 'Bad divorce?'

'Separated.'

'The worst part,' he says. 'By the time the divorce comes around, you can barely remember being married.'

He turns his eyes towards the pump, squeezes gently a few times to make sure he gets the exact amount. Sean does this, even though he pays for fuel by credit card. I can never understand why it's necessary to land on, say, a round sixty pounds, if you're not paying cash. He always does it, though, seems to gain satisfaction from it. Must be a man thing. The guy rattles the pump excessively to prevent any drips and turns his attention back to me.

'Give me a minute,' he says, pulling out his wallet, 'and I'll take you.'

Two hours later, the rain has stopped and I'm parked outside number 7 Wilkinson Street, Bolton. The street is crowded with cars, and this is the only available spot. It's been a bit of a wild-goose chase to get here. Somehow I managed to travel too far along the M61, coming off at completely the wrong side of town, and, instead of doing the sensible thing – doubling back – I decided heading across the centre of town would be quicker.

It wasn't.

Anyway, I'm here now, and parked opposite a primary school. It's an austere building with a small concrete playground and high smoked-glass windows. Must feel like a prison if you're five years old.

Leading off from Wilkinson Street are countless other identical streets; all lined with two-up two-down red-bricked terraced houses. The whole area is swamped in the shadows of a huge, abandoned mill. I assume it's been decommissioned, as its windows are smashed. It's an ugly, monstrous thing, dominating the landscape; a remnant of the industrialized north. Sixteen-hour shifts. Heavens. Hard to imagine now, as it's not clogs and flat caps on the cobbles around here but saris and burqas, people-carriers.

I slap on some lipstick and climb out, head across the street to find number 32. Each house abuts the pavement, no front garden or path, and each window I pass is meticulously clean, as if the window cleaner stops by daily. This is the kind of street where people still sweep their steps, clean the pavements and gutters in front of their houses.

I stop outside number 32, hesitate before pressing the doorbell. The windows are the original single glazing, the wooden frames freshly painted in thick white gloss and the sills in black. The front door is stained an ugly shade of red mahogany, but without a trace of dirt, and there are two giant plastic butterflies adorning the exterior brickwork. Sounds crass, but they do look kind of cheery.

I press the bell and wait.

After an age, and I mean close to four minutes, the door is thrown open and behind it is an elderly woman on a Zimmer frame. She's panting hard and her face is blood red. Immediately I feel terrible for disturbing her, making her suffer what is clearly a marathon of effort.

'Mrs Boydell?' I try, knowing this woman is in no way linked to Eve, but with no other plan available it's the best I can do.

'Who?'

She's deaf.

I enunciate slowly. 'I am looking for Mrs Boydell. Do you know her?'

'Who?'

'Boydell.'

'Shut the door,' she tells me, and begins negotiating her walking frame into a one-eighty. 'I need me ears in,' she says and sets off along the narrow corridor, assuming I'm following her.

Do people not view *Crimewatch*? Don't they know you're not supposed to let strangers into your house?

She takes a left into the front room. The tiny space is practically taken up with a heavy ebony sideboard and two wingback chairs, the type my dad is using at the moment on account of his knees. An old gas fire is lit and alongside lies a weary black dog, breed indiscriminate, greying around the muzzle. It raises its head as I enter; its eyes are cloudy, the pupils turning amber as they catch the light. It's blind, but knowing someone is here its back end begins to rock as it tries to wag its tail.

'Sit down, love,' says the woman. She has a deep, throaty, broad Lancastrian accent. Like Thora Hird.

Automatically, I say, 'You shouldn't let people into your home, you know,' but she doesn't hear me. She's fixing her hearing aid inside her ear and there's a piercing screech like a tea kettle boiling on the stove.

I recoil as she fiddles with it, the pitch rising and falling. 'Am I whistlin'?' she asks, her head cocked to one side.

'A bit,' I say.

'It's stopped?' she asks.

I nod at her to let her know that we're good.

'Righto then,' and before I have a chance to say anything more, she's leaning forward and peeling down her pop sock, fingering the edge of a grubby dressing midway down her shin. 'This is still oozing,' she tells me, grimacing. 'I think it might be better if it gets a bit of air at it.'

She has a leg ulcer. It's a rancid, gaping thing. As though her flesh has been scooped out with a spoon. 'Jesus,' I say, simultaneously transfixed and repulsed. 'Is that *bone*?'

'Aye. It's not healing good at all. Where's your bag o' tricks?'

'Bag of tricks?' And it dawns on me that she thinks I'm some kind of community nurse. 'No, no,' I say, conscious now that the faint fishy odour I noticed on entering the property is actually the smell of rotting human flesh. 'I'm not your nurse,' I say quickly. Perhaps too quickly, because she's mildly affronted.

'Who are you then?' she asks.

'Natty Wainwright.'

She frowns. 'Who?'

'Doesn't matter,' and I shake my head.

I move in closer and look at her straight so she can see my lips moving. 'I need to find Mr Boydell,' I say clearly, almost shouting. 'Do you know where he is?'

'Dead.'

'Oh,' I reply. 'Oh, that's terrible, I didn't know. I'm so sorry. When did he die?'

'Nineteen sixty-seven.'

'Really?'

'Asbestos,' she says, and nods grimly. 'But that were back before they knew it were bad for you, so we got no compensation. Now, Kathleen Moss, her at number 48, she gets an extra fourteen pound a week in her pension. That's 'cause her husband died later on.'

A moment passes where she contemplates this injustice and it seems best to keep silent.

Then I clear my throat. 'Would you happen to know where *Mrs* Boydell is?' I ask, and she does a double take. Checks to see if I'm pulling her leg.

'*I'm* Mrs Boydell!' she exclaims.

'Of course, of course,' I reply apologetically, thinking that this makes no sense whatsoever. There is no way this is the Mrs Boydell I am looking for. For one, she's too old. And it seems almost impossible she could be related to Eve, let alone be her mother. The mother that Eve claimed was long dead. The name must be a coincidence.

Still, I have to ask.

'Mrs Boydell, do you have a daughter named Eve?'

'Eve?'

'Yes,' I say.

'No.'

'I see.'

'I've a granddaughter, though,' she says. 'Nasty piece o' work is Eve. Ran off and never calls her mother. Still, it's probably for the best.'

'So, your son is married to . . .' I pause, working through the lineage to make sure I get this right, 'Your son is married to Eve's mother? Is that correct?'

'What?' she scoffs. 'Our Sharon never married.'

'No?'

'She'd never say who the father was. Some low-life Walter Mitty, she called him. I can't help you if it's 'im you're looking for. She gave the child our name, Boydell, 'cause she didn't want folk knowing who he was.'

'So what you're telling me is your daughter, Sharon, brought Eve up on her own? Around here?'

'In this very house,' she says proudly.

I lean in, excited by what she's saying, anxious about what I'm going to ask next, in case this all amounts to nothing.

'Mrs Boydell,' I say, trying to keep my tone neutral, 'where is Sharon right now? Does she live nearby?'

'Oh aye,' she says. 'She's got a bungalow towards the hospital . . . she moved out when all the Pakis moved in.' Dropping her voice, she taps the side of her nose conspiratorially. 'Now, she won't say owt about it to you,' she whispers, 'and don't you go lettin' on you heard this from me, but our Sharon . . . well, she can be a bit of a racialist.'

29

Eve squirts UHT cream from a can. She places the tall cups on saucers, carefully unwraps the Cadbury's Flakes – sprinkling any leftover shavings on top of the cream – then lays each Flake alongside the hot chocolate. Lastly, she adds a long-handled spoon.

She's not a natural when it comes to this kind of thing, but, standing back, surveying her efforts, she's actually quite pleased.

Alice sits at the table, school tie pulled loose. She has a stark-white Biore blackhead-removal strip across her nose – which would be fine if she actually had any blackheads. Alice uses the strips daily, Eve's noticed. Something Eve finds rather irritating but is prepared to ignore for now. She's going along with it, indulging Alice in her quest to attain perfect skin.

Felicity is at the table also, but sits silently, her head down.

'Why is she *still* not answering her phone?' Alice complains to no one in particular.

'Perhaps your mum just needs a little time to herself,' answers Eve. 'Yesterday must have been really tough for her.'

'But I've left countless messages,' Alice says. 'So now she's, like, totally abandoned us? Is that it?'

Felicity delivers a death stare in Eve's direction. Her jaw set, she stands, grabbing her hot chocolate. 'I'm going upstairs.'

Alice stops texting. 'Felicity, you know you're not allowed drinks upstairs. Mummy'll go schizo if she finds out.'

'Maybe it'll be okay just this once, Felicity,' blusters Eve. 'I won't tell if you won't.'

And Felicity regards Eve coldly before sitting down once more. 'I think I'll stay here after all,' she says.

Alice is now frowning at her sister, and turns her attention back to her phone. 'I'm sending Mummy one last text,' she declares, 'and if she doesn't answer this one, I'm giving up. If she can't be bothered about us, then I shan't be calling *her* every five minutes.'

Eve fixes her hair in the glass of the wall-mounted cabinet. Turning around, she says, 'So, dinner out tonight then, girls?'

'Lovely,' replies Alice.

Felicity lifts her head, watches Eve through narrowed eyes. 'Again?' Her tone is bitter. 'Don't you *ever* cook a proper meal?'

Alice is horrified. 'Felicity!' she admonishes. 'Don't be so rude. It's not Eve's fault she's been marooned here with us because Mummy's done a bunk. She can hardly be expected to cook all our meals and do everything when—'

Felicity noisily scrapes back her chair. 'I've got homework to do,' she says, and leaves.

When she's gone Alice's mouth gapes open. 'What the hell is wrong with her?' she asks, exasperated. 'She's not the only one going through this. She's not the only one upset Mummy was arrested. She's not the *only victim.*'

'Try to be patient with her, Alice. This kind of thing affects everyone differently. It's not easy having what is essentially a stranger in the house . . . when all you've ever known is your parents.'

'But you're not a stranger,' Alice says. 'We've known you for ages.'

'But not as your dad's girlfriend. And Alice, believe me, if I'd had the chance I would have taken this much slower. Teenagers need time to adapt. You can't go barging in, have them think you're trying to replace their mother when—'

'Oh, Eve,' Alice says, jumping up, 'I don't think you're trying to replace her! I don't think that at all. What you're doing here . . . you're helping,' and she hugs Eve tightly.

'Thank you,' Eve tells her, sniffling a little. 'That's so kind, because I don't feel I'm getting it right. I've been thrust into this situation, a situation I really hadn't planned for. And I do feel terrible about your mum being arrested. I really wish I could have kept it from the police . . . but, well, it was recorded on the CCTV. And *of course*, her criminal record flagged up straight away, so . . .' Eve shrugs at Alice as if she had been helpless to avoid what had happened.

Alice drops her head.

At once she appears bruised, and Eve worries perhaps she's pushed things too far. She was aiming to keep Alice on her side. And, Alice being Alice, so open to suggestion, Eve felt confident she would go for it. Now she's not so sure. Now she thinks making Alice feel bad about her mum might not have been the right tactic.

But then Alice speaks up. 'Do you think Mummy will ever tell us the full story of what happened back then?'

And Eve smiles warmly, relieved by Alice's words.

Clasping Alice's hands together in her own, she says, 'I'm sure of it, Alice. But it has to be in her own time. I don't really know what happened exactly, and it wouldn't be my place to tell you even if I did. That's for your mum to do.'

Alice nods seriously.

'She'll tell you,' continues Eve, 'when the time is right. In the meantime, I just hope she's going to be okay.'

'What do you mean?'

'I hope she doesn't become a danger to herself. I spoke to her earlier, and—'

'You did?'

'I didn't want to mention it, because she was terribly upset.'

'What about?' asks Alice. 'Where was she?'

'She wouldn't say.'

'Oh, God!' Alice cries, stricken. 'What if she's hurt, what if—'

'She wasn't hurt, Alice, only upset. Do try not to worry,' says Eve, pulling Alice back to her again and stroking her hair, reassuring her. 'I'm sure she'll be in touch as soon as she's feeling better.'

The sound of the front door slamming echoes through the house. 'Hello?' Sean shouts. 'Who's home?'

'In here, Daddy,' she calls back. 'We're in the kitchen.'

Sean appears and throws the change from his pockets down on the table. He is slightly dishevelled. Ruffled. His usual immaculate appearance is compromised. He has a four o'clock shadow and the collar of his Armani jacket is turned up on one side.

Eve cranes her neck expectantly as he approaches, but he doesn't lean in to kiss her. 'Everything okay?' she asks him.

Sean turns away and moves towards Alice, kissing the top of her head. Regarding the nose strip, he says, 'Haven't you already done that?' in a tone that's slightly sharp for Sean, Eve thinks.

Alice doesn't notice and tells him he knows absolutely nothing about skin care. Particularly teenage skin and how prone it can be to oiliness.

'Have you spoken to Mummy?' she asks him.

'Not today, no.'

'She's not answering her phone.'

Eve jumps in here. Brightly, she tells Sean: 'I've told Alice not to worry, told her Natty probably needs a little time to herself,' and Sean is taken aback.

'Why would she need time away from her own children?' he asks her.

'She wouldn't . . . I just meant that—'

'She's their mother,' he says.

Eve's eyes widen in response. Sean has not spoken to her like this before. It's not a good sign. Quietly, she asks him: 'Sean, whatever is the matter?' and his shoulders heave visibly as he tries to lose the tension from his body.

He shakes his head. 'Bad day at work.'

'Anything I can help with?'

He goes to speak, then changes his mind. 'Honey,' he says, looking at Alice, 'would you mind giving me and Eve a minute alone?'

'Why?'

'Because we need to talk.'

Alice huffs, clearly not happy about being left out of the conversation. 'Okay,' she says finally, slinging her school bag over her shoulder. 'Okay, I'll go.'

When Sean's sure she's out of earshot he turns to Eve. 'There are problems at the hotel. I'm sorry if I'm short-tempered.'

'What sort of problems?'

'Minor stuff. Nothing big. But it all adds up, and it's as if . . .'

'As if?'

He averts his eyes. 'Natty used to take care of the small shit, you know? And now that she's gone it's as if the place is beginning to fall apart.'

'Oh, that can't be true, Sean,' exclaims Eve. 'Nobody is irreplaceable, not even Natty.'

'That's what I keep telling myself,' he says with a rueful smile. 'And while we're talking openly, I know I should have said something about this last night, and I didn't, but I'm truly sorry about what she did to you—'

'Sean, you've already apologized for her ramming me, and I told you it's not your fault.'

'No, what I meant to say is that just because I sorted out the solicitor for her it doesn't mean I condone what she did.' He pauses, searching for the right words. 'I needed to do that for her, if you can understand. To help Natty get out of the mess she was in. Both for her and the girls.'

'No explanations necessary. You wouldn't be the man I've fallen in love with if you didn't feel beholden in some way.'

He nods. Comes in closer and rests his hand on her arm. 'Anyway, back to the problem of work. Perhaps I should hire a second manager ... or maybe you might consider becoming more involved? I don't think I can run the place alone, and it would mean we could—'

'Oh, no.' Eve laughs awkwardly. 'I don't think it's really my thing.'

Sean puts his hands up to his face. 'No,' he says. 'No, you're right. Just a thought,' and he walks towards the fridge. 'I'll put an advert in tomorrow, get another pair of hands, that should do it. Christ, I even had the bank grilling me today over cancelled credit cards, had no idea what they were going on about. As if I've got time to sort that out when the place is full, and we've got eighty in for dinner ... *and* we've got Tony Iommi staying.'

At the mention of the credit cards Eve's left eye twitches.

Sean pulls out a Budweiser, twists off the cap and drinks straight from the bottle. 'I'll need to head back over there later to have a couple of drinks with him,' he says. 'Make sure he's happy.'

'No problem,' replies Eve, relaxing now that Sean's mood is lightening. 'I've told the girls we'll eat out anyway, so you can drop us at home and return to the hotel afterwards. Who's Tony Iommi? Is he a restaurant critic?'

Sean coughs mid-swig and the beer rises up the neck of the bottle fast, spilling on to his hand. Holding it over the sink, he says, 'He's kind of a famous guitarist,' and laughs. He regards her quizzically. 'You've really no idea who he is? You've never heard of Paranoid?'

'Of course,' says Eve, blinking rapidly, thinking it best not to show her ignorance. 'Paranoid are an excellent band . . . Actually, I used to listen to them all the time . . . as a student.'

Forcing a smile, Sean picks up his mobile, kisses her briefly on the cheek and tells her he's off to have a shower.

30

I'VE BEEN WAITING outside Sharon Boydell's bungalow for close to two hours. I'm on the verge of abandoning my post when she returns home.

She reverses her car into the narrow driveway and begins unloading shopping from the boot of her Nissan Micra. As I approach she coughs. It's a rattling, productive cough, ending in a deep growl as she hawks the last of the phlegm from her throat. A smoker.

I loiter for a moment, as she's absorbed in her task. I don't want to frighten her. She's moving chocolate biscuits from one carrier bag to another and is unaware of my presence. She's a wiry woman who moves with fast, jerking actions. One of those women who couldn't put weight on if she tried.

I close in, and she catches sight of me in her peripheral vision. Turning, she regards me directly, and I know instantly that this is Eve's mother. It's Eve after thirty shitty years of hard living.

If you passed this woman on the street you'd say she had a difficult time; most likely been knocked about a bit in her youth. Her skin is stretched over her skull in not quite the right way, calling to mind a mummified corpse. She scowls at me, suggesting she's angered by my presence. I'm hoping it's confusion rather than rage, but when she widens her eyes at me, as if to say: *Well? What is it you want?* I'm left in little doubt.

'Ahem. Sorry to bother you,' I begin, 'but—'

'I'm buyin' nothin', she snaps, and goes back to rearranging her shopping.

'I'm not here to sell you anything.'

She ignores my attempt to explain, cutting me off: 'I am stickin' with British Gas,' she says, without looking up, 'robbing bastards though they are . . . I've got UPVC windows, so as you can see I do not need double glazing, and if it's religion you're selling, I'm a Roman Catholic. So whatever it is you're trying to flog, lady, I've already got it.'

'I'm not selling anything,' I repeat, mildly affronted, because do I *look* like a door-to-door salesperson?

'That's what you all say,' she retorts, throwing me a derisive glance. 'Then you ask me some sort o' daft question like, "Do I think I'm getting value for money from my mobile phone?" I'm absolutely sick to death of you people knocking on my door. So, if you wouldn't mind . . .' and she tilts her head in the direction of the road, indicating I should skedaddle before she really loses her temper.

'Mrs Boydell,' I say carefully, 'I'm here about Eve.'

Immediately she stops. Swallows. She's about to say something nasty. I can almost see the words rising in her throat. But, at the last second, she changes her mind.

'Is she dead?' she asks.

'No.'

'Injured?'

I shake my head. 'No.'

Her face hardens again and she narrows her eyes.

'Has she sent you here 'cause she owes you money?'

'No,' I reply, 'it's nothing like that. Listen,' I say, shifting my weight to my other foot. 'Is there somewhere we can talk?'

'Whatever that girl is up to, I want no part in it. None at all, understand?' and she turns her back to me. Makes out as if she's lost something on the far left-hand side of the boot.

'Please,' I try again. 'I really need your help. Let me talk to you inside. If after two minutes you want me to leave, I will. I promise.'

'Not a chance. Anything you got to say, you say it right here. I don't want you in there upsetting my lad, we've got enough to put up with—'

'Your lad?' I ask, looking over my shoulder at the house. I was certain there was no one home. I've been sitting outside for hours, and there's been no sign of movement from within. 'Mrs Boydell,' I say, 'I pressed your doorbell a good few times earlier and no one answered. I don't think there's anyone home.'

She doesn't look up. 'He must be busy.'

I stand there, helpless. What is it with this woman?

Sharon Boydell closes her boot and reaches down to gather her shopping. I'm running out of ideas.

'You could always put up a sign in the window,' I venture brightly.

'I could do what?'

'If you want to stop people bothering you, put a sign in your front window saying "Do not ring the bell, shift worker asleep inside". I did it when I had a spate of cold callers. It worked instantly.'

She tilts her head as she considers my advice. 'Maybe I will,' she says.

I dip fast and pick up a carrier bag.

'Put that down,' she says.

'No.'

She sighs heavily. Rolls her eyes.

'What are you planning to do,' she asks me, 'stand out here all day?'

'If that's what it takes,' I reply, my voice quivering. I'm trying my best to put on an authoritative air, but it's not really working. This tiny slip of a woman is formidable in the extreme.

Eventually, she says, 'Oh, all right, all right. Grab these,' and she thrusts another two bags my way. 'You may as well make yourself useful,' she adds, before strutting off inside.

After Sharon Boydell has put away all of her freezer stuff, smoked two king-size Lambert & Butlers, removed the lid from a canned Frey Bentos steak and kidney pie and popped it in the oven along with some McCain smiley potato faces, at last she's ready to talk.

I've not yet caught sight of her son, but I am now willing to believe he exists, on account of the potato faces. The place is small, though: whatever he's doing, he's doing it quietly. The house is a 1930s semi-detached bungalow. Not much space, but well laid out.

Sharon stands with her back against the sink in the narrow galley kitchen. Behind her, the windowsill is filled with a selection of pots holding money plants in various stages of growth. She notices me eyeing them and says, 'I do cuttings for people,' then shrugs as if she doesn't know why she bothers.

It doesn't look like Sharon Boydell has a lot of spare cash for home improvements – the kitchen cupboards are brown veneered wood, the edges chipped and exposed, and I'd guess her tea caddy's about the same age as me.

'So, then, what's she done?' she asks when we're finished with the small talk. 'That daughter of mine, what's she gone and done now?'

'Taken my husband.'

She's not shocked. 'Sounds about right,' she says. 'I'd say you're not the first, and you certainly won't be the last.'

'No?'

'It's what she does. Fleeces one poor bugger before moving on to the next. She masquerades as some kind of therapist, so I'm led to believe, but why anyone would take advice from her is beyond me.'

'You say it as if it's common knowledge, as if everyone knows how Eve operates.'

She raises her eyebrows. 'It *is* common knowledge.'

'But I had no idea. And I've been friends with your daughter since I was eighteen. As far as I'm concerned, she's been living happily with Brett for—'

'Who's Brett?'

'Brett Dalladay,' I say. 'Her husband.'

'Never heard of him.'

'Your daughter's married name is Eve Dalladay. That's what she's been going by for the last' – I pause as I count up the years in my head – 'must be around seven years.'

'The only thing you can be sure about with Eve is that everything that comes out of her mouth is a lie.' Sharon grabs her pack of Lambert & Butler and withdraws another cigarette. Shaking her lighter furiously in her hand, she tries to get it to produce a flame. Eventually, she gives up, saying, 'Forgot to buy a bloody new one,' and makes do with using the toaster. I glance at the cooker, thinking, wouldn't it be easier to use the gas? But it's an electric hob.

The conversation stops as Sharon takes a couple of deep drags and the kitchen fills with smoke and a sweet, papery smell from the toaster that is at once both interesting and slightly nauseating.

'Eve will do anything,' Sharon says '– and I mean *anything* – to get what she wants. She has no feelings, she doesn't understand what guilt or empathy is.' I sense from her tone that I've tapped a well that was ready to gush. 'The only time you'll see any kind of remorse from Eve is if she thinks she's in trouble and can't lie her way out of it. Then she'll pretend she's sorry. But that's all forgotten soon enough.' Sharon shakes her head.

I go to speak, because I want to talk more about the inconsistencies in Eve's life story. I want to know if she continued her studies at Salford when she was thrown off her course at Manchester. I want to know about her time in the States. I want to know what is real and what is fake. But Sharon holds up her palm, indicating for me to keep quiet for a moment longer. She's working something out.

'Married for seven years, you say?'

'Yes,' I reply. 'And for that time living permanently in America, as far as I know.'

She nods. 'That'd make sense. It's about the last time I saw her.'

'She's been back and forth to the States most of her adult life,' I tell her. 'She told me she was moving there because she didn't get along with her dad's new wife. She told me you had died.'

Again, this doesn't seem to shock her. 'Eve never knew her dad.'

I nod in agreement, though not letting on that I've spoken to Eve's grandmother. Sharon is clearly a spiky woman and I don't want to antagonize her unnecessarily. She may not take kindly to the fact that her mother let a total stranger inside her house.

'We tried tracing Eve after she disappeared the last time,' she continues, 'but it came to nothing. It was like she was wiped out, never existed.'

'How is that possible?'

'You tell me. I've no idea how a person disappears off the face of the earth.'

'That must have been awful,' I say. 'Did you think she was . . . you know, dead?'

Sharon turns, taps her cigarette in the sink and runs the cold water for a second to rinse away the ash. 'To be frank, I wasn't bothered if she was dead, but I needed to get something to her.' And she looks away, suddenly evasive.

I wait for her to continue, careful not to fill in the break in conversation with chatter which may stop her from revealing useful information.

At last she speaks. 'I needed to tell her something important. Anyway, the upshot of it was I couldn't find her. Tried social services, the police, that kind of thing. A year later, when we still had nothing to go on, I got my friend at the hospital to look at her medical records, but that came to—'

Again Sharon stops suddenly.

'I've said too much,' she whispers. She puts her hands up to her mouth to try to cover her gaffe.

'Don't worry,' I tell her. 'I'll keep it to myself.'

'I promised Anne I'd never tell a soul. Bloody hell.' She's shaking her head at her ineptitude. 'She could get sacked for this . . . she could get worse than sacked for what she did for me.'

'Sharon,' I say firmly, 'I won't say anything. You have my word. What did Anne find?'

'Nothing.'

'No medical notes for Eve after she disappeared?'

Sharon gives a sarcastic bark of laughter. 'Nothing from *before* she disappeared either. There was not one single scrap of information on her.'

'How can that be possible?'

'It was as if she'd never existed,' Sharon says. 'Not even files on her operation from when she was a baby, none of the—'

'Oh, yes,' I say, remembering, 'the aneurysm in her head. That's why she had to retake the first year of university.'

'That's what she told you?'

I nod. 'Yes. She got an infection and—'

'Eve had an aneurysm clip fitted when she was a baby, that much is true,' Sharon says, flicking her ash behind her again. 'But there were no complications later on. That's not why she missed the year at university. Like I said, everything – and I

247

mean *everything* – out of that girl's mouth is utter tripe. She's told so many lies, I bet she can't even remember that . . .' She pauses. 'Never mind.'

I can see there's something Sharon doesn't want to reveal, and I don't want to push her too far lest she closes up on me.

'What made her like this?' I ask.

And Sharon's spine straightens in defence. 'You're asking me if I was a bad mother? If she was neglected? If she wasn't looked after properly?'

'No,' I exclaim, horrified she thinks I'm being critical. 'No, I don't mean that at all.'

'It's fine,' she says. 'I've asked myself the same question about a thousand times. Where did I go wrong? Why did she turn out the way she did? I even asked my GP what was wrong with her, and he told me to go and read up on narcissism. I thought he was joking.' She laughs at the memory of this. 'He told me they used to think female narcissists came about from bad parenting, that they were driven by their need for affection. Turns out it's a load of rubbish . . . now they reckon it's the opposite way around.'

'Meaning?'

'That the condition stems from little girls being over-indulged by their parents, from being told they're special and precious. America's knee deep in 'em, apparently. Anyway, that was certainly the case with Eve. After her operations . . . don't forget this was brain surgery she had . . . well, after that, me and my mother spoilt her rotten.'

'Oh.'

'I know,' she says. 'Who'd have thought? Your child turns into a nutter just because you loved her too much. Doesn't seem fair, does it?'

'Hardly,' I say.

And I'm thinking of my own girls. Thinking of what if? What

if they turn their backs on me for no good reason? What if they don't want to know me any more after I poured all I had into them?

'I've had to harden my heart to my daughter,' Sharon explains, her expression pained. 'Which hasn't been easy. But the fact is, I had no choice.' She takes one last long drag on her cigarette before stubbing it out in the sink. 'I had no choice,' she says again, as if it's something she tells herself, a mantra, to keep sane. 'I had to do it, on account of Danny.'

'Danny?'

'Eve's brother.'

I nod, not really sure how he fits into all this, but at the same time sensing that Sharon's demeanour has quickly gone from defensive, an almost warrior stance, to vulnerable.

She's quiet for a minute and I sense she's readying herself for what she's about to tell me. 'Danny needs extra caring for,' she begins. '. . . He's got a few problems. Cerebral palsy,' and she says this quietly, as though she doesn't want him to overhear. 'It's mild, but, you know, he needs me. Anyway,' she says, gathering herself, 'it is what it is.'

Before I have the chance to impart anything close to sympathy, Sharon adds, 'Well, it's our life. That's what we've got, so that's what we do.' She gives a brave smile. 'And I'm not complaining. Christ, no. I need Danny as much as he needs me . . . it's just, well, you asked why I've given up on Eve and—'

'I didn't say you'd given up on her,' I interrupt.

'No, you didn't,' she replies. 'I did. And I have given up. Because I had to. In the end, I didn't have it in me any longer to keep on loving Eve when all she ever did was bring trouble to our door. It was difficult for Danny. To see me upset would make him upset, so . . .'

'Understandable,' I say.

As if on cue we hear a door closing, followed shortly thereafter by the sound of the loo being flushed. Sharon turns and busies herself taking the lid off the baked beans, fetches the HP Sauce and tomato ketchup from the cupboard.

Sharon leans towards me. 'Don't let on you're here about Eve,' she warns, and I shake my head. 'He misses her. If he hears her name he'll not shut up about her all night.'

A moment later and a huge figure appears in the doorway. Danny is well over six foot, a big bear of a lad inside a Bolton Wanderers shirt. He has the telltale signs of limb spasticity: his left trainer turns in, almost at a right angle, and his right arm is crooked at the elbow, stuck tightly to his side.

'Mum?' he says. 'What time's tea?'

'You finished up Josh's papers?' she asks him brusquely.

'Yeah, I done 'em.'

I'm a little embarrassed she's not introduced us, so I smile and tell him I'm Natty. Tell him I've popped in for a quick chat with his mum.

'Five minutes till your tea's ready,' Sharon says, and he shuffles out. When he's gone she explains how Danny slides the supplements and leaflets inside the *Bolton Evening News*. The kid next door does a paper round and Danny helps out, enjoys the repetitive nature of the task. 'Keeps him quiet for a few hours,' she whispers as we hear the sound of the television coming from the lounge.

'I'd offer you something to eat,' she says, as she lays out the cutlery, 'but you don't get a lot a meat in these pies. And Dan's got hollow legs. He can eat and eat and he's still hungry.'

'No worries,' I tell her. 'I wouldn't want to trouble you more than I already have. I need to be on the road soon and get back to my own children. Thanks for being so open about everything. It's made what's happened a little easier to process. Can I ask you one last thing?'

'Fire away.'

'Was Eve ever violent? I never saw it myself, but I can't help now thinking she might be capable of far worse things.'

'She was. As a child she had terrible tantrums, couldn't control her temper, she had that nasty streak you sometimes see in kids when they can't get their own way. But she did seem to grow out of it. As she got older she liked to take her anger out in other ways.'

I nod, weighing up her words.

'I do wonder, though . . .'

'Oh?'

'I wonder just what did happen seven years ago, to make her need to disappear. I know for certain it wouldn't have been Eve simply wanting a fresh start. She must have run away from something, and I've often wondered what that was.'

Sharon smiles resignedly. 'Anyway, you say you've got kids? Boys or girls?'

'Two girls . . . sixteen and fourteen.'

'Nice,' she says. 'Are they a handful?'

'They have their moments,' I reply. 'I have the feeling they prefer Eve's company to mine right now, though, because—'

'Eve?'

'Yes.'

Sharon takes a step back, an expression of mild confusion on her face as she waits for me to continue.

'There was a misunderstanding . . . an accident,' I stammer reluctantly, not really wanting to admit I was arrested for violent behaviour after just accusing Eve of the same, not wanting Sharon to think badly of me. '. . . There was an accident and it meant my husband and Eve have to take care of the girls for a short while.'

'Oh, she wouldn't like that,' Sharon retorts. 'Eve can't stand kids.'

I frown. 'Well, perhaps she's changed her mind,' I say, 'because she's been trying for a baby. She told me she wanted children but her husband was the one who backed out and that's why they split up. If things weren't the way they were, I'd probably feel quite sorry for her.'

Sharon tilts her head as if not quite comprehending. 'But Eve has been sterilized.'

I shake my head.

'No, that can't be right.'

'It was a while ago,' Sharon says softly.

'When?' I ask. 'Are you sure?'

'Oh yes,' she says. 'I'm sure. I was with her. She was nineteen.'

'Good Lord,' I blurt out, my mind racing. 'Why on earth would she get sterilized at such a young age? It seems so final. How can a person be certain they'll never want a child?' I am dumbstruck by this. 'Surely the National Health Service wouldn't conduct irreversible surgery on a nineteen-year-old? Surely there must be some kind of protocol for—'

Sharon looks at me straight. 'She told them she'd kill herself if they didn't do it, so they didn't have a lot of choice.'

'Good grief,' I say.

My mind is pushed into overdrive again as I begin thinking it through. 'Still, she was very young,' I reason. 'I mean, you have to have counselling for that operation, don't you? Why didn't they advise fitting a coil? That would be more sensible. There are lots of options and none of them quite so final as to actually—'

'Stop!' Sharon shouts out, and I stare at her.

A shocked silence.

Her face is deathly white, and I realize that, unwittingly, I've said completely the wrong thing.

'I'm sorry,' I tell her, embarrassed. 'I didn't mean to upset you, I didn't mean to . . . this really is none of my business.'

'Eve insisted on that operation,' Sharon says, her eyes empty, cold. 'She insisted on it, because she couldn't stand the thought of having another child.'

'Another child?' I whisper.

And Sharon drops her eyes to the floor. 'Eve didn't want to take the chance of having another child like Danny.'

31

I LEAVE EVE'S MOTHER'S house feeling very differently to when I arrived. Before, I was so sure Sharon Boydell held the answers I needed to expose Eve. She certainly gave me the evidence I was searching for. Except – what can I do with this information? I can't do a bloody thing with it.

Danny doesn't know Eve is his mother; he has no clue. And Sharon warned me that should I open my mouth – either now or in ten years' time – she will hunt me down and rip my head off my shoulders. (Her words, and I have no reason to believe she is lying.)

She told me she'd worked too damn hard to give Danny the happiness he deserved. His whole life she had watched him bullied and taunted. She'd watched him go through painful operation after operation to relieve his limb spasticity. This was the reason she'd been trying to locate Eve seven years ago – Danny contracted pneumonia after one such surgery, and she feared he wouldn't make it. Later, when it emerged that Eve had made absolutely certain she could not be traced, Sharon decided it was time to say goodbye to her damaged daughter for good. Time to try to forget about her and move on with her life.

Heading north, in the middle lane of the M61, I am thinking that perhaps Eve and I may be more alike than I'd like to admit. I, too, have tried to shake off a past by living a lie. 'Living inauthentically' is the polite way of saying one has been spinning a web of bullshit to cover past mistakes. This is simply that lie catching up with me. I deserve this after what I did to Sean all those years ago, my head turned by an arrogant, preppy boy.

And Sean stepped into the role of father, became the best dad in the world, compromising his future for a child that wasn't his.

And how had I repaid him?

By becoming consumed with building what, from the outside at least, was deemed to be a successful life, a successful business. And by ignoring his needs altogether.

I can see now that the thing, *the only important thing*, was Sean and I. We formed the bricks and mortar. That's what supports everything else, and if you don't give marriage the attention it needs, cracks appear, and there's sure to be some ruthless woman waiting in the wings, willing to put her integrity to one side, willing to take what's yours in a heartbeat.

Ahead, the traffic is slowing as we hit the busy stretch south of Preston where the motorway joins the M6. A red glow fills the sky as drivers hit the brakes, and I wonder what it would be like to just *let go*. What if I were to let the van careen along of its own accord, ploughing straight into the stationary traffic ahead?

The dead, empty sensation inside me makes this kind of tempting, and for the first time it hits me what a fantastically dangerous activity motorway driving really is; trusting that everyone else on the road is of sound mind and without suicidal tendencies. If I so wished, right now, I could take out not only myself, but potentially another thirty other people along with me.

I shudder at the thought and move my foot over to the brake pedal, shifting down through the gears, the heavy clutch sending a hot sciatic pain all the way up to my left buttock.

The van slows to a halt and, though surrounded every which way by cars, I am more alone than ever.

I take out my phone.

*

255

Eve glances around the restaurant.

To the outside world, they are a perfectly normal family: two parents, two children – shiny, happy people – enjoying a meal together.

The place is busy. The requisite bustling atmosphere of the village Italian restaurant is enhanced by Dean Martin singing 'Volare' from a wall-mounted speaker over by the door, and the owner is shouting orders through to the kitchen, louder than is really necessary. As he moves between the tables he flirts shamelessly with the middle-aged ladies, and they drop their heads, pretending not to enjoy the attention he affords them.

This could be any Italian place, anywhere, Eve's thinking. She fingers the red and white checked tablecloth, watches children's faces beam as they're served vanilla ice cream in a tall glass, a lit sparkler turning the commonplace dessert into a truly magical experience.

Eve turns her attention to the girls. Alice is babbling, as ever. She's wearing the most ridiculous outfit – royal-blue crocheted dress over striped pink leggings – and she's beehived her hair, decorated the auburn up-do with tiny bows and silver butterflies. Eve is at a loss for words.

Felicity wears low-waisted jeans (on account of her appendix scar) and trainers. Eve had asked her to dress up a little and Felicity had told her to go fuck herself. Quietly, though. So nobody heard. Eve had responded to that minor outburst by flashing a nasty smile, which must have put the fear of God into Felicity, as an apology was soon forthcoming. A reluctant one, naturally, but Felicity has not uttered a word since.

Eve is now utterly bored playing happy families and she's zoning out of the conversation. She's wondering just how long she'll have to endure this before she can move on.

She's startled by loud, unfamiliar, tinny music, and for a second her heart sinks as she assumes it's a customer's birthday.

Eve looks towards the kitchen, expecting to see a parade of waiters and kitchen staff shaking maracas and tambourines, faux expressions of joviality plastered across their faces.

This is what she hates most about Italian restaurants.

The music turns out to be Alice's mobile, and Eve picks up her glass and takes a large gulp of the rough red wine. Sean told her earlier there was no point in paying for decent wine in here, because it was all plonk. 'There's no money to be made from food,' he lectured, as Eve perused the wine list. 'They have to import the cheap rubbish no one in Italy will drink, mark it up by five hundred per cent just to make a decent living.'

'Why do you serve food in the hotel then, if there's no money to be made from it?' Eve asked him.

'Because we have to. We don't make a penny on it, the money's all in the beds. I'd add another ten rooms if I could get planning permission to expand the hotel. No chance of that, though . . . building restrictions are tighter than ever in the National Park right now.'

Eve asked for a bottle of red and Sean ordered something Eve had never heard of, which is beginning to strip the lining from the back of her throat. So she puts her glass down and switches to the Prosecco. She watches as Alice tilts her head, gestures wildly as she speaks, acting like this is an important phone call she *absolutely must take.*

'You're on your way home?' Alice is saying. 'Back in an hour?'

And immediately Eve stiffens as she realizes it's Natty on the other end of the line. 'Mummy, I can't hear you too well, you're breaking up . . . you're not *driving*, are you?'

Alice rolls her eyes. 'You're not supposed to talk while you do that,' she tells her mother. 'Where have you been, anyway? I've been calling and calling . . . why didn't you answer?'

Eve pretends to be interested in Sean's starter of chilli tiger prawns, at the same time paying close attention to the exchange between Alice and Natty. Perhaps it wasn't such a good idea to eat out after all. Sean is twitchy and on edge, worrying about the future of the hotel, and he's still full of guilt because Felicity has barely said a word since yesterday – which of course Sean thinks is on account of finding them naked in bed. Though Eve knows it has more to do with her mildly threatening behaviour.

Alice is oblivious to any undercurrent and is carrying on as if she's her mother's keeper – reprimanding her loudly for not keeping in contact.

The other patrons of the restaurant are beginning to stare at her, but in a very British way – hard glares, lots of tutting; no one would be so forward as to approach the table and ask her to lower her voice.

'No,' says Alice, 'we're eating out . . . Italian . . . no, Mummy, I *don't have* the garlic mushrooms any more, that's Felicity, I have bruschetta with tomato, remember? . . . Hang on, I'll just ask them.'

Alice covers the mouthpiece of her phone with her thumb and looks to Sean.

'Mummy's on her way back and wants to come home . . . she's asking you if that's okay? That is okay, isn't it?'

Alice glances shiftily at Eve as if she's not quite sure what the protocol is here.

'Tonight?' Sean says curtly.

'I think so,' she replies, and screws up her face, because she senses it's going to be a problem.

Sean holds out his hand. 'Pass me the phone.'

He takes a breath. 'Natty,' he says, his voice low, serious, 'tonight's not really doable, we're going to need a bit more notice.' He looks to Eve as he suggests, 'How about tomorrow morning?' and Eve nods her head to say that's fine by her. 'Yes, tomorrow morning would suit us much better. Say elevenish? Give us a chance to get packed up . . . I'm stuck at the hotel till late tonight . . . yes . . . drinks with Tony Iommi . . . no, I won't be back till after twelve, I reckon.'

Eve sips her Prosecco and watches Alice's hopeful smile fade as it becomes clear she won't see her mother until tomorrow. Felicity has her face in her food, spearing her garlic mushrooms with her fork in her right hand – something Sean has already reprimanded her for once, telling her not to eat like a savage.

'You've been *where*?' Sean asks Natty, his brow creased in confusion. 'Bolton?' he says. 'What on earth were you doing in Bolton?'

And Eve's glass slips from her fingers, noisily smashing to pieces on the floor tiles of the pizzeria.

Mad Jackie's car is parked outside my dad's in the only space large enough to accommodate his van. I resort to parking the Transit at the top of the street outside an old bloke's house, and he's none too happy. He glares at me through the window as I inch backwards and forwards, trying to get as close as I can to the kerb without mounting it with one of the wheels. Once parked, I take the key from the ignition and give the man my best *You do not own this stretch of road* expression. He narrows his eyes and draws his curtains in disgust. 'Miserable bastard,' I mutter, climbing out.

I'm tired. Bone tired. It's been a long day. I've been on the road since first thing this morning and it's now almost 9 p.m. My body is stiff and leaden, the muscles of my legs taut and inelastic after so long inside the van. My lower back feels as though I've been kicked by a mule.

I walk down the street, the tarmac beneath my feet a wet, glossy black, after what's most likely been another full day of rain. The air has a heavy, saturated feel.

Beyond the main road at the end of the street is the school of my youth and, beyond that, Sheriff Wood. I see the treetops visible and think back to when I was eight or nine: happy days spent beneath the Scots pines, no grown-up cares or worries.

I unlatch my dad's gate and through the glass catch sight of Jackie leaning over to plant a kiss on his forehead. A private, tender moment between the two of them. It hits me, watching the exchange, that they are perhaps closer, more together, than I had anticipated. You do not kiss a person's forehead unless there is love present. I smile at the scene and at the irony of the situation – the first bit of romance my dad has in years and what happens? His daughter moves back in.

'Hello?' I shout, opening the front door, straightening the mat with my foot, vowing to give this place a good vacuum before leaving tomorrow.

'In 'ere,' replies my dad, and I can tell immediately he's already had a few.

'Sorry,' I say. 'Sorry I'm here again. I bet you thought you'd seen the last of me.'

My dad shrugs. 'No bother, love. I expected you'd be bringing the van back at some point. Where did you get to, anyway? I've had Alice on the phone looking for you.'

He has a tumbler in his hand. 'What you drinking?' I ask, avoiding the question.

'Getting through the rest of that brandy,' he says. 'The knees have been bad today.'

Mad Jackie takes away his glass. 'I'll get you a top-up,' she tells him.

Jackie's in her uniform, a length of Tubigrip on her right wrist. She turns to me. 'Joanne said there was some bother?'

'She arrested me,' I reply, yawning. 'Though I wasn't charged with GBH because the solicitor found some CCTV proving I couldn't have caused Eve's injuries. She still had her seatbelt on.' I sit down heavily into the sofa. 'What's happened to your wrist?'

'Sprained it getting a big bugger off the commode.'

I make a face. 'Should you be working if you're injured?'

She laughs. 'No choice. I can't afford to feed myself if I don't.' My dad and Jackie exchange shy glances and, reading between the lines, I'd say it won't be too long before she moves in. 'You look dead beat, love. How about I make you a hot toddy?'

I smile at her gratefully. 'Oh, would you? Perfect. Thank you.'

'Use the cheap stuff for that,' my dad's saying, but Jackie ignores him, waving away his words with her hand, giving him a look as if to say, *Don't be so bloody mean.*

'What about a bite to eat as well?' she offers. 'Bet you've not had nothing all day.'

'No . . . but it's fine, I'll get something in a bit. You shouldn't be waiting on me, Jackie, when you've been on your feet all day looking after others.'

'It's no bother,' she says. 'Anyway, I'm back out again in half an hour. I'm on a late. Just called in to check on your dad.'

'You're going out *again?*' I ask. Goodness, where does this woman get her energy?

She smiles. 'I've got to put two to bed in Windermere, and another out at Crook. One of the new girls has texted in sick . . . she'll not last.'

Jackie disappears to the kitchen and within moments I hear the short stabbing sound of a knife piercing cling film and I wonder which of Jackie's Weight Watcher meals is on the menu. I'm hoping for the salmon and broccoli bake. The microwave pings, there's the sound of the back door opening and closing, and Jackie appears with a tray, on it a steaming hot toddy and a plate of chicken tikka masala. Morris the cat is brushing up against her legs in an attempt to attract her attention.

'There you go, love,' she says, setting down the tray. 'I'll just feed this cat, Kenneth,' she says to my dad, 'then I'm off.'

'What time you back?' he asks.

'Elevenish. Might be a bit earlier. You're sure you want me to cancel Karen tonight?'

My dad nods. 'I'd rather wait for you, my love.'

He says the words 'my love' softly, as if trying them out, seeing how they sound.

'I can help you up the stairs to bed, Dad,' I offer, but he shakes his head.

'You'll be asleep in twenty minutes by the look of you. Jackie can take care of it.'

When Jackie's left we sit in companionable silence. I'm happy to say nothing and Dad's enjoying the respite the brandy is giving from his knee pain. After a while, my eyes drooping, I ask why he's not smoking the discomfort away, as would be his usual way, adding: 'What happened to marijuana as a pain reliever, and all that?' But he tells me he's quit.

'You've given up smoking full stop?' I ask, surprised.

'No . . . just the dope . . . it's not really Jackie's thing,' he says mildly, and I think: Crikey, it *must* be love. I've never known him stop smoking for anyone.

Ready to call it a night, I stand, and he asks me what my plans are for the days ahead. 'Back home tomorrow,' I tell him. 'Then I'm going to make an appointment with a family solicitor and apply for a divorce.'

My dad raises his eyebrows. 'The fight's over, then?' he asks.

'It's over.'

And he nods. 'The only way to come out of this alive,' he says, 'is to move straight through it. There's no point in resisting; you do right to let it go.' He nods again, as if agreeing with his own words. 'Good girl,' he murmurs. 'Good girl, Natty,' and I kiss him goodnight.

After a hot shower it takes me less than a minute to fall asleep.

When I wake, someone is trying to kill me.

32

I'M BEING SMOTHERED. I cannot breathe. As I fight for air, there is a sequence of sharp, knife-like jabs to the skin of my face and neck.

I cry out, desperate.

Please not now. Not now, not like this.

I fight with my hands. Push away the perpetrator and, suddenly, inexplicably, the air floods into my lungs.

But I'm coughing. My mouth and nasal passages are filled with rust and peroxide fumes, and I'm disorientated. I fly from the bed, flicking on the light.

There, on my pillow, is the cat. Which explains my being smothered – so, momentarily, I relax, because no one is trying to kill me after all. It was simply Morris waking me up.

Now, as my eyes adjust to the light, I begin to cough again. And it's then that I see smoke seeping into the room. Violet-tinged smoke, snaking through the gap between the door and the frame. It's acrid-smelling, toxic.

I stare, appalled. It's like something from a bad horror movie. And as I watch, transfixed, my limbs freeze.

I am that person who cannot move even though the ship is sinking. Even though the threat of death is imminent, I am the person immobilized by shock.

My eyes register the danger, but my body does not respond. I feel my conscious mind shutting down, closing in on itself, as if for protection.

I've no idea of the time. Is it morning? Where's Dad? Is Jackie back?

I'm confused, but I'm powerless to do anything about it. My senses are leaving me. Into my mind flutter sepia-toned images of the girls: Alice as a baby, Felicity getting married, Alice *with* a baby . . .

And now I hear crying. Sad, pitiful, strangled-sounding meowing.

Morris.

All at once, I'm lucid. I look around, knowing the second I fully open the door the smoke will billow in and I'll be paralysed by the lack of oxygen. Tentatively, I touch the door handle with my fingertip. It's not hot. No fire outside the door yet.

Christ, what do I do?

Short of a better idea, I push up the window, grab Morris and shove him on to the sill, shouting, 'Help! Help me!' out into the night. It registers somewhere in my brain that there are lighted windows beyond the yard. People are still awake. We have hope of being rescued.

'There's a fire!' I yell, nudging Morris from the sill. He doesn't want to go, so I shove him hard and he screeches, clawing at my arm, but it's only a short drop down on to the roof of the kitchen. I hear a thud and put it out of my mind, because now I'm thinking 999, and start looking frantically for my phone.

That old safety commercial plays in my mind. 'Get out. Call the fire brigade out. Stay out.'

I'll get out when I've got my dad out. Where the hell is my phone?

I close the window, knowing that if it's left wide open then the smoke from the landing will be sucked in here in a split second.

I grab the throw from the end of the bed and put it over my

head like a shroud, pulling the corners across my face, covering my nose and mouth. Then I take the deepest breath I'm able to and open the door.

The smoke hits me at once, forcing me back into the room. Straight away I'm shocked by the denseness of it. It's a wall, impenetrable, almost solid.

I push into the hallway and try to shout, cry out loudly for my dad, but the smoke pushes me back again. It's thick and caustic and I'm completely blinded, enveloped as I am now within it.

I drop to my knees. *Smoke rises*, I'm thinking. Lay low on the floor. Get to Dad.

But I can't.

I start to cry with the realization that I just can't get to him. I don't know where he is. I crawl across the landing towards his bedroom, '*Dad!*' I'm calling, but now I'm hacking and choking. My eyes are streaming, they're raw, and I cannot see my own hands. I can see nothing at all.

Turning around, I make for what I think is the stairs.

And that's when I hear it. The fire is right there at the foot of the staircase, the glow I can sense more than see; it's spreading through the smoke like strobe lighting.

And the heat – the heat is overwhelming.

I suddenly realize the whole house is on fire. The whole fucking house is on fire.

I cannot get past it. I cannot get to my father.

'Dad,' I whimper, overcome now. 'Dad, answer me! Where are you?'

But there is no reply.

33

FROM MY CHAIR in the window I stare blankly out across the lake. This morning the water is a muddy khaki. It reflects the area of thick woodland crowding the opposite shore. Not all the deciduous trees are yet in leaf; some are still bare. The sycamore to the right of our land has just the beginnings of tiny buds; hardly visible unless you're right up close.

The timing of this life cycle catches me unawares every year. I'm surprised by the horse chestnut holding on to its leaves in early December, perplexed now by the hydrangea, still dormant in its winter state into late May. I have in my head – perhaps from childhood TV, I'm not sure – that the leaves fall in October, and the land reawakens in March. But this is not the case here. In Windermere, it happens on its own clock.

House martins return to nest beneath the eaves of the house each spring, and each spring I nag Sean to do something about it. Remove the nest if necessary.

Now I'm grateful he never got around to it. Now I can pass hours – whole days, in fact – watching them dive and swoop. They seem to fly for the sheer pleasure of it.

My dad has gone.

He didn't make it. I got out, and he didn't.

I gaze through the glass, and it's as if time has stopped. I have no sense of anything right now.

I lift my eyes. Focus on the fine haze draping the peaks of

Claife Heights in the distance. In places, the fog merges with the cloud above, giving a sense of two worlds coming together. Those clouds will pass across the lake towards its western edge, droplets of rain will fall against my window and the room will be plunged into shadow.

I am told the fire was his fault. Told it was down to a cigarette falling on to his chair as he snoozed, his senses compromised by the high level of alcohol in his blood as he waited up for Jackie to return.

I am told he didn't stand a chance. That the fumes from the tapestry wingback chair – the chair which I supplied was not fire-resistant, as it turned out – would have overcome him in seconds. Way before he actually . . . No one finishes this sentence.

I'm left to make the leap for myself. The toxic fumes from the sponge-filled cushions would have killed my dad before he realized he was on fire. Before he knew he was burning to death. Before he was cremated inside his own living room.

They tell me that, and I'm supposed to gain comfort. I'm supposed to feel better about the fact that I couldn't get to him. 'Silly old sod,' I can hear people of the village saying. 'Got drunk and set himself on fire, didn't he?' Stupidity like this is not classed as tragedy. He should have known better.

There's a light tap on the bedroom door. 'I do wish you'd eat something, Natty,' says Sean.

I don't face him. 'Thank you, but no. I'm not hungry.'

'Have you taken your medication?' he asks.

Again, without looking, I nod. 'You should go,' I tell him.

'I'll stay.'

Now I do turn around. 'Sean. Go.'

He bows his head a fraction as if to say, *As you wish*, and I hear the sound of soft footsteps on the stairs as he descends.

I have a minor inhalation injury – it's not bad, could have been so much worse – but it is possible that smoke, particularly exposure to burning PVC, may trigger a susceptibility to asthma. So I'm on a course of anti-inflammatories in an attempt to prevent a long-term health issue.

Sean keeps 'popping' in to check on me. He has the look of a whipped dog.

He's so bloody guilty about everything you'd think it was he who had given my dad the chair. Of course, my friend from the nursing home has taken it upon herself to be the real villain in all of this. She is beside herself with remorse. She knew the chair didn't conform to health and safety regulations – that's why it was in the garage, ready to be thrown out.

I've tried telling her it's unlikely my dad would have escaped, regardless, but she's pretty much gone to pieces over it. And, to be frank, I'm too exhausted with my own grief to talk her out of it. The best I can do is tell her: 'You are not to blame,' and leave it up to her whether to believe me or not.

It's the funeral on Tuesday. I'm told it's normal to feel as though you can't face it. Told it will be cathartic, that *I will* get through it, that it's something that has to be done. Still, I don't want to. Because I don't want to feel better. I want to stay like this. I loved my dad fiercely, and I don't want to feel better about his death.

I've not seen Jackie.

That's wrong, I know. She'll be suffering, too, and I know I should see her, try to offer some comfort. That would be the right thing to do. But I can't.

She came to visit me in the hospital, but I sent her away. I don't want to see how my dad's death has affected her. She came into his life late. I've had him for ever. Why should she claim any kind of pity for herself?

And I'd rather not be told by well-meaning fools that I need to be strong for my children. I want to say *Fuck you!* to the world and be left alone. That's what I want.

I hear tyres crunching in the driveway and, ordinarily, I would stand, walk across to the window which looks out over the front of the house, to see who it is. Not today. I'm in my dressing gown and, though there are arrangements to be made regarding the funeral, I am not moving from this room.

The undertaker rang yesterday. Sean dealt with it. He came in asking about coffin style and did I have any preference as to his clothes?

'The undertaker's clothes?' I asked.

'Your dad's,' said Sean softly.

I'd stared at him, my mouth gaping. 'He's charred,' I said. 'My dad's burnt to death, and he wants to know what outfit to dress him in? Has he lost his mind? Get someone else, Sean. That man's clearly an idiot. I don't want him near my dad, you hear me?'

Sean scurried away, telling me he'd resolve the situation, and I was so angry I threw my cup at him. It missed. And I now have a hole in the plasterwork and an arc of tea splashes which I haven't the energy to clean off.

Today I will tell Sean not to come here any more. I'm sick of him tiptoeing around me, walking on eggshells lest I launch at him. He's the only person I allow myself to shout at, so he would be better off not being here. I don't understand why he feels the need to be around anyway. 'You made your choice when you left me,' I told him yesterday evening. 'I don't even know why you keep turning up.'

'Because right now, Natty, you need support. And even though we're not together, I can't go abandoning you after sixteen years of marriage,' he explained.

'Abandoning me? You've already abandoned me. You're just trying to ease your conscience. Go home to Eve. Go home to that bitch . . . she can teach you something about abandonment . . . She's the fucking expert . . .' And I stopped myself before I went any further.

I had made a promise to Sharon, after all. And, as mad as I was about losing my dad, it didn't change that fact.

I hear sounds from the hallway downstairs. An unfamiliar male voice, followed by a woman clearing her throat noisily.

Sean appears. 'Natty, there are some people here to see you.'

'Tell them I'm asleep.'

'I really think you should—'

'Tell whoever it is I've taken a shitload of tranquillizers and you can't wake me up. Tell them that.'

'I can't,' he says.

'Sean,' I say, glaring at him, 'if you weren't here, I wouldn't have answered the door anyway, so what difference does it make?'

'It's the police, Natty. You have to talk to them.'

The anger is rising within me as I hear the sound of feet on the stairs.

How dare the police come around after what's happened. Have they no compassion? Surely, anything to do with the incident between Eve and me can wait until after the funeral?

'Mrs Wainwright, okay if we come in?'

It's DC Aspinall. I scowl and shoot her a look as if to say: *Do I have a choice?*

Behind her, in the doorway, is a short, portly guy with a moustache. He's balding on top and is wearing a Columbo-style mac that's seen better days. He takes one look at the oyster-coloured shagpile carpet and bends down to untie his shoelaces.

'Sorry for your loss,' says DC Aspinall quietly.

I nod by way of acknowledgment.

'This is my colleague, DS Ron Quigley,' she says, gesturing behind her.

And I raise my eyebrows. 'Two detectives?' I say. 'Must be serious.'

'We usually work together,' she explains. 'In pairs.' She pauses as she turns to check on her colleague. 'DS Quigley was away on leave recently, that's why you've not yet had the opportunity to meet.'

DS Quigley raises his head and nods once my way. He's becoming breathless as he removes his shoes, as if this is the first physical activity he's undertaken in years.

'I don't want you to be at all worried by the presence of two detectives, Mrs Wainwright,' says DC Aspinall. 'It's quite rou-tine.'

'Oh, I'm not worried,' I tell her, my tone bitter. 'Just confused.'

'Confused?'

'Yes. As to why you deem it necessary to be here today. Could this not have waited?'

'It couldn't, I'm afraid.'

'You appreciate I'm not in a fit state to go over things with you right now? The funeral's on Tuesday – could you come back when everything's a bit more settled? I really don't see the urgency, since the charges against me have been reduced.'

DC Aspinall doesn't answer, instead she waits on her col-league, who has now removed his shoes and is standing in the doorway in his stockinged feet.

It's warm in here; I have the heating up high. Since I've come out of hospital I feel the cold more – like an old person – and though I've managed to refrain from sitting with a blanket over my knees, I'm sure the room is overly warm for the average person.

Beads of sweat have sprung up across DS Quigley's brow and the top of his head. He's looking kind of awkward, standing there, so I ask if he would like to sit. 'Perhaps over there?' I sug-gest, pointing to the chair in front of the dressing table.

He's apprehensive, as the chair is overtly feminine: pink candy-striped cushions with crimson ribbon piping. It's the chair from the guest room. I switched it when it became obvious that Eve had been sitting in my chair to apply her make-up. And she wrecked all my cosmetics, which Sean says she absolutely *did not*, insisting it must have been Felicity in a fit of rage (the reason for which was not explained). She also managed to smear lotion on the white suede covering of my chair. So of course I had to trash it.

'I'll take my coat off, if you don't mind,' DS Quigley says, dabbing at his forehead with a handkerchief. 'It's pretty hot in here.'

'Mind if I sit on the bed?' asks DC Aspinall.

'Help yourself,' I tell them, giving in to the interview as it slowly dawns on me that they're not going to return in a few days' time to sort out whatever it is they've come here to do.

DC Aspinall perches on the edge of the mattress, as if to sit on it fully would be disrespectful, and she fixes me with a sad smile.

After a moment of silence she says, 'Nice guy, your dad.'

And suddenly I'm knocked for six. All at once my guard has dropped, because I wasn't expecting her to say that. Not sure *what I was* expecting, but a giant wave of emotion surges through me and I'm powerless to stop it.

Trying to hold on to some kind of restraint, I nod furiously in response to her words. 'Yes,' I am trying to say, 'Yes, he was,' but the tears are falling faster than I can wipe them away, and I'm unable to form any coherent sounds. I lift my head to look at her, and my face collapses.

'Hey,' she says, moving quickly from the bed and coming to kneel beside me. 'Hey, it's okay. Don't try to stop it.'

She strokes my arm soothingly. I'm rocking like a child, back and forth, back and forth, as a dam of pent-up grief is released.

Sobbing, I'm able to utter, 'It's all so shit . . . Everything . . . it's all turned to shit.'

'I know,' she says. 'I know it has.'

She stands and strides towards the dressing table, where DS

Quigley holds out the box of tissues for her to take, and then returns to my side. 'Here,' she says. 'Don't try to talk for a minute. Take your time.'

She's got such a kind face. A quiet prettiness that you wouldn't notice on first meeting her. I glance at her hand and, on seeing the absence of a wedding ring, wonder for the first time about this woman's story. Then my thoughts move to her aunt.

'How's Jackie doing?' I ask, blowing my nose.

'Not too good,' she replies.

'She really loved him, huh?'

'It's been hard to watch.'

She holds on to my hand as she speaks. She has a solid grip, and it's comforting. 'This is probably not the best time to bring this up,' she says now, with a certain amount of reluctance, 'but . . . she has the cat.'

'Morris?' I ask, surprised, because I'd been told a neighbour of my dad's had taken him in.

'Jackie can keep him for a short while,' she says, 'but we live in rented accommodation and pets aren't allowed. Jackie wondered if you would be able to have him here.'

'Of course,' I say quietly, thinking how nice it will be to have something of dad's. Everything else was lost in the fire. I have nothing left of his. Aside from a few of my own photographs. Most of the ones of my mother have gone as well. 'Tell Jackie to bring him around whenever's best . . . or I could come and get him. Whichever way, I'd like to see her.'

DC Aspinall tilts her head. 'You're sure?'

'Yes,' I say, a little embarrassed. 'Did she tell you I sent her away from the hospital?'

She nods. 'Jackie understands, though. She can see why it would have been hard for you to see her.'

I take a deep breath in an attempt to settle myself, but there's a sob lingering within my chest and my breath catches as I try to inhale. The linings of the airways are still raw, and I wince as the air fills my lungs.

'I heard you were lucky to get out,' DC Aspinall says.

'Yeah, I heard that, too.'

DC Aspinall pauses at this, looks a little uncomfortable and relaxes her grip. 'That's why we're here, actually,' she says, meeting my gaze.

'You're not here to talk about Eve Dalladay?'

She shakes her head, keeps her tone steady and businesslike. 'The fire . . . it turns out there's evidence of foul play.'

'I don't know what you mean.'

'We need to ask you a few questions, Mrs Wainwright, because it seems as though the fire was started deliberately.'

'No,' I say, pulling my hand out from hers and straightening in my seat. 'It started from a cigarette, my dad, he . . .'

I stop speaking.

DC Aspinall stands. Her face is now clear of emotion, her empathetic demeanour gone.

'There have been small traces of solvent found,' she reports, withdrawing a notepad from her jacket pocket as I stare at her, speechless. 'It's most likely to be lighter fluid, but as yet the result is inconclusive. But they were found on his chair.'

34

'So you're saying you think it was me?' I cry to DC Aspinall, as I jump up from my seat. 'You think I murdered my own father?'

They are speaking, asking questions about my whereabouts that night, but I can't hear them any more. My head feels like it is going to explode. I can't believe someone has done this on purpose. Why would they? I don't understand.

'You think I killed him?' I cry again. 'Why? Why would I do that? *Tell me!*'

'Mrs Wainwright, calm down.'

'No, I won't calm down.' My nose is running, and I'm spitting phlegm as I speak. 'And what was all that about a minute ago? The pretend sympathy? All that rubbish and you accuse me of setting him on fire? You stupid woman,' I sob. 'There's no way on earth I'd hurt him,' I say putting my hands over my face.

I move to the corner, shaking. I can't stand to hear what they are saying. I feel trapped. I need to get out.

'Mrs Wainwright,' DS Quigley says, 'you really need to calm yourself so we can talk.'

'What are you going to do? Take me to the station, like last time? What a charade that turned out to be.' I swing around to face DC Aspinall. 'I think you've already displayed a high level of incompetence, Detective. I don't see any reason why this should be any different.'

Someone has killed my dad. Someone has deliberately killed my dad.

DC Aspinall shrugs as if to suggest my accusation has no grounds. 'I act on the information I'm given,' she says steadily. 'Any officer would have arrested a person under those circumstances. And, by that, I mean a repeat offender.'

'But I didn't *do anything*,' I cry out.

She throws DS Quigley a look of quiet exasperation and refrains from challenging me further. We both know that I did do something. I rammed Eve's car repeatedly. But I did not injure her.

At that moment, Sean comes in. He's heard the commotion and bounded up the stairs and is now standing in the doorway surveying the scene. I am a few feet away from him. He looks between the three of us, unsure of what to do.

Fixing his eyes on DC Aspinall, he asks, 'What's happened? What's going on?'

I don't give her time to answer. 'They're saying I murdered Dad.'

'What?' he says.

DC Aspinall sighs out heavily. 'That's not what was said, Mrs Wainwright, and you know it. Not once have you been accused of murdering your father.'

'So why are you asking me where I was? Why are you asking me what I was doing?'

'Because we're trying to build up a picture of what happened in the few hours leading up to the fire. And for that we need your cooperation. If you're unwilling to reveal your whereabouts in the hours before the fire, that leaves us with a problem. If we can't check out an alibi, Mrs Wainwright, then that person automatically becomes a possible suspect. Simple as that.'

I cast a look towards Sean. His brow is furrowed as he most

likely tries to work out why I would not mention travelling to Bolton. He's trying to fathom what the big deal is – why not just say it?

I told Sharon Boydell I would never reveal the truth about Eve's son, and now both DC Aspinall and DS Quigley are suspicious. They are pressing me to talk.

Eventually, I drop my shoulders. 'I went looking for information on Eve,' I say quietly. 'I travelled to the school of Psychological Sciences at Manchester University. A number of people saw me. They'll be able to tell you I was there.'

'Anywhere else?' asks DS Quigley.

'Then I went in search of Eve's family.' I glance at Sean. By his expression, I'd say he thinks I've lost my mind. 'I talked to her grandmother,' I say, 'and she'd not seen Eve for years. I came home and, as you know, I went to bed. When I woke up the place was on fire.'

'That's it?' asks DC Aspinall.

'That's it.'

Sean walks towards me slowly. When he is in front of me, he rests his hands on my shoulders, holds me at arm's length, and regards me with a desperately sad expression.

'What is it?' I whisper.

He leans in and places a soft kiss on my forehead. 'I'm so sorry, Natty,' he says, before touching my cheek with his fingertips. Then he kisses my brow again, as though to quiet me.

'Sorry?' I ask.

'For everything,' he replies.

'Oh, get the fuck off, Sean,' I snap, and push him away.

DS Ron Quigley decided that, since it was his first day back on the job, he would treat Joanne to lunch.

'Your choice,' he says to her, as she drives, 'but I want more than a sandwich or a thin piece of quiche.'

Joanne picks out her favourite coffee house in Windermere. The food is excellent and the atmosphere informal. Joanne can get something light – she can't manage a huge meal at lunchtime, falls asleep at her desk if she does – and the menu also caters well for the likes of Ron. He's a man's man who requires a proper feed at midday.

Joanne tells the waitress she'll have the goat's cheese-filled field mushroom and smiles to herself as Ron orders the braised pig's cheek *and* the boeuf bourguignon. 'Hungry, are you?' she says, and he replies, 'Always, love.'

'Would you like the *escargots* with the beef?' the young waitress asks him, and he looks at her, unsure.

'Would I like what?'

'Snails,' she says. 'The beef bourguignon comes with a serving of *escargots* on the side.'

Ron stares at her, baffled, shakes his head as if she's asked would he like a side order of rats. 'Why would I want snails?' he says. 'Second thoughts, don't answer that. What beers have you got?'

Joanne grabs a copy of that day's *Gazette* from the next table and flicks through the headlines. Very little happens around here. This week's stories are low-key – 'Motorcyclist injured on wet road'; 'Man exposes himself in Kendal'; 'Farming union angry after Chinese lantern decision'. This arson and murder case will be big news in next week's paper.

'So, that was a bit of a spectacle,' Ron says.

Joanne closes the paper, folds it in half and passes it to an elderly woman nursing a pot of tea to her left. 'Mrs Wainwright can get quite animated,' she says, 'but we just revealed her dad was probably murdered, Ron. She's not going to take it on the chin, is she?'

'Suppose not,' he concedes. 'Do you think she did it?'

'Unlikely.'

278

'So why didn't she come clean about where she was beforehand?'

'Sounds as if she was up to something. But like she said, what's the motive? I can't see one. Problem is, because of her previous run-ins, she'll need to be formally questioned. She won't see it that way though . . . as far as she's concerned, she's innocent of all charges.'

'Mrs Wainwright didn't ask the one obvious question.'

'What?' asks Joanne. 'You mean, if *she* didn't murder him, then who did?'

'I was thinking more along the lines of why would anyone want to murder Ken Odell at all?'

'You think it hasn't yet occurred to her that the fire could've been meant for her?'

Ron nods grimly. 'I wouldn't want to be in the same room as her when she figures that one out.'

The waitress brings their drinks. Joanne's having water and Ron's ordered a bottle of beer – something dark and velvety with a silly-sounding name. What is it with breweries today? When did dark ale, pale ale, Yorkshire bitter, suddenly require ridiculous titles?

Ron pours out the liquid carefully, savouring it, and then takes three huge swallows, downing half the pint in one go.

'Looks strong,' Joanne comments.

'This?' he says innocently. 'Nah, it's driving bitter this, Joanne. Only four per cent.' The creamy head covers Ron's moustache. 'You could drink this all night and you'd be clear as a bell the following morning. It's the additives that give you the headache.'

'Is that right?' Joanne says, smiling, shaking her head.

Ron downs the rest of his beer and sighs contentedly. 'What's your best guess, then?' he asks after a moment.

'You mean about the fire?' she says, and Ron nods. 'I think we ought to start with house-to-house, see who's seen what. It can't have been straightforward to gain access, get a fire going with Ken Odell sitting there in the chair and get out again unseen.'

'Not straightforward,' says Ron, 'but he was drunk, so not totally impossible either.'

Joanne agrees. 'The real question is who'd want to kill him? And if not him, who'd want to kill *her*?'

35

JOANNE FORCES DOWN a slice of apple and almond cake, and Ron just about manages another pint before they finish up and set out to begin their enquiries. Usually, they'd get the uniforms to cover the house-to-house, but after a quick call to DI McAleese, it's decided that since it's quiet at the station and they're already in the area they may as well make a start.

The afternoon is brightening up nicely as they make their way back to the car, and Ron asks Joanne to hold his jacket while he rolls up his sleeves, neatly and evenly. Odd that he's so meticulous about this, thinks Joanne, when he's oblivious to the red-wine sauce splashed down his tie. They climb inside the Mondeo and Joanne hands him a tissue to clean himself off.

'So then, where d'you want to go first?' Ron asks. 'Queens Drive? Or have you got someone specific in mind for questioning?'

'Queens Drive. Let's start with the neighbours,' she says. 'I need to do a bit of research before I act on this thing that's gnawing at me. I want to be better prepared. I'll get on to it when we go back to Kendal, after we've finished up here.'

Ron puts on his seatbelt and squints into the sun before dropping down his visor. 'You're the boss,' he says, and Joanne smiles. Ron is senior to Joanne not only in rank but in his wealth of experience; he's been a detective for getting on close to thirty years. 'You planning on sharing this gut feeling, or am I supposed to guess?'

'Guess away,' Joanne says, and slips the car into gear, pulling out into the slow line of traffic heading to Bowness. The closer they get to summer, the busier this stretch of road becomes with people making their way towards the lake.

There's a short blast of wind and the cherry blossoms quiver. In the space of a second Joanne's windscreen is awash with baby-pink petals, their edges tinged brown, and she uses her wipers to clear them away. Her mind is cast back to childhood, when she would walk along here, gathering flowers in the upturned fold of her T-shirt, ready to make perfume when she got home. Her mother would discover the long-forgotten fetid mess a few weeks later, on a shelf in Joanne's wardrobe, and reprimand her daughter for giving her extra work to do – on top of everything else.

They don't have far to go to reach Queens Drive, but the traffic is stop–start, stop–start. There's a driver in front who is reluctant to overtake the run of stationary cars parked on the left, so they find themselves waiting for him to drum up the courage to pull out.

Ron tuts impatiently. He turns to Joanne, rolling his eyes, and Joanne can smell the sweet, yeasty odour of his breath. 'Why don't you take a left down Brook Road,' he says, 'and go the long way? We'll be here all day if we've got to wait for this joker,' and he leans across and presses hard on the horn, sounding it for a full three seconds.

The driver in front is startled and stares at Joanne in his rear-view mirror as if he's about to cry.

'Jesus, Ron,' she says. 'I hate it when you do that. Look at the poor guy, he's nearly eighty. And now he thinks it's me who's beeping at him.'

Ron shrugs. 'Shouldn't be on the road.'

'You'll be like that one day,' Joanne mutters, and Ron reaches across again, about to give the horn another blast, when she slaps his hand. 'Stop it, Ron, or I'll make you walk.'

There's a period of quiet, which Ron punctuates with impatient sighs, and Joanne switches off, letting her thoughts drift to Eve Dalladay. Could it be possible that she is the one who started the fire? Joanne has found some of Natty Wainwright's behaviour rather extreme, but for the first time she wonders just what the woman has been up against.

If Joanne weren't dealing with the aftermath of the fire, she'd be following up on the possibly self-inflicted injuries of Mrs Dalladay. Perhaps that was the place to start. Perhaps she needed to—

'What you going to do about the DI then?' Ron asks out of nowhere. His voice has a sing-song quality to it, and Joanne is immediately suspicious.

'McAleese?' she replies. 'What do you mean? What am I going to do about what?'

She turns to Ron, but he's not looking at her. He has his eyes fixed forwards, but he's grinning broadly.

'Ron?'

'Oh, nothing,' he says innocently.

'Has something been said?'

'I must have got it wrong.'

'Got what wrong? Have I missed something?' Joanne's a bit rattled. She feels quite hot. Reaching forward, she turns on the air con. 'McAleese has been offhand with me for weeks,' she says. 'Are you privy to something I'm not?'

'He's getting divorced, you know.'

''Course I know. I've not been living under a rock. Is he dissatisfied with my work?'

Ron snorts. Turning to her, he says, 'Is *that* what you think?'

'No, that's not what I think, I haven't done any unsatisfactory work . . . but I don't know why else he should have a problem with me. Other than, you know, messing him about taking some time off for the operation that never was. But it's not as if I could do a lot about it.'

'Joanne,' Ron says, his tone serious now, 'it's not that.'

'Oh,' she says. 'Oh, okay. Good,' and she pulls a left into Queens Drive. She finds a spot around thirty yards along on the left.

Ron is shaking his head, mumbling, 'Call yourself a detective,' and Joanne shoots him an angry stare because, if he knows something, she'd rather he just came right out and said it.

They walk down the street, first stopping to survey the fire damage to the house directly opposite.

'What a mess,' comments Ron, and Joanne murmurs in agreement. 'Don't suppose there's much point dusting for prints.'

What was once a pleasant Lakeland stone semi-detached is now a gutted black shell. The slate roof is gone, and there are only two or three remaining rafters, the rest having been completely destroyed in the fire. The house next door has not come off too badly – part of the roof is damaged and the top windows will need replacing. Other than that, it's mostly cosmetic, thinks Joanne, the whole thing being covered in thick black soot – though she has heard that water damage can be a real headache to fix.

Joanne and Ron watch as a team of men go about erecting a scaffold against the gable end, ready for the repairs. And they're about to cross the street when a voice from behind makes them stop. 'That's what you get if you go mixing cigarettes and alcohol,' the voice says.

Joanne is in the process of taking out her notepad. She turns and nods hello to the woman on the other side of the wall. 'It was a dropped cigarette that caused all that damage, you know,' the woman says, her tone snippy and critical.

'So we've heard,' replies Joanne. 'Did you know Mr Odell?'

The woman winces, retracts her chin, before reaching to pick up a set of hedge shears. 'Only in passing,' she says, but Ron senses there's a history there, as he raises his eyebrows at Joanne.

The woman is early seventies, heavy in the rump, with thick ankles – the type of ankles that come about from water reten-tion. Joanne imagines poking her index finger in, watching as the doughy flesh envelops it right up to the knuckle. The woman takes a few steps and leans in. 'Who are you, then?' she asks. 'Are you from the insurance?'

'We're police officers,' answers Ron.

The woman views them sceptically. 'You don't look like police.'

'That's because we're undercover,' he says, and Joanne gives his foot a nudge with the toe of her shoe. 'Be*have*,' she mouths silently.

The woman starts clipping her box hedge, frowning each time the blades make contact. 'Rain's on its way,' she tells them. 'I need to get this done.'

'Are you okay to answer a few of our questions?' Joanne asks, and the woman pauses.

'If you show me your badges. For all I know, you could be reporters, and I don't want to be quoted saying something I've not.'

Ron and Joanne present their warrant badges, and it's obvious, to Joanne at least, that this woman cannot see anything without her reading glasses.

'Seem to be in order,' she says officiously. 'What would you like to know?'

Ron glances at Ken Odell's burnt-out house, and back to the woman. He does this twice. 'It's not possible for you to see the road from your front window, is it?' he says. 'This hedge must block your view.'

'No,' she says, and Joanne's already mentally moving on to the next house, 'but I can from up there,' and she motions to the window directly above the door. 'That's my sewing room. I sit in there most evenings, the light's better. And my husband likes to have the TV loud, which has been bothering me of late.'

'Were you at home the night of the fire?' Joanne asks.

'I was.'

'And can you remember anything in particular, anything out of the ordinary, happening that night?'

'Always a lot of comings and goings over there,' she says, in a way to suggest she doesn't approve. 'A lot of women, at all times of the night.'

Joanne clears her throat. 'I do believe that Mr Odell had surgery. I'm told those women were there to help care for him, to help him dress and undress. Is that what you're referring to?'

'Hmm,' she says, and puts her shears down by her feet. 'If you say so. But they're a real bunch of undesirables, that's for certain. One in particular is always here, and she's such an overbearing woman, such a loud-mouthed, uncouth—'

'Did you see anyone *other* than the carers?' Ron jumps in quickly, sparing Joanne from what are clearly denigrating remarks about her Aunt Jackie.

'I saw his daughter,' she says. 'She was here.'

'Mrs Wainwright?'

'Yes. She never lets on to me,' the woman says. 'She can be terribly rude. I don't know why, I've known her since she was so high,' and she holds out her hand to her side, palm down. 'I think it's on account of losing her mother at an impressionable age. Kenneth Odell's never seen fit to teach the girl proper manners.'

Ron shifts his weight from one foot to the other, which

Joanne reads as: let's tie this one up fast as we can, and then the woman says, 'Of course, you do know he's a drug addict?'

Ron coughs. 'Who is?' he asks, smirking. 'Ken Odell?'

The woman crosses her arms and nods repeatedly.

Just then, the front door opens behind her. Out comes an old guy in a shirt and tie, blue blazer, pressed trousers and polished shoes. On his head he wears a white summer fedora with a small feather. He makes his way along the short path, unsteadily, and Joanne and Ron smile in his direction by way of a greeting. Joanne's expecting him to stop, speak to his wife – perhaps she'll fill him in on why they're here. Perhaps he'll want to offer his own information, as people often do. But he doesn't. He tips his hat their way, scowls meanly at his wife and continues on, doing a right out of the driveway, making for the main road.

Ron turns to Joanne and winks.

'I'll tell you one thing,' says the woman, watching him go. 'I won't miss Kenneth Odell's cat using this garden as its toilet . . . No,' she says, with a firm shake of her head, 'I won't miss that at all.'

A short while later, and Joanne and Ron have moved out of earshot, stopping outside the house next door but one. Ron dabs the beads of sweat from his forehead. 'So,' he says, eyes glinting, full of mischief, 'Ken Odell's a drug addict then?'

'He smoked a bit of weed now and then,' she explains mildly. 'Jackie told me about it because she was worried he was breaking the law. She reckoned she'd given him an ultimatum.'

'What?' says Ron. 'As in, "It's me or the drugs"?'

'Something like that.'

They decide to work separately, Joanne taking the even-numbered houses, Ron the odd, and have just parted company when Joanne spots the elderly guy in the fedora heading back her way. He's carrying a small white paper bag in his left hand and stops momentarily to catch his breath, holding on to a lamp post with his right. Joanne seizes her chance to talk to him and walks over quickly.

'Been for your prescriptions?' she asks him pleasantly, and his hand moves instinctively to his chest. 'Angina,' he answers.

'I'm DC Aspinall,' she begins, about to explain what she's doing here, when he cuts her off.

'I know who you are, dear. You won't remember, but I was once secretary of the Neighbourhood Watch. We spoke a couple of times back in the day when you were a young WPC.'

'I *do* remember,' smiles Joanne. 'Mr ... Mr ...' and she searches for his name.

'Jerry Gasnier.'

'Yes, of course. Didn't recognize you in the hat.'

'I also used to do a spot of cricket umpiring,' he explains. 'Anyway, what can I do for you, my dear? Is this about the fire? I see you've spoken to Marion.'

'We're just having an informal chat really, with all the neighbours, wondering if anyone saw anything untoward. If someone was seen hanging around the property that wouldn't ordinarily be there?'

He lifts his eyes skyward as he tries to retrieve the memory.

'It had been raining earlier that evening, if that helps remind you,' Joanne says.

He glances to see if she's serious, and when he realizes she's not, gives her a playful pat on the arm. 'Ah, well that does narrow it down for me, thank you.'

'Your wife mentioned there have been a lot of people in and out of the house of late, and it was difficult for her to recall anyone in particular that might have—'

'Marion used to get very upset when Ken Odell parked his Transit in her line of sight,' he says. 'They had numerous bust-ups over the years and, as I think you probably worked out for yourself, there's very little love lost between them. Don't let her cloud your judgement of the man . . . if that's what's going on here. You are investigating his death as suspicious, are you not?'

'We are,' confirms Joanne softly.

'Well then, he was a wonderful man and an excellent neighbour. Marion's not aware of this, but he got our boiler going again more than once . . . she wouldn't have him in the house, so I had to smuggle him in via the utility, when she was locked away upstairs. He is greatly missed by all but Marion, I can tell you.'

Joanne waits as Jerry Gasnier takes a moment of reflection.

'There *was* one thing,' he adds. 'A person who *did* seem a little out of place. I can't remember if it was the night of the fire or earlier, so this might be leading you up completely the wrong path, as it were.'

'That's okay. Anything you can remember is useful.'

'A rather attractive leggy blonde.'

'At Ken's?' she asks.

'I'm not sure. I was bringing out the recycling boxes, it was late . . . I was crouched by the gate, and I *had* assumed she had come from the other house next to Ken's. Didn't look like his usual type of visitor, if you know what I mean, so I made the assumption she'd been visiting Susannah. But I suppose, now that I think about it, she *could* have been at Ken's.'

Joanne writes this down. 'That would have been around what time?'

'Oh, ten at the earliest.'

'Would you be willing to identify this woman if necessary?'

'Certainly, dear.'

'Thank you Mr Gasnier, that's—'

'Jerry, please.'

'Can I give you my card, Jerry? Anything else you remember,

you can give me a call on that number there. Whenever's convenient.'

He takes the card and bids her goodbye, walking the last few remaining paces back to his home.

As Joanne watches him go, she thinks: 'Leggy blonde?' and feels the stirrings of something in her stomach.

36

I HAVE IN MY head a physics experiment. The doddery, bespectacled teacher is stretching a thin piece of copper wire between two points. We're not studying, as one might assume, the properties of various conductors, though, we're studying elasticity. Hooke's Law. The teacher turns a ratchet and we watch as the wire gets thinner and thinner. We are looking for the point at which the wire loses its elasticity and becomes what's known as plastic. This is referred to as the elastic limit or yield point. The material will not spring back to its original shape. It's the point of no return. Things will never be the same again.

I am at this point.

I have reached my limit.

The girls will be home from school in an hour and I'm faced with the task of telling them that there won't be a funeral on Tuesday. Dad's body is now the property of the coroner and we won't have a funeral until – well, I have no idea when.

How do I tell them he was murdered?

Don't. Keep it to yourself.

I did think of that. I thought: Let's make absolutely sure before we put them through further upset. But then I realized they'll find out within a matter of minutes of being home anyhow. They'll be at their laptops, seeing it for themselves. How many times have they said, 'Yeah, we already *know*. Someone put it on Facebook.'

I didn't *know anything* as a child. Wasn't privy to any adult business. My dad watched the news while I did something else. I was kept in blissful ignorance of the world's troubles and I wonder now if the outrage, sadness, helplessness I feel upon hearing news bulletins will not be the same for my children. Have they become so heavily saturated at such a young age that they will grow up to be weary and apathetic? And, if so, will they adopt the attitude of: What's the use in becoming distressed over things we can't change?

I have my head in my hands as I rehearse what I need to say. Sean offered to do it, but I couldn't stand the sight of him here any longer so I asked him to get out. He told me my anger at this was good. Told me I should harness it, turning it into strength, so I could be there for the girls, that it was much better to feel rage rather than grief, that I should—

I told him if he continued trying to find one positive in any of this, I would stab him in the fucking eye.

The doorbell rings.

I ignore it.

It rings again.

I ignore it.

A moment later there's the sound of a key tapping on the glass and I turn, eyes bleary, neck like it's caught in a vice, to see Mad Jackie at the kitchen window.

I beckon her in as I mouth: 'The door's open.' And, seconds later, she's inside, her arms around me, as we cry together into one another's hair.

'I thought you were bringing the cat,' I sob, when eventually we pull apart.

'I've not been home yet,' she explains, 'I came straight from Crook when I got the call from our Joanne about the . . .' Jackie pauses here, can't bring herself to say the word 'murder'. Eventually settles on . . . ' "development". Our Joanne says 'cause of the development, we've all got to present ourselves at Kendal police station sometime in the next forty-eight hours for questioning.'

I stare at her. 'Who?'

'All the care staff.'

'You're suspects?'

'It wasn't an accident, Natty,' and her voice catches in her throat. 'They need to talk to anyone who had any kind of link to the house, and to your dad.'

She pauses as the gravity of what we're facing settles on us both. There will be an investigation, a trial. Christ, I'm going to have to go to court at some point and face the person who did this to us.

'I'll bring Morris by in an hour or so, if that's okay with you,' Jackie says softly. 'Sorry we can't keep him.'

'That's fine,' I tell her. 'I want to have him.'

'Oak Street's not really a place for a cat like Morris,' she smiles. 'I've had to give him a litter tray – there's not a whole lot of soil about, it's mostly yards and decking. I think he might have had a bit of a scrap when he first came as well – he's not really keen on going out now. Be much better for him here, where there's plenty of space.'

'Thank you. Thanks for taking him . . . and, Jackie, I'm sorry I didn't want to see you at the hospital. It was wrong of me, I just didn't feel—'

Jackie lifts her hand. 'Not necessary,' she says. And it's only then I notice she's still wearing the Tubigrip. It's really grotty now. The hole she's cut for her thumb has widened and the top edge is fraying madly.

'How's the hand?' I ask.

'Oh, it'll be better in a couple of days.'

'Have you had it looked at?'

'No need. It's not that bad. I'm only wearing this so I get a bit of sympathy. Gives people something to talk about rather than going on about the fire . . . and your dad. Gets 'em talking about their own ailments. Not that they need a lot of encouragement.'

I smile. Check my watch. 'The girls will be in soon. I've got to tell them what's happened.'

'No easy way to do that. Probably best just to come straight out with it.'

I nod. 'But how? How do I say "Someone tried to kill your grandad?"'

Jackie takes a step back, tilts her head to one side then shocks me into silence.

'What makes you think it was your dad they were after?' she asks.

Joanne and Ron are on their way back to Kendal. They finished up with the house-to-house after it became clear there was nothing more to be gained.

Television crime dramas are for ever depicting people as purposely withholding information from the police. They all have a secret to hide. They will either close up, grow defensive and shifty, refusing to talk, or else they'll become verbally abusive before walking out of shot, scowling menacingly.

If only it was really like that, Joanne muses, as she drops down into third gear, pulling out to overtake a tractor with a trailer-load of sheep. They'd questioned six people this afternoon before throwing in the towel, and even though each knew nothing, had absolutely nothing useful to say, it didn't stop them from trying their hardest to be of some assistance, speculating, racking their brains for the tiniest scrap of information. To the extent that Joanne's now completely out of business cards – the cards she places in the hands of folk to end the conversation politely. *Anything else you can remember, anything at all . . .*

Joanne's not given up hoping that one day, perhaps one day

soon, a suspect *will* grimace, maybe even swear at her, before hotfooting it over a nearby fence. That'd make a nice change, she thinks.

'Why are you driving this way?' Ron asks as they pass the trailer. The sheep have their heads stuck between the bars. It's common knowledge there's a small slaughterhouse further along the Lyth Valley which the local farmers use, and Ron makes an 'Aaw' kind of sound as they draw level. 'Bet they think they're off to Blackpool for a nice day out,' he says. Then he repeats, 'Why are you driving this way, Joanne?'

'I want to check on something before we leave Bowness.'

Joanne swings a right into the gateway of Lakeshore Lodge Hotel, follows the horseshoe driveway around and pulls up outside the grand front entrance. She tells Ron to stay where he is, and he does so without argument, flicking on the radio to listen to the cricket while he's got the chance. The gardener raises his head from the front flower bed and is about to ask Joanne to move over to the car park when he recognizes her. 'I'll only be a minute,' she shouts to him, and he nods, continuing on with his task.

The entrance is awash with blooms, hanging baskets everywhere, pots overflowing with all kinds of plants Joanne doesn't know the names of. Nor does she care to. She spots a fat chef, Formula-1-flag black and white chequered trousers, cigarette between his thumb and forefinger, Marlon Brando-style. Joanne knows he wouldn't be out front smoking if Natty Wainwright were still on the premises.

She heads to reception and flicks the bell on the front desk. Within seconds, a thin, gaunt man emerges from a rear office and greets her. 'Good afternoon, Madam.'

She flashes her warrant badge and the man is startled momentarily but tries to hide it, recovering quickly enough to say, 'I am Raymond, the general manager, how may I be of assistance to you?'

He has an accent, something Eastern European, and a barber's haircut. The kind you don't tend to see any more. Short back and sides, greased into place with shiny pomade.

'Hello, Raymond,' Joanne smiles. 'I'm looking for Dr Eve Dalladay. She wouldn't happen to be here, would she?'

'Ah,' he says, 'let me think. She was here this morning for short time, but now I am remembering she depart. With Mr Wainwright.'

'Oh, that's a shame. I really needed the registration number of her car. Where are they staying right now? Do you have an address for them?'

'No need,' he says. 'Her car is outside. The small Audi, yes?'

'That's right.'

'Is in car park. Mr Wainwright is driving . . . the Maserati – how do you say? – is—'

'In for repair?'

He nods his head gravely. 'Is much damage. If you like, I will find Mr Wainwright?'

'Thank you, Raymond, but no. Maybe later.'

And with that she leaves.

'Call that number in, will you, Ron?' Joanne says, handing him her notepad with the car registration on it. She gives a quick wave to the gardener and pulls away, her brain alive with possibilities. She visualizes a telephone exchange. A round-hipped 50s secretary making connections, pulling out wires and slotting them elsewhere.

At the moment there can be many different outcomes, and Joanne's thinking them through individually, preparing for each alternative conclusion. Whatever happens, though, she needs to head back to the station right away, as she can't get what she needs over the phone. So she puts her foot down, wheels spinning on to the road, and Ron, the phone pressed to his ear, is thrown sideways.

As they pass Windermere Golf Club Ron tells her, 'The car's registered in the name of a Mr Cameron Cox,' and he raises his eyebrows as if to say: *Mean anything to you?*

'At Kirkby Lonsdale?' Joanne asks.

'Yeah,' he replies. 'How did you know that?'

'Lucky guess. He blew his brains out with a shotgun, remember?'

'Yeah,' Ron says, 'I remember. Wife said he'd been having an affair.'

'She told us the mistress in question had cleaned out his bank accounts and scarpered . . . but there was nothing for us to go on. I got the feeling at the time he'd probably been cooking the books, sensed there was a big pile of undeclared cash gone missing as well. But Mrs Cox didn't want us looking at it too closely, in case she had the Inland Revenue breathing down her neck.'

'Sounds about right. So,' Ron says, lowering his window to let some air in, 'you think maybe you've found this mystery mistress then?'

It is perhaps just as well that handguns are illegal in the UK.

Because if I had access to one, if I had it hidden in the wardrobe, kept it in a box beneath the bed – in case an intruder should break in during the night – I'd have already taken that gun and put it to Eve's head. I'd have blown her pretty skull wide open in front of whoever happened to be nearby. Probably blown apart her stomach, took her kneecaps off, too, while I was at it.

As it is, I'm wandering around the house, picking up objects.

I pull out the Honyaki knife from its case and examine the steel. I paid a lot for this knife. It's a chef's knife. It cuts through steak like butter and, as I hold it in my hand, feeling the weight of it, I can almost hear the sound it will make on leaving Eve's chest. It's the sound of a child slurping warm tea. The rush of air across a wet surface.

I won't need to stab her over and over. No, there'll be no bloodbath. With my rudimentary anatomical knowledge, I should be able to do it cleanly. One well-placed cut, at a depth of around an inch, and I will pierce the left ventricle.

I pull a hair from my head. Dangle it high in the air between the fingers of my left hand and, with my right, I flick the blade across it swiftly. Watching as the lower portion drifts down towards the floor. This is how to test a knife.

I repeat the process to be sure.

Then I move to the laundry room. I pick up the Victorian iron we use as a doorstop. It's heavy, black, it's the kind of iron your great-grandmother would have heated on the fire, the kind you might want to bludgeon a person to death with, should you feel the need.

The door swings shut, and behind it I see Felicity's hockey stick. She's wrapped tape around the shaft for a better grip, and I consider the possibilities. I place my weapons gently on the drainer next to the sink. It's the sink I use for soaking grass-stained socks and bloodied knickers, for bleaching my kitchen cloths. It's the sink where Sean once polished his shoes, where he used to whiten the girls' trainers for tennis, where I re-pot my plants when they outgrow their containers.

I pick up the stick – it's heavier than I remember – and I stand with my back against the worktop, holding it like a golf club. Swinging it high over my right shoulder, as I did once in my pre-vious life, but this time I bring it down low. I'm imagining it's Eve's head on the tee, and for some reason this makes me smile. Just before the wood connects, she pleads for her life, and again I laugh.

Now I think about our friendship. About what a joke it really is. I loosen my knees, squatting slightly, line up the hockey stick ready for another swing. If you didn't already know it, you can count up your real friends on the fingers of one hand. Everyone aside from these people are mere acquaintances. Not to be relied on in a crisis. Nowhere to be found when you really need them.

Eve was my friend. Not a childhood friend, and this allowed her to create a whole new history for herself that I never thought to question.

Eve took my husband and killed my father.

Now I shall kill her.

37

I T'S MID-AFTERNOON, AND Joanne sits at her computer, her brow puckered in puzzlement. The sun is streaming through the windows, emphasizing the streaks and filth on the glass, hampering Joanne's ability to read the screen. She gets up, adjusts the vertical blinds, but still has to hold a folder over the computer to decipher the text.

There is absolutely nothing to be found on this woman, Dr Eve Dalladay. She has no National Insurance number, no NHS number, no cars registered in her name, no address, no criminal record, no driving convictions, no record of employment.

On the desk are the transcribed notes of the interview Joanne conducted with Natty Wainwright, from the day she rammed Eve Dalladay in her car. It's pretty clear to Joanne now that the name Eve Dalladay is an alias, perhaps even one of a number of aliases used by Eve, and she could kick herself for not checking her out earlier.

She lifts her head. 'We need to get back to Windermere, Ron,' she says grimly. 'Come and have a look at this.'

Ron goes to stand, grimacing as his knees crunch, and makes his way around to her side of the desk. 'What is it?'

'Eve Dalladay is a ghost,' she says. 'According to this, she doesn't exist.'

Ron considers her words. Not one to get giddy over nothing,

300

he says, 'So, she's given them a false name,' and he shrugs, returning to his chair.

'Well, there's that,' Joanne goes on, 'and the fact she's driving around a dead man's car. Without insurance.' Cameron Cox's car was still registered in his name and to his address in Kirkby Lonsdale.

Ron leans back in his seat and puts his hands behind his head. 'I take it you're assuming this woman is linked to the death of Kenneth Odell, Joanne, because *that is* the case we're working on, isn't it?'

'Of course.'

'So you have a witness who can place Eve Dalladay at Ken's house at the time of the fire?' he asks.

Joanne calls to mind Jerry Gasnier's description of Eve – a leggy blonde – and says to Ron, 'Kind of.'

'Kind of yes, or kind of no?'

'Kind of no. But I'll be able to get a positive ID *at some point*,' she says confidently.

Ron picks up his pen and goes back to work.

'Okay, Ron, look . . . a leap of faith required here,' she says. 'I've got nothing concrete as yet, but there is motive. Maybe Natty Wainwright discovered some dirt on Eve Dalladay, found out something in her past that she's not supposed to know. Maybe that Eve Dalladay *doesn't actually exist*. That's enough of a motive right there for Eve to want to kill her.'

'Not enough to bring her in on a murder charge, though, Joanne, you know that. See what else you can dig up.'

In the transcript Natty Wainwright was recorded as saying that Eve's maiden name was Eve Boydell, so Joanne resumes her search there. It's a common enough name: the database retrieves numerous Eve Boydells with charges against them. It's going to take her an age to sift through them all, Joanne thinks, as she scans the cases, hoping something will jump out at her.

At this point DC Colin Cunningham walks into the office, a little out of breath. 'Joanne,' he says, 'Colette from admin needs to talk to you. Pop down there when you've got a second, will you? She needs to sort out your hours.'

'Thanks, Colin. I'll have to do it tomorrow.'

'Do it now if I were you,' he warns. 'There's a glitch on the payroll. Your wages might not be paid in . . . there's a few people playing hell about it now.'

Joanne heaves a heavy sigh. If her wages aren't deposited into her account, she's screwed. Her rent is transferred on Monday and she's not had Jackie's share of it yet. Jackie's short this month on account of paying two hundred pounds to the vet after Ken Odell's cat needed stitching up. And she won't ask Natty Wainwright for the money – said it wouldn't be right.

Joanne is pushing her chair out from her desk when something catches her eye.

Holland Park. London.

It's the only notably affluent address the database has connected to the name of Eve Boydell. Joanne moves closer to the monitor and clicks on the link, opening the file.

It's a staged suicide. Another suicide, thinks Joanne. They seem to be following Eve Dalladay about.

Jilly Bernstein was found by her eleven-year-old daughter after having, supposedly, cut her own throat in the bath. Eve Boydell, her husband's mistress, had been seen arguing with Mrs Bernstein earlier that day at the Chelsea restaurant Aubergine – two miles from her home.

The coroner's verdict was death by misadventure and Eve Boydell couldn't be traced. She was still wanted in connection with the crime.

Joanne checks the date. Seven years ago.

'Ron,' she says quietly, 'I think I may have something.'

Ron reads the description of Eve and turns to Joanne. 'That sound like her?' he asks, and she nods. 'Best grab your car keys then,' he says.

Joanne makes a quick trip to the loo, smartens herself up a bit. She sprays deodorant under her arms, washes her face in the sink and runs a brush through her hair before securing it into a ponytail. Noticing her shoes are dusty, she moistens a wad of tissue and gives them the once-over. They'll have to do for now, she thinks, making a mental note to get the polish out this evening when she gets home. The whole clean-up takes less than two minutes.

Ron is in DI McAleese's office, giving him an update, briefing him on what Joanne's discovered about Eve Dalladay, telling him they're on their way to question her with a view to bringing her in. Joanne hovers in the doorway, not wanting to get involved in the conversation – one, so that they can leave faster, and two, because she's in the habit of speaking to McAleese only when absolutely necessary right now. She heard an ugly rumour about job cuts. Joanne decided avoidance was key.

McAleese looks at her briefly. 'Joanne,' he says, by way of acknowledgement, immediately returning his attention to Ron.

'Sir,' she replies.

McAleese tells them he'll get Angela Blackwell on the Eve Boydell trail, see what else she can find before they bring her in. 'Joanne, leave your notes with DC Blackwell, give her some idea where to start.'

'Sir.'

'Okay, get yourselves off to Windermere and . . .' He pauses, keeping his eyes lowered on a stack of paperwork. Joanne shifts her weight from foot to foot. They need to go now. Without lifting his head, he says, 'Have you got a minute, Joanne?'

She casts a worried glance in Ron's direction. 'Not really,' she says awkwardly. 'I fear Natasha Wainwright might be liable to do something silly if we don't get back there sharpish. She told us she'd conducted her own investigation into Eve – if she puts two and two together about the fire . . . and comes up with—'

'It won't take long.'

Ron goes shifty and mumbles something before slinking away.

'Close the door, if you wouldn't mind, Joanne.'

'Sir, I don't mean to be difficult, but could we do this another time? I really think it's important that Ron and I—'

'The door?' he repeats.

Joanne takes a steadying breath and does as she's asked.

'Have a seat.'

'I'd rather stand.'

'As you wish.'

He removes his glasses and rubs beneath his eyes. 'I'm pretty tired,' he says absently.

She smiles uneasily.

'You may have heard that Phil Le Breton's off to Durham in August?'

'Are we losing staff, sir? Is that what this is about?'

'Not exactly. We're losing officers, but not from this department . . . yet. I've asked you in because I wondered if you might consider filling Phil's place? Naturally, it would mean immediately tackling the sergeant's exams – you wouldn't have a great deal of time to prepare. And it may mean you'll miss your' – he pauses again, looks down – 'your rescheduled operation.' Quickly, he adds, 'But I think it would be an excellent opportunity for you, Joanne. And I put your name forward, thinking you would be up for the challenge.' He makes an attempt to smile, but it doesn't quite come off.

Joanne must look stunned because he says, 'Would you like to take a few days to mull it over?'

'What?' she says, more abruptly than she means to. 'What? No. Of course not. No. I'll do it. Thank you, sir. Thank you for the opportunity.'

DI McAleese reaches across his desk and shakes her hand. 'Good,' he says. 'That's good.'

They regard each other in a clumsy moment of silence before Joanne says, 'Right. Fantastic. So, I'll go now, shall I?'

And he clears his throat.

'There is another thing, while you're here, actually, Joanne. I don't know if you're aware of this, if it's common knowledge – don't really go in for office gossip myself – but my wife and I are' – he swallows – 'getting divorced.'

'I had heard, yes. I was sad to hear it didn't work out.' Joanne had met his wife only once, a couple of years back at the Christmas party. Seemed like a nice enough woman. McAleese travelled in from Preston, so his home life was kept quite separate from work.

'Well, the truth of the matter is we've been living apart for close to a year, but I didn't want to . . . you know.'

Joanne doesn't know, but she smiles sympathetically.

'And Carmen, my wife, took a job in Bristol, which, to be honest, was the reason we began to have problems in the first place . . .' He stops. Shakes his head to get himself back on track. 'Anyway, the upshot of this is that my daughter will be boarding weekly, in Windermere.'

'Oh,' says Joanne, not at all sure where this was leading. 'It'll be great for her to have some security.'

'Yes,' he agrees. 'That's what we're hoping. She's had a difficult time, what with the hours I work, and her mother being the way she is and . . . anyway, I'm dropping her there this evening, I'll stay on a little while to make sure she's settled in.'

'I'm sure she'll love it, sir. The school's right on the lake, she'll be able to sail and kayak and—'

'Yes,' he says, cutting her off. 'But I wondered if, perhaps, when I'm done, if you're not too busy with this case, or it's not too late for you, I wondered if I might take you out to dinner?'

38

THERE IS A SCENE in *Rain Man* where Dustin Hoffman has to really lose his shit. It's the moment at the bathtub when he relives burning his baby brother with the hot water and was institutionalized as a result. Hoffman dreaded this scene. He knew he couldn't do the thing justice, and what you see on film is not what it appears to be. It's not great acting that gets him in the right space of mind, but frustration at what he perceives as his lack of ability. His torrent of anguished screams, which has such a profound effect on the viewer, is actually Hoffman's frustration at his own weakness, his failure as an actor.

I mention this because, right now, I have a knife, an iron and a hockey stick laid out on the kitchen table, and I am staring at each, frustrated with my inability to come up with a coherent plan of action. I've had three shots of whisky and, this is how my girls found me, five minutes ago, when they came in from school: shouting and pacing, sobbing, unable to think this thing through, to put an end to Eve without putting an end to myself in the process.

Alice and Felicity are certain the wheels have finally come off. That their mother has lost her mind, and as a consequence, out of sheer fear and with no other option, they've called Sean.

I appear mad, though I am not.

I am frustrated. I am angry beyond measure. But I don't know how to communicate this to them.

They want to approach but are giving me a wide berth, and all the while my lips are moving as I play out scenario after scenario. How can I kill her and get away with it? How can I win justice for my dad?

I can just hear that industrious detective in the aftermath: So, Mrs Wainwright, you have no idea how Eve Dalladay could have sustained such an injury? No idea how she managed to trip down the stairs?

I play with the option of hiring someone. But who would do such a thing? How does one hire a hit man? I don't know anyone even vaguely dodgy.

The girls are still standing in the doorway.

'She killed Grandad,' I tell them quietly, so they can hardly hear, and they back away. 'That woman killed your grandad.'

I stare at them, expressionless.

'Do we call an ambulance?' Alice whispers to Felicity.

'No,' she hisses. 'Wait for Dad.'

'But what if she kills herself?'

'She won't. And lower your voice, you idiot, she can hear you.'

'If she can hear me, why is she looking at us like that? Possessed. I say we call an ambulance . . . or at least the doctor.'

'Dad will be here in a minute. Just wait, will you?'

'I don't want to wait, Felicity. I'm scared. What does she mean, "She killed Grandad?"'

'Shut up. Go and sit in the lounge if you have to.'

The front door opens and I hear the murmur of hushed voices in the hallway. Alice goes to greet Sean, and Felicity remains where she is. Before Sean makes his way through to the kitchen Felicity says, quietly, so only I can hear, 'Hold it together, Mum, will you?' Her eyes are pleading.

Sean appears, with Eve behind him. They are smartly dressed, like they've been out for lunch. Sean is wearing his Italian charcoal suit – my favourite – over a white, heavy cotton shirt. Eve wears a red dress. It's short and fitted but very classy. She has a single thread of pearls at her throat and nude-coloured platform shoes – the type the Duchess of Cambridge often wears.

'We came as quickly as we could,' Sean says gravely, to no one in particular. His eyes move from the knife to the iron to the stick, and back again to the knife. 'Felicity, why don't you go and wait through there with Alice? Let us talk to Mum alone.'

Eve is hovering uneasily a few feet away, looking down at the floor. Felicity regards her coldly before saying, 'No. I think I'll stay.'

Sean steps towards me. 'Natty? Are you okay? What's going on here?'

I pick up the knife. 'She,' I say, pointing the blade towards Eve, 'she started the fire.'

Sean swallows. Glances briefly at Eve.

'Natty,' he says carefully, eyeing the empty tumbler over by the microwave, 'are you drunk?'

'Drunk? No.'

'Are you sure?'

'Fuck off, Sean.'

Eve takes this as her opportunity to swoop in. 'What makes you think I started the fire, Natty?' she demands, and Sean tries to shush her. He tells her now is not the time for confrontation, that I'm in no fit state to discuss this with her.

'Sean,' she persists. 'If Natty is accusing me of something, I really would like to know on what grounds,' and she lifts her brow, tilts her head to one side as if to say to me: *Well, bitch? What have you got?*

I shake my head slowly, make like I don't owe her any explanations.

She struts towards the kettle, and for a second I think she's going to begin making tea. She picks up the whisky glass and holds it to her nose. She rolls her eyes at Sean before walking to the sink and rinsing the glass beneath the tap. 'How about you tell us, Natty, because I'd really like to know.' Her tone is mocking, sardonic. She's banking on the fact I don't have any clear proof.

'Why are you all dressed up?' I ask them.

'We've been viewing a new car,' she replies.

'It looks as though the Maserati might be a write-off, after all,' Sean says softly, no hint of reproach.

'*And* we looked at a new house that's come on the market,' Eve adds. She's like a child, showing off.

'That's nice for you,' I reply.

'We've not made an offer or anything, Natty,' Sean says, trying to lessen the blow. 'It's early days yet.'

'Don't play it down, Sean,' Eve snaps. Her posture is con-frontational, reprimanding of Sean. 'There's no point keeping it a secret. We won't be able to rent for ever.'

'Yes, don't play it down, Sean,' I mirror nastily. 'You're going to need more room for that family Eve's so keen on having. You've been longing for a baby for such a long time now. Isn't that right, Eve?'

My words register, but she brushes them off, pretends I'm a babbling fool. Faltering a little, but only enough for me to notice, she regards the table. 'What's with all the weapons?' she scoffs. 'Surely you're not planning to use them on me?'

I scowl at her. 'Where were you the night of the fire?'

'Here. Why?'

'Are you sure she was here?' I ask Sean.

'Yes,' he replies uneasily. 'Where else could she have been?'

'Anyway, regardless of that, Natty,' Eve objects, 'even if I *wasn't* here, what possible reason could I have to set fire to your dad's house?'

'You tell me.'

She shoots Sean a look: *See?* she implies. *See how crazy your wife is?*

'Maybe you wanted me dead,' I add quietly.

Sean closes his eyes briefly before walking over to the drinks cupboard. He pours himself a shot of vodka and drinks it.

'I'd like a drink please,' I say to him but, for now, he ignores me.

'Natty,' he says, as he pours himself another, 'I don't know what's happening, but you're becoming paranoid. Please can you stop with the accusations,' and he pauses, glances towards the door and sees that Alice is now beside Felicity. Both girls are watching intently, so he refrains from speaking further.

'Sean, why did you cancel my credit cards?'

'I didn't,' he replies, full of indignation. His eyes are wide, and I can tell this is the first he's heard of this.

'Well, somebody did.'

'Not me,' he says again and, when it's clear from my expression I'm not about to let it drop, adds, 'Honestly, I wouldn't do that. There must have been some sort of mix-up at the bank.' He looks at me sadly, as if he can't believe what I've become. 'You can't continue on like this, Natty, or people'll think you've lost your mind. Let's get you some help.'

'Perhaps I *have* lost my mind,' I reply. 'You and Eve have driven me insane and—'

At this, Felicity steps forward.

'Or what if she's right, Dad?' she announces, and for the first time Eve's self-satisfied expression drops noticeably; there's a hint of fear in her eyes. 'Maybe Mum's right about Eve sneaking out on the night of the fire. I mean, you weren't here. You were at the hotel, so you don't know for sure what Eve was doing. Maybe what Mum is saying is not so completely outrageous.'

Alice blusters at this and gives her sister a quick shove. 'Felicity, don't be ridiculous! Why on earth would she do that?'

'Yes, Eve,' I mimic, my voice dripping with sarcasm, '*why on earth* would you do that?'

Eve turns and walks towards me, places both hands on the table so that we're opposite each other, and leans in. 'Don't make me do it, Natty,' she warns, and stares at me hard, her eyes full of hate.

Quickly, I go to say, 'No, don't!' but without a moment spared she spins around, spreading her hands wide as if to signal the start of a performance.

Terrified, I look to Sean and see that he, too, has been caught unawares. 'Eve,' he says aghast, 'now is not the time to do this.'

But she ignores us, and we know what is to come.

It's that moment we've circumvented, sidestepped, the moment we thought we'd never have to face. I watch Sean as his shoulders slacken. I can tell by his stance, by the defeatism in his posture, that he never expected her to actually go through with it. His breath shudders as he realizes he has caused this out-come. He, in the pursuit of a pretty new life with Eve, instigated what is to follow.

I ask her to stop; try to plead with Eve's human side. But just as Mad Jackie warned, the gloves are off.

I'm about to ask for mercy, but Felicity has heard our words. 'Don't do what?' she's asking.

Eve smiles in a way to suggest that this is as painful for her . . . She really doesn't want to have to do it but, sadly, there is just no other option.

'All of this nonsense you're witnessing here with your mother, girls,' she says, addressing them both, 'is because she's trying her damnedest to cover up something she doesn't want you to know. She thinks that by painting me as the bad guy, she won't have to atone for the mistakes of her past.'

'What mistakes?' asks Alice, a little worried now.

'See that man there?' and she points to Sean, 'that man is not your father, Alice. I'm so sorry to be the one to break the news

312

but, under the circumstances, what with your mother flinging about accusations, which have no foundation whatsoever, I think it's time you knew. You should have been told a long time ago, in my opinion. Secrets cause problems within families and, left to fester, they can build and build until there is—'

The doorbell sounds and nobody moves. I look to Alice, and she is totally rigid.

'Secrets fester,' Eve continues. 'So, now you know. Now you know the truth, Alice.'

When there is no immediate reaction from Alice, when Alice, being too dumbstruck to speak, stares vacantly ahead, Eve decides she's not yet through. 'Ever wondered why you're so science-minded?' she asks. 'Well, your father was an engineer, a very talented student. Ever wondered why you're nothing like that man over there? Well, now you have your answer.'

Alice is trembling.

Felicity moves towards her, holds out her hand to comfort her sister, but Alice flinches. 'Get away from me,' she breathes.

After what seems like an eternity, she utters, 'I have never wondered about those things. Why would I?'

She doesn't know whether to believe it. Her arms are glued to her sides. Her eyes settle upon me; hatred is coming off her in waves. 'Is it true?' she asks, addressing Sean.

He nods.

'Why was I never told?'

'Because we didn't want you to know!' I cry out, desperate to give her an explanation. 'We didn't want anyone to know. Your dad always loved you, loved you as his own daughter. Nobody needed to know.'

'*I needed to know!*' she flares. 'That's not a thing you hide.'

'We couldn't,' I stammer. 'It wasn't that we didn't want to, we just couldn't.'

'*Why* couldn't you? Why not?'

The hurt in her eyes is extreme. She feels cheated, feels like everything we've based our lives upon is a lie.

I try to speak, but I can't find the words.

Yes, why couldn't we tell her? It seems barely possible that the initial reason had mostly to do with Sean's mother; duping her was upmost in our minds. I don't suppose we ever thought through the long-term consequences. Neither of us imagined it would ever turn out this way.

Alice turns to Sean. 'Is Felicity yours?'

'Yes,' he says.

And she yelps at his response, like she's been bitten. As if there's always been a part of her that knew Sean loved Felicity more.

Which, of course, is not true.

'Alice,' he says softly, moving towards her, 'we were so young, we had just left school. Can you imagine what your grandmother would have said when she found out that you weren't . . .' He pauses, unable to finish the sentence, unable to articulate that she is not his child. 'We were trying our best to get on with it and make a life. We never meant to deceive you. We made a decision that we thought was best at the time and then tried to be the best parents we could be.'

'Who was he?' Alice snaps. 'Who was my father?'

'Somebody who didn't want me,' I reply.

'He didn't want *you*, or he didn't want *me*?'

'Neither of us,' I admit honestly.

At this, Eve scoffs. It's a strange noise she makes – almost spitting. Whatever it is, the intention is clear. It's an attempt at ridicule, as if she means to convey: *Newsflash, why the hell would he want either of you?*

The doorbell sounds again and it's as if in this moment the noise presents something transformational. Alice glowers at Eve. 'Why are you even here?'

'Sorry, Alice, I'm not sure what you mean.'

'Why are you here? We asked my dad to come over today. We phoned Dad, not you.'

'I . . . I was in the car with him when we received the call. You said it was an emergency and asked us to come straight away.'

She glances at Sean, expecting back-up. When none is forthcoming she adds, 'Anyway, Alice, why *shouldn't* I be here? Your mother is clearly demented, why shouldn't I be here to support your . . .' She pauses. She was about to say 'father', but changes her mind. 'To support Sean,' she finishes, a satisfied tone to her voice.

'I hate what you've done to us,' Alice hisses. Her eyes are cold, dead almost.

'Don't shoot the messenger, Alice. I certainly wasn't the cause of all of this,' Eve mutters. 'I was not—'

But Alice already has the knife in her hand.

As quick as that she picked up the knife and is now holding it to Eve's throat. Eve has her chin raised as she screams at Sean to help her.

'Alice!' I'm yelling. 'Put the knife down! Christ, Alice! Step back, step back away from Eve.'

'No!' she shouts, and Eve is inching away, slowly, as carefully as her heels will allow. The blade is resting against her skin.

Fear clutches at my insides. What if Alice slips? What if she moves just a hair's width? Fuck, what if she sneezes?

'Alice, don't hurt her. If you hurt Eve, it's *you* we lose, not her. It's not worth it. Please . . .' I'm pleading with her, but she doesn't hear me. 'Alice, we don't care about Eve, we care about you. Don't do this. You'll ruin your life.'

Sean tries to approach. 'Stay away from me!' Alice warns him. She's shaking now, and the end of the blade is quivering against Eve's neck. 'Why didn't you tell me!' she screams. 'Why did you let me live my whole life as a lie! Both of you!'

Eve's eyes are wild with fear. 'Sean, *do* something!' she hisses. 'Alice, this is not my fault. Let me go before you do something you'll regret.'

'Not your fault?' spits Alice. 'We were all doing just fine before you turned up.' She looks to Sean. 'Why didn't you *tell me*?'

He's frightened. The colour has drained from his face. He's terrified his daughter will slice this woman's throat. I stare at him. *Help her*, my eyes beg.

'I wanted you to be mine, Alice,' he tells her. 'I loved your mum.' He's watching Alice closely, but it's me he's speaking to. He glances my way to let me know he needs me to hear this, too. 'I couldn't believe she had left me for another guy . . . and if this was a chance to keep her, then I'd take it, because I wanted to keep you, too.' His face is anguished, like it's all too much to relive. 'I wanted you both,' he whispers. 'I always did.'

Christ.

'Alice,' I say firmly, 'for the last time, put the knife down.'

'No!' she shouts, but the fight is going out of her; her elbow wobbles as she starts to cry.

'Oh, for fuck's sake, Alice!' comes Felicity's voice from the doorway, like she's had enough of this bullshit.

She marches across the kitchen. My hand flies to my mouth. I'm powerless to stop what is about to occur.

Felicity shoves Eve hard with both hands, shoves her away from Alice's blade, and sends her flailing backwards.

Eve falls in slow motion.

It's as if she's grabbing on to thin air, reaching out with her hands to try to save herself. But she's going down. We watch as she falls, her heels scrabbling on the floor tiles, her eyes searching madly for an alternative, but there is nothing she can do.

There is one dull, sickening thud as the back of her cranium connects with the granite worktop. It's the sound of a bag of sugar falling from an open cupboard. A ripe grapefruit thrown against a wall.

Nobody moves.

Alice gives a small cry as Eve crumples to the floor and, straight away, I search for blood, because she's unconscious, maybe even dead.

The floor is clean.

I look up, and panic sets in. If Eve is dead, our lives as we know them are over. Immediately I start thinking through the full extent of this situation, the logistics of lying to the paramedics, the police, about what just happened here, but I'm halted when something catches my attention out of the window.

It's a shadow.

A shadow passed the window, someone that has more than likely witnessed my daughter Felicity knock Eve Dalladay right off her heels and into lifelessness.

39

'CALL AN AMBULANCE.'

'Is she breathing?' Sean asks me.

'Call an ambulance.'

'Do we move her?'

'No,' I reply. 'She may have a neck injury. If she's breathing, don't move her.'

He pulls out his mobile, dials and, as he waits for an answer, asks, 'What do I tell them? They're going to ask – what do I tell them?'

'Pass it to me,' I instruct, and reach out my hand, grab the phone and hold it to my ear. With my free hand I feel for Eve's pulse. It's shallow and erratic. Her blood pressure is dropping.

Alice is whimpering, wringing her hands over by the fridge. Sean is pacing. And Felicity sits on the other side of Eve's slack body, wearing a look of defiance, as though she's ready to deny anything thrown her way. 'Why don't we just let her die?' she says in a forced whisper.

'Because someone would have to take the consequences.'

The call is answered and before the operator speaks I mouth to Felicity, 'Follow my lead?' and she nods.

'Emergency, which service?'

'Ambulance,' I tell the operator. 'My friend has fallen and hit her head on the kitchen worktop . . . Eve Dalladay . . . No, she's not conscious . . . Yes, she's breathing . . . okay, thank you,' and

I give the address. I stay on the line for another minute, explaining that my husband will, 'Wait on the road to wave them in,' as this address is not always recognized by GPS.

I hang up and tell Alice to stop crying. I return the knife, the doorstop, and the hockey stick to their rightful places. Then, from beneath the sink in the kitchen, I pull out the small wooden stool I use to reach things from the high shelves and I place it next to Eve.

Looking to each of them in turn – Sean, Alice and Felicity – I impart what I need them to know.

'This is what happened,' I say. 'We were discussing the house you looked at this afternoon, Sean, with a view to perhaps selling the hotel. There was no mention of the fire. No mention of the fire being started deliberately. We were not arguing, we were *not* discussing what just came to light' – and I look towards Alice, my expression unyielding, cautionary – 'we were talking about our plans for the future. Eve stepped backwards and stumbled over this stool in her high heels, hitting her head in the process as she fell. Right?'

'Right,' they say in unison.

Sean, frightened, asks, 'What if she wakes up?'

'What if she doesn't, Sean?'

And I give the kitchen a quick examination, checking for anything that would cast doubt on our story.

'What if she wakes up and says she was pushed?' he repeats.

'What if she doesn't wake up, and we admit what happened, and your daughter is charged with killing her?' I fix him with an open stare. 'It's your call, Sean.'

As expected, he responds with 'I'll say it was me,' without hesitation. 'I'll say I did it. I hit her out of frustration and she fell.'

I keep my voice calm. 'You won't need to do that if you do as I say.' I don't wait for his reaction; instead, I turn to Alice: 'Alice, you've got to stop crying,' and I reach down to monitor Eve's pulse again. It's scarcely palpable. 'If the paramedics come in here and see you like this, they'll know something isn't quite right. Look worried and concerned, yes, but do not look hysterical. Go and wash your face if you have to.' She's watching me issue orders, not quite sure how to respond. Surely we should be pandering to her in this moment? Surely, even though Eve is motionless, possibly dead, we should not overlook the enormity of what just took place? *She has been lied to, for heaven's sake.*

I pretend not to notice and address the three of them. 'We've got about six minutes until they get here. Are you all okay with this? Because this is the story we're going to have to go with. If Eve's condition is serious, we'll have to go over it again and again with the police, understand?'

I place Eve's wrist against her breast and move towards Sean.

'Can you manage this?' I ask him quietly. 'Can you lie to help your family?'

'Yes,' he answers. But he's conflicted. The woman he has been sharing a bed with lies before us unconscious, and it was his own daughter that put her there.

I take his hands: 'Thank you,' and I tell him to wait out on the road for the paramedics. Tell him to move his car so they can park the ambulance outside the front door.

He hesitates, and I can feel him trying to get the order of events straight in his mind. He's not certain he's doing the right thing, but what choice does he have?

He picks up his keys and makes for the door.

When he's in the hallway he calls out my name. His tone is anxious, frightened. 'Natty,' he says, 'you need to come and see this.'

I have no idea what to expect, and walk towards him. He's looking in the direction of the stairs.

There, halfway up the steps, back leg cocked vertically, licking his hindquarters, sits Morris.

'That's your dad's cat, isn't it?' whispers Sean.

I nod.

'What's he doing here?'

I don't answer. I go to the front door, my head starting to overload. Five seconds ago I was handling it. Now it's as if there's a ligature wrapped around my forehead, and the tension is mounting.

Just to the right of the door, next to the girls' school shoes, is a box of Tesco's Cat Crunchies and a small aluminium dish.

I turn around. 'Jackie,' I say to Sean simply. 'Jackie must have brought him back.'

'When? Do you think she heard? Do you think she *saw* anything?' His eyes are wide.

'I don't think so,' I lie.

Jackie was the shadow at the window. Jackie must have watched as Felicity pushed Eve, watched her fall against the worktop. She must have seen all this, opened the front door, silently depositing Morris before leaving.

'Move the car, Sean,' I tell him decisively.

I return to the kitchen and ask Felicity, who is loitering near Eve's collapsed body, if she's still breathing. 'Unfortunately, yes,' Felicity answers flatly.

I'm about to go searching for Alice when something occurs to me. 'What exactly happened between you two?' I ask her. 'Did you have a run-in or something?'

Felicity goes shifty. 'Kind of.'

'Do you want to tell me about it?'

She bites the inside of her cheek. 'Maybe later.' Then she changes her mind. Hesitating, she says, 'Mum?' as I'm about to walk away. 'Mum, I need to tell you something.'

I stop.

Almost under her breath, Felicity whispers, 'It was me who sent the note. I sent the note about Eve,' and she waits for me to react.

I regard her trusting face and for a moment I consider gently reprimanding her. I think about feigning shock and chiding her for causing trouble.

In the end, though, I tell her the truth.

'I know you did, honey,' I say softly.

Her shoulders drop. '*How* did you know?'

'I found a pad of yellow paper at the back of your bottom drawer. I was searching for photographs of Grandad – you had some old ones of him, remember? Anyway,' I say looking down, remembering, 'it was after the fire, and it didn't seem all that important by then . . .'

I study her face. I can't tell if she's relieved I'm not angry with her, or if she's upset I didn't mention I knew about the note sooner. 'Good call, Felicity,' I say, holding her gaze. 'Good call. Turns out you had the measure of Eve.'

She nods.

I glance at Eve's lifeless body. 'I did wonder though, love,' I say, almost as an afterthought, 'I did wonder how you managed to get the note to me. It was hand delivered to Grandad's late at night . . .'

She looks away, suddenly evasive. 'I called Raymond and got him to do it,' she admits after a moment.

'Raymond?' I echo back, surprised, because she means Raymond, the hotel manager. 'He delivered it *on his bike*?' Raymond cycles to work every day so his wife can use the car.

'Well, he did have to go past,' she answers defensively. 'It wasn't like it was *totally* out of his way . . . But,' she says, a little more sheepish now, 'I told him it was important. Told him I needed to give you a very important message and he absolutely *had* to deliver it.'

And I have to smile at this, because, I suppose, in the end, that's exactly what it turned out to be. A very important message.

*

It's been more than ten minutes since the call was made and the paramedics have not arrived. I find Alice in the downstairs loo, sobbing hysterically in front of the mirror. I watch unobserved from a crack in the doorway. The cries subside a fraction, and Alice stares at her reflection hard, encouraging the emotion to surge to the surface, until once again she's able to weep unreservedly.

This is how I know the news about her parentage has not actually brought her to her knees. I'm aware that there is a fragment of stagecraft going on here. Because I know my daughter, and she would do this small act of pretence as a child, would make herself cry and cry if she felt our reaction to her state of despair was insufficient. But that's not to say her reaction isn't warranted. It's just to say that the best thing for Alice right now is not necessarily profuse apologies and sympathy.

I nudge the door and the hinge whines, stopping Alice mid-cry. She flicks her head around and upon seeing me does a fast about-face. She stands with her back to me, shoulders shuddering, waiting for me to do what I would ordinarily attempt to do, which is pacify. Pacify, beseech, cajole her out of her misery. Whatever it takes to lessen her dejection. Whatever it takes to make her pain my own. It hurts to watch her in this state, and my instinct is to put my arms around her, but I sense she'd shun me.

'Alice,' I begin.

'Don't.'

I pause, trying to come up with the best way to tackle this. 'What do you want me to do?' I ask her honestly.

'I don't want you to *do* anything,' she sniffs. 'I can't speak to you right now.'

'Can't or won't?'

She spins to face me. 'How could you?' she whimpers.

I walk towards her. Her mascara is running down her cheeks,

her red hair is frizzing at her temples. The muscles in her neck are taut and rigid, two thick straps running along either side of her slim throat. 'How could you?' she repeats, with more anger this time.

'If we hadn't lied, then your Gran wouldn't have let us stay together,' I explain.

'Why not?'

'She didn't want us to be a couple in the first place. She tried to break us up. This would have given her everything she needed to call a halt to it for good. Alice, we fought to stay together and she overruled us. She made us split and go to university promising that we'd stay apart.'

'And you *agreed*?' she asks, truly astonished.

'We didn't have a lot of choice.' I smile weakly. 'If we didn't, she wouldn't fund your dad's studies . . . and, well, he was set on becoming a lawyer.'

She's staring down at her shoes. She hasn't heard the story told this way before. We've always made light of it. Always told the girls we were young and reckless, we waved away any disappointment with the way things played out. 'Don't repeat our mistakes,' we laughed, while at the same time trying our best to convey that it wasn't ever a mistake. Not to us.

Eventually, she says, 'He really wanted to study law, then?' keeping her head low.

'Yeah,' I reply. 'He really did.'

'Does my . . . does . . . this other person . . . does he know about me? You told him about me, did you?' Alice looks at me.

'He knows.'

'And he's never tried to find me? He's not, like, come looking and you've stopped his letters, or anything?'

'No,' I say sadly.

'So, he really doesn't want to know me? That's what you're saying?'

'Love, I can't speak for him, because' – and I shrug my shoulders helplessly – 'I can't tell you why that is. The only thing I know, and this probably isn't the time and place to be having this conversation, but he was a nasty, arrogant fool at the age of twenty-one, and in my experience people don't change that much. People are who they are. You may want to think long and hard before going down the road of looking for him . . . if that's what you're thinking of doing.'

She pushes her foot into the carpet, divides the pile with her big toe. 'But I feel so mad at Dad,' she says.

I go to speak, but she cuts me off.

'That's wrong, isn't it? I know it's wrong, but I feel like he's lied to me, always knowing I don't belong to him. I feel like he must have hated me for being another man's daughter.'

'Have you ever once thought that he doesn't love you?'

'No, but—'

'Well, then,' and I take a breath. 'Alice,' I say to her, 'he showed up when we needed him. I can't imagine what life would have been like for us if he hadn't. And, up until recently, he's been here for you every single day. He brought you up,' I whisper. 'That means he's your dad.'

She bows her head. 'What about Eve?' she asks. 'Why did he need to do something as stupid as that when—'

There's a commotion out in the hallway and I realize we need to move.

I hear the clack of equipment, the deep baritone of an unfamiliar voice.

I move towards Alice, cupping her face in my hands. I'm aware something seismic is taking place here; the fear of discovery has had too strong a hold over me for too long. A load is lifting. 'He really loved us, Alice,' I say, my eyes fixed on hers to make sure she fully understands what this meant to me back then. 'He loved us, and I didn't love him enough back in return.

You want to be furious and disappointed with someone, that person should be me.'

I don't wait for her response. I remove any evidence of the deep relief that's beginning to bloom inside my chest and stride through to the kitchen.

There, I find a bearded, expansive figure crouched down by Eve's side. He has the words 'First Responder' printed across the back of his shirt. He looks up as I enter.

'It all just happened so fast,' I tell him innocently.

40

SEAN AND I SIT side by side, the edge of the moulded plastic chair cutting into my spine. We are in the A & E waiting room of Lancaster Infirmary. Sean rode in the ambulance with Eve, and I followed in Eve's car once I'd calmed the girls. I'm not insured to drive it, but hell, we've got bigger problems right now.

Sean has his head in his hands, and so far we've barely spoken. I arrived only a few minutes after him – the forty-minute drive to Lancaster taking closer to an hour in the rush-hour traffic. As far as we know, Eve has not regained consciousness, and though I've not yet voiced this to Sean, I'm hoping she never wakes up. My one big fear is Eve remembering what happened in the kitchen: Alice threatening her with a knife, Felicity knocking her backwards, and since we don't know the extent of her injuries, I'm imagining the worst. I'm imagining, from the twisted, slumped position of Eve's body, that she sustained a neck fracture and, of course, if she wakes, Felicity will be charged. Every few seconds I close my eyes and see my dad's face. I pray to him with every fibre of my being for him somehow to strike Eve down dead.

The department is busy. It's too early yet for the run of drunks who frequent A & E from early evening onwards, so the chairs are instead filled with whimpering children with various limb injuries, overweight men with breathing difficulties and a couple of people who look as if they've wandered in for no reason, perhaps simply to rest their legs.

We've been here for close to an hour and so far heard nothing. I pick up a magazine from the adjoining chair and thumb through it idly, wondering when I reached the age when I'm no longer able to recognize a celebrity.

As if from nowhere, an apparition almost, a neat, diminutive woman in her early fifties stands before us. 'You're with Eve Dalladay?' she asks.

Sean lifts his head. 'How is she?'

'I'm Vanessa Rose, Senior Registrar. The preliminary X-rays show a fracture at C6. I'm afraid there are some early signs of neurological damage.'

Sean turns to me, worried, and I motion with my finger to the base of my neck. I keep my face blank and without emotion.

'Has she woken up?' he asks.

'No,' answers Dr Rose. 'There's some head trauma – we're not sure of the extent. Sorry, but that's all I can tell you for the moment. I'll come back when I have more.'

And, with that, she's gone.

'What does that mean, Natty?' Sean asks, his voice shaking.

I don't answer.

He closes his eyes, sits back in his chair.

Is he visualizing a life with Eve, a life caring for a woman who will no longer be able to walk? Have limited use of her arms? Is he regretting ever getting involved with her?

Or is he devastated that the future they imagined together is almost certainly not going to happen?

A C6 injury means Eve will be able to breathe for herself, but this is high-intensity care, and twenty-four-hour nursing will be necessary right from the start.

'I fucked up, didn't I?' Sean says quietly.

'You and me both,' I reply.

'The fire?' he says, unexpectedly. 'You're totally sure it was Eve?'

'I can't be totally sure it was her, no.'

'So what makes you think she would do it?'

'To stop me from disclosing who she really is.'

'And *do you know* who she really is?'

I nod.

'But you're not going to tell me,' he says.

'Would you believe me even if I did?'

'I would now,' he says. 'I would've had my reservations before,' he says, 'but after what she just did to Alice? Telling her about us? Not sparing Alice's feelings, and . . .' His words drift off. He's still not got his head around what Eve did back there.

After a moment of silence I ask, 'What about the credit cards, Sean? You must take my word that they were cancelled purposely. She told me herself, said that it was you who orchestrated it.'

He frowns.

'I just don't see how she could have gained access to the accounts,' he explains. 'I'm not suggesting she didn't do it, but I can't see how it's possible.'

'Do you still keep your passwords and log-in information stored on that Word document, the one labelled "Passwords" on your laptop?' I ask.

And he exhales. 'Yes,' he confesses, but I don't push it. He probably doesn't need another 'I told you so' at the moment.

We sit quietly. Observe the comings and goings of the department. I can feel him mulling over events in his mind when he turns to face me. 'There have been other things,' he says, his expression serious, fixed. 'Things that didn't quite add up. I don't think I wanted to admit it, but I knew there was a problem.'

I nod to let him know I understand. 'Do you love her?' I ask.

'I thought I did.'

'And now?'

He hesitates.

'This is going to sound arrogant,' he says, 'but I always saw myself as someone *above* having an affair. I never thought I'd succumb to the flattery.' He pauses, embarrassed by his admission, checks around to make sure no one can hear before continuing. 'I never thought I'd become some clichéd bloke who caved because it felt good to be wanted again, to be desired, to be *virile*. And when Eve came along and I felt all those things, I assumed it was love. The genuine thing.' He scoffs now at the memory. 'Didn't think I was just as fallible as the next man.

'I'm sorry, Natty,' he adds quietly, before I have time to respond. 'That wasn't meant to be a proper explanation. You deserve better than that.'

'It's okay,' I say, reaching out my hand. 'I find myself wondering the same kind of thing. How did I become the nagging, buttoned-up wife? How would it have turned out if I'd focused on you? On us? Instead of stressing about all the irrelevant stuff that gets in the way?'

His eyes fill up. He blinks and looks down as if I've just offered him a glimpse of a life that can now never be.

'What am I going to do, Natty?'

'I don't know.'

'Do I walk away? Or do I take care of her?'

'Depends on what your conscience will allow you to do. You could walk out of this hospital now if you wanted to but, knowing you, I can't imagine you're willing to do that.'

He shakes his head like he can't imagine doing that either.

'It might help to know she did a real number on you,' I tell him. 'On all of us, in fact.'

He lifts his eyebrows in a gesture of *Go on*.

'She's got a whole past that she never revealed, that she's kept hidden. I don't think I even know the half of it.'

'I suppose we all have our secrets, though, don't we?' he says reasonably.

I turn towards him. 'Sean, she has a son.'

'What?'

'A son,' I repeat. 'No one knows about him,' I warn, 'and I promised it would stay that way. Her mother takes care of him. He's around nineteen.'

Sean stares at me, the gravity of Eve's deception perhaps only now beginning to hit home fully. 'Jesus,' he whispers.

I watch as he swallows repeatedly, his face losing colour. He appears stricken, as though his life is unravelling at too fast a rate. A second later he puts his head between his knees in an attempt to remain lucid. I'm about to go and fetch a sick bowl, or call for help when:

'Mr Wainwright? Are you okay down there?'

It's Detective Constable Aspinall.

'Is he ill?' she asks me.

'Worried about Eve,' I reply quickly, trying to mask my horror at her sudden presence here in A & E.

'What happened?' she asks casually, removing her jacket, slinging it over her left arm. She turns and glances towards the front desk, where I see her partner – the rotund, sweating detective who visited after the fire – making enquiries of the admissions clerk.

'She . . . she fell,' I stammer.

I grimace madly as if to suggest how unfortunate this all is, but DC Aspinall's face remains fixed.

'How did she fall exactly?'

'Backwards. She hit her head on the granite worktop.'

DC Aspinall nods thoughtfully.

Sean lifts his head. 'I think I need some air,' he says, standing unsteadily. 'I need to get out of here for a minute, is that okay?'

He is deathly white.

'Fine by me,' DC Aspinall tells him. 'I'll send my colleague along to check on you. If you don't mind me saying so, Mr Wainwright, you look as though you may be liable to pass out.'

Sean tries to smile. It's a brave smile. He walks towards the sliding doors, shoulders hunched, head hanging, and I watch him go before turning back and staring straight ahead.

What is she doing here?

Has she been to the house and interviewed the girls?

Christ, what if they've said the wrong thing? I hadn't had time to prep them properly for this eventuality. What if this detective is here to trick us? To see if our stories match? What if they've already *told her* the truth?

'Mind if I sit?' she asks brightly.

'Not at all.'

The walls of the room begin to close in. I start to sweat. My hands shake, so I sit on them quickly to keep them from jumping around.

'Traffic's bad out there,' she comments.

'Hmm?'

'I said, the traffic is bad through the centre of Lancaster.'

'Yes,' I reply. 'Yes, it is.'

I keep my eyes fixed ahead, on a huge poster depicting the various complications of morbid obesity, squinting as I pretend to read the text.

'What is the news on Eve Dalladay?' she asks. 'Have you been told anything specific?'

DC Aspinall is very relaxed, as though we're sitting side by side in the pub. My heart hammers wildly inside my chest and my instinct is to put my hand to it, try to mask the sound in case she can hear.

I shake my head. 'They're not able to tell us much. She fractured her spine, but they need to do more tests.' I glance her way briefly so as to appear normal, and she nods once again, seemingly unfazed by Eve's condition.

After a moment, she asks, 'You're not wondering what I'm doing here?', a quizzical look on her face.

'Sorry?'

'You haven't asked me why I'm here, Mrs Wainwright. I find that a little strange, to say the least.'

'You do?'

'Yes,' she says firmly. 'I do.'

She waits for me to respond. I swallow. Close my eyes briefly. 'Why are you here, then?' I ask quietly.

'There have been some developments. An old case popped up on the database and I'm here to arrest—'

We're interrupted by Dr Rose. She clears her throat, gives a cursory glance at Detective Aspinall before asking me to follow her immediately. DC Aspinall doesn't protest, so I stand, unsure of what to do.

Do I find Sean?

I look towards the entrance, but I can't see him and Dr Rose is already marching away.

Running a little to catch up, I pursue Dr Rose into a small waiting room, a private space away from the masses. 'We can talk in here,' she says. 'There's been a problem with accessing Eve Dalladay's records,' she says brusquely. 'Is she a resident in the UK?'

'Oh,' I reply, flustered. 'No, she's not. She hasn't lived here for quite a while.'

She looks down at her notes. 'It's not a major problem,' she says absently, 'but you will need to fill out a few forms. Anyway, we'll get to that later. The thing that we must do right now is a scan.'

My breathing stops.

I stare at her.

'A scan, you say?' I repeat carefully.

'Yes, we need to ascertain the reason for Eve's unconscious-ness, to see if there's any bleeding into the brain and, if there is, to what extent it's causing it. We may possibly need to move her to Preston, where they're more set up to deal with head injuries.'

'So you want to do an MRI scan?'

'Yes,' she says. 'That's all right, isn't it? It's nothing to be con-cerned about. The faster we know what's going on in there, the faster we can . . .'

I've stopped listening.

Whatever she says next doesn't register. It's as if I've entered an altered state of awareness. All sound has been shut off, and my immediate environment is eclipsed by an overriding memory, a memory from sixteen years ago.

I'm back at Hope Hospital. I'm a student. I wear maroon trousers and a plain white tunic. The radiographer in the chair next to me wears a similar uniform, but her collar has a stripe, indicating she is qualified to operate the MRI scanner.

She speaks into the microphone. 'Mr Burgess,' she says to the patient lying beyond the glass, 'it will get a bit noisy now, okay? It's perfectly normal and I need you to stay very still.'

Then she turns to me. 'Natasha,' she says brightly, 'why don't you list the contraindications, while we wait for this one to finish?'

I sit tall in my seat, because I know this off by heart. It was the first thing we learned. 'Do not scan if the patient has any elec-tronically, magnetically and mechanically activated implants. Do not scan if the patient has a cardiac pacemaker . . . Do not scan if the patient has surgical clips, wire sutures, screws or mesh—'

'And why is that?' she interrupts.

'Because anything ferromagnetic can interact with the magnetic field. It can cause movement of the device and lead to trauma.'

'And what else?'

'Thermal injury,' I answer firmly, pleased with myself.

'That's right,' she says, and pulls a face. 'You absolutely don't want to *fry* the patient from the inside, do you?' and I laugh.

'No, you don't want to do that.'

I think of the aneurysm clip inside Eve's brain, and my heart races. One of the old metal varieties, Eve said.

I must have a strange look on my face, because at once the doctor stops speaking. 'Are you all right?' she asks, concerned.

'What?' I stammer. 'Yes, yes, of course. Sorry, I was just trying to keep up with what you were saying. Getting a bit lost in all the jargon.'

She smiles. 'Okay, then,' and she reaches for the door. 'If you'd like to take a seat in the main area, apologies, but we do try to keep this spot free so we can speak privately when necessary. I'll authorize the scan and I should have some more news for you within the next couple of hours.'

I thank her and make my way to the general waiting room. DC Aspinall is with her partner at the front desk, and Sean has returned to his seat. Sean looks to me, expectant, and I give him a pained expression, indicating that we know nothing further, and sit down next to him.

I pick up a magazine. Start thumbing my way through and stifle a yawn.

Then I sit back and I wait.

Paula Daly lives in Cumbria with her husband, three children and whippet Skippy. Before becoming a writer she was a freelance physiotherapist. *Keep Your Friends Close* is her second novel.